Praise for Wen Spencer's Ukiah Oregon novels

Bitter Waters

"An engrossing, thrill-filled adventure, full of fascinating alien—and human—weirdness." —*Locus*

"The series is worth the price." —*VOYA*

"Wen Spencer's Ukiah Oregon stories owe more to the Detective genre than to Science Fiction, which is what makes them so compelling. Oh, sure, Ukiah is half alien, a hundred or so years old, once lived as an Indian, ran with wolves, and can't be killed short of incineration, but every PI has baggage.... The SF aspects of it are fun.... But take away the alien parts and you've still got a great action/detective story, which is why you should pick up Wen Spencer's trail wherever her literary muse takes her next." —*SFRevu*

"The rocketing pace ... |

"An exciting science fict
powerful hero who is i
read."

"[Spencer] has blended private investigation, science fiction, and fantasy into a rip-roaring tale.... More books like this would probably expand the Science Fiction and Fantasy genre's readership.... A book that keeps going from strength to strength, the action just won't stop, and it will appeal to fans of a wide spectrum of fiction." —The Alien Online

continued ...

"The continual character development adds another dimension to the story. . . . The tension builds nicely. . . . An exciting chapter to the continuing adventures of Ukiah Oregon."
—Rambles

"Ms. Spencer has a mighty fine imagination."
—Science Fiction Romance

Tainted Trail

"Spencer continues to amaze, cranking up both suspense and wonder."　　　　　　　　　　　　　　—Julie E. Czerneda

"A fun read, definitely worth checking out."　　　　—*Locus*

"Spencer's skillful characterizations, vividly drawn settings, and comic exploitation of Ukiah's deceptively youthful, highly buff looks make the romp high light entertainment."—*Booklist*

"A unique and highly entertaining reading experience."
—*Midwest Book Review*

Alien Taste

"Each and every character is fascinating, extraordinarily well-developed, and gets right under your skin. A terrific, memorable story."   —Julie E. Czerneda

"Revelations ranging from surprising to funny to wonderfully inventive. A delightful new SF mystery with a fun protagonist."
—*Locus*

"Spencer has written an intriguing contemporary science fiction tale. Her characters come alive on the page and their uniqueness will grab and hold you."   —*Talebones*

"The characters are fully developed and understandable. This novel is keeper shelf material."   —BookBrowser

"Spencer takes readers on a fast-paced journey into disbelief. [Her] timing is impeccable and the denouement stunning."
—*Romantic Times* (4 star review)

"A fabulous mix of science fiction, suspense, romance, and the nature of wolves, in a story like none you've ever seen."
—Science Fiction Romance

DOG
WARRIOR

Wen Spencer

A ROC BOOK

ROC

Published by New American Library, a division of
Penguin Group (USA) Inc., 375 Hudson Street,
New York, New York 10014, USA
Penguin Group (Canada), 10 Alcorn Avenue, Toronto,
Ontario M4V 3B2, Canada (a division of Pearson Penguin Canada Inc.)
Penguin Books Ltd., 80 Strand, London WC2R 0RL, England
Penguin Ireland, 25 St. Stephen's Green, Dublin 2,
Ireland (a division of Penguin Books Ltd.)
Penguin Group (Australia), 250 Camberwell Road, Camberwell, Victoria 3124,
Australia (a division of Pearson Australia Group Pty. Ltd.)
Penguin Books India Pvt. Ltd., 11 Community Centre, Panchsheel Park,
New Delhi - 110 017, India
Penguin Group (NZ), Cnr Airborne and Rosedale Roads, Albany,
Auckland 1310, New Zealand (a division of Pearson New Zealand Ltd.)
Penguin Books (South Africa) (Pty.) Ltd., 24 Sturdee Avenue,
Rosebank, Johannesburg 2196, South Africa

Penguin Books Ltd, Registered Offices:
80 Strand, London WC2R 0RL, England

First published by Roc, an imprint of New American Library,
A division of Penguin Group (USA) Inc.

First Printing, October 2004
10 9 8 7 6 5 4 3 2 1

Cover art by Steve Stone

 REGISTERED TRADEMARK—MARCA REGISTRADA

Printed in the United States of America

To David G. Kosak,
little brother of my heart

ACKNOWLEDGMENTS

Gail Brookhart, George Corcoran, W. Randy Hoffman,
Kendall Jung, June Drexler Robertson,
Andi Ward, Aaron Wollerton

Special thanks to Ann Cecil

CHAPTER ONE

**Ludlow Service Area, Massachusetts Turnpike,
Massachusetts
Sunday, September 19, 2004**

Atticus smelled the blood first.

He'd parked the Jaguar under the floodlights, and he had just paused, door open, his cup of hot cocoa on the roof, in order to pull off his leather jacket before climbing back into the still-warm car. A blue Honda sedan came cautiously into the rest stop from the dark highway. The bitter cold wind blasted over the Honda and brought him the reek of slaughter.

He tracked the car's movements without looking directly at it. It paused at the decision point of turning into the parking lot or going on to the gas pumps, the right turn signal flashing a yellow warning. There were four people in the car, three men and a woman. The woman was leaning over the front seat, pointing toward the retro-styled McDonald's with the large yellow arches. Atticus turned his back to the Honda as the driver scanned the parking lot.

On the other side of the Jaguar, Ru picked up on his unease. "The Honda?" Ru pretended to ignore the sedan, seemingly focused on the coffee cup in his hands, tracking the car only with his dark eyes.

"Yes." Focusing on his sense of smell, Atticus grew aware of the Jaguar's hot engine, oil spilled on the asphalt nearby, food cooking in the McDonald's, the taint of the ocean a hundred miles away, and massive amounts of old blood. "They've got something dead in the trunk."

"Ah." Ru sipped his steaming coffee. "Things like that are always a bitch to explain."

"Do you see anything weird about it, Ru?"

The car cooperated and turned into the parking lot. The driver carefully used proper signals and slowly pulled into a nice dark corner of the parking lot, tucked behind an RV.

"Nada." Ru shrugged one lean shoulder, his black bangs falling into his eyes. "Maybe I need a closer look." Ru finished his coffee and walked to a trash can across the parking lot.

Atticus leaned into his car to place his hot cocoa into the front cup holder.

The woman all but bolted from the Honda, hunched over, clutching at her stomach, her face set in pain. She concentrated on walking, eyes focused on the ground. The men followed, intent on the woman, worried. All four were in their early twenties, wearing black running suits with jackets zipped over pistols in shoulder holsters. They smelled faintly of gunpowder, smoke, scorched hair, burned flesh, and blood.

The men had ignored Atticus, half-hidden in the Jaguar, but glared at Ru as he casually stuffed his empty cup into the trash can. Ru read the bulges under the jackets and the tense body language and didn't play any mind games with them. He studiously ignored them, walking back to the Jaguar, pulling on his leather gloves.

"A seriously scary foursome." Ru unzipped his jacket slightly, giving him access to his own gun, as the four vanished into the McDonald's. "I say we see what they've got in their trunk." He made a show of sniffing. "I'm sure I can smell blood now."

Atticus scoffed at the claim, while he considered the car parked upwind. More than the blood, there was a weird niggling feeling that something was drastically wrong with the car. It seemed to exude terror. How could a car feel afraid?

Ru rapped on the roof, his lock picks in hand. "They're not going to be in there very long!" he sang.

Atticus glanced toward the McDonald's. "Let's do it."

He shut the Jaguar's door and walked after Ru, keeping watch on the building.

Ru had the trunk open before Atticus even reached the car, murmuring. "Bingo: one body." Ru stripped off his right glove and reached bare fingertips to the body's neck. "Question is, is he really dead or just— Oh, fuck."

Atticus looked then. The trunk light shone on a young Native American face, battered and bloody, vaguely familiar.

I know this person, Atticus thought with a lurch.

"Atty," Ru whispered. "This is you."

"What? Well, there's a resemblance—"

"Atty, I've seen you dead enough times to recognize your body. This is you. Look, there's blood mice."

This was directed at small forms darting for new cover as Ru shifted the body slightly.

They're just normal black mice, Atticus thought at first. He'd long resigned himself to being a freak of nature; the one-in-a-trillion result of the genetics game played with billions of combinations over millions of years. Like the Elephant Man, he'd been oddly malformed, only his monstrosity remained hidden down on the cellular level.

Then he realized that he could *feel* the mice—little motes of terror moving through his awareness.

They're why the car feels afraid. He looked again at the dead body with the familiar face. His face—just at an angle he wasn't used to viewing. *He's like me?* Atticus laid his hand on the boy's cheek. The flesh was cold to touch, but it was his skin, his cells, his DNA. It felt like half his body was dead and being examined by a part still alive. He jerked his hand back.

"We've got to get him out," Ru was saying. "And into the Jaguar."

He's not "like" me, he is me! Numb, Atticus slowly shook his head. "We call nine-one-one."

"Atty, if we call nine-one-one, they'll take him to the morgue and do an autopsy."

Atticus shuddered at the idea of being not completely dead, but entirely helpless. "We don't know if he'll come back to life."

Ru shook his head. "If he's like you, it's going to take him hours to heal up from this kind of damage. But if he can recover, and we let the coroners take him . . ."

"Oh, fuck." That didn't bear even thinking through. "Okay. Get the Jag."

Atticus would guess the boy to be twenty at most, but Atticus had aged strangely, still looking to be in his teens when he was nearly thirty. Even now Atticus could pass for mid-twenty. Hair as crow black as his own, but long enough for a braid down past the shoulder blades. Boots with a crease mark from shifting motorcycle gears across the top of the left foot. Blue jeans incrusted with road dirt and dead blood. A black T-shirt with small bullet holes punched into the chest. Powder burns indicated the boy had been shot at close range. His arms were handcuffed behind his back, where the bullets had shredded part of the design on the leather jacket. Only the words "Dog Warrior" remained.

Who the hell is this? Why did they kill him?

The damage had been done by more than just bullets. Road dirt, abrasions, paint, and shattered bones indicated that the boy had been hit by a car first. Judging by the angle of entry for the bullets, he'd been lying prone when shot. Oddly, his killers had bound his feet and handcuffed him after he'd died. They'd done a thorough job murdering the boy, but if he was like Atticus, it wouldn't be enough to keep him dead.

Pulling on his leather gloves, Atticus took the handcuffs

and jacket off the boy, leaving them as evidence on the bloody carpet. Ru pulled the Jaguar in beside the Honda and popped the trunk but left the motor running.

"Good compromise," Ru said of the jacket and hand-cuffs. "I need to move the bags. Here." He held out a small cage. "Don't forget the mice."

Some of the Dog Warrior's blood had dried on the car-pet—totally lifeless. The rest had survived spilling out of the boy's body by changing into mice. They scurried out of At-ticus's reach as he shifted the body around, a dozen in all, little bundles of fear and worry.

Come here. He called to them as he would to his own mice. *Come on. Hurry.*

He didn't expect it to work, but they scurried forward and let him scoop them into the cage.

Ru had shifted their bags into the Jaguar's backseat, tuck-ing in the mouse cage last. "Let's get out of here before someone calls the police on us."

Atticus lifted the body up and out of the trunk. As he set-tled the boy into the Jaguar, Ru tugged his right glove back on and closed the Honda's trunk tightly.

It took two minutes to steal the body and stow it safely away. Certainly not what Atticus expected they'd be doing when they stopped for a stretch and something warm to drink. It felt weird driving away, knowing what was in their trunk. Atticus supposed that Ru was used to the feeling, all things considered.

Ru was getting "the grin," enjoying the adrenaline high of doing something outlandishly bold without breaking a sweat. "What do we do about his friends in black?"

Atticus handed Ru his cell phone. "Anonymous tip time."

"You don't suppose they are his friends? Certainly I've driven around with you dead in the trunk enough times. We could be leaping to the wrong conclusion."

"No. They murdered him. The mice are too afraid for them to be friends."

"Ah," Ru murmured. "I suppose I always take the hand-cuffs off you."

"Thank you."

"You're welcome." Ru flashed him a grin, and made the call to weave a mix of truth and fiction.

Atticus hated the house. They crossed Massachusetts on I-90 in a nearly straight shot, dropped down, bypassing Boston until they reached Cape Cod, and then followed increasingly narrower roads until they hooked around a sharp curve and the road stopped altogether. The house sat on a windswept hill, surrounded by sand dunes and nothing else; a contemporary designed for views, it had walls of glass and sprawling, multilevel decks to extend the living space.

All the houses they had seen thus far had been dark on the cold autumn weekday evening. This one, however, was bright, throwing slants of light out into a yard mostly of sand. Kyle's Ford Explorer filled the carport. Obviously they were in the right place.

"You've got to be kidding," Atticus said. "This is Lasker's place?"

"It's all about appearances." Ru zipped up his leather jacket. "Got to have flash."

"Maybe while Lasker was alive. Whose bright idea was it to use his house?"

"I think Sumpter's."

Atticus sighed and got out of the Jaguar. The ocean rumbled close by, like a monster hidden by the darkness, scenting the air with salt. Atticus stood in the freezing wind until he accustomed himself to the bombardment of vastly different stimuli. New places tended to overwhelm him.

The Dog Warrior was still dead. While Ru held the front door, Atticus lifted the body out of the trunk and carried it into the house.

The downstairs was basically one open area with only furniture to denote where one "room" ended and the next

started. A forest of support columns held up the second floor
in the absence of load-bearing walls. To the left a series of
French doors gave access to a sprawling deck. To the right,
a sleek marble fireplace anchored the house. Perhaps Lasker
had used the house merely as flash—bare as a hotel room, it
smelled like one too, tainted only with sea spray, ancient
wood fires, and propane cooking gas.

Kyle was in the kitchen area, counting money. The L-
shaped, granite-topped island was a disarray of computer
equipment, weapons, surveillance cameras, and stacks of
twenties. Despite it being after midnight, he smelled of fresh
soap, and his hair was damp from a recent shower. Somehow,
though he was being stylishly dressed in a charcoal turtleneck
sweater and gray slacks, Kyle managed to look scruffy. It was
more than his perpetual five-o'clock shadow and uncombed
hair—there was a way he held his body, something between a
slouch and a sulk, that defeated all of Ru's fashion tips.

"You hate the house," Kyle called without looking up
from his counting. "It's too isolated, too open, too many
windows, too many doors, and not enough cover. Lasker
was an idiot. You're going to kill Sumpter next time you see
him."

"Yeah, something like that." Atticus paused, considering
where to put the dead body.

"I was starting to worry—the Weather Channel shows a
big storm coming in." Kyle licked his fingers and continued
to count, bobbing his head as he mumbled, "Six hundred,
twenty, forty, sixty, eighty, seven hundred."

"We had a delay." Ru carried in the mouse cage and set it
on a desk built into the kitchen cabinets.

Kyle paused to frown at the mice. "Atty got hurt?" He
turned to look at Atticus and started at the dead body in
Atticus's arms. "Holy shit, who the hell is that?"

"Good question." Upstairs, Atticus decided, out of sight,
would probably be the best place for the boy. He started up
the stairs. "Where's a bathtub?"

"Master bathroom." Kyle followed him. "Top of stairs, to the right, at the end of the hall—but you're not going to put him in there. It's a Jacuzzi!"

"You want him in the shower?" Atticus knew the answer would be no. God forbid they desecrate a shower.

"Oh, gross, no— Shit! I've got security running." Kyle dashed back down the steps.

"Wipe the memory!" Atticus called after him.

The master bedroom looked out over the gray, shifting ocean. The master bath was all black marble and sleek white fixtures. Water still beaded on the glass surround of the dual-person shower. The massive tub sat tucked into a bay window alcove with a foot-wide surround of marble.

The body left a smear of dead blood on the white acrylic when Atticus settled it into the tub. "What a mess."

As Atticus cut off the boy's bullet-tattered shirt, Ru came up with the luggage.

"Here. I brought these up." Ru held out a plastic bag for the black T-shirt. There had been white lettering on the shirt's back, but the exiting bullets had shredded the design; the only thing readable was "Benne" in a thumb-sized font under "Priva" in larger letters. "How is he?"

"Still dead."

As Ru gingerly carried away the bloody shirt, Atticus undressed the body down to underwear. He was always the subject of this exercise—the dead person needing to be nursed back to life. It was a weird, out-of-body experience to be on the caregiving side.

The murderers had stripped the boy of all belongings; at one time, he had carried a wallet, cell phone, keys, change, a Swiss army knife and a pistol—all now missing. Only microscopic traces of them tainted the cotton fabric of his clothes. The bare basics that remained showed that the similarities between Atticus and the Dog Warrior went past genetic makeup and outward appearances. They both preferred

the same hiking boots, cotton boxers, blue jeans, soap, deodorant, and shampoo.

From such an identical foundation, how different could
they be?

The biker jacket suggested the differences could be huge.

Kyle reappeared at the door with the first-aid kit. "Ru
said to bring this up. What are we going to do if he doesn't
come back?"

What a fucking mess that would be. But you didn't say
that to Kyle. While Ru got off on danger, Kyle liked to feel
safe. Kyle had driven straight to the Cape instead of joining
Atticus and Ru in Buffalo, just to avoid the mess they were
dealing with there. "I'll deal with it."

"We've got the buy going down tomorrow night." Kyle
glanced at his watch. "Tonight actually."

"Kyle, I know." Atticus opened up the kit and found the
antibiotic cream. While the bullets probably lodged foreign
material into the wounds, his body usually expelled such
matter while healing. Hopefully—on all counts—the boy
was the same. "I'll figure something out if he stays dead,
okay. Do we have all the money?"

"Yeah, I was just counting it for a second time." Kyle
fidgeted while he watched Atticus apply cream and bandages. "I'm completely jacked in. Phone and cable are up,
and I've got security running. We're set for anything—well,
almost anything." Not counting miscellaneous dead bodies
that might or might not come back from the dead. "I also
stocked the fridge, and put fresh linen on the beds."

"Great! Okay, do me a favor." Atticus told him where and
how they'd found the dead body. "Find out, if you can without drawing attention to us, who killed him and what happened after we left."

"Do you have an ID on him?" Kyle pointed to the boy in
the tub.

"No. He was wearing colors." Atticus described the biker

jacket. "The club name was either Dog Warrior or War-riors."

"Bottom rocker?"

The city named at the bottom of the patch identified the chapter that the member belonged to. Club enforcers, who drifted from chapter to chapter, collecting dues, would have "Nomad" printed in place of a chapter name.

"There was none." Now that Kyle mentioned it, Atticus realized how odd it was. Perhaps the jacket hadn't been a true "gang" jacket.

"See what you can pull up on the name."

"Right." Kyle left in his abrupt manner, locked onto something new.

Having covered the gaping bullet holes, Atticus strapped the broken ribs and splinted the shattered arm; apparently when the car had hit the boy, he had taken the brunt of the damage with his left side. Finally done repairing what damage he could, Atticus washed his hands, and caught sight of himself in the mirror. He studied his reflection for a minute and then looked down at the boy, trying to judge whether they were as identical as their genetics as Ru claimed them to be. While he had stopped being carded long ago, he didn't look the thirty-six years that his driver's license reported. If he seemed solidly in his mid-twenties, what age was this boy who looked only in his late teens? The differences be-tween them were slight. Atticus kept his hair in a short, styl-ish cut instead of the boy's long braid. The boy seemed to have another inch or two to grow before reaching Atticus's height; his youth showed in his chin, the column of his neck, and the depth of his chest. Atticus could remember, though, having this build, this face.

Ru came back with a cocoa blast. "We should get him up if we can, in case Sumpter shows."

One of the bullets had sliced through a major artery, thus the reason for the body shutting down—to keep the heart from pumping out the entire blood supply. Atticus could sense, though, that the wound was healed over. That was promising in and of itself. "Give it a shot."

Ru held the beer stein of warm mash under the Dog Warrior's nose. He gave the stein to Atticus to hold, repositioned the boy's head so the throat was one straight column, and spooned some into the lax mouth. "Come on, come on." After a minute, he shook his head. "No, it's not working." He thumped back onto the tile floor. "This is going to *soooo* suck if he stays dead."

"He's healing," Atticus said slowly. If Atticus could control the mice, and sense the body healing, maybe he could influence it even more. "Let's get him out of the tub."

"Hold on." With practiced ease, Ru cut off the soiled underwear, wrapped it in plastic, tossed it away, and cleaned the boy. It was embarrassing to know Ru had learned the skill on Atticus. Washing his hands, Ru spread a blanket out on the floor. "Okay."

They lifted the body out of the tub and onto the blanket, tucking the flannel around the cool skin.

Atticus leaned over the Dog Warrior, extending his awareness until the boy's still body seemed like part of his own. He could feel the dormant cells patiently waiting for the return of life. *Come on. It's time to be alive. Breathe!* The boy's body arched upward as Atticus forced it hard into the first breath. *Good boy!* He let it go slack and nudged the heart into a beat. *Breathe!* Again the body bent as the breath rattled into its lungs. *Come on. You can do it. Breathe!*

Like a motorcycle being kick-started, the Dog Warrior lurched through the forced breath, gave a sudden half cough, and then gagged as his newly awake stomach decided to eject its contents.

Atticus levered the boy up and over the toilet before he choked, and the boy's stomach emptied. He was ice-cold, and the vomit splashing over Atticus's arm held the same dead chill. The kid was shivering hard, his teeth chattering.

But he was alive. There was a heart thumping hard under

Atticus's palm, pressed to the kid's chest. The kid took deep, deep breaths, like someone who had stayed underwater to the point of drowning and had now come up for air.

"Well, that worked," Ru said. "Whatever you did."

With a wolflike snarl, the Dog Warrior spun to face Ru. Atticus felt the stranger's anger, fear, and despair as the boy started to growl. It was a feral sound, deep in the boy's chest, inhuman in its resonance and savagery.

"We're not going to hurt you," Atticus said. "We're not the ones that killed you."

Atticus had been expecting human reactions. As he started to speak, the boy jerked around to face him even while scuttling away from both of them with stunning speed. A moment later, the Dog Warrior was backed against the bay windows, the pit of the tub between them. His dark eyes locked on Atticus in a steady, unblinking stare that seemed to see into him, to his core, and through, to encompass all that he was and wasn't.

Belatedly, Atticus realized that—because they were physically identical—the boy hadn't realized Atticus was there until he had spoken.

"It's okay." Atticus tried for a calming tone. "You're safe."

Ru started to move, and the boy's stare flicked to him, his lips going back into a silent snarl. Of course, Ru took it in stride, holding out the stein of warm chocolate mash. "Cocoa blast?"

The Dog Warrior sniffed, nostrils flaring to catch the liquid's scent, as he considered the two of them. "Boy" was the wrong word for him. Dead, he seemed a young and helpless human. Alive—even deathly pale, covered with bandages, arm splinted, and shivering hard as his body fought to climb back to normal core temperature—there was no denying that he was something wild and powerful. Slowly, the Dog Warrior uncoiled from the corner, crept forward, and took the large stein in his one good hand.

He drank greedily, getting a dark brown milk mustache,

which he licked off. All the while, he watched them with the all-seeing stare.

"What's your name?" Atticus asked.

"U-U-Ukiah." It was forced out between chattering teeth.

Atticus exchanged a look with Ru; he'd been found as a toddler in Idaho, just over the Blue Mountains from Ukiah, Oregon. "Like the town? Ukiah, Oregon?"

"Y-y-yes."

Atticus waited for him to add a last name, but none was forthcoming.

"W-w-who are you?"

"Atticus. Atticus Steele."

"I'm Hikaru Takahashi, but my friends call me Ru."

Ukiah thrust out the empty stein, the hand trembling, but the eyes locked and steady. "M-m-more. P-p-please."

At least he had manners.

Ru took the stein and murmured, "It's going to be easier to feed him downstairs."

Yes, but the kitchen was full of money and guns. "Go let Kyle know I'm bringing him down."

Kyle hastily packed away the money as Atticus half carried the blanket-wrapped Dog Warrior downstairs; he gave Atticus annoyed looks as he stuffed stacks of twenties into a brushed-steel briefcase. The guns were out of sight, and Kyle's computers showed only log-in screens.

As Ru mixed another cocoa blast using raw eggs, puréed liver, wheat germ, and chocolate sauce, Atticus helped Kyle hide away the money.

"Speaking as someone who has an asshole for a brother," Kyle hissed, "we shouldn't trust him."

Atticus looked to the stranger with his face and feral eyes. *Brother?*

Amazing how one word could explode so much emotion through him. Atticus couldn't even identify all the fragments. Excitement? Maybe something that might have even been joy, but heavily mixed with anger and fear. Family was something Atticus had dreamed about as a child, along with a Santa Claus who would finally figure out which foster home he lived in and deliver several years' worth of misplaced presents.

The Dog Warrior at least had his keen hearing. "B-brother works."

Yeah, right. Still, Atticus couldn't deny that they were genetically identical. *Younger twin brother?* "Who are you? Really?"

Ukiah eyed Kyle, apparently unsure if Kyle was in on family secrets.

"These are my best friends," Atticus said. "I don't hide things from them."

Ukiah picked up a bag of fresh pizza dough Ru had set out of the refrigerator in his search for the cocoa blast makings. "O-our mother was from the Cayuse tribe. Her name was Kicking Deer."

The Cayuse were a Native American tribe in northeast Oregon, over the mountains from where Atticus had been found. According to his case files, the Idaho state police checked with the reservation outside of Pendleton and no one had reported a missing infant. He and Ru had double-checked the summer of their junior year in college. Atticus controlled a flash of anger—he couldn't assume that the boy was telling the truth.

Ukiah fumbled open the bag, and shivered while making the dough into a soft, squishy doll. "Kicking Deer was kidnapped and made pregnant by our father, Prime."

"Prime?" Atticus echoed.

"That's the English version of his name. He wasn't human." Ukiah laid the doll onto the granite counter, and hugged the blanket around his shoulders. "Kicking Deer had a baby. His name was Magic Boy."

"Just one baby?" Ru took sausage links out of the microwave and set them in front of the Dog Warrior.

"I don't get it," Kyle said.

"One of us was this Magic Boy?" Atticus hoped there was a point to this story.

They had to wait while the narrator gobbled down the sausages and licked his fingers clean.

"I-if Magic Boy was hurt," Ukiah continued finally, pinching off a small ball of dough, "what he lost became a mouse." He rolled the ball around on the counter. "Which Magic Boy could recover later by merging it back into him."

"We know about blood mice," Atticus said.

"Ah. Good." Ukiah merged the tiny piece back into the doll with trembling fingers. "Got to keep track of them. They're very important."

Atticus fought the urge to ask why. *Why can't I remember being a baby when I have a perfect memory? Why do I bleed mice? Why do we come back from being dead?* There were so many questions. Would he like the answers? "So I'm this Magic Boy?"

"Well, one day Magic Boy was murdered." Ukiah pulled a cleaver from the knife block beside him. "He was killed with an axe."

Atticus watched with horror as the Dog Warrior hacked the helpless doll apart, reducing it to bits.

"It was quite horrible," Ukiah said sadly, letting the cleaver drop. "All the parts ran in terror. Some went this way." A leg rolled into a ball that went right. "Some went that way." The head rolled to the left. "The pieces scattered away, never to be Magic Boy again."

Ukiah rolled the dismembered torso across the counter to Atticus and then looked at him with the feral stare. "This was you." He leaned back and pointed at the severed leg in front of him. "This was me." His story done, Ukiah ate the scattered pieces of dough.

"That," Kyle whispered, "is profoundly creepy."

Ru moved the cleaver and the knife block out of the Dog Warrior's range.

Atticus stood and walked away. If it weren't for Ru and Kyle, he would have walked far, far away. He settled for prowling the downstairs. This was too much, too soon. This was like the first time he watched his blood turn into mice. This was like the first time he knew for sure that he had died and come back just by the terror on Ru's face when he woke up. This was like the time he blew off the fingers of his right hand and watched them grow back over a week's time. This was one of those huge mind-altering experiences.

He tried to get a handle on it. He and the boy had been one person. The boy was once his leg or his arm. Someone chopped off his leg and it became the boy. He had a brother. One that bled mice, came back from the dead, and aged oddly too. He wasn't alone.

In the kitchen, the conversation continued without him.

"I need to use a phone," Ukiah was saying.

"The phone hasn't been connected yet," Ru lied. "It should be hooked up tomorrow."

"What about cell phones?" Ukiah asked.

"Sorry, I forgot to charge mine," Ru said. "And Atticus doesn't own one."

Atticus glanced back, feeling slightly guilty; as usual, though, Ru was taking all weirdness in stride, calmly putting out food for the boy while fending off requests that could prove awkward.

Undeterred, the boy looked questioningly to Kyle.

"I-I-I forgot mine at home." Kyle made a bad show of patting his pockets.

There was a reason they kept Kyle out of sight.

Sighing, Ukiah wearily laid his head on the counter. Obviously the food was hitting bottom, and his body was focusing on putting it to good use. He'd be dead asleep in minutes, waking up only when his body burned through all the food he just ate. "I need to call . . ." He yawned deeply. "Let everyone know I'm okay."

"I'll plug my phone in after we get you in bed," Ru promised, clearing away dirty dishes. "You can use it when you wake up."

"Hmm." Ukiah didn't move.

"Where should we put him?" Ru asked Kyle. "How many bedrooms are upstairs?"

"There's one downstairs." Kyle made a face over Ukiah's head and pointed urgently downward.

"*Down* is easier than up," Ru studied the boy for a moment before saying, "He's asleep already. Atty, can you carry him?"

Atticus realized that he had actually felt the boy falling asleep; the fading of a *presence* making him aware of its existence.

"Atty?" Ru said, meaning, *Are you okay?*

"Sure." Atticus said, meaning, *I'm fine.*

While not apparent from the driveway, the house was built into a slope, so it had a walkout basement. In one corner was a guest bedroom with glass-block windows. Obviously Kyle thought it made a handy prison; after they tucked Ukiah into bed and shut the door, Kyle produced a latch and padlock, which he installed with a cordless screwdriver.

"Okay." Atticus eyed the padlock. "You've found something out?"

"Come upstairs."

Upstairs, Kyle logged back in to his computers. "The Dog Warriors are one of five biker gangs that make up the Pack. They're not like any outlaw motorcycle club I've ever heard of—not that I'm an expert."

"Outlaw" denoted the one percent of biker gangs, like the Hell's Angels, who embraced being outside the law. Kyle knew enough to distinguish between the "one-percenters" and normal, law-abiding motorcycle clubs; it was a bad sign that he labeled the Dog Warriors as such.

"How so?"

"Well, they don't pretend to be a club. They don't have a

clubhouse, membership dues, charter rules, officers, or any of that stuff. They don't even seem to have a base city or state—they're complete nomads."

Kyle connected with the Internet and pulled Web pages out of his history log. "This is their leader, Rennie Shaw." Under a banner of blazing red that read, "Wanted by the FBI," and a long listing of crimes starting with, "Murder (eighteen counts)," was a slightly blurred photograph of a man with grizzled hair and vivid blue eyes. "His lieutenant, Bear Shadow." Another "Wanted" page, another blurred photo, this of a Native American with feathers braided into his hair and a necklace of bear claws at his throat. "Shaw's girlfriend, Hellena Gobeyn." A compact, dark-haired woman sat astride a fallen log, cleaning a pistol.

Kyle pulled up one page after another. "There are approximately twenty members of the Dog Warriors. All of them are wanted by the FBI."

This was the fear that been eating at Atticus since taking the jacket off of Ukiah. Still, it felt like he'd swallowed cold gravel. "Ukiah too?"

"No." Kyle hated to abandon his fearful suspicions. "He's not listed with the Dog Warriors. The Demon Curs, another Pack gang, has been active in Oregon for the last few weeks, in and around Pendleton and Ukiah; it's spammed all my searches for your brother. Without a last name, I haven't been able to isolate anything about him."

"Wearing a jacket doesn't automatically make him one of them," Ru reasoned. "If he's not listed with the others, then maybe he got it from a thrift store, or found it and didn't know what it was."

They looked at him.

"I'm farting out my mouth here, aren't I?" Ru said.

"Yes," Atticus and Kyle said.

"We're sitting on a quarter million dollars, enough guns to take out a police department, and a *possible* FBI most wanted locked in the basement." Kyle hedged for Ru's sake. "Brother or not, this isn't good."

"Do some more digging," Atticus said. "We need to know who we're dealing with. What about his killers?"

"They're just as scary in a totally different way." Kyle closed up the FBI pages. "I tapped into the state police system. There was a shootout after you left. One of the men was killed, the other three hospitalized. They've identified themselves as Byte, Ascii, Coaxial, and Binary of the Temple of New Reason."

"Ascii and Coaxial? You've got to be kidding."

"No, it's some New Age cult that seems to be on everyone's hit list of 'loonies to arrest on sight.' The members use computer terms for names. The state police notified everyone from ATF down to NSA." Kyle pulled up some files copied from the state police, and scrolled down through them quickly, knowing that Atticus could memorize an entire screen in a glance. "The cult had a public Web site like Heaven's Gate, but took it down. I found an old cache of it. They have lots of weird ideas about the end of the world."

ATF had been notified because the cult was suspected of massing large numbers of automatic and semiautomatic weapons and buying explosives. The NSA were seeking the cult for wiretapping and hacking government computers. The FBI wanted them for kidnapping and murdering several infants in the Pittsburgh area.

"Wait, go back," Atticus said as a phrase leaped out at him. He leaned over Kyle's shoulder to page backward through the reports. He could call it up in his memory, but then Ru and Kyle wouldn't be keyed in to his thoughts. "Here. New York State Police want them in connection with cremated bodies found near Buffalo. Forensics shows that the bodies had been hacked apart with a bladed instrument, probably an axe, and burned, which matches the MO of murder victims found around the Boston area."

"Buffalo and Boston," Ru murmured.

"Do you think that's what they planned to do with your brother?" Kyle asked. "I mean, if they hit him with a car, shot him dead, and then tied him up, maybe they knew that the only way to keep him dead was to burn his body."

Anger flashed through Atticus, surprising him. Certainly no one deserved such brutal treatment, but this was more than general indignation. Why was he enraged? He forced himself to be honest, backtracking to the source of his fury. He found a series of images and impressions that had preceded the anger—like lightning before the thunder.

The boy lying dormant and helpless in the truck, surrounded by the fearful mice.

Ukiah licking the milk mustache from his lips.

His brother in his arms, reduced to helpless and harmless by sleep, so like Atticus that he couldn't tell where his brother ended and he began.

In his mind he knew there was no reason to trust Ukiah. The boy—no, not boy! Atticus forced himself to remember the snarling young man crouched in the bathroom. He couldn't let himself ignore all facts and suspicions; this was a feral, dangerous stranger. For Ru's and Kyle's sakes, he couldn't harbor any feelings toward this person, not now, and perhaps not ever.

Probably picking up on his inner turmoil, Ru checked his wristwatch. "Well, the buy is going down in about twelve hours. What do you think? Call it a night?"

If Atticus didn't go to bed, neither would they. Kyle rarely slept, driven either by insomnia or hyperactivity—Atticus was never sure which. Ru would stay awake, worrying about him—he could be such a mother hen. All things considered, they needed to be sharp in a few hours.

"Let's lock down," Atticus said, "and get some sleep."

A storm was blowing in off the ocean. Atticus stood leaning against the glass wall of the master bedroom, watching the darkness rush over the water as clouds obscured the moon. Light eaten by darkness.

I have a brother. He's a Dog Warrior. A bunch of religious loons tried to destroy him utterly.

The door to the master bathroom reflected in the window, a rectangle of light, the quiet sounds of Ru getting ready for bed. The light snapped off, the clouds covered the moon, and he was in darkness.

"It's like seeing into the past." Ru came to stare out the window with him. "I look at him, and I see you back when we first met."

"Is that how I looked to you? Like some wild creature?"

Ru laughed softly. "Okay, so he's like a wolf-man version of you. That stare he has—it's like he looks right down into your soul." Ru breathed out and his breath smoked the glass. "I wonder what happened to him that he's like that."

The wind gusted and roared against the house.

"This has really weirded you out, hasn't it?" Ru asked.

"When I touch him, I can't tell where he ends and I begin. I can feel his emotions. When I walk around the house, it's like I have a compass needle in me, and he's north. I can't smell him over my own scent. When I touch things he's used, I only feel myself on the item. He's so close that's he's invisible."

"Like he's you and you're him."

"Like we're one person, yes." Atticus sighed. "What are we going to do with him? We can't keep him locked in the basement."

"He's not going anywhere soon. We give him a phone to keep him happy, stuff him with food, and let him sleep. It's only for a few days, and then when we're done here, we can deal with him properly."

"If we let him call the Dog Warriors, they might come here."

"He doesn't know where he is. We picked him up a hundred miles from here, and he was in a car with Pennsylvania plates—who knows where those butchers actually killed him?"

"He'll ask."

"You are just so fucking truthful sometimes it hurts." Ru laughed softly. "We lie to him."

"What if he knows this area? He'll recognize it."

"We improvise. It's what we're good at."

"I don't want you hurt," Atticus said.

Ru reached out and brushed his hand down Atticus's side and paused, letting it rest on Atticus's hip. And they stood a moment in quiet prelude—the wordless question waiting for a silent answer. One would think, after all this time, he'd be less hesitant, more comfortable with their relationship, with himself. There was still that point, though, where love and desire didn't completely mesh. So delicate was the act of engaging both, that a single word could derail him. So they learned this silent dance, temporarily reversing their normal roles—Ru taking lead and he nearly passive—until they could bump over some deep-seated block.

Atticus nodded, and Ru stepped close, hands warm on his back, mouth softly coaxing him into the full unity of love and want.

CHAPTER TWO

Hyannis, Cape Cod, Massachusetts
Monday, September 20, 2004

Kyle's anxious whisper woke Atticus. He stood at the foot of the bed, jiggling the mattress. "Atticus. Atticus."

"What?" Atticus untangled himself from Ru, who was awake but not stirring. Wise man.

"The power is out." Kyle wore pink bunny slippers and black silk pajamas that he plucked at nervously.

Atticus fumbled for his wristwatch. He'd been asleep only four hours. Outside, the howl of the wind drowned out the roar of the surf. "Fuck."

"I can't run the security systems without power. My laptop has only six hours of power, max. The outside line is dead too."

"Fuck," Atticus repeated, scrubbing at his face. "Remind me to kill Sumpter next time I see him."

"What do I do?"

The heat must be off too—the air was chilly. The temperature had dropped outside, sucking the heat of the house through the great expanse of glass.

"Take the Explorer and find a rental place," Atticus told Kyle. "Pick up a generator. Get fuel for it. There's a fireplace downstairs, right? See if you can pick up some firewood."

That was all that was needed. Kyle nodded, calmed by

having a direction pointed out to him. "Okay. It will take me about an hour or two."

Atticus crawled out of bed.

"What are you doing?" Ru grunted, not even opening his eyes.

"Scouting around the house, getting used to the lay of the land."

"I'll come with you." Ru stirred feebly.

"Get more sleep. One of us should be sharp enough to deal. Besides, I want you to stay with my little brother." It felt weird saying that. Little brother.

"Hmmm? Hmm! Oh, yeah. The Dog Warrior. Okay."

Atticus took a cold shower, leaving the hot water for Ru. Dressing, he pondered his taste in clothes. He would have thought such outward choices were dictated by upbringing, not something genetic. Somehow it seemed impossible that Ukiah could be so feral and yet wear the exact same boots. Atticus laid out warm clothes for his brother, and then tried to banish him out of his mind; he had bigger things to think about.

Putting on a windbreaker to cut the cold wind, Atticus went outside to explore the area.

Lasker's place sat on a low bluff, flanked by other luxury beach houses, which Atticus cautiously circled. He found them empty: weekend retreats closed up for the week. While fringed by a stand of stunted hemlocks, the hilltop had only sand and dune grass, giving it an impression of barren isolation even though he could pick out sounds of distant traffic, screened by the trees.

The houses shared a narrow beach facing south, looking out over Nantucket Sound. The storm surf pounded the shore; the water rolled deep green until it broke to white, reeking of salt and a billion fishy organisms, alive and dead. Atticus knew Martha's Vineyard and Nantucket lay out across the water, but the fog hazed the sky to a smothering level.

Atticus had never put his hand in a bag full of scorpions. He assumed that he had too much common sense and intelligence to ever attempt doing so. There was also the little matter of someone finding a good enough reason for him to try. Yet here he was, about to do the equivalent—and worse, it wasn't going to be his hand alone dipping into the bag.

We should just leave. How could this ever have sounded like a good idea?

To be truthful, it never had. It had always sounded like a bag of scorpions.

They were chasing after a phantom, a new designer drug with street names like Pixie Dust, Mojo, Liquidlust, Blissfire, and Desire. They'd first heard about Pixie Dust in raves around Baltimore, elusive as an urban legend. The supply was so erratic and the demand was so high—and still growing quickly—that they'd never even seen a sample of the drug. No one knew where Pixie Dust was coming from. As Atticus and Ru set up deals for old favorites inside the Beltway, others tracked the new drug to Upstate New York. Outside of Buffalo, things had gone horribly wrong.

Atticus had worked with Boyes, Scroggins, and German. Despite what Sumpter might think, the men had given new meaning to the word "paranoid;" it was unlikely that they would have been careless. Whoever ambushed them had done a ruthlessly thorough job, killing everyone at the warehouse, buyer and seller alike, and smashing all the security equipment.

He and Ru had driven up to Buffalo to identify the bodies. Early Sunday morning, he'd slipped under the police tape and searched the warehouse with his inhumanly sharp senses, but there had been little to find. Scroggins and German had emptied their guns—both carried a SIG Sauer P229 in forty-caliber Smith & Wesson—but not into the dead drug dealers, who had been killed with shotguns. The lack of bul-

let holes in the back wall indicated that they'd hit someone—only all the blood splatters matched up with
accounted-for dead bodies. Also there'd been a mysterious
swath of clean floor, as if something had been dragged
across it. During the long drive from Buffalo to Cape Cod,
he'd reviewed his perfect memory, recalling every inch of
the floor and walls in minute detail, and found nothing he'd
overlooked.

Both sides had reasons to keep the meeting secret, so
who would have ambushed the buy and walked away unscathed? Atticus would have suspected the man who had
acted as the go-between—Jay Lasker—but he had dropped
dead suddenly after setting up a second meeting. With
Lasker had gone all the details about the Pixie Dust and the
people selling it.

So here Atticus and his team were: at a dead man's house,
meeting with people who had no names, seeking a drug
they'd never seen. Unfamiliar with the area, they didn't
know the secret ways, the ancient history, and things long
ago buried but not forgotten. And now his brother was
thrown into the mix.

One thing was clear: If things went badly, there wouldn't
be any place to run to, no one to turn to, no place to hide.

When he got back to the house, Ru was up. Still damp
from his shower, he padded around the kitchen, trying to
figure out what to cook for breakfast with the power out.

"I'm going to wake up Ukiah," Atticus told him. "That
way we can feed him and put him back to bed, out of the
way for most of the day."

"Sounds like a plan."

Atticus unlocked the door to the basement bedroom and
opened it, half expecting to find either an empty room or a
snarling, angry stranger. Ukiah, though, still lay in the bed
as they had left him, apparently so deeply asleep he'd not

moved all night. In sleep, his brother was just a young man, badly battered but healing.

He should wake the boy, and yet he stood at the door, watching Ukiah. All the possibilities of the world existed in his sleeping brother. A family. A friend. A belonging complete beyond any he had ever hoped for. A bitter enemy. A cold mirror reflecting back how inhuman he truly was. Once he was awake, time would flow, a single path taken, a course he probably couldn't control. A part of him hardened over the years by the real world foresaw that the cruelest road most likely would be taken.

Atticus stood watching his brother, hoarding this moment before things went wrong. If he stored it away, no matter what, he would have this one moment of peace.

"We're almost out of eggs," Ru called from the kitchen. "So we're going to have pancakes."

Time started again.

"Okay," Atticus called back. "I'll have him up in a minute."

Ukiah was sluggish to get roused and up the stairs. Atticus could feel his brother's bone-deep weariness as his body slaved to knit bones, repair organs, and deal with the massive blood loss that the mice represented.

At the top of the steps, though, Ukiah suddenly veered off toward the back door. The blanket around Ukiah's shoulders slipped to the floor as he opened the door and stepped out onto the deck. Hunching against the stiff cold wind sweeping off the ocean, the boy started for the railing, faltered, and came to a halt. Atticus felt disorientation flooding into his brother, sweeping away both dismay and sense of self.

He's never seen the ocean before!

Picking up the blanket, Atticus went out to rescue him. The feral look was gone, replaced by more human confusion and distress. Naked, the boy was shivering but too overwhelmed to move.

"Come on." Atticus wrapped the blanket around his brother's shoulders and pulled him back inside the house, shutting the door on the roar and the salt-laden spray.

"I could hear it roaring all night." Ukiah whimpered like a lost puppy, his gaze still trapped by the endless gray of ocean. "I could feel it pounding against the land, but I couldn't figure out what it was."

"It's the Atlantic Ocean."

Ukiah tore his gaze away, dismay creeping back in. "Where am I?"

If he'd never seen the sea before, he didn't know the New England coastline.

"Gloucester, Massachusetts," Atticus said. They had decided on the town in case—like Atticus—Ukiah had maps stored in his perfect memory. Gloucester faced water to its south, and had islands across its bay. Not a perfect match for Nantucket Sound, but Gloucester gave them a hundred-mile margin for error. They kept within the state to account for the proliferation of Massachusetts license plates if they had to move him any distance.

"How did I end up here?"

"Ru and I drove in from Buffalo last night. We stopped at the Ludlow service area on the Mass Turnpike and found you locked in the trunk of a car." Atticus described the car, only to get a blank look and a slow shake of the head. "We were hoping you could tell us about it."

"Last thing I remember," Ukiah said slowly, "I was with Rennie in a parking garage."

Through years of experience, Atticus was able to treat the comment as just a data point and file it away to be reacted to later.

Ukiah eyed the cage of black mice on the kitchen's desk. "Are those my mice or yours?"

"Yours." It came out naturally, yet Atticus still found the concept of someone else that bled mice stunning. "All twelve. We've fed them."

On Ukiah's face, desire to remember everything forgotten warred with knowledge of his limits. He was too weak to take back the mice and he knew it.

"Eat and then sleep some more." Ru added water to the pancake mix and then started to stir. "You can deal with them later."

Ukiah grunted acknowledgment of this truth, eyeing the batter hungrily.

"Here." Atticus patted the stack of clothes he'd laid out for his brother. "Let's get you dressed first."

After two awkward minutes of Atticus trying to help Ukiah into the boxers, Ru took pity. "Why don't you cook, and I'll get him dressed?"

So they switched, Atticus lighting the gas burner on the range, while Ru helped Ukiah put on the boxers.

Atticus had always been too hurt to appreciate Ru's bedside manner—he hadn't noticed how Ru could get another man in and out of underwear with such clinical impassiveness. Sweatpants and a pair of tube socks followed boxers.

"Sweater?" Ru asked after watching how carefully Ukiah moved his newly mended arm.

"No, please!" Ukiah winced at the thought.

"Then that will have to do for a while." Ru resettled the blanket around Ukiah's shoulders.

Ukiah fingered the sweater where it lay on the counter, then checked its Lands' End label. "I have this sweater too. Same green color." He inspected his borrowed sweatpants, and then—tugging the front of his sweatpants open—he eyed his boxers.

"Can I take a look-see?" Ru asked.

"What?" Ukiah snapped shut his sweatpants.

Ru looked puzzled and then suddenly grinned. "Your ribs! Can I see them?"

"Oh!" Ukiah opened up his blanket wrap. "There shouldn't be much to look at."

Ru ran light fingers over Ukiah's chest. "It just blows me

away how you two heal. Just apply food and sleep. It ends up being like making bread. Cover the mess up with a blanket and keep it warm, and poof, it transforms itself while you aren't looking."

Ukiah struggled not to laugh. "My ribs still hurt like hell."

"Yes, but they look fine. Here, let me see your arm. Yes, that's healing nicely."

"I've got some use of it back." Ukiah demonstrated. "But the slightest pressure will break it again."

Ru produced a sling and tucked Ukiah's arm into it. "Try not to use it, then."

"Check." Ukiah fiddled to make the sling comfortable.

So the feral Dog Warrior did have a civilized side, once he healed up.

Atticus lifted the first of the pancakes off the griddle and drowned them in syrup for Ukiah. The next batch Atticus split with Ru, but the rest, a monster's share, went to his brother.

After wolfing it all down and licking his plate clean, Ukiah looked longingly at the empty bowl. "Is there anything else?"

"Oh, what pleading puppy eyes." Ru stood and tousled Ukiah's hair, ending the move with a pat on the head. "I had a dog that would beg at the table with that same woebegone look."

Ukiah grinned in response to the affectionate teasing. "Bowwow."

"I could never say no." Ru studied the contents of the dark refrigerator. "How about a steak?"

"Oh, yes! Please," Ukiah said. Whoever raised Atticus's brother had at least taught him manners, despite all the feral appearances. "The power's out?"

"Yes," Atticus said, and then, sensing the coming question, added, "The phone is still dead."

"I did manage to charge up my phone before the electricity went out." Ru slid his phone across the counter. "You can make a call while I get this started. Try to keep it short—it's the only working phone we have."

Ukiah took it and wobbled off across the open downstairs to the farthest corner for privacy.

Ru wore a slight puzzled look on his face as he did a quick wash on a skillet.

"What?" Atticus asked.

"Just thinking on differences."

"Like what?"

"It was weeks before you'd let me touch you that casually." Ru dried the skillet. "You hated it anytime I'd breach your personal space. You still don't like strangers touching you." With a glance toward the roiling surf, Ru added, "And I've never seen you space out like he just did with the ocean."

"I was over the worst of it by the time we met," Atticus said. "I would lose it like that every time they'd move me to a new foster home. It always made a wonderful first impression on foster parents."

The quiet conversation across the room had a familiar cadence—a peppering of questions with lots of silences that indicated listening. Atticus had made many such calls— *What happened while I was dead*?

Ukiah came back, silent and sullen. The feral look was back in his eyes. What triggered the sudden change? He put the phone down beside him on the counter, not offering to return it.

"How do you like your steak? Bloody?" Ru guessed, probably because it was how Atticus liked his steak.

"Yes."

"Then this is done." Ru gave Ukiah a sincere smile, one of the ones that went soul deep, the kind he usually gave only to people he loved.

The feral look gave way before Ru's smile. "Thank you."

Still, he ate with wolflike ferocity.

It was good Ukiah would be sleeping soon, Atticus decided. He found that the boy absorbed all his attention. Surely some of it was that Ukiah was new and unknown—Atticus's own personal ocean to be lost in. He could ill afford the distraction.

Ukiah lifted his head and went still.

"What is it?" Ru asked.

"Harleys. Ten of them."

Atticus listened and heard them now, a rumble of multiple motorcycle engines growing closer. He couldn't tell the make or the exact number, although he could pick out six or seven distinct engines.

The Dog Warriors! Did he call them?

Ukiah glanced at him. "No, they're not Pack."

Atticus frowned. "How do you know?"

"Pack knows Pack."

"What does that mean?"

"Shut your eyes," Ukiah commanded.

Atticus hesitated. He knew how fast he could move—even wounded, Ukiah could probably strike as quickly. He checked to see if Ru was in position and ready before closing his eyes.

"Keep your eyes shut." Ukiah's voice came out of the darkness. "Focus on me."

He could feel Ukiah's presence beside him like an electric ghost. His brother moved, a rustle of blanket, and Atticus sensed that Ukiah had stretched out a hand to nearly touch him, fingers splayed close but not pressing against the fabric of his shirt. Atticus reached without opening his eyes and found Ukiah's hand with his own. Traces of steak. Road dirt. His own saliva. His own flesh. His own blood.

This is right. This is good.

"Looks like we have company," Ru remarked dryly, breaking the spell.

Atticus dropped his brother's hand and stood. The motorcycles had rounded the sharp bend in the road and come into view.

Ukiah grunted. "Iron Horses."

"You know them?" Atticus asked.

"I know of them," Ukiah said. "They're Pack wanna-bes; the biggest one is John Daggit. He's the New England chapter president. Rebar is his sergeant at arms." Which meant Rebar would be the club enforcer. "Smithy and Draconis are both local members, but Animal is a nomad. I don't know the rest. They could be prospects or maybe another club."

The motorcycles roared up to the driveway of the house, sat a moment, scanning the land, gunning their engines, and then silenced ominously.

Who were they? Friends of Lasker? The killers from Buffalo? Or, despite what Ukiah claimed, part of the Pack?

The house felt like a trap, but at least it offered some protection. The treeless sand dunes were entirely too exposed. Atticus went to the door, opened it, and stood waiting for the bikers to come to him.

Atticus had originally thought that "biggest one" meant "the most desirous wannabe" but apparently Ukiah had just meant "huge all over," and the monster of a man on the lead bike was John Daggit.

"You Steele?" Daggit dismounted to swagger toward the house. He topped Atticus by another head with huge, beefy hands. His stock of gray-salted brown hair was shaggy, framing a face that might have been handsome except for the dark inset of his eyes, which made him look not totally sane.

"What do you want?" Atticus kept the door blocked even though Daggit loomed over him. Obviously the big man was used to his size intimidating people.

"Look, asshole . . ." Daggit put out a hand to brush him aside. Atticus caught the hand and used it to bring the big man down to his knees, eliminating the leverage that Daggit's size might have given him.

"What do you want?" Atticus repeated calmly, pushing the hold almost to the point of breaking the arm.

"I'm a friend of Jay Lasker's." Daggit hissed in pain. "If you're Steele, then I've got business with you."

Perfect. The sellers—twelve hours early. Atticus released Daggit, stepping back to let him up.

"Yeah, I'm Atticus Steele."

Daggit got up, wincing at his arm. "I'm John Daggit."

Great. Well, things were so amazingly screwed, but they had no choice but to act as if it were business as usual. "Come in."

"I figured the deal would be off once Lasker died." Daggit ducked into the house, six of his men following. They stank of unwashed hair, old sweat, hot oil, engine exhaust, cigarette smoke, and spilled beer. Atticus scanned them discreetly for weapons. Something crystalline glittered on their hands, clothes, and faces. Pixie Dust? "All I got off him was a name and time."

Which was more than Atticus had gotten. By all signs, Sumpter had focused on the logistics of arranging the buy without getting the intel on the seller, trusting that Lasker would cover those details later. Why was it that the idiots were never the ones that dropped dead?

"Everything is still go." To force introductions and get names attached to the other men, Atticus waved toward Ru. "My partner, Hikaru Takahashi." Then, because he didn't want to get Ukiah more involved than he had to, Atticus made a dismissive noise and added, "And my little brother."

"This is Animal. He's a nomad for the Iron Horses." Daggit named the others—confirming Ukiah's guesses—apparently working from level of importance instead of by whom was standing closest to him. Animal was a wiry man with flamboyant red hair and beard and a slightly manic smile. "Rebar here is my right-hand man." The club enforcer was a bald man whose leather jacket and thick waist disguised a strongly built body. Daggit rattled off the names of the others as if they were of no consequence. "Draconis. Smithy. Quasimodo. Mutt and Jeff."

Draconis was a tall, lanky man with dark hair and beard. Smithy was short, pudgy, and sweating nervously. Quasimodo was as ugly as his namesake. Mutt and Jeff were brothers or cousins; both had the same broad face and sparse, sandy hair.

Atticus committed faces to memory as he kept between the bikers and Ru. He could hear a faint ongoing chiming sound but he couldn't tell the source. As he moved around the room, it stayed elusively faint and directionless. "You're here earlier than we expected. We said dusk, not first thing in the morning."

"Are we screwing up some kind of schedule?" Daggit sneered.

"We were thinking about heading out." Ru reached out and flicked the nearest light switch on and off. "The power is off here. The stove is gas, so we were able to make breakfast, but there's no coffee."

"Yeah, well, it's off for most of the Cape." Daggit meandered through the living room, pausing to open up a drawer and look into it. "A substation got taken out last night in the storm. You'll have to go pretty far out for that coffee."

"Ah." Ru drifted out of the tight corner of the kitchen. "Do you have what we're looking for?"

On the team, Ru was the voice, Atticus was the muscle, and Kyle was the backup—only Kyle was still off getting the generator, and Ukiah, a complete unknown, had been added into the equation. Who knew what direction the Dog Warrior would jump in a situation like this? His brother sat still, seemingly chewing his steak, but Atticus could feel his attention focused on the bikers as they moved around the room.

"Maybe." Daggit had to duck to walk into the kitchen. There was a slight coving to delineate it from the open living room that Atticus hadn't noticed before.

"Nah." Animal's red hair made a nimbus around his head as he shook it. "We just drove all the way out here for our health."

"Do you have it or not?" Atticus snapped, irritated over how fucked-up the situation was. They didn't even know what form the drug came in—pill, brick, dust? They'd have to dance around the word "drug" until they knew.

"Perhaps." Daggit opened the refrigerator, scanned the inside, and helped himself to one of the beers.

Atticus wished that for once a deal could go down without all the coy double talk. He supposed it would make life too simple. "We're not buying 'perhaps' here. Do you have the shit or not?"

Ru gave Atticus a look that said, *What am I missing?*

Daggit had found Ukiah's mice and crouched to stare into the plastic cage. The black mice lined up to stare back.

"What's up with the mice? They look like Pack . . ." Daggit reached out a hand for the cage, but froze when Ukiah growled.

"Don't touch my mice, Daggit," Ukiah said through clenched teeth.

Daggit grunted, abandoning the mice to study the Dog Warrior. "What do we have here? You don't look like you've got bite behind that growl."

On the other side of the room, providing cover for Ru, Atticus was in the wrong place to stop Daggit as he made a grab for Ukiah.

"Don't touch me!" Ukiah snarled, jerking back out of reach with surprising speed, but at a cost. Atticus felt the pain that flashed through his brother as one of the fragile knits splintered. "You've got Invisible Red on you!"

"I have what?" Daggit glanced at his hand, puzzled.

"Blissfire. Drugs."

Daggit twisted open his beer, frowning at Ukiah. "How do you know that?"

"I can smell it." Ukiah growled, hunching against the pain. "It's all over your skin and clothes."

"No, you can't." Daggit shook his head, took a sip, and explained: "It doesn't have a smell or a color. You can't see it."

"You can't," Ukiah said. "Pack can."

Daggit cocked his head. "Who are you?"

"I'm the Pack's Cub," Ukiah said.

"Aaaaah." Daggit's interest sharpened. "So you're the Cub. Man of mystery. We've heard that you existed but not much more; the Pack won't say squat about you. What are you doing here?"

"I'm eating breakfast." Ukiah tore another mouthful of meat off of the steak and made a show of chewing.

Well, that killed any doubt that Ukiah was one of the Dog Warriors.

Daggit flicked his gaze to Atticus and back. "I didn't know that Pack took brothers."

"We're a special case," Ukiah growled.

Daggit worked his jaw as if it were connected to a massive gear that needed to be turned in order for him to think. "This doesn't feel right. You"—he waggled a finger at Ukiah—"I can buy without a doubt. You've got that wolf feel. Him." Daggit pointed to Atticus. "He's Pack. But this one"—the massive finger settled in Ru's direction—"he's all wrong."

"He's not Pack," Ukiah said before either Ru or Atticus could claim otherwise.

"So who is he?" Daggit asked. "What's he doing here with two Pack dogs?"

"That's Pack business," Ukiah growled softly.

Atticus wondered why Daggit and Ukiah included him as part of the outlaw club. *Pack knows Pack.* Did that mean that the rest of the members were somehow like him? But how would Daggit know, since he wasn't Pack?

"You come to our turf and set up a buy," Daggit was saying, and Atticus struggled to keep his attention on the leader of the Iron Horses. "You make it our business."

Daggit got only "the look" as an answer from Ukiah.

The biker jerked his head in the direction of the mouse cage. "Show me that you're really Pack."

"No," Ukiah grunted around a mouthful of steak.

"Shit has gone down, and there are Iron Horses dead," Daggit said. "I'm not going to jump through hoops until I know that I can trust the people I'm dealing with."

"Fine. Don't deal," Ukiah said.

Daggit pulled out his pistol and put it to Ukiah's head. "I said show me!"

Triggered by Daggit, the other six bikers pulled guns and leveled them at Atticus and Ru.

"Just take it easy." Atticus kept his hands carefully clear from his gun but shifted sideways, screening Ru.

Ukiah stilled, eyeing Daggit, then glanced to Atticus protecting Ru. "Okay." He broke the silence. "You, Rebar, Animal, Draconis, and Smithy—I know can be trusted. The other three—I've never heard of them; they don't get to see. Get them out."

Daggit lowered his gun. "You heard him. Out."

Licking his fingers, Ukiah stood up, shrugging off the blanket. Half-naked, his borrowed sweatpants threatening to slide down off his slim hips, his torso a patchwork of bruises and bandages, dwarfed by Daggit, Ukiah suddenly seemed battered and vulnerable. A fear for his brother took root in Atticus, yet there was nothing he could do but watch as Ukiah limped around the island to the desk, Daggit looming over him. The mice sensed Ukiah's intent and fought for his attention, all wanting back, to be a part of him again. He opened the lid and plucked one out. A second slipped out. "Nah, nah, back in," Ukiah said gently. "I'll get you later."

The unwanted mouse scurried back into the cage.

The mouse in Ukiah's hand shivered with anticipation, a tiny spark of joy.

Ukiah covered it lightly, screening the true process. The spark faded, lost in the larger presence of his brother. After a moment, Ukiah opened up his hands, showing they were empty. "There. I won't do any more tricks for you."

"Looks like someone had you playing dead." Animal smirked, indicating the bandages.

Ukiah snarled silently in response, like the defiance of a wounded dog.

"Are we still dealing here?" Ru struggled to pull the conversation back on track.

"We're dealing," Daggit said. "How much do you want?"

"A hundred grand, to start," Ru said.

With a large buy, they'd learn better how close the bikers were to the source of the drug; the rest of the quarter million would be held in reserve for follow-up buys.

"A nice even number," Daggit said, without indication that it would be a problem to fill. Then what Lasker reported was true—the bikers had ties to the manufacturer.

"Do you have it?" Ru pressed for an answer.

"Not on us," Daggit said.

Atticus and Ru glanced at each other and came to a silent agreement on how to proceed.

"What is this bullshit?" Ru said. "Time is money. Are we supposed to sit around with our thumbs up our butts without so much as a sample?"

"A sample we can provide." Daggit reached into his back pocket and slipped out a thumb-sized self-sealing plastic bag. "This is a nickel bag." He held it up to glitter in the weak sun.

"It's empty," Ru said.

Atticus shook his head. "There's something in it."

"It's invisible." Daggit tented open the bag. "Well, except to Pack. It has no smell. No taste. You can barely feel it."

Daggit stepped forward, offering to pour it out into Ru's palm. Ru raised his hand to accept it, but Ukiah moved—fluid motion at fast-forward speed—to suddenly be standing beside them, Ru's hand trapped in his own. A growl so low it was nearly subsonic came from his brother.

"If you love Ru, don't let him touch it," Ukiah said, and it wasn't until Atticus started to ask why that he realized that Ukiah hadn't opened his mouth, moved his lips, or spoken aloud. *"If one of you must handle it, it should be you—and then don't touch him."*

"Hey, don't pull any freaky Pack shit," Daggit snapped. "Talk with your mouths. You want a sample or not?"

"It's okay." Animal seemed reluctant to annoy either Atticus or Ukiah. "This is good shit. It's not going to hurt him."

"Don't be a wuss." Rebar made a noise of disgust. "This is the safest shit to hit the street. It makes Ecstasy look like heroin."

Intervening between Daggit and Ru seemed to have sucked the last of Ukiah's energy out of him—he started to sag. Ru moved to support Ukiah, either as an excuse to occupy his hands or simply to keep him from falling over—Atticus couldn't tell which.

Atticus put out his hand to receive the drug. Daggit shrugged and spilled out the contents into Atticus's palm. The bikers were right—except for an impression of being slightly greasy, even he could barely feel it. He expected something fairly simple like cocaine, but its molecular structure was vastly complex and strange. For a moment it lay on his skin, and then he felt it seep into his flesh and enter his bloodstream like liquid fire. A dozen heartbeats and the drug surged through his entire body, unfolding into a jangling erotic buzz. He became aroused, suddenly aware of the warmth of Ru's body beside him, his heated scent. The chiming went from nearly imperceptible to so loud it threatened to drown out the conversation around him.

Ukiah leaned against Ru, head against his shoulder, arm about his waist. Ru held his brother lightly in return. It was a disturbingly intimate pose.

"Well?" Ru eyed him worriedly. "Atty?"

"It's real." Atticus gasped.

"So, you want to deal?" Daggit asked.

"Okay," Ru said slowly, still watching Atticus. "Let's try this again, but with money and the real shit."

"No go." Daggit made a motion that took in the house and the ocean. "Not out here. Not after what happened in Buffalo. We pick the place."

"Where?" Atticus snapped.

"There's a town closer to Boston, called Hull. We'll be at Hawg Heaven on Nantasket Avenue. Meet us there at seven."

"Fine," Atticus said, anxious to be done. His thoughts kept straying to Ru—and Ukiah was about to drop over completely.

Daggit followed his gaze and smirked. "Well, you three have fun. We'll see you tonight."

Eternity passed before the Iron Horses roared off on their Harleys.

"Why shouldn't Ru handle it?" Atticus snapped as Ru muscled his brother to the couch.

"It's death." Ukiah sagged back onto the cushions.

"They said that it's harmless," Atticus said. "They all use it."

"They're wrong." Ukiah slid sideways so he half lay on the couch, eyes closed, his feet still on the ground as if he were too weary to move them. "They're all dead men."

"How do you know?"

"It's Invisible Red. It's . . . it's . . ." Ukiah mumbled and then made a raspberry. "It's too hard to think. I just know."

"Will it hurt Atty?" Ru swung Ukiah's feet up onto the couch so he was fully lying on it.

"No," Ukiah said. "Not that little, no."

"It has affected me," Atticus said from across the room, keeping his distance from Ukiah and especially Ru.

Ukiah breathed deeply as if asleep for a minute, and then

mumbled. "You're a . . . a breeder . . . it will make you want to have sex . . . but it won't hurt you . . . you're a breeder . . . it was made to make you breed."

And then he was truly sound asleep.

Atticus took a cold shower, scrubbing the last traces of the drug from his skin, but could do nothing to remove what raced through his blood, filling him with artificial desire.

Ru waited outside the shower, towel in hand and a worried look on his face. "Are you okay?"

"I'm just horny." Atticus accepted the towel.

"When are you not?" Ru teased lightly, but his smile didn't reach his eyes; he was worried.

"I'm fine."

"Lasker dropped dead after using it only a couple of times. The autopsy said he died of an aneurysm."

"I come back from the dead." Atticus scrubbed his short hair dry.

"We don't know if you come back if you're poisoned." Ru picked up another towel and wrapped it around Atticus's waist.

It was the barest brush of Ru's fingertips over his hip, the warmth of his touch gliding across skin, that undid Atticus. It was like a large wild animal awoke in him and shoved him aside to use his body for its own pleasure. It pushed Ru roughly against the wall, bruising his mouth with Atticus's lips, tugging impatiently at his clothing with Atticus's hands. Tasting blood, he tried to stop, but his body continued, leaving him mentally crying *No, damn it, no*! Only after the first, frantic, rough union did he manage to wrestle control back.

"Oh, shit, Ru, I'm sorry."

"Oh, don't you dare think I'm not enjoying this." Ru pulled him back, and he was lost again, but this time he didn't care.

•   •   •

Kyle returned with a generator and had it set up before the drug wore off. Atticus caught him up to speed, explaining the Iron Horses, the drug, Ukiah's identification and caution of it, and the buy scheduled later in the day.

Kyle had only one question. "What are we going to do with your brother *during* the buy?"

Atticus jerked to a full halt as every quick answer he thought of fell flat. Take Ukiah with them? They couldn't put him in with Kyle—they needed Kyle to act as backup, not babysitter. Nor could Atticus and Ru take Ukiah with them in the Jaguar—the last thing they needed in the middle of a buy was someone who could read Atticus's thoughts. Even if Ukiah's telepathic ability wasn't that profound, his presence would be like trying to do surgery while someone jiggled his elbow.

Yet leaving Ukiah locked in the basement seemed dangerous. There was a risk that he'd leave or call out or be found—none of which would be good.

Ru guessed the reason for his silence. "We could lock him back in the Jaguar's trunk."

"Don't tempt me," Atticus snapped. "But, he could easily wake up and cause a problem."

"Well," Kyle said, "we could kill him."

"Kyle!"

"He'd get better."

"No, Kyle."

"Well, I could rig some remote alarms. We'd at least know if any of the doors were opened."

"Even with the phones down?"

"Oh, yeah, I'd link them to a hub that could page my PDA if anything got triggered."

"We're going to be over an hour away," Ru said. "We might know something went down, but we're not going to be able to do anything about it."

"We can't take him with us." Atticus wasn't going to endanger Ru and Kyle to keep Ukiah safe. "Can you search on 'Cub'? That's his street name."

Kyle shook his head after several minutes of searching. "No, nothing is coming up under that name. Did you get a last name out of him?"

"No, the Iron Horses showed up before we had a chance to ask. He did make a call on Ru's phone."

"Ah, tricky." Kyle typed on his keyboard to cue up the recorded conversation.

The number had a 412 area code. Pittsburgh, Pennsylvania. It rang seven times before being picked up, and a sleepy male voice grunted into the phone. "Hmm?"

"It's me," Ukiah said with all confidence his voice would be recognized. And it was.

"Ukiah! Oh, thank God."

"I've got a broken arm, broken ribs. I've been shot about five times. I've got a dozen mice on my hands . . . and I'm at the ocean. What the hell happened?"

Who had Ukiah called? Rennie Shaw?

"The cult nailed you yesterday evening. The police called early this morning; they found your jacket on the Mass Pike but there was no sign of you. We've been worried sick that the cult torched your body. Are you still with them, or are you safe someplace?"

"I think I'm safe. I got yanked out of the trunk, dead, by . . ." There was some mysterious grunting on the other end of the line. "Max?"

No, not Shaw. Atticus leaned over Kyle's shoulder, substituted "Max" for "Cub" and hit return.

"Oh, I'm just trying to get my PDA," the mysterious Max said. "It's—damn it—I hate hospitals. There! Give me the number you're at."

Ukiah read off Ru's number. "Is everyone else okay?"

A woman's voice, distant but growing closer said, "Hi, I'm Deb, your physical therapist. I need to clear you on crutches before you can be discharged."

"Ummm, I'll talk to you later about that. My physical therapist is here." Obviously this Max didn't want to discuss murder and mayhem in front of hospital personnel.

"Max, was anyone hurt?"

"Don't worry, kid. They took you down in Ohio with the Dogs."

"If you want to be released today," Deb said impatiently, "you're going to have to get off the phone."

"Hang tight, kid. And be careful. You're too vulnerable right now to believe anything that anyone tells you. These loons specialize at getting people to trust them. If you were"—a pause as the word "dead" was caught before being said aloud—"if you've got that many mice, your 'rescue' might not be what it seems. I'll call you back as soon as I'm done here."

"Okay."

The line went dead.

Well, that explained why Ukiah had come back from the phone call sullen. The conversation only raised more questions. The search for Pack members with the name of Max had come back empty. So who was this? What was his relationship with Ukiah? Why was he in the hospital? If the "Dogs" were the Dog Warriors, why had the cult attacked them? When did religious groups start wars with biker gangs?

"The number was a private room at Mercy Hospital in Pittsburgh," Kyle complained. "I'll have to hack their database to find out who was in the room."

Ru read the call log off the computer screen. "This Max has called back a dozen times since Ukiah called him." He kept his phone on silent mode; it must have vibrated unnoticed. "If we leave Ukiah here, he might disappear back to Pittsburgh, or wherever he came from."

"We can't take him with us," Atticus repeated.

Ru glanced at his watch. "He'll probably wake up soon after we leave."

"If we get him to take back all his mice, he'll be asleep the rest of the day."

"You think he'll be safe?" Ru asked.

"The only ones who know he's here are the Iron Horses—and they seemed fairly respectful. He should be safe here. We can't take him with us."

By the looks on Ru's and Kyle's faces, the one he was trying hardest to convince was himself.

CHAPTER THREE

The town of Hull sat on a narrow dogleg of land that jutted out into the Atlantic Ocean. On the way to it, they passed signs for "World's End," which seemed appropriate as they drove down Nantasket Avenue, water flanking either side of the road. To their left, the water was nearly pond still, fringed with trees dressed in fall colors. On their right ran an empty parking lot, a sandy beach, and the ocean. Seasonal businesses were closed up, and no one was out on the rainy cold afternoon.

They scouted the area in the drizzling rain before dusk started to set in, not that there was much to be learned. The bar sat on a lump of land in the middle of the narrow peninsula, between the mainland and the bulk of the town on the bulbous tip. Nantasket Avenue split around the bar and its parking lot, with traffic going out to the land's end running in front of the bar, and the lanes heading for the mainland lying behind it. Motorcycles already sat in the bar's parking lot, so they had no chance to scout the inside before the buy.

When it came time, they parked the Jaguar where Kyle could keep watch on both it and the bar and yet stay out of direct sight. They had the money in a backpack on the theory it would draw less notice than a briefcase. Atticus slung it onto his back, made sure it didn't interfere with drawing his pistol, and then led the way into the bar.

Steppenwolf leaked out around the door, wailing about heavy metal thunder. Atticus opened the door and the music flooded out on a wave of warm air, thick with cigarette smoke, beer, and hot grease. Obviously the bar was the refuge of men who had nothing better to do than sit around and abuse themselves with diluted poisons. Atticus stepped in far enough to give Ru room to enter, and paused, letting all the little details sink in. Once the bar became known, his senses would work on automatic, acting like a "spider sense," alerting him to danger as long as he didn't get too deep into focus on something.

"Born to be Wild" beat against his skin. The banks of smoke came from Winston, Old Gold, and Marlboro cigarettes. Off to the right was the clack of billiards, the table screened by bodies. The beer on tap was Samuel Adams and the whiskey of choice seemed to be Jack Daniel's. Unlike other bars he'd been in, this one was heavy with cured leather and blue jeans embedded with the exhaust and engine oil of motorcycles. After the bars and raves of the Beltway, the men were shaggier, dirtier, and more heavily armed. He picked out knives—and in lesser numbers pistols—hidden in boots, in pockets, and under clothing.

It was a WASP blue-collar bar. He and Ru had dressed down in blue jeans and T-shirts and leather jackets, but everything from the shape of their eyes to the color of their skin set them apart.

One of Daggit's Iron Horse peons, Draconis, leaned against the bar, looking up when they came through the door. Recognizing them, he ground out his cigarette, picked up his beer, and sauntered across to greet them.

"Daggit is waiting for you in the back room." Draconis gave a jerk of his head to indicate a doorway behind him. After getting a nod from Atticus—interestingly Ru didn't rate attention—Draconis led the way down a long narrow hall past restrooms reeking of urine to a back room.

The walls muted the music, the bass thumping like the heartbeat of a giant beast.

Five of the Iron Horses sat around a poker table; a single shaded light hung down, throwing harsh shadows on their faces. Crushed cigarette packs, overflowing ashtrays, guns, and crumpled bills littered the table.

Animal was dealing out cards, making them flash across the table in easy, well-practiced throws. He had a pile of bills in front of him, while the others wore surly looks. "Seven-card stud, black deuces and red fours are wild."

A groan went up from the players.

"If you're going to do wild cards, j-just make it one or the other," Rebar cried as the first card landed in front of him. His complaint came too late; his first showing card was a two of diamonds. "Crap. This isn't poker; it's a kid's game."

"They're here," Draconis announced.

Daggit's showing cards were a five of clubs and a nine of hearts. He glanced at his hole cards, frowned, and shoved them back toward Animal without revealing them. "Game's over. Everybody clear out."

"Ahh, I had two queens," one complained, flipping over his hole cards.

"I had three kings," another said, showing a king of hearts, the two of hearts, and the four of spades.

Animal laughed, flashing his gold tooth. "*Black* deuces, *red* fours."

"But last time—"

"Was last time, and this time is this time." Animal tucked away the bills in a wallet already fat with hundred-dollar bills.

The sheared lambs fled, leaving the wolves behind to deal a different type of game.

Atticus gave the opening bid, playing the heavy. "Could

you've picked a place more public? We'll do this deal, but next time we pick the place."

"This is how I do business. My turf. My rules." Daggit took out a revolver and laid it on the table and then produced bullets with dramatic flair. They were self-loaded shells with silvery tips. "I know about Pack and I'm ready for you."

Only confused by the odd display, Atticus glanced to Ru. There was laughter dancing in his partner's eyes.

"Silver bullets?" Ru guessed.

"Damn right!" Daggit loaded the bullets into the revolver. "The only way to deal with werewolves."

"Werewolves?" The word slipped out before Atticus could stop himself.

"Do you think we're stupid?" Daggit ticked factoids off with his fingers. "The Pack. Dog Warriors. Demon Curs. Hell Hounds. Growling like a rabid dog anytime you're pissed off. Howling at the full moon? Jesus, you might as well have it tattooed on your arm: werewolf."

Howling? Atticus had never felt the urge to howl.

"They can't do tattoos, dickhead." Animal snickered. "Their bodies reject the ink and heal over. They don't fucking scar."

That's true, Atticus thought.

"They could use silver ink." Daggit used one of the bullets to imitate the rapid jab of the tattoo needle, complete with a soft *tat tat tat* sound effect.

"Silver only works as a bullet *in* the heart," Animal said. "If it just goes *through* the heart, you're screwed. You're going to get your face torn off by a pissed-off Pack dog."

"Whatever." Daggit waved it off. "Where's the Cub?"

"He's sleeping." Ru gave a safe answer.

"Someone fucked him over good." Animal tapped out a cigarette and lit it. "Who is this walking dead man?"

"The Cub doesn't remember what happened," Ru told them; they'd decided against mentioning Ukiah's real name

to the bikers. Annoying as it might be, they were safest dealing under the Pack's cover.

"He lost that mouse, eh?" Daggit ignored Ru's presence
and addressed Atticus instead. "Or hasn't he taken the mice
back yet?"

"That's why he's sleeping. He took them all back." Actually, they had released the mice into bed with Ukiah. Nature
would take its course, keeping his brother asleep longer than
any drug would. Still, it was startling that the bikers knew
things Atticus thought were secret. Was what they were
telling him about werewolves true?

"Someone's going to get their ass kicked, then." Animal
gave a breathy laugh, eyes going wide with anticipation of
such an event.

"You're Pack too, aren't you?" Daggit finished loading
his revolver and gave the cylinder a spin. "You have that
look."

Atticus glanced towards Ru—he didn't like talking during these things. Normally he stood in the corner, looking
menacing while Ru closed the deal. Because of his Pack
connection, though, the Iron Horses seemed to want to talk
only to him. Ru glanced upward in an abbreviated roll of his
eyes, meaning that they had little choice but to reverse their
roles. "I didn't know we had a look."

"You're lean and mean." Daggit patted his paunch. "You
never see a beer gut on Pack. Six-pack abs. It's all part of the
magic."

"Like voodoo," Animal intoned. "The werewolf curse."

"It's one of the reasons that these dipshits are all drooling
over the idea of being Pack." Daggit shook his head as if not
understanding it. "Ask any one of them if they were willing
to run the risk to be Pack, and they'd sign up for a mauling
in a second."

"Not you?" Atticus asked.

"Hell, no." Daggit borrowed Animal's cigarettes and
tapped one out for himself. "Any retard can do the numbers.

A couple dozen can take the walk in the woods with the Pack, maybe one will come back out *changed*, one of them."

"A Get," Animal said with reverence.

Daggit shot Animal a disgusted look, and then continued. "These dipshits see one of their brothers go all toned without lifting a weight, able to throw a bike around with one hand, and take any amount of shit and get back up, and think, 'That's so cool; I want that too.' They can smell the power, without thinking it all through."

"Hell, I'd do it. Like that!" Animal snapped his fingers.

"Yeah." Daggit lit his cigarette, took a deep drag, and blew out a column of smoke. "And if you do come back, there's a stranger looking out through your eyes."

"Look." Animal pulled out his wallet and thumbed through it to pull out a photo. "Look at this."

Daggit took the photo and studied it a moment. "So?"

Atticus intercepted it before Daggit could hand it back. Unlike the blurry photograph on the FBI Web site, this was a clean shot of Rennie Shaw and a young Animal with a Mohawk haircut. The nomad faced the camera while the Dog Warrior was focused on something else. On the back was written, *Mike "Animal" Ross, Rennie Shaw, 1984 Gather.*

"I was seventeen in that picture. Look at Shaw. The fuck hasn't aged a day. He still looks like he's in his mid-twenties. They live forever, Daggit. Shaw was in the fucking Civil War, man."

"Come on; that's all bullshit. Urban legend."

"And the chicks," Animal went on, undeterred. "Prime babes. Not an ounce of fat on them, and that sexy wild-thing look. They only spread for Pack dogs."

If the conversation had sunk down to sex, then they weren't going to get more useful information—if you wanted to call the werewolf theory useful—out of the bikers.

"Let's do this." Atticus unslung the backpack and thumped it down on the table. "Show us the goods."

Animal reached under the table to pull out a black leather duffel bag. He unzipped it and lifted out resealable plastic bags, the contents shifting like invisible sand. Empty, the inside of the duffel bag glittered faintly from a dusting of the drug, meaning that the plastic bags were probably coated too. Atticus warned Ru off with a look and reluctantly examined the bags. The chiming in his ears had started the moment Animal opened the bag, releasing tainted air. As Atticus handled the bags, the chiming grew louder.

Ru unloaded the backpack, stacking up the bills. He gave Atticus one worried look and then kept his focus on the bikers. The bikers, in turn, thumbed through the stacks of twenties, examining the bills to see if they were real, and even checking for sequential numbers.

Animal produced a scale and they weighed out the bags. Normally Atticus would open the bags and check the contents—his system shrugged off most drugs—but there was no way he was going to do that now, not if he wanted to stay in control. As the drug burned through him, all his senses took on a *sharpness*, making irritating little cuts into his patience. It was like wading through sawgrass. He packed the plastic bags hurriedly into the backpack, trying to handle them as little as possible.

"We're going to want more," Ru said. "Double this. How soon can you get it?"

"More?" Animal looked to Daggit, who shrugged. "You'll have to give us a couple days."

"This is Monday. By Thursday?" Ru asked.

"Saturday," Daggit said.

"If the Pack are werewolves," Ru, seemingly causal, asked, "does it mean that pixies literally make this shit? Do you hold them upside down and shake hard?"

The bikers laughed, showing teeth yellow from cigarettes, filled with silver.

"Just about," Animal said. "The Temple are all fucking fairies."

Temple of New Reason? The religious cult that murdered Ukiah was their source? Suddenly Ukiah's hate of the drug became clear. The police reports, detailing out bodies being hacked apart with an axe and cremated, flashed into Atticus's all too perfect memory. He felt sudden dread; the bikers knew where Ukiah slept alone at the isolated beach house. "Did you talk to them after you left us?"

"That's none of your business," Daggit sneered. "The middleman stands in the middle, you don't go around him. Pack or not, you're not cutting us out."

Atticus lashed out, grabbed Daggit by the hair, and slammed his head face-first into the table. Everything littering the table leapt up, as if startled by the violence. The smell of blood blossomed into the room. "What did you tell them about us?"

Daggit tried to rise but Atticus kept him pinned, grinding his bleeding nose into the cigarette ashes. Daggit flailed for his pistol, and Atticus caught the hand by the wrist and jerked it up behind Daggit's back.

Ru snatched up the pistol and aimed it at Animal, who was starting to rise. "Easy, easy. Atty?"

It was more the awareness of Ru's exhale, the air warmed by his body and carrying his scent, than Ru's words that made Atticus realize it was the drug pushing him to act.

"What did you tell them?" Atticus managed a calmer tone.

"Fuck off!" Daggit cried. "I'm not telling you nothing about them."

"I didn't ask about them," Atticus said. "I want to know what you said about us! Now tell me, or I'll rip your arm off."

"Nothing! Not a goddamn thing."

Atticus could tell by the slight jump in the pulse under his fingertips that Daggit was lying. Clearly, though, he would have to pretend to believe him or beat the information out of him. He was already putting the whole setup at risk for what—a stranger he just met yesterday? A man who might be the coldest bastard on the planet?

Letting go of Daggit, he stepped back out of Daggit's reach as the big man surged to his feet. The room suddenly seemed claustrophobic, taken up by the angry biker, the seated Animal, and the table blocking the exit. There was some part of him, that punk kid he used to be, that wanted Daggit to come at him so he had an excuse to beat the snot out of him. An older, wiser self, nearly swamped under the drug's influence, knew that would be a bad thing. Guns were already in the mix, and Ru could easily be hurt.

"Daggit, he's Pack," Animal drawled, seemingly undisturbed by the violence or the gun that Ru held. "That's a losing hand. Just fold."

Daggit froze, hands clenched into massive fists, panting out breath tainted with beer, blood, and years of cigarette smoking. He glared at Atticus like he meant murder. Atticus stared back, ready and waiting to see how things played out. They stood statue-still for a minute, like samurai testing each other's will. Finally, Daggit wiped his bloody upper lip with the back of his hand and looked away.

Ru took it as a sign that danger was past. He thumbed the revolver's cylinder out and rejected the silver-tipped bullets; they rained onto the tabletop. "You don't want us to know about them. We don't want them to know about us. It seems fairly simple—mum's the word, all the way around."

Daggit grunted.

"We lost three men at Buffalo," Ru reminded Daggit as an explanation of Atticus's reaction. "You lost three too."

"Four." Daggit spat out blood and wiped his thumb over his lip. "No one's heard from Toback since; whoever hit the place took him."

"You sure he wasn't in on the hit?" Ru asked.

Daggit glanced to Animal and shook his head. "I don't know him that well. He's part of the Buffalo chapter."

"Big, stupid, and loyal as a dog," Animal said. "That was David Toback."

So the nomad Animal was the link between Buffalo and Boston.

"Did you tell the Temple about the Buffalo deal before it went down?" Atticus asked.

Animal thought a moment this time before shaking his head. "No. Core got really creepy in the spring, moving out to Buffalo and talking about the end of the world. Let's just say I don't drink around them—just in case they're in the middle of doing a Jonestown thing."

When members of the People's Temple staged a cult suicide with cyanide-laced grape Kool-Aid, not everyone had drunk willingly. It wasn't a good sign that the outlaw bikers—with their loose grip on normal—considered the Temple of New Reason unstable.

"So they're based in Buffalo now?" Atticus asked.

Animal eyed him warily and then shrugged. "They moved again. To Pennsylvania or Ohio. No forwarding address."

Ohio was where they killed Ukiah.

"When we do this again on Saturday, we're not doing it here," Atticus said firmly. "Do you know the Boston Harbor Hotel?"

"It's hard to miss," Animal said.

"Use the guest phone and ask for Steele. We'll meet you there Saturday, at eight o'clock."

Atticus slung the backpack over his shoulder, and they beat a hasty retreat then, the drugs weighing heavy on Atticus's back because of his hyperawareness of it.

Kyle started up the Explorer when they walked out of the bar and sat idling, waiting for them to reach the Jaguar.

"We'll need to bag this and wash my hands." Atticus hated the delay, but he wanted it off him before they got into closed confines of the Jag.

While Atticus kept watch, Ru got out a large plastic bag and tented it open for Atticus, so he could slide the backpack in without touching the bag itself. Luckily they always kept bottles of water in the car. Ru emptied two over Atticus' hands before Atticus sensed that the drug had been washed away. Decontaminated, they got into the Jag and headed for the interstate. A few minutes later, the Explorer's lights appeared in the rearview mirror.

"No one's following you," Kyle said over the radio, after Ru turned off their wires. "What the hell happened in there? It sounded like Atticus jumped someone."

"I did," Atticus snapped. Ru wisely said nothing.

"Sumpter called. He wanted to know when we're dropping the drugs to him."

"We can do it tomorrow morning," Atticus said. "I want to get back to the house."

"They managed to reconstruct some of the records from Buffalo," Kyle said. "He's got a DVD for us."

They'd stopped at a red light, giving Atticus time to shuffle through his options. Sending Kyle to see Sumpter was a no-go; oil and water mixed better. Nor did Atticus like the idea of sending Kyle back to the house alone. If Ukiah was awake and not as harmless as he seemed, Kyle—or Ru, for that matter—would be no match for the Dog Warrior. Ru could take the drugs to Sumpter, but there was a slim chance that they had a tail that Kyle hadn't spotted. Besides, Sumpter was an officious prick and would probably throw a fit if Atticus, as team leader, didn't show. Normally Atticus couldn't care less, but he wanted the DVD—which Sumpter might refuse to hand over to just Ru.

Atticus took comfort that Daggit probably wouldn't endanger his status as middleman. Whatever the biker leader said to the cult, it probably hadn't included specifics on how to find them. Atticus sighed. "Fine. We'll make the drop."

•   •   •

Ukiah slept deep and heavy as the dead, reabsorbed memories unfolding as dreams.

The Dog Warriors hunted like wolves. They ran silent and intent through the autumn night, the moon full and the wind wild, covering the sound of their passing. Ukiah could feel the Pack as they slipped through moonlight and shadows. Grim as their mission was, they were pleased he hunted with them. He made them feel complete: wolves showing their young how to hunt.

Fields of shorn hay. Pastures of sleeping cattle. Rich, freshly plowed earth, ready for the winter wheat. They searched for their prey, the Temple of New Reason; more specifically, for the deadly alien machines—the Ae—that the cult had stolen out of storage. Their informant, ex-cultist Socket, could give them only general directions; she'd been given exact change for getting the U-Haul truck through the tollbooths of the Pennsylvania and Ohio turnpikes, and knew that the trip would take roughly two hours. The cultists had mentioned a chain of convenience stores in Ohio by name, telling her one was close to their destination. She wasn't of the "inner circle," so the cult told her nothing more about where they were going, or the plan once they got there.

With perfect memory and a century of roaming the countryside, the Dog Warriors were able to narrow the possibilities to a twenty-mile radius. They checked the hiding places the Pack knew and found them empty. So now the Dog Warriors searched on foot, with nothing between them and clues that the land might hold, using no motors that would alert their prey.

In a low fold in the land, they found the burned remains of a bonfire, built from old telephone poles, heavy with creosote. The fire would have burned hot and long. Ukiah crouched there, smoky ghosts of the bonfire filling his senses as he shifted fingers through the fine ash, finding bits of bone.

The man had been short, dark haired and dark eyed, Italian in heritage, born of a human mother and father, middle-aged, perhaps a parent himself—and long dead before the cult killed his body. The bone fragment showed that he'd been infected by the Ontongard and replaced, cell by cell, until he was fully alien in stolen human form. The cremated man had been Hex's Get long enough that all of the bone had not only been replaced but improved upon, a creature of inhuman speed and strength, healing faster than Ukiah could; the Get should have been nearly indestructible.

Rennie came out of the darkness, silent in his passage.

Ukiah handed the bone to him. "We're close."

The tall, lean leader of the Dog Warriors examined the fragment, reading Hex's familiar stamp on what once was human. "They're good at this game."

Rennie meant the Temple of New Reason, who had discovered the alien Ontongard and deemed them demons. Not that they were far from wrong—the Ontongard certainly fit the description of evil personified. The first Ontongard, Hex, had extended himself into hundreds by infecting humans over the centuries; a hundred thousand more humans had died when their immune systems resisted the virulent infection.

"The Temple is successful only because the Gets never see them coming," Ukiah said. *In the way that Pack knew Pack, the Ontongard could sense the Pack. The cult, though, could lose itself in the sea of humanity and strike without warning. Unfortunately, the Pack was as blind as the Ontongard to the cult, and thus just as vulnerable.*

Seeing themselves as holy warriors, the cult believed the ends justified the means of saving the world. Ironically, with the stolen Ae, they could accidentally destroy all life on the planet.

A train whistle echoed out over the land, drawing Rennie's attention to the east. "We're losing the dark." *Rennie tossed the bone aside and took off at a run.*

The dream skipped, plunging into darkness and resurfacing . . .

Ukiah's cell phone vibrated, and he paused to answer. An unfamiliar phone number showed on the display. "Hello?"

"Is this Joe?" a female voice asked.

"No. You've got a wrong number."

"Is this . . ." She read off a number, but the last two digets were transposed from his.

"No. You messed up dialing the number."

"I'm sorry; I just got this new phone. Sorry."

The line went dead. Storm clouds cloaked the moon; the night grew darker. The lone headlight of a train crossed his path, a quarter mile ahead . . .

. . . the freight cars flashed by, the rails ringing up and down the sonic range. He was the only one on this side of the track. The diesel engine roared on, too far ahead for him to catch. Somewhere a mile or more in the opposite direction, the end of the train had yet to come into sight.

"Go on," he thought to Rennie, who had paused in his hunting to check on Ukiah. "I'll catch up in a few minutes."

Rennie's memories played back over the countryside they'd just searched, reconsidering it for hidden dangers, finding none. "Come when you can."

Ukiah ran alongside the train, looking for something that went over the tracks, or under . . .

. . . Ukiah's cell phone vibrated. Who now? He took out his phone. The same number as last time showed on the display. He thought about answering and growling at the clueless woman, but he settled for turning off the phone completely . . .

. . . He paused on the berm of the highway, squinting as the headlights of an oncoming truck hit his night-sensitive eyes. He fumbled out his flashlight, knowing that he'd be night-blind for several minutes after the truck passed—a hazard of having eyes that shifted to night vision. At the fringe of his awareness, he sensed sudden intensity from the

*others—they'd found something. He went still, focusing on
them. The Dog Warriors gathered around a farmhouse, windows dark, hunched under towering oaks. The wind brought
the smell of C4 and the taste of red.*

*Movement warned him too late, and he snapped out of
the focus as the truck suddenly veered toward him.*

*It hit him on the left side, smashed him to the hard road,
and rolled over him. Caught between the truck and the road,
he tumbled. His flashlight flipped alongside him, showing
frightening glimpses of the trailer's undercarriage. Strut,
axle, gears flashed by. Somehow the big wheels missed him
but his flashlight went under the last set and was crunched
flat.*

*It lasted only seconds but it seemed like forever. Finally
it was over. Ukiah lay sprawled facedown on the pavement,
dazed and broken. The truck shuddered to a stop, its engine
dropping to the low rumble of an idle. The air was heavy
with the smell of smoking rubber.*

"Cub?" *Rennie's thoughts pushed through the pain.*
"What happened?"

*Good question. Ukiah tried to lever himself up and dis-
covered with an explosion of new pain that his left arm was
shattered.*

"Cub?"

"A . . . a . . . a truck. A truck hit me."

*Cars were stopping on the highway; people were getting
out. For a moment it seemed like a normal accident. Then
Ukiah recognized one of the cars: Goodman's dark blue
Honda. The cult had taken the car after dismembering their
rogue kidnapper.*

"Rennie! Rennie!" *He could only think of the bonfire victim, chopped up and burned to ash. He fought to stay conscious, to try to crawl away. They were certain to do worse
than kill him.*

Ice swung down out of the truck's cab and headed toward

him, in long, determined strides. "He's probably not alone. We have to act quickly. Kill him."

"But if we're right about him—" a female cultist started to protest.

"Then he'll only be dead a little while." Ice handed her a pistol. "And ye shall chase your enemies, and they shall fall before you by the sword . . ."

Ukiah bolted awake. Even with his eyes open, though, he could see the muzzle flash suddenly brilliant in the rain-cloaked night, feel the bullets hit him with a force that nearly matched that of the truck.

He looked around the room, trying to fill his vision with something else. He was safe. He was with his brother. He was safe.

Then he realized he was alone in the house, his panting the only sound except the rumble of the surf and the wind buffeting the walls of glass.

Atticus left?

Implications of the dream dawned on him. He had his memories back. Atticus must have put the mice in bed with him. That skunk!

Wondering what time it was, he checked the waistband of his boxer shorts. Yes, Ru's phone was still where he'd slipped it during the Iron Horse's arrival. Eleven-thirty—Atticus and Ru had done their drug deal, and probably were on their way back. The call log indicated eight missed phone calls.

Working through the phone's unfamiliar menu system, he discovered that most of the calls were from Max, but the latest was from Indigo. The display showed that the battery was low and the phone was picking up only a weak signal from the carrier.

He left Indigo's number showing and hit the talk button.

"Special Agent Zheng," Indigo answered.

"It's me. I just woke up."

"Good, you're still with the phone," Indigo said cryptically.

"The battery is low, so it might cut out at any point," he told her.

"Are you safe?"

"Yeah."

"Hang up then. Save the power."

Trusting her, he did.

Ukiah sat up and took inventory of his newly healed arm, bending and flexing the fingers, wrist, and elbow. The knitted bones were still weak, but he could use it if he was careful. Under the bandages, the bullet wounds had healed to scabs. It would be another couple of days before the skin was unmarked, but he was strong enough to leave.

The door, though, was locked.

They certainly didn't want him leaving.

He rested his head on the door. Was he strong enough to break the dead bolt?

Outside, a vehicle pulled up to the house. Was Atticus back? His sleeping memories marked the departure of a Ford Explorer and the snarl of a sports car. This engine didn't sound like either. Someone else had found him.

The Jaguar's navigation system said that they had an exit coming up on the right. A proliferation of signs, though, stated that the road was closed and suggested they use unfamiliar roads.

"Figures," Atticus muttered. "Our luck is running true lately. All bad."

The navigation system also seemed decidedly annoyed by the detour, insisting that they take the exit as they flashed past the barricaded roadway. Beyond the heavy fortifications, the pavement came to an abrupt halt at a vast pit, seemingly a mile square—a forest of cranes and a jumble of structures, none of them linked, that refused to take any logical form.

"What the hell are they building there?"

Ru made a noise to indicate he was clueless.

"It's probably the Big Dig," Kyle said over the radio.

"The what?"

"The largest urban construction project in the history of the modern world. Forty-two miles of underground highway in a path over two hundred feet wide."

"Oh, yeah. I guess I've heard of it," Atticus said. "Mostly that it's overbudget and way behind schedule."

"Well, they're basically building the Panama Canal through the heart of Boston."

"I heard that in some places they'll have, like, four tunnels stacked on top of themselves," Ru said.

"Four? What the hell for?"

"One for cars, one for buses, the subway system, and the last . . ." Ru searched his memory. "Oh, yeah, the subway station itself."

The detour sent them off on a newly constructed road that the navigation system didn't acknowledge existed, and minutes later they were lost in a maze of small one-way side streets. Atticus cursed softly under his breath as the navigation system struggled to plot a new course. Hopefully finding their way back to the beach house wouldn't be as complicated and time-consuming; he wanted to see for himself that Ukiah was safe.

The Iron Horses had described the Boston Harbor Hotel as "hard to miss," and they were right. The street in front of the hotel was an obstacle course as the old elevated freeway was being dismantled. The hotel itself, though, was surprisingly beautiful: crowned like a princess with an elegant rotunda and a four-story archway through the heart of the building to a harborside courtyard and yacht-lined wharf.

They parked in the hotel's underground parking lot and rode the elevator up to the lobby. There it stopped and Kyle stepped off.

Atticus stuck his hand out to catch the doors before they could close. "What are you doing?"

"There's a business center here. I'm going to connect to the Internet and do some searches on the cult."

"You can do that after we talk to Sumpter."

Kyle fidgeted in place. "I don't want to talk to Sumpter."

"I don't want to talk to him either," Ru said.

Atticus gave Ru a hard look. "Neither do I, but we have to."

"You two talk to him. I don't need to be there. I'm just backup."

"Yeah, we're a team," Atticus said. "Come on."

Kyle shook his head, getting his mulish look. "No."

Atticus sighed. "Fine, fine, we'll talk to him. We're going to make this quick, twenty minutes tops."

"I'm just downloading stuff to my laptop for later." Kyle patted his shoulder bag.

"Ten minutes." Atticus let the door shut.

"I don't blame him," Ru murmured as the elevator started up again.

"Sumpter is an asshole," Atticus agreed.

He and Ru rode the elevator to the top floor and found Sumpter's room.

"Yes?" Sumpter called from within the room when Atticus rapped on the door.

"It's Steele and Takahashi."

Footsteps neared the door, there was a pause to use the spyhole, and then the door opened. The wave of air brought out the reek of Sumpter's cologne, Old Spice put on heavy.

"Come in!" Sumpter murmured. He glanced beyond them. "Where's Rainman?"

"Who?" Ru chose to misunderstand him.

"Johnston," Sumpter said.

"Kyle isn't autistic," Atticus stated as calmly as he could.

"Well, there's something wrong with the dweeb."

Atticus stepped close to Sumpter. "Don't . . . insult . . . my . . . backup."

"Did you make the deal?" Sumpter ignored him, heading back into the hotel room. It was a large suite, with windows overlooking Boston Harbor. The door they came through opened to a living room with a sofa, desk, easy chair, and coffee table. A door into a second room revealed a king-size bed, slightly rumpled.

"Yes." Atticus examined the plastic bag containing the backpack a second time, looking for the drug's telltale glitter. He'd checked it downstairs in the garage while writing his name on the tape sealing it shut, but he was feeling paranoid. "We've got some information on the drug. It's a lot more dangerous than we've been led to believe. It's possible that it's lethal with one dose."

"And it's transparent—nearly invisible," Ru said.

"Invisible?" Sumpter frowned, eyes narrowing. "Are you sure you weren't gypped?"

"This is the real stuff." Atticus held out the bag. "It should be handled only while wearing plastic gloves."

"Check." Sumpter took the bag and added his name to the seal.

"We set up another buy on Saturday, but we changed the location to here."

"Here?" Sumpter asked.

"Lasker's beach house is too exposed. Also the sellers won't deal out there."

"You've made contact with them; that's all that matters." Sumpter disappeared into the bedroom with the bag. The closet door slid open, and a moment later slid closed. He returned with a DVD in hand. "The case and circuitry of the digital video recorder's hard drive were trashed, but the platters were salvageable. A few hours in a clean room and the boys in the lab managed to recover most of the drive. They burned about ten days of data onto this DVD for us." He loaded the DVD into the laptop set up on the desk. "I've scanned through the disk, and it looks like the last few minutes is the only thing worthwhile."

The Buffalo team had used a standard eight-camera system, recording the last minutes of their lives. One camera focused on the desolate parking lot in a mostly abandoned industrial park, carefully set to pick up license plates and faces of people sitting inside the cars. Four others covered different angles of the staged "office" area, well lit and painted a sharp white for better contrast. The last three cameras had been scattered through the shadowy warehouse with motion sensors and silent alarm systems attached.

Sumpter started the video with the team waiting for the buyers as caught by camera four.

The kid, Jason German, juggled while telling a joke; he arced four small cloth sacks through a continuous graceful loop. Tracy Scroggins sat on a battered desk, still and patient, quirking his mouth into a smile at Jason's nervous antics. Walt Boyes, the backup, wasn't visible, most likely stationed at the monitors in the concealed room, judging by how the camera zoomed in and out on the kid. The time stamp ticked off the seconds until they died.

". . . and she says, 'Whatever you gave me, Doctor, didn't work.'" Jason was midjoke as the video started. "'While my farts are still perfectly silent, they now smell awful. Thank goodness that no one can tell it's me farting, because they could peel the paint off walls!' 'Good,' shouts the doctor, 'now that we cleared up your sinuses, we can start to work on your hearing!'"

There was an odd noise from off camera.

"I think you just killed Walt," Scroggins said. "You okay back there, Walt?" A muffled laugh was the only answer. "You've heard that one before, haven't you?"

"It's funnier this time," Walt Boyes called from his concealed room.

"I don't know whether to be complimented or insulted."

Jason sent one of the balls looping over his shoulder and deftly caught it.

"Heads up!" Boyes announced the buyers' arrival.

Jason caught the cloth bags he'd been juggling and put them aside, saying, "It's about time."

Tracy nervously checked the draw on his pistol.

The door opened. Four men entered dripping slightly from rain, just as the Iron Horses had claimed. Atticus had seen the bodies of the other three bikers, so he focused on the missing man. He was a big black man with a sleepy look to him. He leaned against the back wall, tucked between two support columns. Nothing about him suggested that he knew what was coming. While Jason and the lead biker exchanged presale banter about the heavy rain outside, Toback literally picked his nose out of boredom.

"Who gives a fuck about the rain?" Scroggins gave the banter a shove toward real business. "Are we going to do this, or talk ourselves to death?"

"Tracy! Jason! Incoming!" Boyes shouted. "Incoming!"

Sumpter reached down and slowed the playback, murmuring, "This goes too fast to see otherwise."

The door flew open and a man walked in, shotgun at his shoulder. He fired as he walked, shooting the bikers even as they turned. Others filed in after him, six in all, faces set and emotionless as they fired. The bullets slammed the bikers' bodies around like puppets with their strings randomly jerked. In the slowed replay, the blood splattered gruesomely. Scroggins and German had flung themselves behind the steel desk. The camera showed only the tops of their heads as they returned fire, pinned behind the desk. Two of the shooters went down, but the other four rounded the sides of the desk and fired point-blank. The police would find later that Scroggins had tried to shield German with his own body.

The time stamp had ticked through twelve seconds.

But the shooters had missed Toback, who had cowered

between the support columns. While they started to reload, he charged, a long steel pipe in hand. The foursome glanced up, and one, handing his gun to another, stepped forward to engage Toback hand-to-hand.

The shooter ducked the steel pipe casually, and then caught hold of it. There was a momentary contest of strength that the big man should have won, but the shooter wrestled the pipe away and struck Toback down with it.

The other three stepped forward, guns now loaded, and aimed down at the prone biker. They checked, apparently reconsidered killing Toback, and turned away. They turned toward Boyes's hole instead, leveled their guns, and opened fire. They systematically shifted their fire, visibly working left to right. Atticus recalled the line of bullet holes, how they ran with machine precision across the back wall; he thought that only one marksman had made them. He watched now, stunned with the knowledge that three men had acted in unison. How were they coordinating their shots? He realized then that so far they hadn't uttered a single word.

Behind them, the impossible happened. The two dead shooters scrambled to their feet. One picked up the bags containing the money and the drugs. The other stooped down to grab Toback by the ankles and dragged him outside, leaving the swath of clean floor that would later puzzle Atticus. The shooters' clothes showed bloody bullet holes and gaping wounds, entrances and exits indicating paths through vital organs, but they seemed unhampered and unperturbed by the massive damage done to them.

Walt Boyes started to scream, a wordless howl of anger and pain, like a wounded animal. The guns thundered, and the screaming stopped, and then the video ended.

Sumpter took the DVD out, put it in a jewel case, and held it out to Atticus. "That was the best angle to view the shooters. You'll want to study all the angles."

Atticus took it numbly. Two images chased through his

mind: the shooters standing up, ignoring their wounds, and Ukiah coming back to life. His brother had known about the drug, known the bikers, and they found him on I-90, a straight shot from Buffalo. It was the cultists who manufactured the drug and killed Ukiah. Who were the bad guys here? Was it the cult who hit his brother with a car and then shot him? Or was it the Pack, who might have staged the shooting in Buffalo? He was going to get answers from his brother, even if he had to beat them out of him.

Ru talked them out of Sumpter's room. There was an older couple waiting for the elevator, so they rode in silence, watching the floor numbers count downward. They found Kyle in the business center, downloading information to his laptop.

"That was not twenty minutes," he grumbled, typing furiously on the keyboard.

"Change of plans," Atticus said. "You and Ru are staying here."

"What?" Ru gave him an angry look.

Kyle glanced up to eye them standing over him and then bowed his head back over his keyboard. "So the video was that bad? I, for one, would rather not see it, but I know I'm going to have to digitally enhance it until my eyes bleed."

"There's no reason for all three of us to go," Atticus stated, answering Ru and ignoring Kyle because he was completely right.

"And we'll be safer here?" Ru added, as if he were finishing Atticus's statement.

Yes. He knew what Ru would say to that, so he didn't say it aloud, not that it mattered. Ru knew him well enough to guess what he was thinking.

"I'm going with you," Ru said.

"I'm just going to pick up Ukiah and come back," Atticus said.

"Don't get stupid because of what happened to the Buffalo team," Ru said.

"The Jag only seats two comfortably," Atticus said.

"We can take the Explorer," Ru countered.

"It needs gas," Kyle interjected the information quietly into conversation.

"I'll be fine alone," Atticus said.

"We don't even know if there are rooms available here." Ru waved his hand to indicate the hotel.

"Two rooms." Kyle paused in his typing. "Should I reserve them?"

Atticus glanced at the screen and saw that Kyle had the reservation form for the Boston Harbor Hotel up, the request for two rooms already filled out, his hand hovering over the enter key. "Do it."

Kyle tapped downward. "You two fight it out." He shut down his computer and unhooked it with swift efficiency. "I'm checking in."

Ru sat back on the desk as Kyle escaped. "I'm coming with you. This is different this time. These people know what you are. They know what it takes to really kill you. The playing field is level here, and I'm not going to let you go without backup."

Atticus sighed, recognizing the pattern. He was being overly cautious, and Ru was asserting his right to put everything on the line. If Ru didn't want danger—and the accompanying adrenaline rush—he'd have been a lawyer like his father had wanted him to be. "Fine."

Atticus decided to take the Jag, as it was faster. Ukiah would have to suffer in the cramped space pretending to be a backseat—if the Dog Warrior was even still at the beach house. It was possible that he had woken up, found them gone, and left. Atticus funneled his anger and fears into the car, and they roared down the highway at speeds that made it more low-altitude flying than driving.

They were nearly to the house when the car phone rang.

Ru answered it, putting the call on speaker. "What is it, Kyle?"

"It's the house security," Kyle said. "The front door has been triggered."

Atticus glanced at the GPS system showing their location. They were still twenty miles from the house, nearly fifteen minutes at the speed they were going.

"The door down to the basement just tripped," Kyle said.

Atticus swore. If it were Ukiah leaving, the doors would have opened in the opposite order.

"The bedroom door is open," Kyle reported. "Should I call 911?"

"Shit!" Atticus considered all the messy entanglements that calling the police would involve. It would jeopardize their whole operation.

"Atticus?" Kyle asked after a minute's silence.

Chances were that Ukiah could survive any attack until they got there. They owed him nothing. But if it was a normal human Atticus had just put in harm's way, wouldn't he do something?

"Call the Hyannis police."

There was a pause. "And tell them what? That we have a man that was shot five times locked in a dead man's basement?"

Atticus glanced at the GPS system again. "No. Forget it." He and Ru would be there before they could talk Kyle through a safe report.

The house was dark, no sign of any vehicles.

Atticus slammed the Jag to a stop and leapt out, pulling his gun.

The doorjamb of the front door was broken and the door hung open. He went in, gun leveled, splinters of wood under his shoes. The house was silent and still.

He knew he should go slowly, but he found himself moving quickly and quietly for the basement stairs. *Let him be there! Let him be in the bed. Dead is fine, just be there!*

The bedroom door had been smashed open. He crept to it, afraid of what he would find.

The room was empty, the bed innocent of blood.

What had happened? Who had broken into the house and taken him?

I shouldn't have left him alone. I should have found a way to keep him safe . . .

For the first time in his life, his senses failed to give him warning of an attack.

Atticus stood staring into the room, sick with fear for his brother, and someone slammed into him. In that hard collision of bodies, he lost his pistol. They smashed through the sliding glass door and tumbled out onto the sand. They rolled across the sand, the stranger growling a deep rumble.

Ukiah? But no, Ukiah would have felt identical to him, and there was an "otherness" to this man. Atticus twisted and wrenched himself out of his attacker's hold and scrambled backward.

Rennie Shaw stood grinning, teeth and eyes gleaming in the moonlight, his breath misting in the cold. Shaw topped Atticus by several inches—taller than Atticus expected from Animal's photo. Lean and fit as the Iron Horses described, the Dog Warrior wore biking leathers with savage style. With dark hair grizzled with silver, he smelled like a wolf and radiated the same prickly awareness that Ukiah had against Atticus's senses.

Pack knows Pack.

"So you are like two peas in a pod," Shaw murmured in a deep, carrying voice. "The question is, at the heart of it all, are you the same man that your brother is?"

"Where's Ukiah? Is he safe?"

"It's a little late to worry about that, boy."

What did that mean? Did the Dog Warriors have Ukiah,

or had someone else come and taken him? If his brother was
safe with the bikers, why had Shaw attacked Atticus?

"I want to scratch your surface a little." Shaw sneered.
"See what's underneath."

Shaw lunged at him with inhuman speed, and his punch
felt like being hit by a high-powered bullet. Atticus countered with two punches, both of which Shaw dodged as
though the fight were choreographed, allowing Atticus to
come so close to hitting that he could feel the heat of Shaw's
skin.

"Come on, boy, you're thinking too much." Shaw struck
him again, knocking him down the sand dune. Atticus tried
to duck the next blow, but Shaw, grinning, landed it anyhow.

Shaw battered him down the hill and to the water's edge.
Atticus fought with silent desperation, but his kicks and
punches kept failing to land on their target. Shaw was as
elusive as a shadow, always a fraction of an inch out of
reach.

*"If you're going to fight someone who can read your
thoughts,"* Shaw said into his mind, *"you have to fight without thinking."*

Atticus went still with shock. He'd been gathering information on the Dog Warriors, watching the evidence mount
up that they were much like him, but he'd somehow denied
the deep truth. He wasn't one of a kind—he was part of a
race that he knew nothing about. The vast shifting of his universe stunned him to his core.

With a scoffing laugh, Shaw tackled him into the surf.
The water sucked them out, away from the shore, and then
tumbled them back to the land.

A score of men and women lined the shore, waiting for
them. Even standing still, they were sleek, dark, and dangerous in the way of poisonous snakes. The moonlight
gleamed in their eyes, and the scent of wolves overrode that
of humans. Over the roar of the surf, he could hear their

growling, their hostility pressing against him, as irritating as his own anger.

His brother stood on the shore, flanked by Dog Warriors, wholly one of them.

CHAPTER FOUR

Hyannis, Massachusetts
Monday, September 20, 2004

Ukiah had only heard the car arrive, but he felt the Pack's arrival as they swept in behind it and broke down doors to get to him. Rennie reached him first, cuffing him lightly in rough affection. Then awareness moved through the Pack and they made way for an outsider among them. He recognized Indigo by her scent as she picked her way through the dark house to him. When he folded her into his arms, he found that she wore a plain black leather jacket, all signs of her being FBI hidden away. She clung to him hard and parted reluctantly.

She peered at the splintered door frame, smashed into the room and hanging drunkenly on a wedge of drywall. "Direct as usual, Shaw."

"It's faster to break them down than try to pick the locks," Rennie rumbled, anger pushing him to nearly growling. He didn't like that Ukiah had been locked up, or the silent reports from the Dogs upstairs on what they were discovering.

Ukiah realized then what their combined presence—Indigo and the Dog Warriors—meant. She'd brought them as backup. "You're working together?"

"We weren't sure what we'd be walking into," Rennie said, but meant, *what Indigo would be walking into alone.*

Ukiah flashed over his conversation with Max that morning. No, what he'd told his partner hadn't been too reassuring. He hadn't explained being rescued by his brother; to be truthful, though, he wasn't completely sure how safe he'd been with Atticus. "How did you find me?"

"We used the GPS on the cell phone you're using," Indigo explained. "Who is Hikaru Takahashi?"

"He's my brother's lover."

"What?" she cried as the Pack went still around him.

"I have an older brother. His name is Atticus Steele. He's the one who rescued me out of the trunk."

"Why did he lock you in the basement?" Her voice held the suspicious anger echoed by the Dog Warriors.

"And why is the upstairs dusted with Invisible Red?" Rennie added.

"I think . . . I think he's a drug dealer."

Into the following silence, Indigo's phone rang. She answered it with a brusque, "Special Agent Zheng." She listened to the thin voice coming through the cell phone, her brow gathering into annoyance. "Okay, I'll be there shortly.

"The two male cultists wounded in the shoot-out just died," Indigo told them. "I need to go deal with that. Here." She handed Ukiah his wallet and then a hotel room key card. "I'm at the Residence Inn in Framingham; I've got it stocked with food."

The cult had left his photo ID and Evans City Library card, but taken his cash and credit cards. One of Max's ATM/Visa cards, however, had been tucked into his wallet.

"My gun . . . and cell phone?"

"The cult kept your gun," she said. "We've reported it stolen. We found only pieces of your cell phone, but that's probably just as well—the cult used your cell phone to track you."

He flashed to the undercarriage of the rental truck, the flashlight lying flattened beside him on the road, and shuddered with recalled pain. "Keep yourself safe."

"Let me remind you that I haven't been shot or killed once this year," she said, without adding that he had. In fact, he'd lost count of how many times. She reached up, pulled him down to her, and kissed him, full of fearful passion. "Don't," she whispered huskily afterward, their foreheads still lightly touching, "do that again."

"I won't," he promised, even though he had no clue how to prevent it from happening again. He'd promise her anything to make her happy.

"Good." She released him then.

As Ukiah walked Indigo to her car, Rennie gave silent orders to Murray and Stein, who gave her an unrequested— and perhaps unwanted—protective shadow.

"I'll see you at the hotel."

He nodded rather than lie, then watched her drive away, trying to keep down feelings that he was betraying her. The phone call had distracted her from Atticus. Also she probably thought the drugs his brother was dealing with were of the more mundane type, not Invisible Red. Like one creature, the Pack's mind stayed firmly on Atticus, with a growing determination that he'd be tested in accordance to Pack law, and if found wanting, destroyed. Ukiah didn't want to get her involved, forcing her into impossible choices.

"Atticus is coming back soon," he told Rennie as her taillights vanished. "He left to buy Invisible Red off of the Iron Horses."

"After that massive dose of Invisible Red the cult gave you three days ago, your resistance to it is still low. We'll have to make sure you don't get exposed to any more."

Ukiah winced, memories of his rape while under the influence of the drug cuttingly sharp. "I can hang back until you've got the drug off him. But I want to be there when you test him."

"And if he doesn't pass?"

What will you do if we have to destroy him? was what Rennie was asking.

"I think he'll pass," Ukiah said. "He was part of Magic Boy. He seems even more human than I am. He loves Ru."

"But if he doesn't pass?"

Ukiah shied away from the question and instead tried to find more evidence that his brother was worthy of living. He suspected that, if nothing else, Atticus was a far more complicated person than he was. Atticus seemed to think in multiple layers, and while the surface level had been damning, there had been occasional glimpses at something deeper and truer beneath. Unfortunately, Atticus seemed mostly annoyed at Ukiah, as if he disdained his existence.

"Cub?"

"I know he's flawed, but if he's worse than I think . . ." He didn't want to say it. It was a cold and heartless thing to think of destroying his own flesh and blood, but if Atticus was hiding a heart as barren of emotions as the Ontongard's, then Ukiah couldn't allow himself to be trapped by the word "brother." "We'll do whatever is needed."

Rennie nodded, keeping his thoughts to himself.

Atticus arrived a short time later, broadcasting his concern for Ukiah. In typical Pack fashion, Rennie made sure Atticus had no Invisible Red on him prior to their reunion by knocking him into the ocean. It was a bitter thing to feel Atticus's concern for him wash away with the salt water.

His brother stood now in the surf, face closed and emotions so tightly controlled that there was no clue what he was feeling. How did Atticus learn that, isolated as he was from his own kind? Was it that he merely didn't allow himself to feel?

"What do you want?" Atticus shouted over the surf.

"It's Pack law, Atticus." Ukiah wanted Atticus to understand more than he had when the Pack tested him. "You need to be tested, to see if you're human—or monster."

"Tested?"

"We need to know what kind of person you truly are."

"Go to hell."

On Rennie's silent signal, the Dogs swept in. Atticus was a better fighter than Ukiah; it took four of the Dogs to drag him out of the water, struggling in their grip. Once they got him to the land, the fight went out of Atticus, and he knelt in the sand where they forced him to, panting, eyeing Ukiah darkly.

In that moment, Ukiah would have given almost anything to change history. If only he'd found Atticus at some other time, gotten to know his secret heart without this violence.

Rennie's lieutenant, the Cheyenne warrior Bear Shadow, came down the sand dune, pulling Ru along by the arm. Ru's face was carefully neutral; the man guarded his inner thoughts as closely as Atticus did. Ukiah noticed that Ru rubbed his right hand, as if Bear had disarmed him with force.

"I don't want him hurt," Ukiah silently told Bear.

"He'll witness everything." Bear meant that he could testify against Ukiah, if the Pack killed Atticus.

"I don't care." Ukiah took Ru's arm and pulled him out of Bear's hold. *"Either Atticus loves him, or, if Atticus is a heartless monster, then it was Ru who decided to rescue me out of the trunk."*

"Ah." Bear nodded slowly. *"He won't be hurt then."*

Ukiah kept hold of Ru's arm, just in case the Pack forgot.

Hellena stepped forward, caught hold of Atticus's head, and held him still, cocking his head back to look up at her.

"Take a deep breath." She locked eyes with Atticus.

"Fuck you," Atticus hissed, trying to twist out of her hold.

Hellena pushed her will onto his body. "Breathe!"

And against his will, Atticus took a deep breath.

"Again." Together, the two took a breath and released it.

Synced with his body, Hellena pushed into his memories. Atticus grunted with pain as his body resisted another's control. Ukiah and the Dog Warriors reached out mentally, bonding with Hellena as she forced a union of minds. Instantly, they were all one. They were Atticus.

... *the knifepoint of pain cut straight into him. He wouldn't give them the satisfaction of screaming. He tried to shut his eyes, but couldn't. He couldn't even look away. The knifepoint reached bottom and twisted and ...*

... *the game room had a vinyl floor that mimicked red and terra-cotta bricks in a random pattern, embedded with memories of the ages. He had been stacking colored blocks. He'd play with similar blocks later, in other houses with other families: green quarter blocks, square blue half blocks, rectangular red full blocks, and lemon yellow wedges. That week he had learned to stack one on top of another to build towers. Mama could stack them ten high, but his chubby, graceless hands could manage only three. He'd grasped that his hands were supposed to be larger, more like Mama's, and the night before had pushed his growth as far as his dinner would allow. To Mama's great height, the change seemed marginal, but Daddy called him a big boy before they left him with Jilly and the blocks. Still, this new size was awkward and he struggled to adjust, building and rebuilding his towers.*

Focused on the blocks, he hadn't noticed dusk setting in, or the first knock at the door, or the stream of people gathering in the remote living room. The porch grew dark except for the glow of the muted TV. Night filled the kitchen and dining room beyond. Only a slant of light from the far living room's doorway cut the still darkness.

Finally, he realized that he was alone. Where was Jilly? Thinking back, he realized now that she left him to answer the door and hadn't returned. Strangers were in the living room, the taint of their scent finally filtering through the house to him.

He abandoned the blocks and ventured into the darkness.

All the lights in the living room were on, and people towered there, ignoring the furniture, talking excitedly. He paused in the doorway, still in the dark, looking into the harsh light at the confusion.

"The Caddy swerved around a pickup pulling out of the ice-cream stand and went head-on into them. They never knew what hit them . . ."

A stillness moved through the room as the strangers realized he watched from the doorway.

"Oh, oh!" Jilly sobbed, tears pouring down her face. "What's going to happen to Johnnie Doe?"

Ukiah's life had been simple—decades of running with wolves followed by eight years of living as a child with his mothers. When the Dog Warriors tested him, Hellena had flipped through his memories rapid-fire, quickly finding proof of his humanity.

Atticus's memories, though, started when he was still a toddler, confused by a world where no one was like him, being shuffled through foster homes. Hellena abandoned this early memory and chose another, moving much slower, trying to get a sense of who Atticus really was, as life had shaped him.

. . . He lived in the land of the giants. These people so different from him towered over him and shuffled him from place to place without seeming to realize he wasn't one of them. He was lost in the bombard of new. His newly shorn scalp reported that he had only a quarter-inch of hair now, the rest buzzed off during the haze of a barbershop visit. His shoulders and neck itched from the uncomfortable reminders in the form of dead hair, lifeless parts of him pressed against his skin. Mixed in were ghost traces of everyone shorn by the cutters since their last thorough wash. In a hot car, vinyl seats covered in old tears of unwanted children, ghosts of strangers lay on his shoulders and whispered genetic secrets. The car stopped, the back door opened, hands undid his seat belt, and he was pulled from the vehicle.

Only later, late at night in the new bed in the new house

*of the new family, would he be able to pick out what the gi-
ants said in their thunderous voices.*

*"This is Johnnie Doe." The social worker herded him
firmly into a house.*

*"They said he was two years old. He looks more like
three to me."*

*"It's just a guess. He was found abandoned in a rest-
room. They thought he was only eight months old, but now
they think he might have been over a year old."*

*A face loomed close. "He seems very . . . confused. Is he
retarded?"*

*"No. They say he seems to have some kind of sensory
problem; he doesn't process well. It will be a few days before he comes out of his shell. They say he's quite sweet,
once he warms up. He's been through so much for one so little, first abandoned and then the couple that wanted to
adopt him were killed . . ."*

The Pack grieved for lost opportunity. If they had only
been able to find Atticus, things would have been different.
Regret moved through the Dogs as they watched Atticus
flounder through life, moved from one foster home to another in rapid succession. The joyful toddler grew into a
troubled second grader.

". . . tell me about your picture."

*He eyed Dr. Holland. He'd been lost in his own drawing
and remembering. Normally he had access to only crayons
to draw, and they were useless at capturing the details he remembered. Dr. Holland's colored pencils did a better job,
but still his ability fell far short of reality. He had been focused, trying to capture real trees on paper. "It's just a picture." He'd learned not to talk about the time in the woods,
but Dr. Holland was a nice giant.*

"Is this a little boy?"

"Yes."

"Is he you?"

"No, but he's just like me."

"Ah. And what's this? A dog?"

"No. That's me."

"Why are you a dog?"

"I don't know. Something bad happened and I ran away. I wanted to go back, but this part of me became a little boy and we couldn't go back together, so I stayed with him, protecting him, trying to get him to come back, but he'd forgotten almost everything but being scared."

"I see." Dr. Holland nodded as if he did understand. *"Where is he now?"*

"I don't know. I forgot where I left him. I know I've forgotten a lot of things since then, so much drained away before I realized what was happening, so I think about this so I won't forget."

"I see." Dr. Holland nodded again. *"Did you like being a dog?"*

"No."

"Why were you a dog?"

He lifted his shoulders up into a shrug. *"I don't know."*

"Why did you stop being a dog?"

He shrugged again. *"I don't know. I've forgotten."*

"Why did you draw this picture?"

He looked at Dr. Holland. The giants never ceased to confound him. *"You told me to."*

"I see," Dr. Holland said.

Perhaps Dr. Holland said that when he didn't see at all.

"Why did you hit all those boys?"

"They were teasing Bobby Hyzen. He can't help the way he is. He would change if he could. But he can't."

"Why did you draw this picture instead of one of Bobby Hyzen?"

"Because I wish I could find him again, the boy just like me."

The end-of-school tone sounded, alerting everyone that buses were arriving.

"Can you sign it for me?" Dr. Holland pointed to the lower left-hand corner.

He put his new name down.

"Clark?"

"I don't want to be John Doe anymore." His last set of foster parents explained the meaning of his name.

"Why Clark?"

He didn't want to tell Dr. Holland that it was because it was Superman's secret identity. Not because he was afraid Dr. Holland would laugh, but because he'd write it down and someone else might find out. He was discovering many of the mistakes he thought he left behind at the last foster home and the last school somehow showed up to haunt him. It would be best not to say . . .

A jump forward in time, an angry sixth grader in another office, fingering a broken nose that was rapidly healing.

". . . what's this about you wanting to be called Parker? What kind of name is that?" vice principal Henry asked.

He'd decided that Clark was a stupid name. Aliens that looked exactly like humans? Only one man on the whole planet smart enough to know it was going to explode but too stupid to send a guardian out with his baby? And that whole kryptonite thing was stupid—how could that much stuff get to Earth?—and a little unnerving. Did he have his own personal kryptonite? Besides, the new Superman movies made his choice way too obvious.

He chose Parker over Peter because he'd seen how Peter Johnson suffered once kids realized all the nicknames for penis. Just like Spider-Man, he had inhuman abilities—but what had been his radioactive spider?

"I don't want to be John Doe," he told the vice principal. *"I don't like the name; it's like a big sign that says I don't know who I am."*

"You can't change your name until you're of legal age."

Ah, yes, the magical age of eighteen, when he was free of

so many annoyances. "Anthony Cercone Junior goes by
Tony, and everyone calls James Walton J.J."

"That's what their families call them. We all need to stay
on the same page, John."

"I can have my foster parents call me Parker."

"What about your social worker, and your case files, and
the state? Your foster parents are being paid to take care of
a John, not a Parker."

He'd come to recognize insurmountable obstinacy. Luckily, he only had to deal with it until the next set of foster parents and the next school.

Flashes of junior high school followed, an endless flow
of fighting in the halls, in streets, and on playing fields.
Hockey was an excuse to legally hit the other kids.
Wrestling. Basketball. Football. Atticus's natural skills got
him onto sports teams. His aggression got him thrown off.
An angry teenager, he refused to see that his actions dictated
much of how the system treated him. One too many fights
landed him in juvenile hall, and the fights became a necessity for survival.

When Hellena tested Ukiah, he had been aware only of
his thoughts. Now he could see how she directed the search,
suggesting a topic and then pulling up the strongest response. What had brought up the funeral of his adopted sister's pet rabbit? He would have to ask Hellena, if things
went well. He sensed regret growing in the Pack, though, as
they saw a near future where his brother's murder would
taint their relationship with Ukiah.

There were areas where Atticus resisted invasion, somehow turning aside Hellena's probes. What he let her search
through were fights in dark alleys, crowded barrooms, and
even illegal fighting rings for bare-fisted fighters.

"Ru," Ukiah murmured to Hellena. "Have him remember
Ru."

. . . *Was there anything louder, drunker, randier than a
party of college boys? Atticus couldn't decide if coming*

tonight had been a mistake. With the recent gay bashings, he didn't like his roommate walking alone, but Atticus was the only straight person at the party. And apparently there was some confusion over that. On the theory that a moving target was harder to hit on, he drifted through the party. Perversely, he felt like Goldilocks, critiquing each area: too loud, too crowded, too drunk, way too intimate.

Where the hell was Ru? Atticus felt a prick of jealousy that probably someone else was with his roommate. Ru had been moody and withdrawn since winter break and the whole mess with the stabbing.

At the time Ru had been surprisingly calm and efficient. He said the mice were cute. Instead of being upset about Atticus not being human and able to come back from the dead, Ru seemed to focus on the fact that he was the first person Atticus ever told his secret to. He invited Atticus home during the break, and introduced him to his parents and three little sisters. What had happened? Even with Atticus's perfect memory, he couldn't pinpoint the sentence or the gesture where it all went wrong. And it hurt like hell. Ru was the best friend he'd ever had, and it really felt like he was losing him.

No one was in the backyard. While there was a fire going in a brick grill, it was dark and cold: a perfect spot to sulk. Ru found him there a short time later.

"Hey!" Ru breathed out a haze of wine, snuggling against Atticus's back. "What are you doing out here?"

"Sulking." Atticus immediately wished he'd said something else. For a moment, things had been right, with Ru playfully affectionate. He liked the closeness they had, despite what it was doing to his image.

Ru, though, pulled away. "Whatever for?"

"The mice weirded you out—didn't they?"

"Why would you say that?"

"Because . . . Nothing, just forget about it."

"You sorry you told me?" Ru asked warily, putting more distance between them.

"No. It's just things seem broke between us. And it sucks."

"Yeah, it sucks."

So they fell into silence except the crackling of the fire.

"Yeah," Atticus whispered finally, "I'm sorry I told you. I hate this."

"Atty, this has nothing to do with the mice."

He looked at Ru, dubious.

"This is about you and my sisters," Ru explained, or rather, didn't.

"What?"

"All the girls you dated last term were complete babes, but my sisters . . . I couldn't deal with that."

"Ru, what the hell are you talking about?"

Ru gave him a look of pure agony. "You'll hate me."

"What, you've taken up killing babies and torturing puppies when I wasn't looking?"

Ru laughed, and then sobered, falling back to the hurt look.

Atticus didn't know what to say. He never knew what to say. He tried to bridge the gap between them; he went to Ru, awkwardly embraced him, and asked quietly, "Tell me what's wrong. Until I know, I can't do anything to fix things."

Ru's heart started to hammer, and he let out a trembling sigh, as if he were going to start crying. "Oh, Atty, sometimes you're just so clueless."

Just as Atticus was going to ask him what he meant, Ru reached up to undo Atticus's top three buttons, leaned his head down, and dropped a kiss in the hollow of Atticus's neck. His kisses moved upward, strange for their maleness.

It all clicked for Atticus. Ru was in love with him, and Atticus was straight. Things had been fine as long as Atticus was unattainable, but then they'd gone to Ru's home and Atticus had flirted with Ru's sisters. With Ru's long hair, and his sisters' relatively flat chests, the only difference between the siblings was an X chromosome and some southerly plumbing. He felt stupid not to have realized it before.

Shaking now, Ru whispered, "I love you."

Ru, who knew that he wasn't human, who had seen the mice form and be reabsorbed, who watched him die and come back to life, loved him. A jolt of something as pure and blinding as joy flashed through Atticus, stunning him.

Ru kissed him, then, firm male lips against his.

Atticus was fairly sure he was straight-straight; as totally aware of being driven by pheromones and animal instincts as he was mystified that he could not be human and still so desperately want to mate with a human female. In his blackest moods, he felt similar to a randy little dog that humped visitors' legs, driven over the boundaries of his species by lust. But he had no species of his own; he was a solitary creature, a freak of nature.

And Ru loved him just the same.

Ru kissed him again, tasting of tears, and then, realizing that Atticus wasn't responding, tried to pull away. Atticus tightened his hold, sensing that if he let Ru go now, it would tear a larger rift between them. The slight pressure was enough to check Ru. As they stood in the cold darkness, neither wanting to let go, it started to snow. Huge white flakes drifted down silently around them.

Could he maybe not be as straight as he always thought? Certainly he'd never tried . . . that. Never had the desire to. But if he really were entirely straight, why'd he never rebuff Ru? Why would the thought of Ru loving him hit him with lightning-intense happiness? And if asked—just minutes ago—for a word to describe how he felt about Ru, wouldn't he have used the word "love"?

Ru traced the line of Atticus's jaw with his fingertips, snowflakes in his long black hair.

What was the depth and width of his love? For Ru, couldn't he bend a little?

Wetting his lips, Atticus tilted his head to Ru and kissed

him. Strangely, while his senses told him that this was just another set of lips, with an X chromosome instead of a Y, there was something different—some electricity that had nothing to do with taste or smell or touch. Was this love?

So while the snow sprinkled them with cold kisses, they tested the possibilities, Atticus unsure and hesitant, Ru eager and growing bolder.

After having Ru as a roommate for months, his body was imprinted on all his senses, and yet it was like Atticus was discovering him for the first time. His musky scent. His soft skin over hard muscle. His silky black hair.

Ru fumbled with Atticus's belt, undid his pants, and slipped a hand down the flat of Atticus's stomach and into his boxers.

Do I really want this? Can I do this?

There was no denying that what Ru was doing felt good— he grew erect in Ru's hand. Encouraged, Ru slid down his body, freed Atticus from his underwear, and, with a slight groan of want, took Atticus into his mouth.

Am I really ready for this? *Atticus didn't know, but his body did as it took up the rhythm of sex.*

Ru looked up at him, and in that moment of union it seemed like Atticus could see straight to his soul and knew— Atticus loved him.

Relief and puzzlement went through the Pack. How did Atticus get to college? How did he go from the angry teenager to this protective and sensitive man? And how did he end up selling drugs? How long had he been dealing in Invisible Red? Atticus resisted Helena's probes until she used her personal knowledge of the Iron Horses—and what Ukiah had told the Pack earlier—to dig out memories of tonight's buy. She glossed over the biker's theories about the Pack and focused in on the information on the cult.

"We lost three men at Buffalo," Ru said. "You lost three too."

"Four," Daggit said. *"No one's heard from Toback since; whoever hit the place took him."*

There was a weird echo in the memory; Atticus hadn't known the name when Daggit said it, but he'd put a face to the name since then, so the reference had new meaning to him. Hellena pushed into the echo, and Atticus's memory jumped to a hotel suite overlooking the Boston Harbor. Atticus stood with a man, watching a massacre on a computer screen.

Why would drug dealers record a drug buy?

Hellena went digging for an answer. Atticus resisted, trying to divert to other thoughts. They played cat and mouse for a moment, and then Hellena caught hold of a memory and dragged it forward with a cry of dismay from Atticus.

Atticus was starting to hate hospitals. He stopped, found the right room, and glanced in. The now familiar scene of a young man strapped to machines doing the living for him, a family desolate with grief. Hopefully this time he could get some useful information.

He rapped on the door, catching the attention of the father. "I'm sorry to bother you, but I need to ask you a few questions." He took out his ID and held it out to them. "I'm Agent Atticus Steele with the DEA."

"I don't understand," the father said.

"We believe your son took a new designer drug. It has several names. Pixie Dust. Liquidlust."

"Our son would never do hard drugs."

"The word on the street is that this drug is harmless, safer to take than Ecstasy, but we've seen a growing number of deaths in young men like Paul here who frequent the rave and dance club scenes. We think this new drug is the cause."

Atticus thrashed in Hellena's hold, desperately trying to escape her power. He tried to turn his thoughts from the memory, but Hellena kept firm, pushing on to see what he was hiding now.

*. . . footsteps sounded behind Atticus. He knew the length
of the stride, the scent . . .*

"No." Atticus groaned. "No."

*. . . the father's eyes shifted to the newcomer. Without
turning, Atticus indicated the man behind him . . .*

"No!"

"This is my partner, Agent Hikaru Takahashi."

With a roar of anger and fear, Atticus yanked himself out
of Helena's control and surged to his feet. The Pack melted
backward, having seen enough to convince them, their relief
obvious. Ukiah felt his brother's fear for his partner and
stepped back, clearing a path to Ru.

Atticus and Ru communicated in some secret language, a
look, a touch of left hands, and relief swept through Atticus.
Ukiah sensed that Atticus ached to hug Ru tight, as if all his
body wanted part of the reassuring contact, but his brother
ruthlessly shoved the desire away to focus on the surrounding Dog Warriors. The two DEA agents put their backs to
each other and faced the Dogs. Despite the rush of terror for
Ru's safety, part of Atticus filled with calm; Ukiah realized
that as Atticus protected Ru, his partner guarded Atticus's
heart.

But was there anyone else in his brother's life? Atticus
had seemed to view Kyle as an odd mix of friend and child;
someone protected with affection and yet kept at a slight distance. Ukiah supposed that was the nature of children, that
the act of protecting them built a shell around them, keeping
them from your own dark thoughts of disappointment and
despair. And in Atticus's memories, there had been no one
else. What a desolation of a heart. For Ukiah, in the wilder-
ness, there had been only the rough affection of the wolves.
How much harder it had to have been for Atticus, surrounded with examples of what he lacked. From Jo finding
Ukiah in the woods, onward to the Pack and Indigo, he'd
been blessed with those who loved him.

"We're not going to hurt you," Ukiah said.

"I don't believe you." Atticus stood panting, one arm still out flung to shield Ru. "You set us up, you little bastard. I can't believe I was fucking worried about you."

"We only wanted to be sure you're a decent man." Ukiah didn't need to check for a vote; he sensed the lack of dissension among the Dogs. "You passed."

Atticus clenched down on a curse, but still it struck like stones against their minds. *Fuck you. Fuck you all.*

"Atticus." Ukiah stepped close, attempting to merge back to one mind, to explain. *"We don't care that you're DEA. You're family. We test everyone. They even tested—"*

"Get out of my mind!" Atticus hit him with the force of a truck, smashing him off his feet.

Without thinking Ukiah put out a newly healed arm to catch himself as he fell. The many fragile knits shattered in an explosion of pain. As the Dogs closed back in with a snarl of anger, Ukiah fought to stay conscious. *"No! Don't hurt them!"*

"I said stay out of my head!" Atticus roared. "We're not family! I'm not one of you, and you don't have any right to do this fucking mind rape! You have no right to go in, mess with my head, and pass judgment on me!"

"We're brothers," Ukiah whispered.

"We're nothing but an accident with an axe. I don't know you. I don't *want* to know you." Atticus caught Ru's elbow and hurried him toward the waiting Jaguar, radiating his anxiousness to get his all too human partner away from the Dog Warriors. "Stay out of my head, stay out of my life, and stay out of my investigation, or so help me God, you'll find out how little I value our family tie."

CHAPTER FIVE

Boston Harbor Hotel, Boston, Massachusetts
Tuesday, September 21, 2004

Why, Atticus wondered, did life continually try to confound him?

The sudden addition of an outlaw brother had been bad enough, but an entire species of criminals? Hypocritical ones at that—judge if he was a good man? Unlikely. What had they really been after?

The answer came while they were at a truck stop off of Route 3, where Atticus changed into dry clothes while Ru filled the Jaguar with gas. Atticus had just gotten back in the car when the Jag's phone rang.

Atticus pressed the talk button. "What is it, Kyle?"

"The Dog Warriors just raided Sumpter's room. They've taken the drop."

"Damn it! Are you okay?"

"Yeah, they didn't come down to our rooms."

Because they knew from Atticus's memories that Sumpter had the drugs.

"What about Sumpter?"

"He's pissed."

Which meant he was at least alive.

"We're on our way back."

"I tried both of your phones and you didn't answer."

His phone had been killed by the dip in the ocean. Ru's

phone had gone missing sometime during the day. "We're fine. I'll explain later. We'll be there in twenty minutes."

The door to Sumpter's hotel room was smashed open in a manner that was entirely too familiar. The room had been thoroughly searched; all the dresser drawers were pulled out and couches overturned. The computer, Atticus noted, was gone from the desk. On the floor was the plastic evidence bag that had held the drugs; his signature was still readable on the tamper-proof tape. They found Sumpter in the bathroom, nose bloodied, checking the tightness of his teeth.

"Steele, you asshole." Sumpter grimaced at his reflection as he found a loose molar. "You were followed here after the buy."

"Yeah, something like that." Atticus scanned the room. "What did they take?"

"Everything, even my sheets and blankets."

That puzzled Atticus until he remembered that the FBI reports stated that the Dog Warriors were known to camp outdoors and Ukiah was without a sleeping bag. He felt a moment of remorse, remembering the flashes of pain as bones splintered; it had been like he did the damage to himself. Angrily, he pushed the sense of guilt aside. Yes, he hurt his brother, but look what the Dog Warriors had done after raping his mind.

"They took my copy of the surveillance DVD." Sumpter wet down a hand towel and dabbed at the blood on his face, wincing in pain. "It's only reasonable to assume that they did it to cover up their involvement in the Buffalo shooting."

Bitter as Atticus was at the Dog Warriors, that didn't seem right. The images on the DVD had been fairly clear; none of the shooters had been the Dog Warriors at the beach. Ukiah and the Dogs had been full of feral grace, something that the shooters lacked. "I think it would be wrong to jump to that conclusion."

"Why else would they be involved in this?" Sumpter snapped.

Because Atticus stole his dead brother out of a trunk. It was annoying that his sense of right and wrong had gotten him into this mess. "According to the Iron Horses, the source of the drug seems to be the Temple of New Reason. I think the cult—"

"You're going the wrong direction." Sumpter threw the bloody towel into the sink. "The Iron Horses set us up here. Obviously, they're working with the Pack. They've got the money and now the Dog Warriors have the drugs."

"That's possible." Atticus could easily believe that. It would explain how the Dog Warriors found the beach house when Ukiah himself was clueless as to his location. "But I don't think they're our shooters."

Sumpter harrumphed, taking one last look at himself in the mirror, frowning at the bloody mess of his shirt. "Where the hell were you, anyhow?" He turned and saw the matching bruises on Atticus's face. "What the hell happened to you?"

Atticus's encounter with the Dog Warriors had left him battered enough that a change of clothes and the healing done during the drive couldn't disguise it. "The Dog Warriors jumped me at the beach house."

"You?" Sumpter studied Ru, who was unscathed beyond a bruised hand. "Where were you during this?"

Ru's face went to neutral, but Atticus recognized the signs of guilt and hurt carefully hidden away.

"He was smart enough not to pick a fight with them," Atticus said.

"He's your partner," Sumpter said.

And the pain etched deeper into Ru's face.

"Give it a rest," Atticus snapped.

"Just because you don't fill out the forms, doesn't mean I don't keep track of the number of times you've been hurt," Sumpter said. "I can read between the lines on your reports.

He always slacks off and lets you take the brunt of the danger. He's going to get you killed."

Atticus turned and walked out of the hotel room. It was the only way he could keep from hitting Sumpter.

"Where are you going, Steele?"

"I need a drink!"

He was thankful the elevator appeared moments after he slammed down on the button. Ru huddled in the corner, trying to keep his hurt to himself.

"He's not right," Atticus said to the numbers counting down. "He doesn't know jack shit about me."

"I screwed up big-time at the house. I've gotten too lax. I count on you being able to take anything the perps deal out."

"You didn't do anything wrong," Atticus said. "I rushed in like an idiot, and there were just too many of them. We lost it the moment I got out of the car. Hell, when I left the hotel." He reached out and tried to smooth away the worry line on Ru's brow. "You didn't let me go alone, and that's all you could have done, and that's all that matters." Ru gave him a sad smile as the elevator stopped on their floor and the door opened. "Let's get Kyle and go down to the bar."

Normally, Atticus didn't drink. It never solved anything, and his body rejected the poison violently, but he did it when he was depressed. Tonight he intended to get smashed.

The hotel bar had wood floors of cherry with narrow strips of maple and deep red walls. It was cool and elegant, not at all comforting.

"It was just like Daggit said, werewolves," Atticus said after they'd filled Kyle in. "I could smell them. I could feel it." He rubbed his fingers together. He'd scrubbed the evidence away but his perfect memory held the recall of the genetic pattern, so like his, but with a thread of wolf DNA running through it. "Part human, part wolves."

"Yeah, but you're not," Ru said.

He shot Ru a look and went to buy himself another bottle

of whiskey. The problem with trying to get drunk was that it was expensive; his body rid itself of the alcohol nearly as fast as he drank it. He carried the bottle back to their table.

"You're not a werewolf," Ru continued as if he hadn't left.

"But everything fits. The whole healing thing. The heightened senses."

"You don't turn into a wolf."

Atticus poured himself a shot of whiskey, ignoring him, trying not to think of the memories he saved from before he was found—those of running on four legs. If he looked hard enough, he could find that thread of wolf in himself. "I can remember . . . something."

Kyle was ignoring them in favor of his PDA, a sure sign that the conversation was bothering him greatly.

Atticus drank the whiskey, letting it burn its way down and blur the edges of his razor-sharp—wolfish—senses. "And I can remember Ukiah. At least I think it was him. I've always felt like there was . . . someone . . . out there. Someone I lost."

"What was the whole stand-around-and-stare-at-you thing, anyhow?" Ru asked.

"They went through my memories. It was like a television, and they kept changing the channels. I couldn't stop them."

"Then they know . . . ?"

"Yeah, they know. They know everything important." He felt like he had been raped. There wasn't a dark secret in his soul that they didn't uncover and fumble through.

"What do we do next?" Ru asked.

Atticus glared at him. He knew what Ru was doing. "We get drunk."

"And tomorrow?"

"We'll think about it when we get up."

"One thing's for certain." Kyle broke his silence. "The Dog Warriors are going to be after the Temple of New Reason."

They looked at him in stunned surprise.

"Well, the cultists killed your brother, and they're the ones with the drugs that the Dog Warriors want, so of course they're going to go after the cult."

"Damn," Atticus swore. "Ukiah knows that the stuff came from the Iron Horses. They'll hit them next."

"The Iron Horses will probably roll over for them," Ru said. "They idolize the Dog Warriors."

"I don't know," Atticus said. "There's a lot of money involved. It's not like they're going to turn over the cash cow."

It would be safest to assume that the Dog Warriors had already blown their cover with the Iron Horses. It was stunning that the Pack had left the two agents alive. During their "test" he couldn't even see; it was like the Dog Warriors had focused his eyes inward. Atticus had been helpless—a new and uncomfortable feeling for him. Not one he wanted to repeat. They'd have to get ahead of the Dog Warriors and stay there—but how?

"What did you find out about the cult?" Atticus asked Kyle.

Kyle made a noise of disgust. "Trying to find out anything was like wading through a flood of sewage."

"What happened to the cultist picked up at the rest stop?"

"They've identified the one killed in the shoot-out: John Pender of New Hampshire. He joined the cult two years ago. Apparently the Pennsylvania State Police pulled over a cult member," Kyle frowned at his PDA. "Dmitriy Yevgenyevitch Zlotnikov was arrested earlier this month while driving Pender's car. Zlotnikov died in a holding tank without explaining where Pender was. Pender's parents listed him as missing after Zlotnikov died, and provided dental records. There's a flag on Zlotnikov's records indicating that his hobbies included high explosives, and abandoned cult property might be booby-trapped."

Atticus grunted.

"I'm not sure who to pity in this war," Ru said, "the cult or the Dog Warriors."

"What about the two wounded cultists?" Atticus asked.

Kyle shook his head. "They're now two dead cultists. They both went into grand mal seizures and died this evening. Still no ID on them beyond the cult names of Coaxial and Binary."

The seizures were just one of the side effects of the Pixie Dust poisoning. The vast array of deadly symptoms had made it difficult to first determine that the deaths of so many young men were linked. Oddly, not a single woman had fallen victim to the drug.

"So that leaves the female cultist."

"So far the police have no ID on her beyond her cult name of Ascii," Kyle said. "She's been transferred to Massachusetts Correctional Institution in Framingham."

"So we can get to her tomorrow," Ru said.

"Most likely," Atticus said. "What else did you find out?"

"Well, the Temple of New Reason was founded by a William Harris, who called himself Core. Harris and Zlotnikov were both originally from Butler, Pennsylvania. Homeland has been tracking the cult for about a year; during that time, they've been in Boston, Buffalo, and Pittsburgh. According to the *Pittsburgh Post-Gazette,* Core was killed early Saturday morning when the boat he was driving at high speeds hit a barge. FBI reports are weirdly muddled about what happened, but apparently the cult planned to do some kind of human sacrifice on an island and there was a shootout, an explosion, an extensive fire, two boating accidents, a drowning, and then some kind of vandalism of the crime scene afterward."

"Everything but cotton candy and fireworks," Ru muttered.

"That was just Saturday morning. Friday there were two other bombings linked to the cult." Kyle checked his PDA again. "An Iron Mountain storage facility and a mansion in Butler where the cult had been living."

"Any forwarding address?" Ru asked.

Kyle shook his head. "The FBI thinks that Harris's second

in command, a man they know only by the name of Ice, has taken the cult into hiding. The Pittsburgh police have a cult member who has turned state's evidence; she says that Ice and several of the surviving cult members are from the Boston area."

"Ukiah was in Pittsburgh," Atticus realized. "He called the Pittsburgh hospital and the car that we found him in had Pennsylvania plates."

"Oh, yeah, your brother's name is smeared all through this." Kyle waved the PDA.

But they didn't know his name—did they? "What is his name?"

"Ukiah Oregon."

"Like the town?" Atticus had asked. "Ukiah, Oregon?"

Atticus groaned. Ukiah had told him his name—he just hadn't realized it. "Did you run a priors on him?"

"There was a missing person's report filed on Sunday by a Samuel Anne Killington of Pendleton, Oregon—I'm not sure what *her* connection to him is—but other than that, he's clean."

Atticus sagged back in his chair. Clean. What the hell was he supposed to make of that? A Dog Warrior who wasn't wanted?

"According to the report," Kyle continued, "Ukiah had been in Ohio when he disappeared. There was another explosion in that area—a farmhouse leveled Sunday night—and another bonfire site found on the land yesterday morning. The owners of the farm are missing, presumed murdered. Dental records on the human remains found at the bonfire site are being checked."

Okay, the cultists were vicious little bastards, all the way around.

Ru made notes on his PDA and eyed them now. "So it looks like Ice fled Pittsburgh for Ohio, and Ukiah followed. The cult and the Pack fight, Ukiah is killed, and the cult heads back to home turf."

"Looks like." Kyle nodded his consensus.

Atticus frowned. "We'll skip over 'how does the cult know he'll come back from the dead.' After talking to the Iron Horses, it's obvious that my healing abilities are not as secret as *we* thought they were. But why did the cult take Ukiah with them?"

"Maybe they were going to ransom him," Kyle said.

"Maybe they planned to hold him hostage against the Pack," Ru guessed. "The Pack certainly seem like they'll plow through anything to get him back."

That would be more gratifying if it hadn't been *him* that they had plowed through. This led Atticus back, however, to the need to stay ahead of the Dog Warriors.

"There's two things here," Atticus said. "First is that the cult might be our shooters. We need to run through the DVD, pull out mug shots of our perps, and compare them to known cult members. Just to be thorough, we can check against the Pack too, but I didn't see a match."

"Check," Kyle said.

"The second is seeing what the state police, the FBI, and any other organizations have on the cult in the Boston area. They might have returned to an old haunt."

Ru nodded and made a note.

"My finding my brother doesn't change anything. This drug is a poison killing everyone coming in contact with it. We've got to shut it down fast."

CHAPTER SIX

Massachusetts Correctional Institution at Framingham
Tuesday, September 21, 2004

Framingham proved to be a sprawling industrial town with a heavy Brazilian population. Leaving Kyle to dig through databases, Atticus and Ru used the Jag's GPS system to thread through the heart of the town to the women's prison.

Like the state of Massachusetts itself, MCI Framingham was small and orderly. Screened from the road by a stand of cattails, the prison was a modern redbrick facility with pale gold bricks highlighting the windows. Exercise yards winged the buildings, and a triple row of concertina wire shimmered bright silver in the weak sun. Storm clouds scudded across the sky, cloaking it with gray.

There was a bite of winter to the brittle morning. Atticus's breath frosted as he locked the Jag, and he remembered with a flash of remorse that Ukiah had spent the night out in the cold with a shattered arm. It seemed like his brother was never far from his mind. It had taken ruthless determination last night to ignore all the answers on Ukiah they might find in Kyle's data flood and focus instead on the cult activities in the Boston area.

As he and Ru stopped to sign in, they found David Brukman signing out. They had worked with the ATF agent a number of times; drugs and guns were a common mix, with one often used to buy the other.

Atticus nodded to Brukman, letting Ru do the shaking of hands and the friendly greeting, while he occupied his hands with signing in. If he could, he avoided pressing flesh with people.

"What are you doing here?" Ru effortlessly made small talk.

"I was transferred up to Boston last year." Brukman took back his gun from the guards. "Pittsburgh FBI field office notified us Monday that a gun-happy religious cult just moved back into the area and they bombed the hell out of Pittsburgh when they left."

"Temple of New Reason," Atticus guessed.

"You here for Ascii too?" Securing his gun, Brukman knew them well enough not to push for a handshake from Atticus. "We heard you took a hit in Buffalo but no details. Who went down? Anyone I know?"

Ru glanced to Atticus. The DEA was sitting on the information to protect Atticus's team. If the ATF was after the Temple of New Reason, though, they might be caught in the crossfire between the cult and the Pack.

"It was Scroggins' team," Atticus said quietly. "All three dead."

"Shit." Brukman's gaze hardened. "The Temple were the shooters?"

"We don't know yet." Ru dropped his voice to a whisper. "Scroggins' team was set up to buy a drug that we've since traced back to the cult. They're using bikers as go-betweens."

Brukman nodded, glancing about to see if anyone was listening.

"The shooters are heavily armed and ruthless," Atticus warned. "No ID on them yet, but we just found out that the Pack is going to war against the Temple."

Brukman surprised Atticus by admitting, "The Pittsburgh FBI field office gave us the heads-up on that. I don't know what the hell the Temple was thinking, except maybe they didn't know anything about the Pack. You don't fuck with them."

Atticus laughed at the truth of this, but Brukman misunderstood.

"Don't try anything with them, Steele. I know your team is good, but the Pack has spotted every undercover agent we've ever tried to get close to them and we've lost a lot of good people to them—one way or another."

"What do you mean?" Ru asked.

"Usually they disappear without a trace." Brukman shook his head, seeming confounded. "But sometimes—and this never makes sense, no matter how many times I say it—they join the Pack."

"*. . . a couple dozen can take the walk in the woods with the Pack, maybe one will come back out changed, one of them . . .*"

Had the Pack somehow transformed the ATF agents? Made them inhuman? Made them . . . werewolves?

"What do you have on the Temple?" Ru changed the subject away from the Pack.

"Not much," Brukman admitted. "We were just starting to investigate them earlier this year when they dropped off the face of the planet. Homeland tracked them to Buffalo but they moved again; FBI says that the Temple grabbed a Homeland agent and maimed him." Brukman made a *snick* noise while chopping down on his left wrist. "They've reattached the hand but—you know—it's never the same."

Perhaps the cult didn't understand Ukiah's nature if they routinely kidnapped and brutalized people.

"Any idea where the cult is now that they're back in this area?" Ru got a shake of Brukman's head. "What did you find out from Ascii?"

Brukman shook his head with a look of disgust. "So far she's clammed up tight to everyone; no one has been able to get her to say anything past her name and some Temple of New Reason rhetoric."

"Who all has talked to her?"

"Me, the state police, and an agent from the Pittsburgh FBI field office. Special Agent Zheng. Oh, there's a real number for you. Very cool. Very collected. You get the impression ice wouldn't melt in her mouth."

"Ouch."

Brukman glanced over Atticus's shoulder and jerked his chin up to indicate someone walking up behind him. "Speak of the devil."

Atticus turned to follow the gaze.

Agent Zheng wore FBI black with stylish perfection. She came only to his shoulder, but there was nothing fragile about her; under the black silk of her expensive pantsuit, she had a trim, athletic body. Her hair was perfectly straight, glossy black of Asian stock, but her eyes were gray and only vaguely Asian in shape. She looked at him with a gaze that gave nothing away about what she was thinking.

"Agent Steele," Agent Zheng greeted him. "They told me I could find you here."

They must have given her a very good description of him, though he supposed there weren't a lot of Native American federal agents in New England.

"Agent Zheng," he said to prove that she didn't have one up on him.

"The DEA wants a go at Ascii." Bitch though she might be, Brukman seemed eager to please the FBI agent.

"I heard." Agent Zheng kept her gray gaze on Atticus. "I need to speak to you about that. Can we talk privately?"

"In regard to?" Atticus wondered how she had heard when they had told no one.

"To be quite frank, I believe you're the only one who has a chance of getting anywhere with Ascii, but perhaps only in the first minutes of your discussion. Considering that you'll be able to ask only a handful of questions before she shuts down again, I would like to see that advantage be utilized to the utmost."

"Meaning?"

Agent Zheng flicked her gaze to Brukman, who was listening to their conversation. "I mean that in all probability, I can answer any question you may have, and there are questions of vital importance regarding things you know nothing about that need to be answered."

"While the FBI might think itself the fount of all knowledge, I doubt very much you know the answers to my questions."

"You might be surprised."

Frankly he was getting sick of surprises. Certainly there was one piece of information he knew that she didn't.

"The biker jacket in the truck of the cultist's car—do you know what they did to the Dog Warrior who wore it?"

"Yes," Agent Zheng said.

He should learn not to play word games—a case of going unarmed to battle. Atticus waited for more information, but none was forthcoming. Prosecuting attorneys must love her on the stand.

Ru took pity on him and asked, "What do you know about Pixie Dust?"

Agent Zheng flicked a look at Ru, and then returned her focus to Atticus. "Invisible Red?"

That was what Ukiah had called the drug.

"Yes," Atticus said.

"I know that the cult is manufacturing it," Zheng said. "And selling it to the Iron Horses, who are in turn redistributing it up and down the East Coast."

"How do you know that?" Atticus asked.

"I have my sources. If we're going to continue this conversation, I suggest we move to a more private place. We could walk outside."

She leveled a cold look at Brukman.

The ATF agent took the clue and saved face by glancing at his watch. "Well, I've got to run. Have fun, kids." With a wink, he took off.

Just beyond the parking lot was a small pond with Canada geese and a fence to keep out visitors. Zheng led Atticus and Ru around the prison to a country road that ran behind the prison. Across the road were horse pastures and well-kept barns. A sign identified the farm as the home of the National Lancers, and a memory attached to the bright sound of marching bands told him that they were a mounted honor guard.

"What do you know about Invisible Red?" Atticus asked Agent Zheng.

"The cultists raided a stash of bioweapons and stole four machines." Agent Zheng took out a pencil sketch and handed it to him. "This is a drawing of the machines. They're identical except for this design here." She pointed out an odd symbol in the center of the machine. "This is Loo-ae—Air Death. The other one"—she pointed out a second symbol in the corner of the page—"is Hu-ae—Little Death."

"Let me guess," Ru said. "Hu-ae makes the sex drug."

"Yes," Agent Zheng said.

"What language is this?" Atticus asked. "Who made these machines?"

"Let's stick to basics," Agent Zheng said. "Their names and what they produce are all you need to know about the Ae."

"I'm sick of being in the dark." Atticus thrust the picture to Ru to study. "I want to know where these machines came from."

Agent Zheng sighed. "About two hundred years ago, an alien spacecraft entered our solar system. It was a seed ship for a race called the Ontongard. Its sole intent was to land on Earth and replace all life here with its genetic code. Due to a rebel in their ranks, most of their force was decimated, but some survived and are in hiding among us now. They brought the Ae to Earth. The Temple of New Reason believes that the Ontongard are demons and are on a holy crusade against them. By wiretapping the aliens, the cult learned of the Ae's existence and stole the Ae from the Ontongard and, after years of study, have managed to get Hu-ae to work."

"W-w-what?"

"Shall we go back to the basics?" Agent Zheng asked. "There were four Ae. Two have been destroyed. Hu-ae makes Invisible Red. Loo-ae produces a deadly airborne virus that could kill every man, woman, and child on the planet. It's vital that we find this machine and destroy it before the cultists manage to use it."

"That sounds fairly basic to me." Ru handed the sketch back to Agent Zheng.

"We also need to find out what the cult intends to use as a key," Zheng said.

"Key to what?"

"The Ae won't work without a genetic key. The cult kidnapped five children in Pittsburgh, whom they were going to use as blood sacrifices. I want to know if the rescued children are still in danger from the cult."

"You haven't asked Ascii yourself?" Atticus asked.

"I've asked her," Zheng said. "She wouldn't answer me."

"Why do you think she'll talk to me?"

"Because she might mistake you for your brother."

How did she know about Ukiah? Was she here in Massachusetts because of Ukiah's jacket? If so, why was she chasing after his brother? How was Ukiah involved in the cult? And what did it mean for Atticus now that the trail led to him?

"Aliens and demons," Atticus scoffed. "Do you expect me to believe that?"

"Why not, Agent Steele? You are a half Ontongard, created by them to be a breeder. You were to be their tool for taking over the human race—only they misplaced you."

It took him a full minute before he could breathe again.

"Yesterday," Atticus countered as calmly as he could, "I was told I was a werewolf."

Why had it been so much easier to know that the bikers considered him inhuman? Because they couldn't truly inflict harm on him?

"Lately I've been keeping an open mind about old legends." Stunningly, Zheng seemed neither afraid of him nor hostile.

"What does the FBI plan to do about me?"

"Nothing," Zheng said. "The FBI doesn't know about any of this. Not about the Ae, the Ontongard, or about you and your brother. Only I know about this."

For a moment he was relieved, and then annoyed.

"You've got a group of madmen with a bioweapon they could set off in a city with a population of half a million, and you haven't reported it to your superiors?"

"I've let the FBI know that I suspect that the cult has biotoxins, type unknown, origin unknown. I've let them know that Boston is a possible target."

"You know a hell of a lot more than that."

"What am I supposed to say?" Zheng's voice went brittle with anger. "That the cult has stolen a device from aliens that they think are demons and are trying to prevent the Second Coming?"

Atticus glanced at Ru for suggestions. Ru shrugged, looking slightly panic-stricken.

"Currently they're wanted by the FBI for the kidnapping of five infants and the murder of two. ATF wants them for illegal weapons. NSA wants them for wiretapping and hacking government sites, including some top-secret spy satellites. Every law agency in this country is looking for them."

"This has the possibilities of being bigger than nine-eleven."

"I realize that. I also realize that the moment that aliens and demons are mentioned in my reports, my validity will be questioned. The cult has biotoxins. Their target is unknown. That anyone can believe and act on."

Agent Zheng glanced at her watch. "The public defender will be here shortly. If we want to get answers out of Ascii without him acting as a filter, we have to do it now."

Atticus studied Agent Zheng. If she was telling him the truth, their goals were identical—finding the cult. He considered the possibility that she was lying, but he couldn't ignore the simple fact that she'd known he wasn't human. "Okay, let's do this."

Atticus paused by the door into the questioning room, gazing through the two-way mirror to the room beyond. Sunlight shafted down from a high barred window, motes of dust making the light seem substantial as it cut down onto Ascii.

The cultist was as he remembered her from the turnpike: a pale, thin blonde. The black running suit had been exchanged for prison grays, making her look more colorless than before. She seemed nearly void of color, a watercolor stain on plain paper. Strangely the insubstantial look flattered her, her fragile features becoming ethereal. She sat composed at the questioning table—hands folded in her lap, staring off at the left-hand corner of the room, eyes unfocused.

She didn't seem like a ruthless killer, but Atticus had found that few murderers did.

Agent Zheng stood beside Atticus, a dark reflection of Ascii: black hair, expensive black pantsuit, focused with bitter intensity on the woman within. "There's no telling which way this conversation might go. You're going to have to stay sharp."

"Takahashi usually does the talking," Atticus said.

For some reason, that summoned a Mona Lisa smile, making Atticus aware of how tightly composed she kept herself. The smile slipped away.

Ru had been watching the exchange, and a small wrinkle of jealousy creased his brow.

Atticus opened the door, stepped into the room, and closed the door behind him.

Ascii didn't look up until he slid into the chair across from her, and when she did, stunned amazement took over her face. "You!"

That answered any question of her mistaking him for his brother.

"Oh, oh, forgive me," Ascii cried, hands hovering near her mouth in distress, as if she was torn between pleading for forgiveness and keeping her silence. "Please. Ice said we had to take you by force. It seemed so wrong to kill an angel of the Lord, but Ice said it was the right thing, but Ice wasn't touched by God like Core was, so . . . I'm sorry that we raised our hands against you."

What did you say to something like that? Atticus thought of Ukiah, battered, shot, bound and dead in the trunk, and rage went through him. Even a Dog Warrior shouldn't die like that. "It was an evil act."

"We weren't sure if you were really an angel. You're the first we've found. Even when the mice formed, we weren't sure if you weren't just a new type of demon, but then, when the police opened the trunk and you were gone, I knew. I knew. You'd ascended to heaven to take your place in the glory of God, and I was sore afraid."

He found himself standing, putting distance between himself and her.

Wan as she was, her eyes were vivid green, luminous in her pale face. "Forgive me, for I have sinned."

"Why would you do something like that? What if he . . . what if I were just a regular man?" *And not a Dog Warrior.* "Thou shall not kill; it doesn't get any clearer than that."

"Surely you of all beings can see the necessity—that the needs of the one or the few are nothing to the needs of the many. We are sacrificial lambs for the good of mankind. We will kill to protect, taking the sin upon ourselves to save the world. The demons are winning this war, and God might choose at any time to wipe the slate clean once more."

He wanted out of the room, but he still needed to ask Agent Zheng's questions. "Where is Loo-ae?"

"Ice has the founts."

"The founts? Is that what you call Loo-ae?"

She hesitated a moment, before asking. "Is that the wrong name?"

"We call them the Ae." When did it become "we"? Somehow with a flash of the badge, Agent Zheng had established herself as sane.

"Ohhh. I get it," Ascii said. "Loo-ae. Hu-ae. Doh. We've been calling them Huey and Louie. And there was Chewie and Dewey, but . . ." She eyed him, chewing on her bottom lip. "Core said they were like the Ark of the Covenant, most holy of relics. We called them the founts, because from them God's will would flow."

"Where are the founts?"

"I don't know. Ice didn't tell us where he was taking them. We were to go to the parking lot of the Salem train station and wait. We didn't know what vengeance we might be calling down upon ourselves in slaying you, so we who did the killing kept ourselves separate from the rest. And we were right to. Within hours I lost my child, and the others were dead, and despite our efforts, you were gone."

It would seem miraculous, except that Ukiah's ascension had been via Atticus's keen nose and Ru's lock picks. Ukiah had gone to a luxury beach house instead of heaven. If Atticus were inclined to believe in miracles, then one would be that he had been at the Ludlow rest stop, standing out in the parking lot, when the cultists arrived. Just a few seconds later, inside the Jaguar and out of the wind, he wouldn't have caught the smell of blood.

"We've long suspected that angels might walk the world," Ascii continued as if the dam had broken and the floodwaters would not stop. "Time and time again we'll find a demon nest ransacked and all that is left will be ashes. When we had you in our power at Eden Court, though, only Core recognized you—but he was touched by God."

"What?" The cult had held Ukiah prisoner at one point? But if he was going to keep pretending to be Ukiah, Atticus couldn't ask straight-out. He scrambled for another question. "Were you there—at Eden Court—when I was?"

"I'd gone on to the Western Reserve." It took Atticus a moment to realize she meant northeast Ohio, the infamous western reserve of Connecticut. "I wasn't there when Ice first captured you and Core shared you with Ping." Her voice dropped to a whisper. "They say that's why the house was destroyed—because Core drugged you and took you against your will."

They had raped Ukiah? "Why?" He caught hold of her by her prison uniform and could barely keep from shaking her. "Why would you do that to anyone?"

She didn't seem to notice the violence of his actions, gazing up at him without flinching. "We wouldn't have attacked you if the need wasn't so great!"

"What do you mean?"

"There has been a quickening to the demons' plans. A shift. Something has changed and we don't know what. We thought it was the events of June, but wiretaps we've translated recently mention Boston, and something of great importance. We might be too late already. It's taking us too long to work through the translation. We had to have help. We needed you!"

"What are the demons trying to do in Boston?"

"We don't know. We can't translate their conversations. We've tried to torture the information out of the demons, but it's quite impossible. They shatter down to mice without talking."

"So coming to Boston had nothing to do with Loo-ae?"

"Ice says if we have to, we will use Louie—Loo-ae—to kill everything that moves in Boston."

Ru rapped a signal on the door. Time was up.

Atticus scrambled to squeeze in Agent Zheng's second question. "What are you planning to use as a key for Loo-ae?"

Ascii gazed up at him, eyes wide and bright with religious fervor. "You."

CHAPTER SEVEN

MCI Framingham, Framingham, Massachusetts
Tuesday, September 21, 2004

The public defender who was assigned to Ascii stormed into the room. "I don't know what the hell you think you're doing. Anything she's said isn't admissible in court."

"So far all she's talked about is angels and demons." Atticus retreated to the door. He didn't want to discuss in front of this man the madness that suddenly was his life.

"Really?" The attorney made a note on a legal pad. "Then insanity is a possible plea."

Atticus fled the room. He knew that what made America great was that everyone was assumed innocent until proved guilty and that it was an honest attorney's job to do everything in his power for his client, but still, it grated. By her own admission, this woman had run a man down, shot him in the chest while he was helpless, and stolen his dead body. All evidence said that if Atticus hadn't rescued his brother, she would have hacked him to pieces and burned him to ash. All that, though, was inadmissible. She'd do a little time, if any, and be released. Yet all the time in the world wouldn't erase her discovery that it wasn't that hard to kill; and like everything else in life, it would only get easier with practice.

The guard who had been absent when Atticus entered the room stood quietly now in the corner. Agent Zheng waited beyond the two-way mirror, making notes in her PDA, no clue of what she was thinking on her face. It bothered him that he couldn't read her.

"This is insane," Atticus whispered to her. "Werewolves. Aliens. Angels. Demons. Everyone seems to be running with their own version of reality."

"Yes." Zheng put away her PDA. "But that's the way it's been from the beginning of time."

Inside the questioning room, the public defender introduced himself. Under his polished manner, he put out mixed signs of anger, impatience, and concern. The intercom was turned off, yet it was clear that the muted conversation ground down as the attorney met a stone wall of silence from Ascii.

Zheng had been correct when she guessed that Ascii would talk only to Atticus.

"I'd rather not be here when he gets tired of beating his head against the wall." Zheng picked up her black trench coat. "Let's find someplace private to discuss this."

He nodded—he had a million questions to ask her. Atticus expected another walk around the grounds of the prison, but storm clouds filled the sky, pouring down sheets of gray rain. They paused in the doorway, judging the rain and each other, being jostled by damp visitors dashing in from the downpour.

"I've got a suite at the Residence Inn," Zheng said, naming a hotel chain. "It's about a five- to ten-mile drive. We can talk there."

"We'll follow you," Atticus promised.

Zheng turned up the collar on her raincoat and went out, unhurried, into the rain.

"I don't know about you," Ru said as he watched the FBI agent stride purposely across the parking lot, "but she really creeps me out."

• • •

Atticus drove on mental autopilot, following Zheng in an SUV with Massachusetts plates—apparently a rental car. Angels. Demons. Evil aliens—Ontongard, Zheng had called them. What did this make him? Where did the Pack and Ukiah fit into this mess? Nothing in the reports Kyle pulled up suggested that the outlaw biker gang was hell-bent on global domination. And how did this fit into the shooting at Buffalo?

"The Ontongard," he murmured.

"What?" Ru asked.

"What if the shooters weren't Pack or the Temple of New Reason, but this third group? The Ontongard."

"The demons?"

"Yes. The cult steals Hu-ae from the Ontongard and starts producing Invisible Red and sells it via Animal. Only the drug leaves a trail back to the Iron Horses. The Ontongard tracks it back to the Buffalo chapter and ambushes the buy, looking for the cult and their machines."

"So you believe Agent Zheng's claim that the cult is using these alien machines to make Invisible Red?"

He had no problem accepting it. Why? Once he considered the drug's structure, he realized it was far more complex than anything he'd ever dealt with before. "Most drugs are a couple of molecules hung together off of sugar. This stuff . . . it reminds me of DNA; it's an incredibly dense lattice. And it can change. Daggit and I handled the same substance, and it reacted to us both as it came in contact with our skin. With me, it seemed like it was simplifying. But with Daggit, it grew more complex, like thorns growing. It was sensing us, and . . . and . . . unfolding . . . differently."

"Unfolding?"

"I think it's like a computer program. Parts of it were being triggered, going active, while other sections . . . terminated."

"So for you, it's safe to take, but it's going to kill Daggit?"

"Possibly."

"It's death," Ukiah had said. *"They're all dead men. You're a breeder. It will make you want to have sex but it won't hurt you. It was made to make you breed."*

Did Agent Zheng know what his brother meant by "a breeder?" How safe was it to discuss what little Atticus knew with her? He'd always kept his differences hidden from everyone but Ru and Kyle, afraid of some dangerous fallout if the wrong person discovered how inhuman he was. Afraid that someone would see him as a monster. Afraid because it was often hard for him not to think of himself as one.

Suddenly he saw the Pack's "test" in a new light. Was that why they were testing him? Were they also afraid of being monsters?

Apparently, Ru had started out following the same line of thought, but diverged off in another direction. "What are we going to do about Zheng?"

"Call Kyle. Tell him to dig into her records. I want to know everything about her. I want to know how she knows all this shit about me."

Ru picked up the car phone, pausing before he dialed. "You okay?"

"I didn't think I would want to go back to being just a werewolf."

Agent Zheng had a room on the first floor of the hotel in the back. They found ready parking and dashed to the covered entrance; she opened the door with her card key. Ten steps and they were in her room, totally unseen by any other guest. He couldn't have picked a better room himself.

The hotel was maid-neat but still tainted with Zheng's scent. She hung up her black trench coat, asking, "Coffee? Root beer?"

"You have root beer?" Atticus found it surprising. Not many people stocked root beer, much less thought to offer it.

"I've been here a couple of days." Zheng ripped open a package of gourmet coffee and poured it into the filter of a coffeemaker. "I like this hotel chain, since it will do food shopping for you. No matter what time you get back to your room, there's decent food. No candy bar or pizza dinners."

"There are advantages to working with a team," Atticus said.

Zheng tilted her head, acknowledging this. "Do you want that root beer or not?"

"Yes, thank you."

The root beer was even IBC in the dark glass bottles. She had the refrigerator stocked well enough to feed a small army. How long did she expect to stay? She unloaded carrots, dip, blocks of cheese, a deli bag of sliced roast beef, buns, lettuce, brown mustard, and a massive bag of seedless grapes.

"I've got more than enough. Help yourself," Zheng said.

Out of habit, Ru dallied while Atticus sampled the fare, although it was unlikely that an FBI agent would drug the food. Finding it innocent, Atticus considered the woman herself. She gazed at him levelly over her cup of freshly brewed coffee, eyes a gunmetal gray. Judging by their vaguely Asian shape, she was at least partially Chinese. Her composed gaze went beyond normal law-officer stoic to something nearly Buddhist in its level of calm.

He had a million questions he wanted to ask her, starting with, "How do you know all this?" But in the world of drug dealing, admitting to ignorance rarely got you information and always put you in a weaker position. How much could he trust this woman—and perhaps as important, how much did she trust him? He was, according to her, the child of the enemy. Did she hold that against him? When his team invited someone into their hotel room, they always had the place bugged. Was this a trap? Had she offered them food to throw them off balance and admit to hidden cameras exactly what he was?

"You're completely right about the advantages of working with a team," Agent Zheng said. "That's why I propose we combine forces."

"Work together?"

"I'm not a fool; it would be suicide for me to continue searching for the cult in an unfamiliar area by myself. But my options are limited."

"And we look like handy fodder."

Agent Zheng gave a slight exhale that could have been a sigh. "I would rather you didn't confirm my opinion that all male federal agents are egotistical jerks. I would be far more disappointed than you could imagine."

And what the hell did that mean? Judging by the darkening of Ru's face, it could be taken as a pass.

"I have to consider the welfare of my team first," Atticus said. "I know nothing about you." Yet. "Far as I know, you're a maverick who rushes into dangerous positions without an ounce of precaution." He stepped close to stress that he was a nearly a foot taller than her. "Some would say you're a fool to bring two strangers to her hotel room."

"You're Atticus Steele. No middle name. You were found abandoned as an infant in 1973. You joined the military in 1988 with what must have been a forged birth certificate and served for six years. In 1994, you were given an honorable discharge, and you applied to the University of Maryland . . ."

"Okay, so you did your homework, but that doesn't make us—"

". . . where you met your current lover, Hikaru Takahashi." Zheng played her hole card. "You two have been together for ten years and own a T Street row house in Washington that you've been renovating over the last five years. I'm told that you just refinished the floors and they're beautiful."

Atticus's opinion of her went from annoying to terrifying.

"Did you do a full background check on us?" Ru snapped.

"I was discreet," Zheng said. "But yes. You originally came on my radar screen as drug dealers. It wasn't until this morning that I learned you were actually undercover agents."

Atticus relaxed slightly. "I'm impressed. The agency provides us with fairly fireproof backgrounds so perps can run their own checks and we still come up clean."

"I have my resources," Zheng said.

Atticus glanced to Ru, who didn't look happy but nodded his agreement. "Okay. So you're good, and you're way ahead of us on this." And most likely the only way she'd catch them up to speed would be by their agreeing to work with her. Of course, agreeing wasn't the same as trusting. In some ways, it would be just another undercover assignment. "We're in."

Zheng accepted the announcement with a serene nod. Putting down her coffee cup, she took a folder out of her briefcase. "We have an ex-cultist working with us in Pittsburgh. Her cult name was Socket. She's a Boston-area heiress whom the cult recruited specifically to gain access to her fortune. Her total worth is ten million dollars, which is in a trust she can't touch—but it gives her a yearly income of a hundred thousand dollars. As one of their cash cows, the cult didn't subject Socket to the most brutal of their brainwashing techniques, but that also means she wasn't part of their inner circle."

"So, unlike Ascii, who will tell the FBI nothing, Socket spilled her guts, but there's not much there?"

"Exactly," Zheng said. "This is the only photo we have of Ice, current leader of the cult." It seemed to have been taken from a bank surveillance camera. In the grainy black-and-white photo, the tall, lean blond male was partially obscured by a potted plant. "Socket worked with us to create composite sketches of him and the other known surviving cultists."

Twenty laser printouts of pencil drawings followed. The cult favored military-short haircuts, and accepted a wide range of ethnic groups. Of the twenty, five were women and the rest men. All were identified only by single computer terms: Ice, Firewall, Mouse, Ether, Diskette, Ram.

"What do we know about this Ice?" Atticus asked.

Zheng consulted her PDA. "He's approximately six-one, a hundred and eighty pounds, blond with blue eyes, in his early twenties, and has black tribal tattoos on his back. He's skilled in martial arts and served as the cult's weapons trainer. While they didn't discuss it openly with Socket, she got the impression that he also taught the cult how to forge driver's licenses, pick locks, and steal cars. He was the cult's tactician for ambushes on the Ontongard Gets. The founder, William Harris, was the one with the vision—Ice was the one who made it happen."

"We don't have any real names for these people?" Atticus asked.

Zheng produced another artist sketch with a Polaroid attached. Atticus recognized him as the driver of the Honda. The photograph was of the man's dead body on the coroner's table. "We've identified him as John Pender, originally of New Hampshire. He joined the cult two years ago, breaking ties with his parents."

"I would think," Ru said, "that he's a total dead end."

Zheng's full mouth curved into her Mona Lisa smile and her eyes softened—there was warmth under that cool exterior. When not hard as steel, her gray eyes were surprisingly beautiful. "Perhaps. Perhaps not."

Atticus realized his paranoia was slipping and hugged it a little closer. Until he knew more about Zheng, he had to keep in mind that they weren't necessarily on the same side. "So far, you've not given us much to go on."

"Socket also gave us this list." Zheng shuffled through

papers in her briefcase. What wasn't she showing them? Atticus controlled the urge to snatch up her briefcase and dump it out. "Through dummy corporations, the cult bought a good deal of property in New England. The only one they openly owned was a farm in New Hampshire, and they used it as a front for anyone investigating them." Zheng found the paper she was looking for and laid it on the table between them. "The top addresses were the ones that Socket knew about. I had the records pulled on these sites, and then found other property bought from the same bank accounts."

There were two dozen addresses listed scattered throughout New England. The first had notes after them: *Farm— sold? Warehouse. Safe house. Offices. Burn site.* Atticus compared the last with his photographic memory of the police report Kyle had found on the crime scenes of cremated bodies. Same place.

"So you think they might be at one of these locations?"

"One can hope," Zheng said. "The turnpike basically splits the state in half. Your team can take north or south, and I'll cover the other."

"By yourself?" Atticus said as Ru said, "Without backup?"

"I have backup." Zheng didn't explain further. "Because you look like your brother, Atticus, you're going to have to approach the cult with caution. They hunt Ontongard—they have gotten ambushing someone with your talents down to an art."

Atticus considered the list. Ascii had said that she and the other three cultists were taking Ukiah to Salem, which was north of Boston. None of the addresses were in the town famous for witch-hunts, not that that signified much. While the train station might have been a convenient meeting site, Ascii could have been lying about their destination, or the cult had a place that Zheng hadn't found, or Zheng herself was lying. Still, it was someplace to start. "We'll take north."

"Then I'll take south." Zheng glanced over what that left

her. "It will take the rest of the day to do these. We should meet tomorrow and compare what we find." Zheng consulted her PDA. "I've arranged to meet with the NSA to discuss the cult at nine-thirty. What about eight?"

Mark up one basic difference between DEA and FBI: Atticus's team mostly worked evening and night hours. Drug dealers tended to be night owls.

Ru made a noise of disgust at the early hour. "Then it should involve coffee."

"And real food," Atticus added.

"Fine. Breakfast. Where?"

The trouble with two out-of-town teams: Neither knew of the good, cheap places to eat. At least it could be expensed.

"Our base—Boston Harbor Hotel."

"Fine." She made note of it in her PDA.

The rain had passed, leaving behind a gray sky filled with ominous clouds and bitter cold wind. They walked out together and paused beside Zheng's rental.

"Call me if you find anything." Zheng handed Atticus her business card, lightly perfumed with her scent.

Atticus glanced at it and handed it to Ru. "The Pack killed my phone last night."

"That sounds like them," Zheng said as Ru offered up one of his own carefully worded cards that they used while they were undercover. She tucked it away without glancing at it.

They watched her drive away.

"Indigo Zheng," Ru read off her card. "I wouldn't have guessed Indigo, but I don't know; it suits her."

"She still creeps you out?"

"Oh, yeah."

A sound like baying hounds made Atticus look up; Canada geese went overhead, flying in a ragged V formation, honking loudly. He wondered if they were the same ones they had seen earlier, resting on the prison's pond.

When he looked down, Ru was grinning at him from the other side of the Jaguar.

"What?"

"Gabble Ratchet."

"What's that?"

"The sound of wild geese supposedly heralds the arrival of the archangel Gabriel."

"I am not an angel—nor is my brother."

"If you say so."

He got in, started up the Jaguar, and dialed Kyle. "What did you find out about Agent Zheng?"

"Nothing," Kyle said with disgust. "Sumpter pulled me off it to"—he paused to make a noise of irritation and tap something into his computer—"look into something else. Someone did a deep sweep on you and Ru. Credit history. Priors. The works."

"We know." Atticus growled. "Agent Zheng did."

"Oooh, sexy woman," Kyle said. "The first hit was on Ru's phone about nine o'clock last night, and went from there. I'm getting trip-wire reports off everything here. She probably knows how deep his belly-button lint is at this point."

"I feel vaguely violated here," Ru complained.

"Your Agent Zheng is versatile. She hammered on Ru until well past midnight, and this morning she chewed into Atticus. No hits on me, though."

"You originally came on my radar screen as drug dealers. It wasn't until this morning that I learned you were actually undercover agents."

"Kyle, check Ru's call log," Atticus said.

"What am I looking for?"

"My brother had Ru's phone last night." And most likely still had it.

"A couple unanswered calls in, and one outgoing call," Kyle said, and then read out the number. It matched the cell phone number listed on Agent Zheng's business card.

"The bitch." Atticus searched back through his memories and found Zheng's scent tainting the basement's air. "She was at the beach house with the Dog Warriors before we arrived. She's working with them."

"She's dirty?" Kyle asked.

Unsure, Atticus glanced to Ru, who shrugged. "I don't know if it's that straight-forward. See what you can find on her, and anything you can dig up on a group called the Ontongard."

"How do you spell that?"

"I have not a clue."

"Ooooooookay. Do you have a first name yet for Miss Sexy Agent?"

Atticus found himself thinking of her Mona Lisa smile, her compact body, and the tantalizing flashes of camisole under the sheer white of her silk blouse. He shifted uneasily, slightly aroused by the memories. *Where the hell did that come from?*

"Indigo, like the color blue," Ru reported.

"And what do I tell Sumpter?" Kyle asked.

"Tell him that the FBI tripped over us." Atticus saw no reason not to stick to the truth

CHAPTER EIGHT

Cape Cod Campground, Massachusetts
Tuesday, September 21, 2004

Ukiah woke, naked and bundled against the cold. He lay under a lean-to, deep in rain-soaked woods of stunted oaks and maples, night cloaked tight around him. Beside the sturdily built shelter a small fire burned, hissing when water dripped from leaves overhead. The ocean was somewhere nearby, pounding on the earth, filling the air with salt and the faint aftertaste of fish. Harley motorcycles growled counter to the ocean's rumble, and headlights swept through trees. While Ukiah was alone by a small fire, he felt the Dog Warriors scattered in the darkness. He found Rennie's familiar presence, just beyond the shifting light thrown by the flames. *"Is it the Iron Horses?"*

"Seems to be."

Instead of tracking down the wanna-bes scattered to their mundane lives, Rennie had sent out word where the Dog Warriors would be camping instead. Judging by the weave of headlights, every member of the local chapter plus some had arrived.

Lambs to a slaughter.

"We won't hurt them if they tell us what we want to know." Rennie slipped through the shadows, staying hidden until the visitors' identity was fully known.

Ukiah sat up stiffly. All the bones of his left arm were

once again knitted whole but not yet sound. The massive scabs covering the bullet wounds on his chest and back were hot and itchy; his body was still healing at its furious rate. His stomach knotted up, emptied during his long sleep. Surrounded by the Pack in a womb of safety, he had most likely been awakened by hunger.

Tucked beside him where it would be safe from the rain was a stack of clean clothes. By her scent and the selection—his black T-shirt, his favorite blue jeans, and his "Property of FBI" boxers—it was obvious that Indigo had been the one who raided his closet at Max's. Sitting in the lean-to, Ukiah pulled on his boxers and pants as the bikers settled around him, drawn by the fire.

Daggit had been in the lead, and he eyed Ukiah suspiciously as he killed his engine. "You here alone, puppy?"

"No," Rennie answered, drifting out of the darkness, his eyes gleaming from the reflected headlights. "He's not."

"Shaw." Daggit grunted. "So he is yours."

"Yes." Rennie paused beside Ukiah as he sat tying his boots and lightly touched the top of Ukiah's head. "This is our Cub."

"Does he have another name?"

"Not for you."

"What, you think we're going to cause trouble for him?"

"I think you're smarter than that."

Daggit understood the implied threat with a flash of fear that he shrugged away. "Whatever. Cub it is."

The bikers wandered into the campsite, loud and careless. They carried bottles of alcohol and offerings of food—they seemed to be expecting a party. Ukiah wondered what Rennie told his contact. Animal came into the light, carrying a bucket of Kentucky Fried Chicken and a bottle of expensive scotch.

While the Pack rarely drank, it made an exception for fine liquor, and the scotch qualified.

"Hey, Shaw, where have you been?" Animal shouted out

with alcohol-tainted breath. "You haven't been in this area for a coon's age."

Rennie took the bucket of chicken, and flicked the lid into the fire. "We had Pack business."

"Which means we'll never know," Animal complained.

Rennie grunted at the truth of this and tilted the bucket to Ukiah. *"Don't touch the sides of the bucket."* A few stray flecks of Invisible Red glittered on the red-and-white container. "Eat."

Ukiah grabbed out a deep fried thigh and bit deep into the juicy dark meat.

"More," Rennie commanded. After Ukiah took a breast, Rennie selected a drumstick and passed the bucket to Bear.

Animal gazed at Ukiah with an odd look on his face. "Where did he come from? I've never seen him at a Gathering."

"Who he is," Rennie growled, "and where he came from is Pack business."

"You know, some of us have been loyal for years, waiting for our turn to be made . . ." Animal's complaint trailed off to slack-jawed drooling in a display of sexual desire that would have been cartoonish if Ukiah didn't know the strength of Invisible Red.

Ukiah glanced over his shoulder to follow Animal's gaze.

Hellena had stalked out of the woods, black leather pants clinging like a second skin, black silk camisole highlighting the shape of her breasts, long black hair spilling down over her shoulders in loose curls. She was lean, strong, and sexy.

"I-I-I've got an anniversary VRSCA V-Rod Harley." Animal pointed to his bike. "It's only a year old. I've got less than a thousand miles on it. I'll trade you."

Rennie frowned a moment, and then he too followed Animal's gaze.

"It's like being surrounded by rutting dachshunds," Hellena thought.

Rennie laughed at Hellena's silent comment, though

anger flashed through him. "We don't trade our women. You should know that."

"Yeah," Animal whimpered. "But I hoped if I made the pot rich enough . . . I can throw in a pair of Desert Eagle pistols and a dozen nickel bags of Pixie Dust."

A growl rose from the Dogs. It was one of the differences between the Pack and the outlaw biker gangs that followed them; the humans treated women as objects to be traded and sold. Even if the Pack weren't morally against such debasement, there was the matter that the women of the Pack were physically equal to the men.

"Okay, okay, okay. I know 'no' when I hear it." Animal held up his hands.

Rennie tossed the bare drumstick toward the trash pit and hit it unerringly. "Where is the Temple of New Reason?"

"Those fairies?" Animal asked.

"Yes," Rennie rumbled.

"They're—"

Daggit gave Animal an angry shove to silence him. "Is it Pixie Dust that you want?" Rennie's silent snarl made Daggit try for a lighter tone. "Look, you can buy through us. We'll give you a good price."

Rennie struck Daggit with savage speed, catching him by the back of the head with a fistful of hair, and the other hand yanking him down to his knees until the leader of the Iron Horses crouched in the dirt in front of Ukiah. "Look at what the Temple has done to our Cub. They ran him down with a truck and shot him full of holes."

Daggit hissed in pain, but managed. "So it's true what they say—you can't keep a good man down."

"Where are they?" Rennie growled.

"I don't know," Daggit's voice went sharp as Rennie put pressure on his arm.

"He knows," Animal said quietly. "He won't tell you. But I can tell you everything I know."

"You don't know shit!" Daggit snarled.

"Who did they contact first? You? No, me!" Animal thumped on his chest with his index finger. "Me!"

"You don't know where they are," Daggit said.

"Yeah, but I know how to get ahold of them."

"We don't want to talk," Rennie said.

"I can set up a meeting."

"Shut up, asshole!" Daggit snapped, and hissed as Rennie tightened his hold. "You know what they're going to do to those idiots."

"I want to be Pack," Animal said. "I want to be fast and strong and cool."

"Dumb fuck," Daggit muttered and squirmed in Rennie's hold. "You don't have to fuck them over, Shaw. Your Cub is fine."

"Make me Pack, and I'll gift-wrap the bastards for you."

"Do you have any idea what you're saying?" Ukiah pulled on his shirt.

"My cholesterol is through the roof," Animal said. "I've got rheumatoid arthritis in my knees so bad I can barely sit on a bike, and all the men of my family die before they turn fifty. I figure I only have, like, ten years or so left. I'm willing to gamble."

Ukiah sensed the direction of Rennie's thoughts. *"No. We can't make him a Get."*

"We need to be quick and dirty," Rennie thought. *"We need to find the cult before they can use that damn machine."*

"No."

"Do we beat the information out of them instead? Torture them? Men can stay amazingly silent for lots of money."

Ukiah thought of the bundles of twenties that Kyle and Atticus had stashed away.

"The drug is killing him," Rennie pressed on. *"The only way he's going to live is by becoming a Get."*

"If he survives the process."

"There is that."

Ukiah studied the bikers, their clothes glittering with motes of Invisible Red. The concentration of it on their groins puzzled him until he noticed that they absently rubbed themselves, the lingering effects of the drug still stimulating them. There was not one unmarked by the shimmering dust—doomed by the exposure to Invisible Red. Rennie was right. They had to shut down Hu-ae and get Loo-ae back as soon as possible. *"Okay."*

Rennie shoved Daggit away and drifted back into the darkness. "Come." He motioned to Animal. "Walk with us."

"Animal!" Daggit tried to catch Animal's arm, but Smack blocked him. "Mike! Shit, man, think about this."

"I've thought about this for twenty years." Animal followed Rennie into the woods.

A half mile from the campsite, they stopped in a marshy clearing. While there was no house in sight, a knee-high stone wall meandered along the edge of the woods. The night sky overhead had cleared, but fog drifted through the trees, as if the clouds had sunk down out of the sky to hide. Some of the Dogs—Stein, Heathyr, and Smack—had stayed behind to keep an eye on the bikers. The rest ranged through the darkness, grim with the knowledge of what was about to happen.

"Okay!" Animal threw open his arms, welcoming the experience. "Make me Pack!"

"Tell us about the cult first," Rennie commanded. "Who's your contact? Where are they now? Everything you know, and then we'll do the mauling."

"Ahhh." Animal raked his hand through his wild red hair. "My sister has a boy, a stepson actually, Eddie." He shrugged his lean shoulder as if the boy were nothing of consequence. The lack of blood connection equaled lack of affection. "The kid gave her a lot of lip when she first got married, and his real mom didn't want to deal with him, so they shipped him off to military school. They brainwashed him on that God-and-country shit."

Animal took out a pack of cigarettes, tapped one out. His hands were shaking, and he laughed nervously as he fumbled with lighting it. "Look at me. Shaking like a virgin with his first whore." He took a deep drag, the tip of the cigarette glowing angry red in the darkness.

"What about Eddie?" Ukiah pushed Animal back to the cult.

"After graduation, Eddie joined the army or marines or one of those but got kicked out. He moved back with my sister for a few months, and then dropped out of sight completely. Didn't even show up for his father's funeral. It turns out he'd joined this cult—Temple of New Reason."

"Do you know his cult name?"

"Ice." Animal laughed, shaking his head. "I've met some of the others and they've got the shit-stupidest names: Mouse, Link, Ether, Ascii, and Io. What a bunch of dweebs. Though Socket and Ping are hot babes."

"Eddie what?" Ukiah tried to fit "Eddie" to the ruthless Ice.

"Eddie Howard," Animal said. "He got hold of me at the end of last year. He knew that I sold reefer and speed and sometimes handled cocaine, that I know people like Jay Lasker. He wanted me to sell this new shit. He gave me a free sample. After my first hit, I knew it was pure gold."

"Where is the cult?"

Animal shook his head again. "Eddie got really paranoid. He wanted everything set up without anything that could be traced back to him. Like it was some fucking *French Connection*."

"So you don't know where he is." Shaw glanced back to where Daggit was being detained.

"I know how to get ahold of him! We'd use the personals on the Internet." Animal named the Web site they used, an online dating service. "I'd post under the name Pokey102 and he posted under Gumby666."

Ukiah did not recognize the references for either one. "Why those names?"

"You don't use 'drug runner' and 'drug lord' as handles and expect to stay hidden from the narcs," Animal said. "You don't mention drugs or money or city or anything like that in the message. Usually I say something like, 'Drop me a hundred' and he'd post back, 'Cam noon Sunday.'"

"That was your last buy?" Rennie asked.

"Cambridge." Animal nodded. "I hadn't set up the next buy yet."

"You have preset places to meet? Cambridge sounds too general."

"Cambridge is the Cambridge Bridge. For the drugs, the buy is always on the bridge, and the drop weighted, so if the narcs try to bust us, we'd throw the bag over the side of the river, and it sinks. No evidence, no conviction."

"Which bridges do you use?"

"Cam is Cambridge. LF is Longfellow." Animal named a few more bridges, but the list was short.

"That's the complete list?" Ukiah asked, surprised that there were so few.

"This isn't Pittsburgh," Rennie said.

"But it's got a river and a harbor, right?"

"Pittsburgh went a little nuts when it came to bridges."

Rennie returned his attention to Animal. "What does Daggit know? Can he call and warn them?"

Animal started to swear that Daggit knew nothing, but then, with a hard look from Rennie, retracted the claim. "I'm not sure what Daggit knows. He's been selling them stuff like guns, explosives, and shit like that—hard-to-get equipment—while I've been running the drugs down to Philly, Baltimore, and places like that. But I really doubt Daggit knows crap. Eddie's a paranoid little shit. He doesn't even do the drug deals—he uses peons from the cult."

They questioned him further, but found out little else. Animal and his sister had had little to do with Ice most of his life before he joined the cult. With the exception of occasional weapon purchases, Animal had dealt with lower-level cult members.

"We are doing this? Right?" Animal dropped his cigarette and ground it out with his booted foot. "I've been steady for the Pack, right there, with whatever you guys needed. Guns. Bikes. You name it and I've supplied it. You fucking owe this to me."

"Not everyone survives this," Ukiah told him. "You can die."

"Or I could live forever," Animal said. "Life is a fucking crapshoot. You've got to play to win. So are we fucking doing this?"

"We're doing this." Rennie growled. He lifted his head, sniffing the wind, extending his Pack sense. While they'd talked, the other Dog Warriors had ranged out in all directions, making sure they were alone in the woods. They tensed now, hating what they must do, but resolved.

With the exception of the Kicking Deers, who had been made perfect hosts via Magic Boy's blood, most attempts to make a human into Pack led to death. Rennie had been the first to survive the process; he'd been shot in the shoulder and pinned under his dead horse on a Civil War battlefield. After countless failures, Rennie guessed, wolflike, that the weak made better prey than the healthy. He picked the sick and the wounded, and sought comfort in the knowledge that those who died had already been doomed.

Surviving, however, was not the same as thriving.

Ironically, the outlaw bikers proved to be not only willing, but also quite successful as Gets. They loved the life—the fighting and the nomadic existence—finding it a natural extension to a life they had already chosen. The bikers expected an initiation rite, and the Pack couldn't always afford to wait for one to become conveniently ill or hurt. Thus the maulings became a hated tool of necessity.

Animal shifted nervously. "Well?"

"Run," Rennie growled.

Animal's eyes went wide and he edged away from Rennie.

"Run!" Rennie roared.

And Animal bolted into a run.

"He's covered in Invisible Red," Rennie sent a hard thought Ukiah's direction. *"Stay out of this."* And then he was gone, loping after the running man.

Ukiah stood a moment in the empty clearing, feeling the hunt move through the woods without him. Rennie's howl went up, calling out the trail, and Ukiah felt the pull of kinship.

No, he wouldn't hunt, but he would stand witness.

Animal had said that he understood what a mauling entailed, but he couldn't really. The biker laughed as he ran, heavy footed and nearly blind, tripping and falling often as the Dogs paced him easily.

There was a mile of woods until the berm of a highway— the Dogs let Animal run half of it before the first hit. Bear had been running silently behind the biker; he surged forward and knocked Animal off his feet. As the biker scrambled in the wet dead leaves, churning up the rich black dirt to scent the night, Hellena broke his left arm with a hard, precise kick.

Animal cried out then, falling back into the autumn leaves. With carefully judged blows, they beat on the fallen biker, hurting him but not killing him.

Rennie stood over Animal, holding a syringe full of the Pack blood that would make the biker a Get or kill him, his thoughts on the red-haired boy with the mohawk who had come to the Gather nearly twenty years before. Rennie had seen the look of envy in Animal's eyes then, and known this was the probable end. "This only gets worse. If you want, you can stop it here, and we'll see that you get to a hospital."

"Fuck you," Animal whispered hoarsely. "You promised."

"So be it." Rennie pinned him and stabbed the needle home.

Silence fell except for Animal's harsh breathing and the distant roar of the surf.

"It's done." Rennie stepped away. "It's in God's hands now."

Animal died before sunrise.

CHAPTER NINE

Truck Plaza, Massachusetts
Wednesday, September 22, 2004

Fog had thickened the air into a cold, damp blanket. Sunrise only paled the world. Leaving Bear to deal with Animal's body, the Dog Warriors had taken Ukiah north, away from the killing grounds. They stopped for gas, and Ukiah took advantage of the truck plaza's bank of pay phones to call Max.

"Bennett." Max answered the phone with his normal snap, and then groaned slightly. "Oh, God, what time is it?"

"Six thirty," Ukiah said. "I'm sorry, Max, I've been up all night . . . and . . . and . . ."

"Ukiah? What's wrong? You sound upset."

And with those simple words, Ukiah was torn. He desperately wanted Max there—morally steadfast in the most confusing of times. Yet at the same time, he was glad Max wasn't there to be tainted by the gray. He was ashamed to admit what he'd witnessed. Ashamed to admit having done nothing to stop it. He was tempted to lie to Max, but couldn't bear the thought of staining his trust.

"Things I can't talk about over the phone," Ukiah said finally, rubbing at his suddenly burning eyes.

"Ah."

"I'm sorry for calling you so early."

"No, no, I've been worried sick about you. When you

didn't call back Monday, Sam and I did a background search on the owner of the cell phone you'd used—Hikaru Takahashi."

Ukiah groaned slightly. "He's Atticus's partner."

"Yeah, Indigo dropped the bomb about your brother yesterday. She called us to say they'd found you and to call off the background search."

"Which bomb?"

"It was a multiple strike. That you had a brother. That he was DEA. That the Pack had tested him. That the Pack raided the DEA and took their shipment of Invisible Red. She sounded pretty pissed—for Indigo, that is."

Ukiah winced. When he'd called Indigo early yesterday morning—to let her know that she'd be tripping over the DEA in the guise of his brother—he'd caught her between the postmortems of the cult members. She'd been focused on the discovery that Boston-area doctors had seen enough Invisible Red–related deaths to actually recognize the symptoms. They were, however, still mystified as to the cause.

The conversation had turned bitterly cold as he explained what had happened after she left. "Yeah, she is. I let her go knowing full well what could happen to Atticus."

"She's not angry enough to . . . ?" Max paused, searching for a tactful question. Ukiah realized that Max was still looking for the cause of Ukiah's distress, and hoping that the source was as mundane as a fight with his lover.

"I don't know." Ukiah thought of Animal, dead, even now being settled into a shallow grave. What was he going to tell Indigo?

There was a sudden blare of a deep horn from Max's side of the conversation.

"What the hell was that?" Ukiah asked as Max swore.

"A barge. We took the boat downriver a ways and slept on it. Just in case. The horns, though—they about put me through the ceiling every time."

We? Ukiah said nothing. Any precaution on Max's part was well justified at this point.

"You're coming home today?" Max asked as if the answer were an automatic yes.

"No. I need to see this through."

There was a long silence from Max, another blast of the barge horn echoing up the distant Ohio River valley in the background.

"I know you feel like you have to do something," Max said, "but if you want a life with Indigo and to be a father to your son, you can't run with the Pack. You can't do both. If you keep walking the edge, you're going to fall off."

"I know. But there's too much on the line here. Too many lives at stake."

Max sighed. "What can you do that the Pack can't?"

"Well, I can ask you to help me set up a trap for the cult. Computer literate, the Pack isn't."

The only problem with working undercover was dealing with the hours. Not so much the long hours, though occasionally that sucked, but the guilt of not spending every waking moment working when you were undercover. It wasn't a job you started at nine o'clock and did your eight hours for. No matter how late you stayed up the night before, as soon as you woke up, you felt the need to do battle with the forces of evil.

The clock read six thirty and they had an eight-o'clock meeting with Agent Zheng. It was, though, a perfect morning, and Atticus didn't want to stir. He and Ru were tucked together just right, the morning light through the window sublimely pale, and the cries of gulls mixed with the deep horns of ships. He could lie, watching Ru sleep, and feel a fragile peace. So fragile that moving, let alone questioning it, would shatter it all.

Then Ru stirred, opened his eyes, and smiled sleepily. "Morning."

"I love you," Atticus whispered.

"Good." Ru kissed his jaw and snuggled back down into the blankets. "Because I love you too."

And then Ru was asleep again, and the moment hadn't passed so much as changed. Atticus's happiness solidified, and he felt now that he could get up, shower and let in the world.

Kyle was waiting when he came out of the shower, two sweaters in hand.

"What do you think, the gray or the green?"

"What?"

"Which looks better on me?" Kyle held up first the green sweater. "The green brings out my eyes—don't you think?"

"What's the special occasion?"

"We're having breakfast with Indigo this morning." Kyle overlaid the green sweater with the gray. "This is much more macho, though, don't you think?"

It took Atticus a moment to connect "Indigo" with "Agent Zheng." "You've got to be kidding me. Agent Zheng?"

"She's a complete babe." Kyle ducked back into his connecting room and returned—sans sweaters—with a color photo of Agent Zheng. "She's really sharp. She has a mind like a diamond."

"Who uses a machete to cut through red tape," Atticus sang.

"Are you saying I don't have a chance?"

"I'm not saying that."

"If she knows you two are . . . you know . . . it's not like I have to compete with you."

Atticus sighed. He hadn't counted on Kyle wanting to join them at breakfast. "She knows. What did you find out about her?"

"She's twenty-six, like *moi,* and an Aries, extremely compatible with a Virgo like me. Her tax records claim that she's single and owns a luxury one-bedroom *studio* condo in

Pittsburgh." Kyle crooned the word "studio." "You know what that means—no live-in boyfriend. Her hobbies are science fiction and mystery novels, motorcycles, and cooking."

Cooking? The stocked refrigerator in Zheng's hotel room took on new meaning. "My God, she's a nerd's dream come true."

Undeterred, Kyle went on. "She's got a Suzuki Katana and a Ford Mustang, a black belt in judo, and is the Pittsburgh field office's top scorer in pistol."

Atticus shooed Kyle back into his room so Ru could go on sleeping. They'd been out late, working through the addresses Agent Zheng had provided. The places were so scattered that they drove nearly two hundred miles just to hit the first two.

On Kyle's laptop various windows were open to lingerie models.

"And the lingerie relates how?"

"These are all things she ordered last month from Victoria's Secret."

He was going to have to have a long talk with Kyle about what the words "find out everything" really entailed. "I don't know, Kyle. Women wear things like that when they have someone to show it off to."

"You think so?"

"Yeah."

Kyle dropped into a sulk.

"What about the Ontongard?"

He looked unhappier. "Either Indigo sanitized her reports completely or there just isn't anything. She joined the FBI in 1999, and I've been searching through five years of reports, but so far, officially, the only 'aliens' she's dealt with are Russian Mafia and Chinese Tongs. I'm sorry, Atty; I'll do some more digging."

Atticus went to gaze out Kyle's window, looking down on Boston Harbor. Fog masked all but the wharf at the foot of the hotel and its collection of sailboats and cabin cruisers.

It felt like the fog extended through his soul; Atticus knew he wasn't human, but who was telling him the truth? Could he believe Agent Zheng merely because she was on the side of truth, justice, and the American way? Was "alien" any saner than "werewolf," "angel," or "demon"? Who knew the truth and who was deceiving themselves?

In the long run, did it really matter? After what he and Ru found yesterday, he knew that the cult needed to be stopped.

Deciding that Ice's instruction to Ascii might indicate a general direction to look, they investigated the northernmost addresses on the list. The New Hampshire farm had indeed been sold and the new owners were an investment banker from Boston, his pregnant wife, and their two children. After what they learned at the next site, Atticus nearly drove back to the farm and told the banker to pack up his family and flee any chance of interacting with the cult.

Zheng's list had innocuously noted: *burn site*. The police report had been dryly worded. What they found was little more than secluded acreage on the edge of extensive wetlands. There had been cinder blocks stacked around the bonfire, making crude fire tunnels, but they'd been numbered and hauled away to FBI crime labs. The ash had been gathered for bone fragments, the ground scraped for evidence, and all that was left was scorched earth and the scent of long-dead fires.

He searched anyhow, crouching in the cold wind, fingering the marshy edges of the clearing. In the break between two slightly singed bushes, he found where a woman had crawled through, missing a left arm and a right foot, burning hot enough to scorch the ground she scrabbled over. In a low hollow, fifty feet from the incinerator, she broke into a collection of mice—but that hadn't saved her. The cultists had smashed the mice with sledgehammers, doused them with gasoline, and burned them. The police missed or ignored the pitifully small, charred bodies. Atticus steeled himself to pick one up, breaking open the heat-mummified remains to find intact DNA.

The cult killed the mice while they were still caught between two species. This cell was a mouse. That cell was . . . well, one couldn't call it human.

"Is that what I think it is?" Ru had whispered from behind Atticus.

"Yes." He dug a hole in the damp, loose soil and buried the mice. There was nothing else he could do; he couldn't take them to the police and say, "These were a woman—someone just like me."

It was a chance encounter with the incinerator's neighbor that exposed the rest of the horror.

"They did it at night—to hide the smoke," she'd said only after they'd shown her ID. She had the doors of her car locked, and the window cracked only a finger width. "The wind usually blows west to east—so it goes out over the wetlands, but one night last fall I could smell it—I live the next lot down the lane—so I called the fire department. They needed to bring in a psychologist for the whole department—it was like something out of a Nazi death camp."

Ru tsked. Atticus hung back, letting Ru finesse her. People liked Ru and opened up to him. "It must be terrifying to have something like that so close to home."

"We've bought a dog and a gun and had alarms installed on all windows and doors."

"Very intelligent of you," Ru murmured.

"I wouldn't have stayed except we would have taken a terrible hit trying to sell our house—it was all through the news, and no one wanted to live next to that."

Ru made more encouraging noises.

"I can't believe those monsters were so close to my house—that I might have passed them in the car and looked them in the face."

"Have they caught any of the ones responsible?"

"No, no." She scanned the empty road, either becoming

aware they were alone on the country lane, or looking for monsters in the form of men lurking in the bushes, or maybe both. Ironically, she'd probably mistake Ascii as an ally against the monstrous. What would she make of Atticus? "The police keep asking us, insisting we must have seen something. There were cars every now and then—and trucks of firewood—but I thought those were deliveries for someone farther down the road. The McBeals or the Henrys."

Ru showed her the artist sketches of the cult members, but she didn't recognize anyone.

"Is this drug related then?" She seemed incredulous, as if unmotivated murder was simpler to understand than drugs being sold in her neighborhood.

"That's what we're trying to find out."

In the end, she could enlighten them only about the aftermath, not about the murders themselves. She repeated her tale of calling the fire department, and expanded on the story, telling about the police canvassing the area to see if residents were missing, and how the local paper still carried stories each time a victim was identified. "They think there were thirty to forty bodies cremated there. Once the news came out, I called everyone I knew, just to check on them— even one thieving cousin I won't let in my house; he might be a bastard but I wouldn't wish that on him."

Was this where they had been taking Ukiah? Had the victims been other family members Atticus now would never meet? Or had they been humans who fell prey to the cult insanity?

Since they were operating on the assumption that their cover was blown, they gave her their business cards and asked her to call them if she remembered anything, or—in the way of a mild warning—noticed any new activity at the site.

The smell of coffee pulled Atticus out of the memory. Kyle had opened up a bag of instant coffee and poured it out into the filter of the hotel room's coffeemaker. The rich, dark aroma blossomed to fill the small room as few things could; it was a good thing that he liked the smell of coffee, if not the taste. Atticus shifted his attention to his room—Ru was up and in the shower.

"The police have apparently identified some of the victims of the cult," Atticus told Kyle. "Do you have the records on that?"

"Of course." Kyle transferred the water from the carafe to the coffeemaker, and started the coffee brewing. "But I haven't really done anything with them."

"Unless Zheng's come up with new leads, we're running out of options."

After the burn site, he and Ru worked their way south, hitting a house gutted by fire, an empty town house, and finally an empty storefront in Kendall Square that once housed the cult's recruitment center for Harvard and MIT students. The cult had only leased the last and the landlord more than willingly let them search the dusty interior. They found neither Zheng's supposed alien doomsday devices nor any leads to the cult's current location.

"There's a possibility, though, knowing the cult is behind the murders," Atticus said. "That we might be able to find a common factor among the victims which might pinpoint something not on Zheng's list."

Ru padded in from the adjoining room. He was naked except for the towel cinched around his slender waist, and a bejeweling of water. "You know, I was thinking in the shower," he said while scrubbing his fingers through his thick black hair, spiking it on end. He smelled of everything right and wonderful in Atticus's life. "It was listening to the boat horns this morning—we're on the coast."

"Doh," Kyle muttered at the keyboard.

"Salem is a harbor. What if Ice was going to meet them there with a boat, load Ukiah onto it, and abandon the car?"

They glanced at each other, weighing the idea.

"Yeah," Atticus said.

Kyle opened a search window and a moment later had a map and satellite photo for Salem displayed. "Bingo. This triangle here is the parking lot for the train station." He slid his finger over to a featureless gray area. "And this is open water."

"Deep enough for a boat?"

"Maybe; there are little pierlike things," Kyle murmured, tapping man-made structures jutting into the water. He zoomed in as much as the software allowed and panned northward from the train station. After a moment of fiddling, he swore, minimized that window, and started to call up others, quickly running through Salem Harbor Channel and then Danver River Channel and finally Collins Cove. "It would help if I knew anything about boating."

He hadn't minimized the lingerie ads, and they peeked around the edges of the other windows as he filtered through the massive information on the Internet, looking for the grain of data.

"What's with the panties and bras?" Ru whispered to Atticus.

"Our little boy is in love," Atticus whispered back.

"With who?"

"Agent Zheng."

Showing that Ru had heard Atticus singing earlier, he sang, "I want to love you madly; I want to love you now."

Atticus laughed. "You know, when I was growing up, I thought there was some weird affliction that made humans burst into song whenever they were in love."

"*Kaiwaii!*" Ru cried, which was Japanese for "cute." "Is this why you're so into karaoke?"

Was it?

Kyle sighed, apparently deciding that he had reached the balance point of time invested to payoff. "It's possible, but unlikely. Look at this chart. It shows the channels in and out of this river area. None of them point into this cove—although there are several rocks indicated. This document here talks about mooring field A located at the convergence of this channel and Collins Cove—which is the body of water beside the train station. It says there are roughly a hundred and eighty moorings—but that's up here at the mouth of the cove, and the train station is down here, but we're only talking . . . feet."

"Assuming there is a boat," Atticus said, "where did they get it, and where is it now? It's not on the list of purchases that Zheng had."

"And where were they going to take Ukiah?" Ru said.

"Legend has it that vampires can't cross running water," Kyle said.

Atticus looked at him with horrified dismay. "No, don't add vampires to this."

"I thought we might as well cover all bases."

"Don't even go there."

"But the cult might lump demons and vampires together," Ru said.

Kyle's laptop played a sound clip from a Japanese anime film; "Ringu, ringu, wakey, wakey."

"Ack." Kyle started to save information and close windows. "I still need to shower and shave before we meet with Indigo!"

At a quarter to eight, Atticus called time for heading downstairs to meet with Zheng. Kyle, for once, had his five-o'clock shadow in check and borrowed some of Ru's cologne.

"Are you sure this isn't going to . . . you know . . . weird you out?" Kyle asked as he dabbed it on. "I mean, me smelling like Ru?"

"It combines differently with your body chemistry." Atticus shrugged into his shoulder holster and then his leather jacket to hide his pistol. "You don't smell the same."

"Really?" Kyle sniffed himself. "Not in a bad way? I smell good, right?"

"Better smell good, considering what I pay for that." Like Atticus, Ru had on his leather jacket with his shoulder holster underneath. He filled his pockets with his wallet, DEA ID, keys, change, PDA, and the team's backup cell phone.

"Cell phone!" Atticus snapped his fingers. "I forgot!" Which earned him a look from his partners. No, perfect recall wasn't the same as perfect memory. "Let me borrow your phone, Kyle." Atticus glanced at the hotel room's phone to memorize the number. "After breakfast, get hold of Darcy and have her FedEx us two new phones."

"Geesh, she's going to love that." Kyle handed over his phone. "Don't play any of the games, okay? Don't mess with the settings—it took me forever to download the various rings—and don't break it."

Atticus took it. "Can I at least set it to silent ring?"

Kyle took it, changed the ring, and handed it back.

They'd been prepping the rooms so all of them could leave at once. Ru had the bag with the money. Kyle had his laptop. Atticus had a heavier bag with all their most expensive equipment. They locked up the connecting doors, scanned the hall through the spyhole, and, seeing the way was clear, undid the dead bolts and security chain, and left.

It was nearly a perfect break.

When the elevator door opened, however, Sumpter stepped out, folder in hand. He nearly brushed past them before realizing who they were. He jerked to a surprised stop. "Where are you going?"

So much for arriving at the meeting site before their adversary.

"We've got a meeting with the FBI." Atticus let the elevator doors close. They'd found that Sumpter would follow them at great lengths to merely to finish a conversation. They would have to brush him off before getting on the elevator, or they'd have him at the meeting.

"Since when?" Sumpter asked.

"The background check on us was FBI stumbling over our sting," Atticus said.

"Johnston told me." Sumpter ignored the fact that Kyle was standing beside him. "But it's still not clear to me where they popped up. You didn't mention any Chinese men earlier."

Kyle chose the wrong moment to speak up. "Indigo's a woman. A real babe."

"Hmm?" Sumpter said with interest. "Where are you meeting?"

Atticus tried to be truthful with Sumpter, to save lying for important dodges. "Downstairs."

"Okay." Sumpter punched the down button. "Shall *we* see what the FBI has to say?"

Riding with Sumpter was like riding with a stranger, only worse. Sumpter stood watching the numbers count down as Atticus and his team silently communicated.

I called her first. Kyle's face plainly said.

What do we do? Ru asked subtly with a nervous glance to Sumpter and a slight twitch of his upraised palms.

Fake a call, Atticus told them, thumb and pinkie extended to form a receiver, with a slight shake as if it vibrated with a silent ring.

Kyle started to sulk, as he was the one who normally set up such a ploy.

Ru took pity on him. He used the Japanese hand signal of pointing to his nose to indicate himself, a habit he got off his mother and grandparents. *I'll do it.*

Atticus nodded. Ru was more devious than Kyle, by far.

How soon? Ru asked by raising his left wrist and giving Atticus a querying look.

Atticus flashed all ten fingers and then repeated the phone sign. A time delay would keep suspicion off of Ru.

They hit the lobby and got off the elevator.

Ru made a show of searching his pockets. "Shoot," he

said aloud for Sumpter's sake. "I think I left my phone and PDA upstairs."

"Lax, Takahashi." Sumpter sighed.

Ru handed Atticus the money. "I'm going to run back upstairs for it. I'll be back down in a couple of minutes."

Atticus urged Kyle toward the restaurant with a look. "Go see if Zheng is here yet." Atticus handed the money to Sumpter. "Could you put this in the hotel safe?" And then, to give him a little nudge, "Sir. We won't need it until Saturday."

A sharp glance from Sumpter indicated that the "sir" might have been over the top, but he took the bag without a word.

Having delayed Sumpter, Atticus felt he should make sure that Kyle had given the heads-up to Agent Zheng that Sumpter was outside the loop. Normally Kyle could be trusted to keep his eyes on the ball, but this time his eyes would be likely elsewhere.

A prickling awareness made Atticus check his stride. He focused and found he perceived a presence beyond the wall of the hotel, pretending to be relaxed, watching and waiting.

Pack.

"Good morning, Boy." Another's thoughts brushed against Atticus's mind with the impression of grizzled fur and a curious working nose. Atticus struggled to put a face to the psyche. *"I'm Murray."* And a face was supplied, picked from a perfect memory, created by a glance into a mirror: an unruly head of salt-and-pepper curls, a neatly trimmed beard, and dark eyes framed a nose formed by Jewish ancestry. *"They call me Mouthpiece. Onetime lawyer, public defender, now Pack member. Going from one necessary evil to another."*

A Jewish space alien?

"What are we?" Atticus wondered if he could trust Murray's answer any more than that of the Iron Horses or Agent Zheng. *"Werewolves, space aliens, demon, or angel?"*

"Angel is new." While the idea seemed to amuse Murray, there was no indication it was correct.

"Any of them true?"

"What we did to you on the beach, we did because you can't lie mind to mind. You can't create a believable memory any more than you can have a fully textured dream."

"So?"

"If you want the unassailable truth, you can examine our memories. See how our kind came to this world."

"Yeah, right." He wasn't about to let them back into his head. This casual intimacy—a stranger's emotions raw and honest—grated like sandpaper against his sense of privacy. It had been barely tolerable with Ukiah; despite everything, he had to admit—reluctantly—he'd been excited about finding his brother.

"You're the one who has to live in ignorance." Murray gave a mental shrug. *"If you change your mind, we are denning tonight at Ponkapoag Camp, outside of Randolph."*

How did you shut someone out of your mind? Atticus had never learned the trick of not listening that humans seemed to easily achieve. He stalked across the hotel lobby, hoping that distance could block Murray out.

The hotel had two restaurants. Breakfast was being served at the one named—ironically enough—the Intrigue Café. Kyle was hovering nervously by the door.

"I thought I would be able to recognize her." Kyle motioned at the various businesswomen already seated. "She's not one of these, right?"

"Not even close." Atticus took out his—Kyle's—phone and found the time was five minutes after. He dialed Zheng's number and was dropped immediately into voice mail. Her phone was either busy or off.

"Think she blew us off?" Kyle checked his own watch, and then compared it to his PDA. "Or maybe she got into trouble?"

If she was working with the Pack, wouldn't Murray have

mentioned if Zheng had gotten into trouble? But when Atticus considered this, he realized that Murray was *guarding* Zheng. She was somewhere close by. If she was on her phone, then perhaps she had sought out someplace private to talk.

"Get a table." Atticus patted Kyle on the shoulder. "I'll find her."

Now that he was focusing on her, he caught her scent on the air by the door. He drifted through the café. She must have left the doorway moments before the elevator delivered them to the ground floor. While the front of the hotel faced an elevated highway (which Kyle had told them would be torn down once the Big Dig was finished), the back was directly on the waterfront. Sleek yachts and sailboats were tied up to the U-shaped wharf, shrouded thick with fog. Globe streetlights still burned, extending his range of vision. A glass rotunda sat at the far end of the wharf, and a female figure stood within it.

Zheng? Atticus pushed out into the chilly, damp morning. Her scent led toward the building that signage identified as the Ferry Pavilion. She stood in profile to him, looking out into the fog, but her attention was on the cell phone she held to her left ear. Tension filled her body, although the only sign on her face was a slight gathering of her brow. The glass wall blocked her voice until Atticus pressed his hand against it and caught the vibration.

". . . felt better if you'd slept with me last night," she was saying.

Who was she talking to? There had been only a queen-size bed in her room at the Residence Inn. Had she worn her lingerie? Atticus considered Murray's presence and wondered if there were some Pack-to-panties correlations; maybe Zheng's involvement with the Dog Warriors had begun at the same time she had started to buy fancy underwear.

If so, who was the lucky Dog? He couldn't imagine the

sleek and elegant Zheng with any of the Dog Warriors, but they said opposites attracted.

Judging by her body language, Atticus wasn't the only one having trouble hearing the other end of the conversation. Zheng pressed the phone closer to her ear and focused on the words.

"I'm fine. It just unsettled me. I hate walking blind into them—though Socket is right; it's like they're one person wearing borrowed skins. We should have expected this after Butler— *I'm fine*. Murray is here with me. Where are you now?"

Zheng paused to listen, rubbing her brow to soothe away the slight signs of distress. In a moment, she regained her serene composure. "What are you going to do about—are you on a pay phone? Call me when you can talk without being overheard." She glanced at her phone to check the time. "I'm going to be late to this meeting. Is that spelled how it sounds? H-o-w-a-r-d?" She started to turn toward Atticus. "Okay, I'll check my—"

Atticus rapped on the glass before she fully faced him, making it seem as if he'd just walked up and signaled immediately for her attention.

Interesting to note, her first reaction was to go for her pistol. As she registered his presence, she slipped her right hand into her trench coat, stopping only when she recognized him. More surprisingly, she actually blushed.

"I have to go," she murmured. "Call me later."

She hung up and stepped out of the pavilion. "Sorry to keep you waiting."

He wanted to grill her on the phone call and Murray's presence, but the longer they stood outside in view of the café, the more likely Sumpter would come looking. "My superior is sitting in on this. He's not in the loop."

"What does he know?"

"We're after a drug that the cult is manufacturing. That's it. I'm not even sure how he'd handle the whole alien invasion thing. I suspect he'd laugh in your face and yank us back to D.C."

"What does he know about your brother?"

Atticus felt a prick of guilt. Why did he continue to protect his jerk of a brother? "Nothing."

"This him?" Zheng indicated the café door with her glance.

Sumpter stood in the doorway, about to come out, kept inside only by the bitter cold.

"Yeah." Atticus motioned that they should join the others in the café, even though somehow it felt like walking into a lion's den.

Zheng introduced herself to Sumpter with the calm authority of someone expecting to be taken as an equal. The only thing feminine about her handshake was the pearl gleam of her carefully manicured fingernails.

"Randolph Sumpter." Sumpter did his impersonation of an undercover agent, Mr. Joe Cool. "It's good of you to meet with us and combine efforts on this."

"Thank you." The slightly rattled woman on the phone had vanished behind calm professionalism; whatever Zheng thought of Sumpter didn't show on her face or leak into her voice.

"You've met Agent Steele. His partners, Hikaru Takahashi and Kyle Johnston."

Sumpter had commandeered a large corner booth. Kyle had his laptop out and was immersing himself in calming data. Ru was finessing superior service out of the waitress.

On their introduction, Ru gave a smile without getting up, clearing the path for Kyle's bid.

Kyle stood and offered a handshake. "Kyle Johnston. I'm their hole man." He realized the possible sexual implications of the phrase. "I mean, backup man."

"Good to meet you." Was that a warmer greeting than the one she gave Sumpter?

Ru coughed slightly and indicated the steaming cup of coffee at the place setting beside Kyle.

"I got you coffee," Kyle said. "Hope you don't mind."

"Thank you." Her Mona Lisa smile appeared and vanished, proving that she did appreciate the kindness. She slid off her trench coat and folded it over the back of a chair. Under it she wore the same pantsuit and strand of pearls but with a different white silk blouse. Thanks to Kyle's research, Atticus recognized the "Angels" lace camisole under the sheer fabric and wondered if she wore the matching panties.

Ru noticed his gaze, and—judging by the slight frown— guessed his thoughts.

It was Atticus's turn to blush.

Ru had the waitress hovering, so they glanced over the menus. Sumpter waived his turn to see what Zheng ordered. Atticus ordered two eggs scrambled, bacon, and French toast. Ru went with coffee and a bagel with cream cheese on the side. Kyle kept to his standard of hot oatmeal, raisins, brown sugar, and milk.

"A poached egg, plain wheat toast, orange juice." Zheng glanced down over the menu. "And the fresh fruit."

"Ah, a woman with a healthy appetite," Sumpter murmured. "Steak and eggs for me, double order of white toast. Very rare on that steak; just let it shake hands with the fire." Obviously Sumpter missed the fact that Zheng's breakfast was low-fat and well-rounded. He did catch the hard look she leveled at him. "Most women would just get coffee and a bagel and talk about watching their weight."

Atticus winced, as that described Ru's order and reasoning.

"I run five miles every morning," Zheng said. "Weight-train three times a week, and study Muay Thai kickboxing."

"I thought," Kyle said slowly, "that you studied judo."

Atticus tried hard not to wince at Kyle's slip.

"I studied judo in high school." Zheng switched her cold

look to Atticus. "I wanted something that offered more attack moves, so I switched to kickboxing."

Sumpter often talked about liking aggressive women. It was amusing to see him quail in the face of a real one. "What does your boyfriend think of the kickboxing?"

Zheng's gaze flicked down to Sumpter's left ring finger and noted it was bare. "Subtlety, I see, is not your forté."

Touché.

Fortunately, the hotel proved its four-star rating by having the food arrive quickly. The presence of the waitress as she handed out plates, refilled water glasses, and topped off various coffee mugs curtailed conversation down to a game of "who do you know," as they compared people they'd worked with in each other's agencies. Zheng proved it was possible to eat elegantly and talk at the same time.

They had just rid themselves of the waitress when Sumpter's phone rang. He answered with a voice half an octave lower than normal. "Speak to me."

Atticus caught a puzzled "Who is this?" from the caller and recognized the department's administrative assistant, Darcy.

"Sumpter here."

"Randy?" Darcy said with an equal mix of surprise and accusation.

The cool composure cracked and Sumpter stood up. "Excuse me; I need to take this call."

Laughter danced in Ru's eyes as Sumpter hurried away, which confirmed Atticus's suspicion that his partner engineered the call.

"I couldn't help but overhear part of your conversation," Atticus confessed to Zheng. There was no telling how long Sumpter would be gone, so he had to cut straight to the point. "The disadvantage of having sharp ears is that you often hear things you weren't meant to," he covered with a partial lie. "What happened in Butler? Who did you run into?"

Irritation flashed across Agent Zheng's face and was quickly smoothed away. "The Ontongard had the Ae stored in shipping crates at an underground storage facility north of Butler. The Temple of New Reason stole the Ae several years ago; they booby-trapped the crates with high explosives and left them behind—so the cult would know when the theft was noticed."

Kyle had said something about an explosion at a storage facility on Tuesday night while Atticus was trying to get drunk.

"Iron Mountain?" Atticus earned a nod. "And there was a second explosion at the cult's mansion."

Zheng nodded again. "Rennie Shaw and Ukiah accidentally triggered the booby trap, and the explosion made live coverage for several hours. We know that the cult had memory mice in the mansion's basement. What we think happened is that the Ontongard, on their way through Butler to check on the Ae's condition, sensed the mice."

"What was the cult doing with mice?" Kyle asked.

"According to Socket, they had trapped several Gets and rendered them down to mice to perform experiments. They tested poisons, narcotics, stun weapons, tear gas, suffocation, and drowning on the mice."

"Eeewww." Ru wrinkled his nose in distaste.

Atticus thought of the cremation sites and felt sick. "So you're saying the cult didn't blow up the mansion? The Ontongard did?"

"We think so. Two cultists who had been patrolling the grounds of the mansion had been killed in a manner very atypical of the cult. The fire marshal verified yesterday that there're no bodies in the wreckage, so it means at least two cultists are definitely missing."

"Which ones?"

Indigo produced two photographs out of her briefcase. The first was obviously a senior high school photo of a blond young man. "This is Parity. His family owned the mansion. His real name is Thomas James DeMent."

DeMent? Poor kid. The name sounded like a flavor of Pepto-Bismol or "demented." Parity was an improvement.

"He's really this young?"

"Nineteen. His parents thought he was still at college. They flew back from Europe on Monday."

House leveled. Son missing. They couldn't be happy campers.

"This is Ping."

Atticus had noticed the absence of Core and Ping from the mug shots that Zheng gave them earlier and thought them both safely dead. He realized now how relieved he had been not to have to put faces to his brother's rapists; the lack of messy details kept it all nicely distant. He braced himself for Ping to be hulking, muscle-bound, ugly, and, most important, male; so he found himself oddly unprepared for the beautiful young Asian woman in the Polaroid photograph. She wore a nightgown transparent as smoke and a fuck-me look. The edge of the picture was singed, as if it been plucked from a fire.

"Wow," Kyle murmured.

Yes, but how had Ukiah felt about being shared between her and Core? Atticus recalled Ukiah, on the point of collapse, leaning on Ru as he warned them away from handling the drug; relaxed to the point of intimate. What direction did his brother swing?

"We don't have another name for her yet." Zheng had tried for a neutral tone and failed. The cold brittleness crept back into her voice. "She was extremely devoted to Core and would do anything for him; he used her more than once to lure recruits into the cult, including Parity."

She kept her gaze down, trying to hide the hurt and anger.

What had Ping done to Zheng? Or was the fact that the girl was missing the problem? "How does this relate to what happened to you yesterday?"

"I spotted an Ontongard near a house that the cult owned in Uxbridge," Zheng said, naming a town at the southern edge of the state. "It means that the Ontongard are definitely hunting the cult. It was a site known to all of the cultists, so Parity could have been the source of the Gets' knowledge. Ping was inner circle; she would know all the cult's secrets."

"So the clock is ticking."

"Yes. I'll be honest with you. You have not a clue how dangerous this is. The Ontongard Gets view themselves as completely disposable. They're fearless. They will attack until they're destroyed. If they kill you, Atticus, they'll either mistake you for a Dog Warrior—and burn your body— or they'll recognize you for what you are—a breeder—and break you down to mice. It's imperative that you never fall into their power."

Without conscious thought, Atticus stilled, expanding his focus away from Zheng and the table to the room and beyond. Instantly he knew the location of every human in the café, including Sumpter, walking through the lobby toward them. Once he realized what he'd done, he pulled back his awareness and took a sip of water. "I'm an undercover narc; I'm well used to dealing with danger."

Zheng frowned at him as Sumpter returned, dropping into his seat with a mumbled "Sorry about that. Now where were we?"

No longer talking about aliens.

"We searched these sites." Atticus steered the conversation to a safe subject by indicating the locations they had visited and found empty. "The cult hasn't been to any of them recently. We have a theory. Right, Kyle?"

"Oh. Um." Kyle pulled up the satellite photos he had searched out earlier. "We know that Ascii was to meet Ice at the Salem train station parking lot. See how close it is to the harbor? We're thinking that perhaps they had a boat."

"What was wrong with the train?" Sumpter asked.

Kyle gave Ru a desperate look; they couldn't mention

that the cult had arranged to move a body if the police hadn't found one in the car.

"They were covered with blood," Ru said. "That's what tipped off the people at the rest stop. That and the barely concealed weapons."

"If we can find the boat," Atticus said, "we might be able to find the cultist. It's going to be easier to find than a car—there's only a limited number of places they can dock it."

"When we thought that the cultists were going to poison the Pittsburgh water supply, we searched for any connections they had to boats," Zheng said. "Parity's family had a speedboat, but the marina where they docked it said that the family took it out of storage last summer and never returned it."

"And this helps us how?" Sumpter asked.

"Parity attended Harvard," Zheng said. "He might have brought the boat up with him."

"That's just across the river," Atticus said. "He would probably dock it someplace close by."

"That's what I'm thinking." Zheng sorted through her briefcase and pulled out a laser-printed photo of a sleek boat. "This is a picture of the model, a thirty-four-foot Sea Ray Sport Cruiser. It's named the *Nautilus*."

"Follow the money." Kyle turned his laptop so Zheng could view the screen. He had run a standard credit report on Parity. "The Charles River Yacht Club did a credit check on him on July seventh, 2003, and currently he's fifty-two days late on August 2004's fee."

Taking out his borrowed cell phone, Atticus dialed the marina. A machine answered immediately. "You have reached the Charles River Yacht Club," a cheerful female voice said. "We're either out on the docks or on another line. Please leave a message and we will get back to you." He hung up without leaving a message.

"It's just across the river. Ru and I can duck over and look to see if the boat is there. See if anyone knows anything."

"I think you're right in that they were heading for a boat, but you've got the wrong reason," Sumpter said. "There's tons of places they could have ditched the car and changed clothes without being noticed; you've got a list of sites right here that they know well. No, they need the boat to get someplace. An island."

Atticus hated when Sumpter finally got his head out of his asshole and used his brain; it made him so unpredictable. Would Sumpter be a raving idiot, or Sherlock Holmes's lost grandson? The most annoying thing was that Sumpter was completely right.

"With the number of ports they have to choose from, the question becomes why Salem?" Sumpter continued his brilliance. "Either it's the port nearest to the island or one that they know well."

"They had to know it fairly well to know you can easily reach the harbor from the parking lot," Zheng pointed out.

"How are they buying gasoline for cars? Cash or charge?" Sumpter asked.

"Charge." Zheng expanded the answer with, "They practiced identity theft on a large scale. After forging a change of address, they would apply for new credit cards to be delivered to a rented post office box. They've had at least twenty or thirty identities they can tap."

"Can you give a list of known credit card numbers to Johnston to cross-reference to marine fuel stations?" Sumpter asked. "If they're making frequent runs from the mainland to an island, it's going to show up in fuel purchases."

"I've got those here." Zheng took out her PDA and indicated she could transfer them to Kyle's laptop. "I'm meeting with the NSA to see what they have on the cult's wiretapping activities."

"Takahashi, it would be more efficient if you visit Boston DEA and ask them about local islands. Update them on the case and keep them in the loop."

Ru glanced to Atticus, who nodded.

"I need to go," Zheng announced as Kyle's laptop confirmed the receipt of her files. Her plate was clean. She took the last sip of her coffee to empty her cup.

Sumpter looked longingly at his nearly untouched steak and sighed. "I'll come with you."

CHAPTER TEN

Charles River Yacht Club, Cambridge, Massachusetts
Wednesday, September 22, 2004

The Charles River Yacht Club, as its name suggested, was on the Charles River alongside Memorial Drive in Cambridge. It required Atticus to hunt for a parking space and then walk across four lanes of fast-moving traffic. None of the fifty or so boats tied up seemed to be the *Nautilus*, so he detoured into the marina's office.

A young suntanned woman sat behind the counter, taking a detailed message, with a series of "uh-huhs" as she scribbled on a message pad. He judged her to be nineteen or twenty. She had her blond hair braided into two short pigtails, and she grimaced with her wide, mobile mouth as the caller continued to talk. She wore deceptively simple clothes whose quality material meant money, and a large diamond engagement ring.

She rolled her eyes, held up a finger to indicate he was to wait, and finished with, "Okay, I'll let her know. Thank you."

She ripped free the message, shoved it into a bin on the edge of the counter, and looked expectantly to Atticus. "Can I help you?"

"Thomas James DeMent rents a boat slip here," Atticus said, giving her Parity's real name. "Can you tell me the boat's current location?"

She wrinkled up her nose. "I-I-I don't know if I'm allowed to do that."

He pulled out his ID and showed it to her. "I'm not going
to search the boat; I'm just trying to determine where it is."

"Oh!" She thought a moment, eyes focused over the
water, her tongue tracing over her upper lip. Atticus wondered if she knew how erotic it appeared, and if it was the
cause of the engagement ring. "I suppose that can't hurt."

A moment of checking books, and she found the information Atticus wanted.

"He's still renting slip number ten. His boat is the *Nautilus*." She hiked herself up onto the counter and leaned far
out to study the pier. "She's not down there."

"She?"

"The boat. It's the second slip to the end." She pointed.

"Do you remember the last time it was tied up?"

"I'm not sure. I think it was there yesterday. The phone's
been ringing off the hook this morning, and I haven't been
paying attention. You can check with the dock staff."

Between the thick fog and the bitter cold, it came as no
surprise that the docks were nearly empty. The only person
in sight was a man waxing the flying bridge of a fifty-foot
yacht.

"Nice boat," Atticus called up to him.

"Thanks," the man said without stopping. "It's a lot of
work, though. It's taken me three days to wax the whole
thing. Some vacation."

Atticus pointed down the jetty to the empty slip. "Do you
know anything about the *Nautilus*?"

The man halted to look down at Atticus. "Who's asking?"

Atticus produced his ID. "DEA."

The man shook his head. "I keep my nose out of other
people's business."

"Look." Atticus held out Parity's photo. "The kid who
owns the boat is in trouble. He fell into the wrong crowd and

last weekend his parents' house was firebombed and he's gone missing. It's possible he's dead. The *Nautilus* might be the only clue we have to finding him—helping him."

The man frowned at the photo. "He wasn't one of the men who took the boat out this morning."

"This morning?"

"Yeah, there were, like, five men and a woman. They pulled out maybe an hour ago."

Atticus took out his PDA and brought up the scanned copies of the artist sketches for the cult. "Are any of these people the ones who took the boat?"

The man clambered down off the boat to study the PDA screen. "Yeah. This one. And him. Maybe him. And she's the woman. I really didn't get a good look at the other two men." He'd picked off Ice and the cultists named Mouse, Link, and Ether. "They seemed to have scuba gear with them."

"Did you see which way they headed?"

The man waved toward the fog-shrouded river. "They would have gone downriver. The *Nautilus* is too tall to fit under the Harvard Bridge."

Atticus took out his business card. "Do me a favor—if they come back, call me. Don't try to approach them—they're quite dangerous."

The man looked dubious but took the card.

The river water gurgled quietly under the wooden planking as Atticus walked down the dock to the empty boat slip. While it was doubtful that the cult left any clues to where they were headed, they might have slipped up somehow. Wedged in the cracks of the decking, Atticus found a hypodermic needle filled with a clear liquid, its tip capped with wax. He recognized veronol, a powerful barbiturate sedative, from traces of drug on the outside of the syringe.

The cult was out hunting their demons again. But what was the scuba-diving gear for?

Atticus called their hotel rooms, eyeing the hypodermic

in his hand. Thrusting the needle into flesh obviously would push the tip through the protective wax. How safe would it be to carry in his pocket?

Kyle answered with a faintly suspicious, "Yeah?"

"Ice was here an hour ago and took the boat out." Atticus filled him in on the other details.

"I'll get hold of the coast guard and have them keep an eye out for the boat, but in this fog, I don't know what luck they're going to have."

The Longfellow Bridge was just a smudge in the fog, crossing the water into whiteness. Atticus heard more than saw the T train cross over it along with the heavy Boston traffic. "That's the truth. I'm going to head back and hook up with Ru at the DEA."

"Ru called a little while ago. He's out in the Explorer somewhere."

"Somewhere?"

"Something about making a wrong turn onto Sorrow Drive, which is limited access. I'm not sure why he called, he hung up after telling me he was lost."

Unlike the Jaguar, the Explorer didn't have a navigation system.

Atticus sighed. "I'm heading for the DEA. Let him know."

As Atticus hung up, a blare of horns came from Memorial Drive. A man was crossing the four lanes of traffic, barely noticing the cars honking at him. He had an odd, mechanical gait. As Atticus watched, a second man made his way across the street. For a moment Atticus thought them twins, and then realized with a start that body-wise, they were nothing alike—only the second man had managed to completely mimic the first man's way of moving.

". . . it's like they're one person wearing borrowed skins."

Atticus scanned the area quickly. If these Ontongard had the same abilities as the Pack, they'd be able to match Atticus's speed and strength. And Rennie, at least, could match him too in fighting ability. He spotted at least three more on the other side of the highway, stiff and awkward as stick puppets.

Shit! Well, he would have to bluff his way through them. Zheng had walked into them and managed to slip away unnoticed.

Atticus started forward. A blond boy in a black running suit crossed the highway and joined the two males on the dock. The boy met his gaze and recognition jumped between them.

Parity?

For a supposedly kidnapped man, he seemed unfettered.

The boy looked startled, saying, "Wolf boy!"

Alerted, the two adult males focused on Atticus. A presence that was like Pack, and yet totally different, hit him, and the recognition went to a full knowledge of what he was. An all-encompassing hate followed the understanding, a flood of rage with the intent to destroy.

"Pack Dog!" The first male surged toward him.

All of Atticus's body reacted, recognizing a primal enemy. Adrenaline washed through him, sending his heart racing. "Oh, hell."

At least he didn't have to be worried about hurting them too much. Remembering how Rennie Shaw could anticipate his moves, Atticus closed his thoughts tight on the real him, going mentally into deep cover. *I am nothing. I am invisible.*

The male actually hesitated in midstride, off balance, as if Atticus had vanished from sight. Atticus punched the male in the face, putting all his weight and strength into the swing. It broke the male's jaw—Atticus heard it crack and felt the slight shift of bone as it snapped. The male stumbled, registered pain, but kept coming.

"Shit," Atticus swore. The second male and a newly arrived female were coming down the dock and would be on him in a moment. He realized that he still held the hypodermic filled with veronol from the demon-hunting cult. He stabbed the tip into the male's shoulder and pushed the plunger home. The male jerked back away from him—and kept falling, hitting the dock in an awkward sprawl of unconsciousness or death. *Oops. Hopefully not dead. Oh, well.*

Tossing the syringe aside, Atticus ducked under the punch of his second attacker. *I am void. I am emptiness.*

There was a boat hook on the dock beside where the boater had been waxing his boat. Atticus snatched the boat hook up as he dodged the blow and let it go where it wanted, flashing it through the nothingness achieved through years of martial-arts training. A power sweep shattered a knee of the second male. The woman, however, caught the hook's shaft. They stood a moment, both muscling for control of the steel-capped pole.

Atticus *sensed* the second male behind him, the shattered knee reknitting itself with stunning speed. He could feel too the movements of the others around him; unlike the Pack, where the bristle of minds around him had been like electric auras of the individual Dog Warriors, these aliens merged at the mental level. They gathered around him, six bodies but one huge mental presence, like a multilimbed monster. One limb—specifically, one attached to the last man bearing down on him—held an axe. The monster planned to hack him down to mice.

Time to flee.

Atticus let go of the boat hook, knocked the off-balance female into the river, and scrambled over the boats to leap for the shore.

It was a simple trap that Ukiah devised. Animal had said that his nephew never made the drops himself, and without Animal they wouldn't be able to meet with whomever Ice sent. With his flaming red hair and thin frame, Animal had been too distinct for one of the Pack to pass as him. Since most of the cultists Ukiah knew on sight were dead or in jail, the Pack wouldn't be able to pick the bagman out of the crowd. They decided that setting up a normal sale and hoping to catch scent of the drugs was too risky.

So Ukiah decided for a straightforward tactic. Max had relayed from Indigo the result of Atticus's interview with Ascii. Apparently the cult's attack had been more than just simple malice; they wanted him to translate recordings of Ontongard conversations. Wanted him badly. The message to Ice had been simple: *Wolf Boy desires to meet with Ice.*

Max had reluctantly agreed to act as the go-between, posting the messages and reporting back that the cult wanted to meet on the Longfellow Bridge at ten A.M. "Remember, kid, you don't know this city at all, and this is their stomping ground and their choice of meeting place. Get to know the area, and keep the Dog Warriors between you and them."

There wasn't really time to learn the city well. Luckily Ukiah had Rennie's memories of Boston; they stretched from the late eighteen hundreds to the last time the Dog Warriors were through Boston. Rennie escorted Ukiah to Charlesbank Park, just downriver of the Longfellow Bridge, as the Pack roamed the surrounding area, reporting changes they found. Having never seen Boston for himself, Ukiah found himself disoriented. All of his borrowed memories—from those of horse-drawn carriages crowding the streets onward—held equal value. Every part of the city was at once familiar and strange.

At this point the Charles River, between the Longfellow Bridge and O'Brien Highway, was dammed into a wide lake with only a narrow slit giving it access to the river's mouth and the inner harbor beyond. The park was one in a series edging the river and obviously popular; despite the thick fog and the near-freezing temperature, dozens of joggers used the path encircling the park.

"Cambridge is over there, beyond the fog." Rennie pointed across the river as sculling boats cut out of the fog, gliding like knife blades through the water, ranks of oars dipping in time. They sliced by and vanished again into the fog.

"Bunker Hill," Rennie continued. This too was across river, but farther downstream.

"Wasn't there a battle there?"

"That was before my time," Rennie said. "My grandfather fought in it. My father was a drummer boy at the battle of 1812, down in New Orleans. Seems my family has fought one battle after another to be free."

Rennie turned away from the river to point inland. "Over there is the Old North Church; it used to be the tallest building in town. But now you couldn't see it even on a clear day—too much is in the way. That's the North End." He continued to turn, orienting Ukiah's memories as he indicated landmarks. "Beacon Hill. Boston Commons is beyond it."

"They call that a hill?"

"All the hills were taller once, I'm told. Again, before my time. Apparently since the first colonist landed, they've graded down all the hills to landfill the Back Bay and enlarged the city. They've always been big on urban development projects in Boston."

That would explain the mass of road construction that the Pack found cutting off favorite streets, making the entire downtown traffic scene a snarled mess. Rennie had memories of the start of the project they called the Big Dig, but they were jumbled in Ukiah's recall with those of the original highway project in the 1950s that tore down complete neighborhoods to cut a swath through the heart of the city. After a century and a half, Rennie barely paid attention to the changing world except where it related to killing Ontongard. Born in a simpler time, Rennie found the world too complex and crowded to do otherwise.

Now that Ukiah thought about it, he had had much in common with Rennie even before the Pack leader shared memories with him.

Rennie had followed his thoughts and grinned now, tousling his hair. "It will be time soon. Eyes sharp. Keep yourself safe."

The Pack gathered loosely around Ukiah, far enough out to make it appear he was alone, but close enough to rescue him out of any trouble that might arise.

Ukiah settled on a park bench, watching the joggers. Max jogged on a treadmill every morning, along with lifting weights, to keep fit. He bemoaned the lack of a nearby park to run in—he would have liked the wide, level paths along the serene river. Even with the Pack around him, Ukiah missed his partner's sane, level presence.

Senses filtering for the unknown and thoughts on home, Ukiah missed Ru's approach until his brother's partner was nearly up to him.

"What are you doing here?" Ru asked.

The sight of Ru flushed Ukiah with surprising delight—it was like drinking down heady wine. True, Ukiah had grown to like the man at the beach house; Ru had shown him open friendliness. But somehow being exposed to his brother's memories during his test, Atticus's feelings had reinforced his own; Ukiah recognized what he felt was love—as deep and true as what he felt for his moms, Max, and Indigo. He smiled his honest joy at seeing his brother's partner.

Ru frowned at him with open hostility and suspicion.

Even as Ukiah's smile faded, Ru's anger changed to puzzlement.

"Why are you here . . ?" Ru paused, scanning the park to spot the various Dog Warriors mixed with the joggers and bicyclers. "I was going to say 'alone', but that's not the case."

"I'm . . . we're . . ." As Ukiah formed the words, he realized it might be a bad idea to admit their plan to trap the cultists. The Pack had insisted that they exclude Indigo, and reluctantly he'd agreed. Dealing with the Ontongard ruthlessly had been one thing—that the cultists were human put her on unstable ground. "You probably would be better off not knowing."

"Let me guess." Ru studied the park for a minute. "You're waiting for someone and you expect trouble." He turned to Ukiah and swept a gaze down over him. "You're the bagman."

"How can you tell that?" Atticus's memories hadn't warned Ukiah how clever Ru was.

"You're at the center of the pattern. Who are you meeting?"

"You should just go."

"Because what you're going to do is illegal?"

"Because I don't want you to be hurt."

Ru looked surprised. "Why do you care what happens to me?"

"I like you. And Atticus loves you; it would destroy him to lose you."

Disbelief and the desire to believe him warred on Ru's face. Abruptly he asked, "How's your arm?"

The question threw Ukiah off balance. "My arm?" Ukiah extended his hand to Ru and showed him how he could flex and bend his arm without pain. "It's all healed."

Ru took his hand and ran his thumb up the bone, inspecting the knits. He gave Ukiah another measuring look. "Here, let me see in your ears."

"My ears?"

"Yes, your ears." Ru turned Ukiah's head to peer into his ears. "Ah, yes."

"What?"

"There's something I want to check." He held Ukiah's head still and peered into his eyes, making little doctorlike noises. Ru took out a small pen flashlight and made Ukiah wince by shining the light into his eyes.

"Ru, why . . . why are you doing that?"

"They say that the eyes are the windows into the soul." Ru gazed into his eyes. "I'm looking at your soul."

Ru's eyes were black, almond shaped, with the elliptical fold under thick black eyebrows. There didn't seem to be anything mystical about them, and yet Ru seemed serious.

"What do souls look like?"

Ru leaned closer, as if to see better. "Oh, souls come in a range. Some are quite black. Some are dark blue. Others are red. The soul of a child is pure white."

"What color is mine?"

"Are you worried about the condition of your soul?"

"I-I'm not totally sure I have one. Magic Boy had one— but there's more than one of us now."

Ru winced. "You have one, babe. And it looks all nice and squeaky-clean to me."

Ukiah stared at Ru, trying to tell if Ru was telling him the truth. Ru gazed back, unwavering, so close that his breath brushed warm against Ukiah's wind-chilled cheek. It was the directness of Ru's gaze that finally convinced him—Ru was doing everything in his power to appear truthful. "You're lying to me."

"Of course I am." The façade breached, Ru gave a mischievous grin. "But the fact you weren't sure only goes to prove I'm right." He glanced off, over Ukiah's shoulder. "Are you hungry?"

Ukiah followed his gaze to the hot-dog vendor; just looking at it made his stomach clench up tight, reminding him that his body had been working on overdrive to heal him up. "The cult took my wallet. I don't have any cash."

Ru eyed the hand that Ukiah had pressed to his stomach, trying to soothe away the knot. "That was an offer—I'll buy you a couple of hot dogs."

"Thank you, but— Ru! Ru!"

The DEA agent had already started for the cart, ignoring Ukiah's protest. Rather than shout after him, Ukiah trailed behind, at a loss for how to handle the situation. The Pack had listened with their sharp ears and now radiated mild amusement. Affection seemed to be a viral thing for the

Pack—the Dogs had also been affected by Atticus's memories. It built on their gratitude that Ru's loving acceptance had kept Atticus mentally stable and provided a safe outlet for Atticus's sexual drive. That Ru was now treating Ukiah with kindness only sealed their opinion. It made Ukiah wonder about their affection for Indigo and Max—did his feelings make the Pack love them too? Was there a rebound effect, if his relationships soured? His moms talked about the difficulty of staying friends on both sides of a divorce.

He should keep it in mind.

Ru ordered him two chili dogs, fully loaded, and a root beer without asking his preferences—but it was what he'd normally order. He supposed that Ru—via Atticus—knew what he liked, just as Indigo or Max would know.

"Ru, there isn't time for this."

"It's chili dogs." Ru paid the vendor, collected the chili dogs, and handed them to Ukiah. "Not the Four Seasons. Eat them"—Ru cut off another protest—"before the chili falls off."

Ukiah bit into the sandwich in his right hand. In his post-battering state, it was the best chili dog he'd ever tasted. He suspected, though, that anything short of roadkill would be appealing; it was a trick his body used to get him to cooperate.

In certain ways, Ru was no different.

"What are you doing here?" Ukiah asked around a mouthful of chili, cheese, and bun.

"I made a wrong turn and ended up driving by." Ru waved toward the parking lot. The team's Ford Explorer with its Maryland plates sat among the cars bearing Massachusetts plates. "I saw you and thought I'd stop to talk."

"Why?"

"Because I like you," Ru echoed back Ukiah's reason; Ukiah wanted to believe he meant it. "And you're Atticus's brother—and much as Atticus currently wants nothing to do with you, that's important to him."

Ukiah sighed. "This has been one screwed-up reunion. I suppose it could have been worse, but frankly I'm not sure how."

"There's some rule of nature that says family reunions are supposed to be traumatic; I've never been to one that wasn't—but then, I'm gay, and that comes with interesting baggage."

Ukiah thought of how his Mom Jo's extensive family treated his Mom Lara. When the two presented themselves merely as college roommates, everyone had warmly accepted Lara. Gatherings became quiet battlefields after his moms confessed their true relationship.

He finished the first chili dog and asked, "Does your family know about Atticus?" Do they accept him? Or do they blame him for making you gay?" Which was what Mom Jo's family accused Mom Lara of.

"I figured out in junior high school that I was gay, and I told my parents then." Ru opened the can of root beer and held it out to Ukiah. "They wanted their kids to be unprejudiced, so I was kind of clueless about what I was announcing to them. Gay people were okay in my parents' book, so I thought it would be okay for me to be one. After that little bomb went off, they were a little more specific as to what 'okay' constituted. You know, Catholics are nice people, but don't marry one."

Ukiah took a deep gulp of root beer and felt it wash sugary goodness through his calorie-starved system. "What is wrong with Catholics?"

"I'm not sure! Part of my parents' 'unprejudiced' campaign was never telling us anything *bad* about other religions and races. After I told them I was gay, though, it became clear that they only wanted me to marry a straight, Japanese Buddhist—they were hoping this being gay stuff was a phase I was going through. High school was rough, and I made it rougher by rebelling against the norm at every step. They were afraid to send me to college—that either I'd self-destruct or the big wide world would chew me up and swallow me down without a trace. By the time Atticus showed up, they were glad to see him. He grounded me back to someone they could relate to."

"I'm glad then." Ukiah finished the second chili dog and the last of the root beer. "I wish I could have been there for him when he was growing up. Being alone nearly destroyed him."

Ru gazed at him for several minutes, as if searching for some truth in his eyes. If he loved Ru because of Atticus's memories, what did Ru feel, with Ukiah having Atticus's face? "What about the future?" Ru broke his silence. "Are you going to be there for him from now on?"

"You said yourself, he doesn't want anything to do with me." Ukiah stood. It was nearly ten. He held out his left arm to Ru as a reminder. "He made himself fairly clear on that point."

"He was scared, and that made him angry." Ru clasped Ukiah's hand. "I could talk to him—make it right between the two of you."

Possibilities unfolded for Ukiah. He could be the brother that Atticus always wanted. He could share with him Magic Boy's memories. They could go to Pendleton together, and meet their many nieces and nephews, giving Atticus all the family he always wanted, had desperately needed as a child. "You could?"

"You'd have to work with me." Ru tightened his hold on Ukiah's hand. "Tell me what you're planning. Keeping us out is not going to build trust, and I think that's all that's needed here. Honesty and trust."

What Ru said felt right; Ukiah couldn't argue that.

"We've set up a trap," he said reluctantly. "For Ice—he's the leader of the Temple of New Reason. I'm the bait."

"Are you insane? After what they've done to you?"

"They want me to translate some . . ." Ukiah paused as he felt a distant jolt of fear and surprise. He turned to gaze across the river, reaching for Atticus and finding a tight knot of Ontongard Gets.

"What is it?"

Distant gunshots thundered and a flash of pain came from Atticus.

"Atticus!" Ukiah cried, and started running.

"Cub! Cub, no!" Rennie's will pushed against him, trying to get him to stop. *"Stay; we'll deal with it. We can't risk you falling to Hex too."*

Ukiah paused, recognizing the wisdom of what Rennie said, but he could sense Atticus pitching a running fight, heading away from him. Already Atticus was at the edge of what he could sense, and he was the one most connected to Atticus. His brother lacked the bonds Ukiah had with the Pack, from Rennie's blood mouse to months of close acquaintance; the Dogs were reacting to Ukiah, not Atticus. Wait—Ru might know where Atticus was. Ukiah turned back, surprised to see he'd covered a city block and stood at the foot of the bridge. The park bench was empty and the Explorer was gone from its parking space.

"Shit." Ukiah ran a hand through his hair, looking back across the bridge to the sprawling city where Atticus was. He could sense the Pack already across the bridge, racing toward Atticus. His brother was a more experienced fighter than he was, he reminded himself. Still, he started across the bridge at a sprint, dodging pedestrians.

Suddenly one of the joggers slammed into him, jabbing a hypodermic needle into him. Ukiah jerked back, surprised and then panicked as he felt some drug surge through his system, carrying numbness.

Oh, this is bad.

Other joggers veered toward him, and he realized he'd been seeing them for over a half hour, circling him on the paths around the park. The cult had laid their own trap and he was neatly in it.

As his legs folded, the cultists caught hold of him,

pressed him up against the railing, and then flipped him over.

The Charles River expanded to fill his vision, and he hit hard, a flash of stunning pain. Then he was flailing in the icy water.

Oh, God, this is so bad.

There was someone in the water with him, snagging something onto his jacket. As he was dragged upward, he considered slipping free of his coat, and then realized that in his current condition, if he did, he'd drown. Moments later they broke the water's surface, and he coughed and sputtered for air.

The boat loomed up beside him, a wall of white, and hands were tugging him upward.

"Well, look what we landed," Ice drawled as Ukiah was dragged aboard. "An angel fish."

CHAPTER ELEVEN

Atticus ran like a fox before the hounds. The chase went through the quiet treed lawns and stately old brick buildings of MIT's campus, and out onto its busy main street. He was used to dashing through cars and crowds—although usually running *after* someone rather than *from*—but the principle was the same. The trick was making eye contact with drivers and other pedestrians and convincing them with a hard stare to keep the hell out of your way.

He'd just made the opposite side of the street when a bullet struck him high in the left shoulder. He stumbled and fell, the window above him shattering as a second bullet missed him. He hit the sidewalk in an explosion of pain that threatened to black him out. A bullet kissed the sidewalk beside his cheek and ricocheted off in a whine. Another tugged at him as it plowed through the leather of his jacket. He rolled and fumbled out his pistol. He hated to use a gun in an urban situation, but he had no choice.

He scrambled to his knees, braced himself, and aimed down on the shooter, who was nearly on top of him. His first bullet took the shooter square in the chest, sprawling the man backward onto the sidewalk with a meaty, lifeless thump. Recoil sent a shock of fresh pain through Atticus. Gritting his teeth, he aimed at the second man. His pistol kicked pain through him as he fired, the first bullet only grazing the man's shoulder. Unlike a normal human, the man—no, *creature*—didn't even flinch, coming straight at him as if pain and death didn't matter. Atticus squeezed off two more shots, nailing his attacker this time.

His SIG Sauer had a magazine of twelve bullets plus one in the chamber. As he lined up the axe man, he counted the bullets down. Nine. Eight. Seven.

Six bullets left, he thought as he lurched to his feet, ears ringing. Three down, but would they stay down? There were rats forming in the pooling blood from the first, and he sensed the body knitting together heart muscle at stunning speed.

The other two—Parity and the woman—were closing. He could wait and shoot them, but then what? He'd be out of bullets and the first man would be healed. He needed breathing room and more of a plan.

He ran east, along the busy street. Behind him he sensed the first dead man come to life and start after him.

A human Atticus could outrun, even if he was hurt. Wounded, against these creatures so like himself, he could sense the gap between them quickly closing. There was the Jag, though, parked close by; if he could get to it, he'd be home free.

Bullets whined past him, striking storefront windows, marking his trail with fractured flowers of destruction in the safety glass.

He was running past a red-trimmed building when a bullet caught him in the leg. He stumbled out of his full run, and the female Ontongard tackled him through a window. They dropped down a stairwell beyond. Atticus hit worn tile a story and a half below, the female on top of him, a smothering blanket of hate in human form.

They were on a subway station platform, and the handful of people waiting were startled by their sudden, violent appearance. An outbound train had just pulled in, its doors clattering open. From the dark tunnel of the inbound line came the ominous roar of an incoming train.

Not good.

The gunman and axe man he'd shot, the ones who should still be dead, dropped down to land lightly beside him.

Atticus lashed out at the woman, slamming her off him and coming up in sweeping kick to take out the axe man. He couldn't reach the gunman in time.

This is going to hurt.

Suddenly Rennie Shaw was between him and the gunman, wearing a black leather jacket with the picture of a snarling dog and the words "Dog Warrior." The gun thundered, booming in the enclosed space. The bullet punched through Shaw, exiting out of his back in a fist-sized hole. Blood splattered Atticus and crawled, gathering together into a tiny mote of snarling anger.

The female punched Atticus hard in his wounded shoulder, distracting him from the sentient blood. He caught her arm and broke it as he swung her into the axe man. Humans would have fumbled, but the two dodged each other with choreographed ease. The female grasped Atticus's arm, her bones already knitting, and held him as the axe man swung back his axe. Behind them the inbound train thundered into the station.

With a snarl, Hellena Gobeyn dropped from street level to the axe man's feet, picked him up, and flung him into the path of the oncoming train. The man vanished under the bright steel wheels with a bloom of blood scent. A moment later, rats swarmed out up out of the pit.

Another Ontongard and a wave of Dog Warriors rolled down the stairs, already locked in battle. The subway platform became a mass of snarling, struggling bodies.

The door-closing chime sounded on the outbound train and Atticus found himself suddenly hauled up and thrust into the subway train.

"Go!" Rennie Shaw barked, producing a sawed-off shotgun from under his duster like in a magic trick. He turned, firing at one of the Ontongard in a roar of sound and a cloud of gunsmoke.

Then the door closed and the train pulled away from the carnage.

Atticus grabbed a pole to keep from falling. His phone vibrated. He pulled it out to discover he'd missed two calls already.

"Steele."

"Where are you?" Ru cried through the phone. "Cambridge looks like a war zone! What the hell happened?"

"I'm on a subway train." Atticus turned to ask the other passengers the train's destination and found that they had crowded to either end of the car, as far away from him as they could. "Where are we going?"

"C-C-Central is the next station, " the nearest of the passengers stuttered, "then Harvard, and . . . oh, God, I don't remember."

"Porter, Davis, Alewife," someone behind Atticus said, but when he turned, he couldn't tell who. Everyone had big doe eyes of fear.

The train pulled into Central, and when the doors opened the passengers bolted, throwing frightened glances back to see if he was getting off too. He didn't have the heart to follow them; he couldn't stand them looking at him like he was a monster. The door-closing chime sounded. The doors closed and the train pulled out of the station.

"Atty?" Ru's voice pulled his attention back to the phone.

"I'm on a train going to Alewife." Atticus sighed and sat down in the now empty car. "Come get me there."

"Okay."

He hung up and sagged back in the seat. What the hell was that? Zheng had warned him, but with quiet, reasonable words. She had left out that they would recognize him from a distance and how profound their hate for the Pack ran.

Why? Weren't they the same race? What the hell was that all about?

Usually Ru bandaging him up was a soothing activity, but Atticus found his mind racing over the last few days, the little scraps of information that he'd pieced into an imperfect patchwork quilt of knowledge. He was finding gaping holes in his knowledge. He wasn't even sure which theory to believe about himself: werewolf, angel, demon, or alien? Who did he trust to tell him the truth? Agent Zheng? The Pack?

"You know," he said to break the silence of his own thinking, "Batman was just a nutcase."

"Hmm?"

"No, here he was, stinking rich, huge house, no need to do any work at all, and what does he do? Get a wife? Adopt some needy kids whom he doesn't bend to his own vigilante lifestyle? No. He sulks around at night, breaking the law, ruining crime scenes, and destroying any chance of building a criminal suit against any of these lowlifes. No wonder the badly run insane asylum was full—by the time he stomped through a case, the only thing you could legally do with these criminals was commit them and then lose the paperwork."

Ru paused in stripping the sterile wrapper from an oversize bandage. "Is this a 'we should get a life and go on vacation' speech?"

"What?"

Ru shrugged and gingerly pressed the bandage in place. "The line of reasoning usually goes: He let a petty criminal define his life, he should have moved on, all that money and he never kicks back and enjoys it, let's go to Bermuda."

"You missed that he should at least have bought a few politicians and pushed through stronger gun-control laws and three-strikes-you're-out programs."

"Oh, yeah, that too."

Atticus considered the battered neighborhood around the Alewife train station's parking garage, bleak and cold with autumn rain. "Yeah, Bermuda might be a good idea, but that wasn't the point I was trying to get to."

"It wasn't?"

"No. I never told you this, but I've always hated Batman because he's racist. At least in the new canon."

"Really?"

"Yeah, he distrusts Superman because he's not human. Sure, he'll fuck Catwoman, a cheap petty criminal, but trust an alien that has done nothing but risk his life for others, nope, nope, can't do it."

"Sooo?"

"Well, it doesn't stop him from joining the Justice League and fighting with Superman."

"And this relates how?" Ru asked.

"I don't trust Zheng to tell me the truth. Superman, when he needed to know about who he really was, he retreated to Fortress of Solitude and sought knowledge from the source."

Ru busied himself putting away the bandages, radiating unease.

"What?"

"Atty . . . you know . . . sometimes it worries me that you get your moral guidance from comic books."

"Where else am I going to go? Everything else assumes you're human."

"*Sou desu.*" It was a Japanese phrase meaning "that is so," which neither agreed or disagreed with the speaker, just confirmed the facts.

"I need to talk to the Dog Warriors."

"They know you're a DEA agent."

"Yeah, but there's a bigger picture here that I'm not seeing, and I think not knowing is going to get me killed."

•   •   •

Ponkapoag Camp—once they figured out how to spell it—proved to be an eighty-five-hundred-acre wildlife reservation just fifteen miles from Boston. Its Web site claimed that the campground was a collection of twenty rustic cabins dotting the shore of Ponkapoag Pond.

As he drew close to the reservation, he could feel the Dog Warriors, a hard, angry knot of Pack presence. There were motorcycles lining the campground's road, dozens of them, and an occasional pickup truck. Men walked the road, reluctantly moving to the edge to let him pass. They wore leather jackets, and the club badges identified them as various New England motorcycle clubs, from Gold Wing Riders to Hell's Angels.

The Pack was having a party.

The partygoers had built a bonfire on the edge of Ponkapoag Pond, the flames reflecting in the dark water. The bikers had brought a portable stereo, and it thumped out, ironically enough, "Smoke on the Water."

Atticus pulled in and got out of the Jaguar. Coming now felt like a mistake. He was glad, though, that he'd been able to talk Ru into staying with Kyle, playing his backup instead of his voice. He wanted to be alone when he heard all the dark secrets the Pack might tell him.

"Hey." Someone—a regular human—shone a flashlight onto the Jaguar, seeking him out. "This is a private party."

"And he's invited," a voice rumbled out of the dark. The flashlight flicked to the speaker, and hit Rennie Shaw as he drifted out of the shadows. The light reflected in his eyes with the greenish gleam of a wild dog's. There was a bullet hole in Shaw's leather jacket—a reminder of the Dog Warrior's intervention that afternoon. "This is our Boy."

The light jumped back to Atticus, finding his face. He squinted against the glare, as his eyes had been getting accustomed to the dark.

"Oh, I see," the wielder of the flashlight said, and the light snapped off.

The hairs on the back of Atticus's neck rose. *Am I that much like them?*

"Mouthpiece said you might be coming around, Boy." Shaw motioned that Atticus was to follow.

"You're having a party?" Atticus covered his disquiet.

"We're having a Gathering of the clans." To the bikers, Shaw called back. "Nothing happens to the car, or you'll be the ones we track down."

"Does that mean we have to stand here and guard it?" One of them whined, and was immediately cuffed by the man standing beside him.

"Okay, Rennie," the wielder of the flashlight said. "You can count on us—sir."

"Hell's Angels calling you sir." Atticus murmured as he and Shaw moved into the woods. "That's pathetic."

"They have their uses. Mostly that the cops have to wade through them to get to us."

There were knots of parties scattered through the camp-ground; the largest concentration of people being down by the bonfire. He could *feel* solitary Pack members moving through the crowds like herd dogs. It surprised him that he recognized some as they brushed against his awareness.

The humans carried flashlights, or stumbled through darkness. He and Shaw moved quietly through the trees, eyes growing accustomed to the dark, the night becoming vivid grays.

Atticus eyed the bullet hole in Shaw's jacket, the leather scorched by the muzzle flare, tainted slightly by burned blood. Shaw showed no sign, though, of being wounded. The Dog Warriors must heal as readily as himself—or perhaps faster, like the Ontongard. Still, it had to hurt. "Thanks for the save."

"We're your family. You're our Boy."

Another time, Atticus would have snapped a denial to that, but now . . . what did he know? "Am I?"

"Here. Take my hand." Shaw paused to hold out his right hand, as if to shake. "Go on. I don't bite—much."

Atticus reluctantly reached out and took Shaw's hand. The fingers closed like a steel trap on his, holding him tight.

"Do you know how to use those senses of yours?" Shaw asked. "Can you feel down deep to the pattern of life?"

During their fight on the beach, Atticus had sensed that Shaw wasn't human, but hadn't focused on how. Now, without distraction, he could study Shaw's genetic pattern. Whereas his own DNA was one smooth pattern, alien as it was, Shaw's was a mass of confusion. There was a scant human part—like a veneer—of a tall, lean, Anglo-Saxon man. Under the man, though, ran a thread of wolf and mouse, and then, like a raging river under it all, was something fully alien. Yet he could find familiar landmarks, similarities that lay in himself.

His family.

"So what are you to me? Uncle? Cousin? Brother?"

"The answer isn't that simple."

"Why not?"

"Because we don't reproduce like humans." Shaw started to walk again.

"How do you reproduce?"

"Actually, as little as possible."

After a minute of silence, it became obvious that Shaw wasn't going to elaborate. He tried another line of questions. "What happened after you put me on the train?"

"Do you really want to know? It's a grisly tale."

"Yes, I do."

"We had the advantage of numbers. Eighteen to four."

Eighteen? Then the Dog Warriors weren't there in full force. Zheng must still have her Pack backup. And four was wrong too.

"There were six." Though Atticus did leave the one drugged, possibly dead, on the docks.

"Once the police started to arrive, we didn't have the luxury to search for stragglers. We grabbed the ones we could and went to the city pound. They cremate the dogs they put down. We borrowed the facilities."

He thought of the woman, so like himself, crawling through the weeds on fire, and felt slightly sick.

"Don't pity them!" Shaw snapped. "They're the enemy of all life on this planet. They won't stop until they're put down, or they've corrupted everything into their image."

"Okay, so I don't know what the hell is going on. Why don't you tell me? What the hell are they? What are we? Werewolves? Demons? Angels?"

"You're asking for a history lesson that stretches back thousands of years and covers multiple star systems."

"So we're aliens?"

"Mostly."

Atticus jerked to a halt. "Just give me a straight answer, damn it."

"You didn't fight four men this morning," Hellena Gob- eyn said, moving ghost silent through the trees to join them. "You faced one creature." She reached out and took Atti- cus's hand in hers. "As you have five fingers that can act as one fist"—she curled his hand into a fist—"the Ontongard act as one being."

"One body—ten bodies—a thousand—it doesn't make a difference," Shaw said. "It's one monster with one thought— to *grow.*"

"But we're like them." Atticus freed his hand from Hel- lena's. "They heal like us, and the mice."

"Prime—the first of us—was a mutation of Ontongard," Hellena said. "He had a will of his own. He had hopes and dreams and desires of his own making."

"You're a lot like him," Shaw said. "An angry young male, surrounded by beings that seem like you but aren't, made a loner by the very fact that you aren't one of them. He hated the Ontongard." Shaw gave Atticus a questioning look. "Do you hate humans?"

"No," Atticus snapped.

Shaw pushed against him mentally, seeking the truth.

"Don't do that!" Atticus backed away from him, unsure how to break the mental contact.

"Don't lie to me then." Nevertheless, Shaw backed off. "I've seen into your mind. You enjoy beating the hell out of them."

"No, not all of them. I couldn't hate the entire race. For every shitheel that crawls the earth, there are a dozen good people worth protecting."

"Ah, there's the difference then. For Prime, there was only one being, and it was a monster. He tried his best to kill them all."

"He almost succeeded," Hellena said. "At least, as far as Earth is concerned. Prime sabotaged the seed ship so it would self-destruct and then joined the crew of the scout ship. When he crashed it into the Blue Mountains in Oregon, he killed all but one—Hex."

"But one was too many," Shaw said. "Oregon, late seventeen hundreds. There was nothing there that could stand against Hex. Arrows with stone heads. Hell, we can barely stand against his Gets now, and we're on an even footing."

"In his dying minutes, Prime made us, the Pack, to carry on his fight," Hellena said. "We've fought Hex and his Gets for hundreds of years."

"Made? How did he make the Pack?"

"The Ontongard reproduce virally, Boy. They might look human, but you're looking at a million of them in one body. That's how we can make the mice—shape or size isn't important—though it does affect intelligence. They inject themselves into a host—a human—and take the body over."

They walked out of the woods at last, into a clearing. It was like stepping back in time. A small cook fire was the only source of light. A deer carcass hung from a high branch; cuts of it were being grilled over the wood flame. Beings pretending to be human dressed in leather and carrying guns moved through the flickering firelight. When they looked up, their eyes gleamed in the darkness like wolves'.

His family. God had to be laughing at him now.

Shaw pointed to the nearest man. "This is Grant; he leads the Wild Wolves." And from there, he continued, spilling out names to which the owner nodded in greeting. Wild Wolves. Dog Warriors. Hell Hounds. Devil Dogs. Demon Curs. Shaw meant it when he said the clans were gathering.

"What is your fixation on dogs?" Atticus asked after the last of them were introduced.

"Prime didn't infect a human." Degas, who led the Demon Curs, answered with a look toward Shaw, as if rebuking him for not being clearer. "His only Get was a wolf; it was the wolf that created the Pack."

"We have him stamped on our minds," Shaw admitted. "His DNA laced through our genetics—his instincts threaded through our soul. Sometimes when we dream, we run the dappled green on four furred feet."

"There are those who are most comfortable running around like packs of wolves." Degas made it clear with his sneer that he excluded himself. "Some of us, though, aren't totally happy with embracing the way of the beast, Boy."

Atticus understood then that they had given him a nickname, one as stupid as Cub: Boy. "No, I'm Atticus. Atticus Steele."

Degas smirked, apparently pleased that he'd nettled Atticus. "Where's your chew toy?"

It took Atticus a moment to realize Degas meant Ru. In a flash of anger, Atticus lashed out, striking without holding back as he normally would. He caught the clan leader totally unaware and Degas dropped with a sickening crack of his neck. Atticus had always had a morbid curiosity of what he could do with his full strength—the day had been a continuous lesson.

"He will get better from that?" he asked guiltily.

"Shortly," Hellena murmured.

Shaw snorted a laugh. "Except his pride. He did ask for that."

"I-I didn't realize I could hit so hard."

"Degas would have killed you if he could. He tried to kill your brother—it was a close fight."

Atticus glanced about, realizing whom he most wanted to see. "Where's Ukiah?"

A low growl rose from the Pack, rage and anger unifying them nearly as tight as the Ontongard had been. They stood out, though, as individuals in their fear, anxiety, and worry.

"They have him," Shaw said.

"What? Who?"

"Those religious nutcases!" Shaw snarled. "We've spent the day looking for him."

"How did this happen?"

Hellena explained their plan to trap Ice and how they'd been distracted by the Ontongard's attack on Atticus. Her distress grew as she talked until there were tears in her eyes. "Somehow, they took him so quickly, he didn't get a chance to call for help. We scoured the park and found no trace of him."

Shaw put a hand to her shoulder and she grasped it tightly.

Had the cult killed Ukiah again? Would they burn him, as they had done with the others?

Atticus pushed away memories of the burned mice to focus on what he knew of the cult. "Ascii said that they need him to translate something. He's probably safe as long as he's useful to them." But that was far from comforting. If the cult had grabbed him instead, thinking Atticus was also an angel, he wouldn't be able to translate diddly. "Does Ukiah understand the Ontongard language? Can he translate like they want him to?"

"Yes, I gave him one of my mice." Then, seeing that Atticus didn't understand, Shaw explained. "Our memories are genetically coded. Absorbing another person's mouse adds their memories to yours. I gave Ukiah all my memories, which extend back to the beginning of the Ontongard race."

His brother's life was so weird. "He can do it then?"

Shaw looked away.

Atticus turned to Hellena. "Can he or can't he?"

"Our Cub . . ." Hellena's voice quavered with strong emotions. "He believes strongly in doing what is right—no matter the cost to himself."

And a wave of sorrow and anger went through the Pack.

They know Ukiah won't cooperate.

From the pond's edge, the bikers started into a drunken chorus.

"Why aren't you out looking for him?" Atticus asked. "What are you doing here—having a party?"

"We've tried looking blindly all day," Shaw snapped. "Now we're waiting."

"For what?"

Stillness ran through the Pack. Atticus could sense them listening, focused on the rumble of incoming motorcycles.

"It's them," someone near the road mentally reported.

The Pack melted into the woods, leaving him alone with Shaw, Hellena, Degas, and the Demon Cur's alpha female, Blade.

"You should leave." Shaw gave him a slight push toward the clearing's edge, back toward the Jag.

Atticus resisted. "What's happening?"

"We don't have time for niceties anymore. Things are going to get messy."

"What are you going to do?"

"Daggit knows where the cult is. We're going to do everything short of tearing his head off his shoulders to get that information. And the only reason we're stopping there is because dead men don't talk."

"You can't torture him."

"We're in this mess because that's what your brother

said," Shaw said. "Go home. Better yet, go back to Washington."

"No."

Oddly, Shaw's stare was neither as feral nor penetrating as Ukiah's. "Don't interfere. We will kill you and drop your body with your team if you try. We won't let even you stand between us and getting our Cub back."

"Fine."

The Iron Horses entered the campground cautiously, but the noose was already tightening around them. The Pack moved silently through the woods, surrounding the bikers, communicating mind to mind.

They took Daggit down hard, knocking him from his bike. After disarming him of various knives and guns, they dragged him kicking and swearing to the clearing. Having suffered the same treatment just days before, Atticus found himself wincing in sympathy.

As the Blue Öyster Cult sang "Don't Fear the Reaper" on the distant stereo, two Dog Warriors—Bear Shadow and David Stein—flung Daggit to the ground in front of Shaw, and the Pack closed ranks around the man.

"Let's try this again, Daggit," Shaw rumbled, his voice full of menace. "Where is the Temple of New Reason?"

Daggit scrambled to his feet, his sweat sour with fear, his nose running with blood. Still he managed, "Go fuck yourself, Shaw."

"They have our Cub, Daggit." Shaw began to circle Daggit.

"You should have watched him a little more carefully then." Daggit backed as far away from Shaw as the watching Pack allowed, turning to keep the Pack leader in front of him. "You knew they were after him."

Shaw lashed out, faster than even Atticus could see. In a blur of savage motion, he had Daggit down on his knees, right arm dislocated and forced up behind his back. As Daggit flailed at him with his left arm, Shaw leaned down and growled into Daggit's ear. It wasn't the sound of a man imitating an animal, but the deep chest growl of a true beast that raised the hairs on the back of Atticus's neck.

"I'm not going to tell you squat!" Daggit cried.

"We're not going to take 'squat' as an answer." Shaw shifted his hold and broke Daggit's right pinkie.

Daggit grunted but otherwise remained stoic in the face of the pain. The ring finger broke with the snap of a dry branch. On the middle finger, Daggit cried, "I don't fucking know!"

"Animal said you knew."

"Animal was wrong." Daggit panted and peered at the encircling Pack. "Funny thing, I don't see him here."

"Focus. Your life is on the line, Daggit. Blink wrong and you're dead. Now, where are they?"

"I don't know." This time Daggit's voice quavered with fear.

"After we break your fingers, we'll cut them off. And we'll keep cutting till we hack off your dick." Shaw snapped the next finger.

"Okay! Okay, okay! They've got this island. They were talking about it last time I saw them. They've been digging in. They wanted claymores and napalm. They were getting ready for a fucking war."

"Not good enough." Shaw growled, drawing a bowie knife.

"I really don't know!" Daggit shouted. "It's out of Salem, like out by South Goosberry, or Bakers Island, but farther out! I think it's like three or four miles from shore! A little shit of an island. There's just one fucking house on it!"

Shaw ignored him, putting the blade up against the base of the broken pinkie.

"Wait." Atticus caught Shaw's arm. "Parity kept a boat on the Charles River. Ice took it out this morning. That's what I was doing in Cambridge. And Ascii was taking Ukiah to Salem, before I got him out of the trunk."

Shaw grunted and released Daggit. The big man cradled his broken hand, glaring at the Pack. "If you're lying to us, Daggit, we will hunt you down and cut out your liver and feed it to you."

As Stein dragged Daggit away, Atticus's mind was filled with images of the Pack waging war with the cult, leaving a trail of stolen boats and dead humans floating in their wake. "I'll set up a raid with Zheng. We'll get Ukiah back. Just give me twelve hours."

"No," Shaw growled.

"What about the Ontongard? Why do you think they were in Cambridge? They were down at the marina. They're hunting the cult. If you go after the cult, you'll be caught between them."

"All the more reason for us to go, not you and Zheng."

"You can keep the Ontongard busy. That's what you were made for, right? To fight the Ontongard."

Shaw snarled as an answer.

"There's the problem of finding Hex's Gets," Grant said. "We know where the cult is."

"If the cult really have been killing and burning these Gets," Atticus said, "then a profile of the victims from the cult's burn sites probably will give last known addresses and such. All you have to do is get close, right? Then you can feel them? My team's already working on the information."

Consensus moved through the Pack, with hard knots of resistance coming from the Dog Warriors, who knew Ukiah best.

"Fine, twelve hours," Shaw said. "Make it noon tomorrow."

"Well?" Ru greeted him when he pulled the Jaguar in beside the Explorer.

Atticus could feel the Pack following behind him, waiting for the information he'd promised. What the hell was he thinking? "We have to pull rabbits out of our ass to save my brother." He explained the situation as quickly as he could. "They think Ukiah is too moral to cooperate with the cult."

"Possibly. He's actually quite sweet."

Atticus frowned at Ru. "Based on what? We barely got to talk to him."

"I ran into him this morning. Things got so crazy, I forgot to mention it." Ru hesitated, looking troubled. "But there's something wrong with him."

"Which is he? Sweet or screwed in the head?"

"I gave him a street test. He failed so bad."

"Street test" was what Ru called his method of seeing how street-smart a kid was. A lot of kids who crossed their paths were already hardened criminals. Others, though, were good kids about to be swallowed down; those were the ones they tried to steer toward havens, getting them off the street before they could be eaten.

"So he's naïve," Atticus grumbled.

"I've never seen a kid over the age of ten let me go this far. He's a complete babe in the woods. He let me do the fucking penlight in the eyes, Atty."

Atticus found himself thinking of the sturdy naked toddler he'd protected in the forest as a wolf. He tried to ignore it. Ukiah probably only looked younger because of the odd way they aged. "If he's like me, then he's perfect. He could be just pretending to get on your good side."

"Are you sure? Think about when he first woke up in the bathroom. That wasn't an act. It was like he's feral."

Yes, that was true. Even the Pack with their wolf taint didn't seem half as wild.

I left him in the woods—how long did it take for someone to find him?

CHAPTER TWELVE

Ukiah woke with something warm and furry gently touching his cheek. He opened his eyes to find a yellow tabby kitten sitting beside him, patting at his face. Its eyes seemed over-size for its large head, and all its fur was puffed out in a wild, disorganized manner. It was a tiny scarecrow version of a cat.

"You're a lot nicer than what I'd expected to wake up to." Ukiah heaved himself up to a sitting position, which made the room spin.

Said room was ten foot square and made of cinder-block walls, a steel door, and no windows. Except for the bare foam pad he sat on, a plastic twin food-and-water dish for the kitten, and a yet unused litter box, the room was empty. Light came from single bare bulb. The air was stale, as if circulation was limited. "Yeah, this is more what I expected."

The kitten clambered over his bare knees, needle-sharp claws coming out sporadically as it needed more traction. Ukiah petted it absently, generating a steady rough-engine purr, as he searched for Pack presence.

"Rennie? Bear? Hellena?" he silently called, and then, truly desperate, *"Atticus?"*

But there was no one there to reach. He was utterly alone in this desolate corner of the world.

Things could be worse, he reminded himself. He was at least alive and not a prisoner of the Ontongard—only a cult of homicidal lunatics.

"In circumstances like this," he told the kitten, "you have to keep things in perspective."

The cult had stripped him out of his soaked clothes and dressed him only in a pair of dark flannel boxers. If his situation weren't so dire, he'd mourn the loss of his black tracking shirt and favorite blue jeans. Maybe the cultists were just washing his clothes. His body reported massive bruising and demanded food. Closing his eyes and shutting out the kitten's furry warmth, he could sense the pounding of the surf in ceaseless rhythm and the heaviness of air that he'd come to associate with Massachusetts. How far from the coast did you have to get to escape those effects?

The kitten, which had been licking his thumb, decided to chew on it instead with tiny sharp teeth.

"Ow, ow, ow, stop that!" Ukiah jerked back his hand and checked to see if he was bleeding. Even a small amount of his blood could transform the kitten to a hybrid of himself. "And we don't need that on top of everything, now, do we?"

Outside, footsteps came quietly up to the door. The walker was wearing something soft-soled, like tennis shoes. Ukiah breathed deep, expecting to catch the person's scent, but the stale air reminded him that the room was close to airtight; there wouldn't be advance warning by that means.

Thus he was mildly off balance when a slot at eye level on the door slid open, revealing Ice's steady gaze.

Did Ice know that Ukiah had been fighting with Core when he'd been killed? Did he blame Ukiah for his lover's death? Did he hate Ukiah?

"They say eyes are the windows of the soul," Ice whispered after several minutes of silent study, echoing Ru's comment. Knowingly? Unknowingly? Ice's eyes were the color of the winter sky, a blue paled nearly to white. If Ukiah was seeing Ice's soul, it was a cold and emotionless thing.

"I'd been so busy looking at the lost fount, the spoiled plans, the fleeing time, and Core's desire that I missed you completely. If I had just *looked*, I'd have seen that you were not human, and avoided all this."

What was "this"? Ukiah was afraid to ask.

"The question is," Ice continued, "what exactly are you?"

Ice seemed to want an answer.

"I'm hungry," Ukiah said. "And I need to pee."

"We left you a litter box, water, and food."

"That?" Ukiah pointed to the kitten's food to clarify that they were referring to the same thing. Yes, Ice meant the cat food. "I'm not eating that."

"What, it's not good enough for you?"

"If I eat it, what would the kitten eat?"

"Schrödinger Five? He's food too."

It took a moment for Ukiah to realize he meant the kitten. "I'm not eating him!"

"Perhaps if you get hungry enough, you will."

The view slot slid closed.

Ukiah used the litter box, and was surprised at how well it absorbed the smell of urine. Afterward, he distracted his empty stomach by playing with Schrödinger. What was the point, he wondered, of kidnapping him if the cult only planned to starve him to death?

He'd been awake for approximately four hours when someone came furtively up to the door. Ukiah felt half-blind, unable to guess who was on the other side. The slot slid open, letting in a male's scent. The eyes looking in were dark brown; they glanced first to the kitten in Ukiah's lap and then rose to meet his gaze.

"Are you still hungry?" the man whispered.

"I'm starving," Ukiah said truthfully.

"Shhhhh." The man turned his head, showing that his hair was dark brown, straight, and cropped tight around his ears, making them seem too large for his head. The cultist looked down the hall for a minute, apparently trying to judge whether their conversation was being overheard. "I have something you can eat," he whispered once he was convinced that it was safe. He poked a candy bar in through the narrow slot and jiggled it.

The smell of chocolate pulled Ukiah across the room to snatch the candy bar quickly before the cultist could change his mind.

"Thank you," Ukiah mumbled out of habit around the warm, rich hit of complex carbohydrates. It was a stupid thing to say, he realized, considering the situation.

"I'm Mouse," the cultist whispered.

"Why are you giving this to me?"

"I wanted to ask you a question."

"What?" Ukiah asked, leery of answering any of their questions. He'd die before he gave up Kittanning or allowed the cult near his moms.

"Is Joachim Wolf correct in his theory of holon principles?"

Ukiah paused in chewing, confounded. "Hmmm?"

"Well, he points out that people living in a two-dimensional world would perceive a sphere passing through their plane of existence as a circle that grows larger and shrinks. And that if a number of cylinders were scattered onto their dimensions, they couldn't perceive that those lying on their sides—appearing as rods—were the same objects as those standing upright—thus seeming to be circles."

"Yeah," Ukiah said, meaning he understood.

"So if a four-dimensional creature intersected its hand into their plane," Mouse illustrated with his fingertips and the slot, "the two-dimensional inhabitants would see the fingers as separate beings and not as a unified whole."

Ukiah stuck to an "uh-huh."

"So it's reasonable to correlate that humans are in essence all members of an über-being that we can't perceive, yet is immanently in us. Just as flocks of birds fly together because of the über-being of birds, and schools of fish swim together because of the über-being of fish, so do humans follow lines of thinking when there is no apparent means of communication. The same idea occurs to individuals who aren't exposed to the same materials or line of thought—as if there's an ether-space that we share."

Mouse said this with the fire of someone who considered himself correct, but then squelched the fire with, "Right?"

"I suppose that's how it would seem," Ukiah said carefully.

"Well, it would explain why the Fallen all seem to be one creature. They are, in essence, evil intersecting our plane of existence—one creature, appearing as many—yet, when you look closely, you can recognize each piece as part of the same whole."

Since Mouse was right and wrong, Ukiah decided to stick with saying he was completely right. "Yeah."

"Wow," Mouse whispered. "Can you touch me?"

From his scent, Ukiah recognized him now as one of the cultists on the boat. Surely they'd come in contact several times, but apparently Mouse wanted something much more focused.

Why was it that as individuals the cultists seemed, by and large, good people, yet as a whole the cult was ruthless and deadly? Was there something to this über-being theory, where the cultists had been massed together into something more dangerous than any one alone would have been? Ukiah extended his fingers into the slot and touched Mouse's hand resting on the sill beyond.

"Thank you," Mouse breathed. He eased the slot closed with obvious reluctance and scurried away.

Mouse proved to be the first in a series of odd conversations. A pale-eyed woman by the name of Ether came whispering questions about string theory, offering up a sausage wrapped in a pancake. Luckily ancient memories from the

Pack held information of how the universe worked from civilizations that had greater knowledge than Earth.

The third cultist was a green-eyed man called Link, who wanted to know if his father, a soldier, was in heaven. The light dawned on Ukiah: The cultists, suddenly finding themselves in possession of an angel, wanted to tap his holy knowledge.

"Yes" seemed the best answer to give Link.

"Even though the commandment is: 'Thou shalt not kill'?"

"A father gives his children rules, so they can know 'good' from 'bad,' but he also forgives them when they do wrong, because he knows that it's part of growing up. What child can be perfect?"

Link gave him a pack of gum as a treat. Ukiah rationed himself to one, crinkling up the silver wrapper to make a cat toy for Schrödinger.

Ukiah recognized Ice's stride when he returned. He got to his feet, wondering what would happen now.

Ice opened the door this time and gazed at Ukiah with an odd, uncertain look. While Ice didn't point it at Ukiah, he carried a stun baton. The kitten, Schrödinger Five, darted about their feet, blissfully unaware.

"We only suspected that you were an angel, but you know, you don't really look . . . holy." Ice swept his gaze down over Ukiah, and shrugged. "Perhaps the Mormons are right."

"How do you know . . ." It felt wrong to claim he was angelic, so Ukiah let the question trail off.

"Demons are usually easy to spot," Ice explained. "They all hold their bodies the same. It's like one person wearing different skins. They shuffle around like automatons." Ice slowly circled Ukiah. "But you . . . you've got that wild-animal grace, so we didn't spot you. And then there's the matter of the Blissfire—you could pour a bag over a demon and it might as well be water. You reacted."

"No, it doesn't work on them," Ukiah observed truthfully.

"And when you capture a demon, it's like a rabid dog. There's no reasoning with a demon, and certainly you can't intimidate it."

And the cult had done both with him.

"So when we caught you and took you to Eden Court, we thought you were just a human, guarding over the nephilim." Ice shook his head. "We'd only dug into your past deep enough to find your name and address. Something made me double-check our information, and there it was, like handwriting on the wall—in June you'd been shot dead."

"You didn't sound sure that I was an angel before."

"The cat was the last test."

"Schrödinger?" Ukiah glanced down at the small tuft of fur currently chewing on Ice's shoelaces.

"You put a living animal in with a demon, and it's dead in minutes." Ice picked up the kitten and examined it. "Demons can't stand to have life near them." Ice handed Ukiah the kitten. "Usually they'll eat the cat."

Schrödinger Five, as in, numbers one through four had already been killed.

"Come," Ice said. "We'll find you something to eat."

Ice led Ukiah down a hallway lined with steel doors. Ukiah eyed them, wondering what else the cult had hidden behind them. The Ae? If nothing good came of this mess, then at least he had a much better chance of finding and destroying the Ae before the cult could use them.

"Where are we?" Ukiah asked.

"This is our ultimate haven," Ice said. "We call it Sanctuary."

They went up a flight of stairs and through another steel door into a large and surprisingly elegant kitchen. Natural stones formed the exterior walls. Floor-to-ceiling windows looked out over roiling surf, revealing that the building sat on a bluff next to the Atlantic. A dozen cultists were gathered in the kitchen, working on a meal. Ukiah recognized Mouse and Link from talking to them. Some of the cultists he recognized from Eden Court, their names gleaned from conversations there: Meta, Ray, Cursor, Qwerty, and Boolean. The other five Ukiah didn't know.

Ether entered the room carrying a bright yellow bottle of laundry detergent and a stack of folded clothing. "Link, you said you needed a buoy for the new lobster pot? I emptied the last of this out into a quart jar and"—she saw Ukiah and went shy— "rinsed it well."

"Thank you." Link took the empty bottle. "Cool, neon yellow. That will be easy to see."

"Here." Ether held out the clothing to Ukiah, blushing.

"Thank you," Ukiah said out of habit, and found that while the clothes were his, they no longer felt right; the seawater and harsh detergent had washed away everything familiar.

"You can . . ." Ether started to say something but then, glancing to Ice, fell silent.

She had been about to offer him privacy, Ukiah guessed, but Ice had stopped her. Angel or not, Ice still wasn't about to trust him. Putting the kitten down, Ukiah dressed, aware that the cultists watched him, some with awe, others with guarded suspicion. He had the package of gum tucked into his waistband. As he took the pack out, Ice stopped him long enough to see what he had in his hand. The cult leader gave Link a hard look, but let Ukiah pocket the gum.

Like Atticus's beach house, Sanctuary was an open, sprawling home. From where Ukiah stood, he could see into a living room with a vaulted, rough-timbered ceiling and a dining room that could seat twelve people without squeezing. Like the kitchen, the windows of both rooms looked out over the ocean.

He was zipping up his pants when the realization hit him. "We're on an island!"

"Yes." Ice watched him with the cold blue eyes.

Ukiah went out the kitchen door to a flagstone patio. The stone house had been built on the highest point of the low-slung island, probably sometime in the eighteen-hundreds. Ukiah could see that from the north to the south points, the island was a mile long and a quarter of that distance from east to west. Grass and low shrubs made up most of the vegetation—less than a dozen pine trees dotted the island. The only creature moving seemed to be a solitary seagull riding a stiff wind overhead; its cry echoed his inward cry of dismay.

A thin veil of fog hazed the sky, obscuring the horizons. To the west he could make out tiny barren islands and then an immense nothingness of water and fog. To the east the land curved around a small bay with a dock and a garage-sized boathouse. Two boats sat tied to the docks; one was the one that the cult had used to kidnap him. Four cultists, heavily armed, guarded the boats.

Of the mainland, Ukiah could see nothing. Never in his life had he felt this alone.

Ice and Mouse had trailed out behind him, apparently not afraid he would try to escape. Escape to where?

"How far is it to the mainland?" Ukiah asked them.

Mouse glanced toward Ice. "Too far to swim, really it is."

Rennie had shown Ukiah a map of New England—yesterday? Tuesday? He'd been losing track of days since the cult entered his life. If they were north of Cape Cod, swimming west would get him to the mainland. If they were south of the Cape's peninsula, however, he could swim for days before reaching land.

What should he do?

Ukiah retained enough of Rennie's memories to know that, in his place, Rennie would have tried to kill as many of the cultists as he could before they took him down, snarling and biting. Animal's recent death, however, strengthened Ukiah's abhorrence of killing a human. And even if he wanted to kill the cultists, he wasn't sure he could—so far they were seriously outclassing him in fighting.

What would Max do in his situation? Try as he might, Ukiah couldn't imagine Max ever being mistaken for an angel by homicidal Christians.

Atticus? His brother would pretend to cooperate, gather information, and wait patiently for the chance to put it to use.

Mouse nervously gestured to the kitchen door. "Come. Get some food."

Ukiah's stomach clenched tight on the thought of food, so he let himself be led back into the house to eat. The seating at the table had obviously been carefully planned. Ice took the thronelike chair at the head of the table—angel or not, the new cult leader wasn't giving up his position to Ukiah. Surprisingly, it was quiet Mouse that sat to Ice's right, and Ether to his left. The remaining cultists sat in the ten chairs flanking the table.

The only chair left open for Ukiah was the one at the foot of the table. Ukiah sat, wondering whose place he was filling. Core's? No, he would have been at the head in the throne, with Ice to his right.

"Let us say grace." Ice held out his hands to Mouse and Ether.

The cultists joined in a chain of hands and burly Meta and diminutive Qwerty shyly held out their hands to Ukiah. He eyed them uneasily for traces of Invisible Red and could see no telltale glitter. He reached out and clasped them loosely.

"Our Father, who art in heaven," Ice prayed aloud. The other cultists had closed their eyes, but Ice kept his cold blue stare on Ukiah. "We—your chosen, your holy warriors—give thanks for our daily bread and the new weapon you've put in our hands. Guide us to use him wisely. Watch over us and protect us as we face evil. Amen."

Ukiah silently said his own prayer. *Oh, God, help me find the Ae before these idiots do something stupid. Amen.*

"Amen," the cultists echoed.

The cult had been taking advantage of the sea and land; the table was laden with lobster bisque, baked cod, late squash, roasted potatoes, and pumpkin bread. For several minutes the food sucked in all his attention. Luckily the soup came first, and after its jolt of creamy calorie richness, he managed to pull his focus back to the cultists.

They'd been watching him with a mix of shy reverence and intense curiosity. Silence reigned at the table, broken only by the chime of silverware on china and the soft slurping of soup.

"So, if you . . . know"—Ukiah almost said "think" but decided that "know" was a safer word—"that I'm an angel, why did you attack me? What is it you want from me?"

"We need your help," Ice said. "Or at least, we hope you can help us. Can you speak the language of the demons?"

"Of course he can." Mouse flinched from the hard look Ice gave him. "Well, he's an angel."

Was it safe to admit he did, or was this another test? "I don't understand. There aren't any demons here."

"We have recordings of their conversations," Ice said. "We knew from the start that it would be suicide to try to take out the demons where they nest. Studying their habits, finding their weaknesses, and exploiting them are the only intelligent methods."

Ukiah nodded at the soundness of this.

"By doing statistical modeling," Mouse said, "we've identified certain patterns in their behavior."

"The number of the beast is six-six-six," Ether said with bright eyes.

"Um, yeah." Mouse was momentarily derailed. "What

that means is that the demons usually perform any function in a collective of six."

"Unless a demon is trying to pass as a human—then they go solo," Ether inserted.

Mouse bobbed his head to agree that this was true. "Six of these collectives gather into nests for a total of thirty-six individuals typical for any one nest. And each geographic area will have six nests, arranged in a hexagonal figure."

"So any one occupied area will have two hundred and sixteen demons," Ice said. "And we can't take on that number by ourselves."

This was news to Ukiah. While Hex acknowledged that he was most comfortable as six individuals, Ukiah suspected that the adherence to the multiples of six was totally unconscious. With their memories of the Ontongard, the Pack assumed they knew everything they needed to know about their enemy without realizing there were things that the Ontongard didn't know about themselves. "You mapped the nest locations and noticed a pattern?"

"There seems to be some variation to that which might be caused by geographic anomalies." Mouse rearranged the silverware, stealing some from those near him, to form a six-sided figure of forks and knives. "Normal hexagon." He placed a saltshaker at one point, and then dimpled the lines of that corner. "One with a body of water, highways, or whatnot in the way."

"Mouse, I'm sure he knows all this," Ice said.

Apparently there were some drawbacks to pretending to be a perfect being.

"Well, I just want to make sure all our assumptions are sound," Mouse said. "This has all been guesswork."

Ice sighed and waved his hand, inviting Mouse to continue.

"Well, we experimented on burning them out of a nest to see how they chose nest sites." Mouse removed the saltshaker and reformed the hexagon. "We discovered that we could predict where they move to. Their movement is very simple and organic, and we created a computer program to mimic it. If you burn one nest, they'll abandon all the surviving nests except one to maintain the hexagonal shape and yet avoid the area of the destroyed nest." Mouse shifted the hexagon around the point that once held the saltshaker. "They always keep the nest farthest from the burn, rotating it in this manner."

Ice made a noise of disgust. "Destroying them would have been faster if we could have done a full assault on the nests."

"Their senses are very keen, so laying traps for them once they're settled in is nearly impossible," Mouse said. "Also there's the slight problem of getting into a nest after they establish it. But by being able to predict where they'll move to, we can prep a nest, bugging all the rooms and wiretapping the phones."

"The bugging devices are useless," Ice said. "They don't talk to one another. We think they have some type of telepathy that allows them to act as units without premeditating their actions."

"They do," Ukiah said.

"But they do use the phone," Mouse said. "We think there's a limited range to their telepathy, which the nests fall within. The only time they use the phone is to communicate with demons not at one of the nests."

"When we firebombed one nest, the other five nests reacted instantly," Ice said. "We did a hit-and-run operation and still barely escaped. They definitely have some type of ranged telepathy going on."

"They're very insectlike," one cultist noted. "Like bees in a hive making honeycombs, they exhibit the same behavioral patterns again and again. I'm not even sure that you could term them intelligent in the same manner that we classify humans."

"Let's not get into the intelligence fight," Ice snapped.

"They don't spend a lot of time talking on the phone," Mouse continued. "When they do, it's in a mix of English and demon tongue. What seems to happen is that they need to talk about something that doesn't have the equivalent English word available, and they switch into demon tongue until an English word will yank them back out. Because of their switching back and forth, we've been able to create a dictionary of sorts."

"But the conversations are cryptic," Ice complained. "It's more like they're dictating notes to themselves than having actual dialogue. Never any chitchat: How's the kids, what's the weather like."

Because in truth, Ukiah thought, *the telephone acts more like an artificial neuron, connecting two halves of the same brain, than a device that two very different people use to communicate.*

Schrödinger Five chose that moment to climb up his leg, all needle-sharp claws extended.

"Ow! Schrödinger!" Ukiah caught the kitten before he could wreak more havoc. "What? Are you hungry? Here." Ukiah offered a bit of his baked cod to the kitten, which it needed to sniff cautiously for a full minute before deciding it was fit to eat.

The cultists had gone silent. He looked up to find them watching him with nervous intent. Letting him live, he suddenly realized, was a supreme act of faith and courage for them—they knew what a Get was capable of. His existence had balanced completely on the well-being of the kitten. They watched now—with bated breath—to see if they'd been wrong.

Blissfully ignorant of his importance, Schrödinger rumbled into a tiny, contented purr.

"I'm not one of them." Ukiah carefully selected another bite of fish for the kitten.

"You are too gentle to be one of them." Ice was a man whose vision was limited by his belief. He knew evil, recognized it at a distance. But his universe contained only two types of good: human and angel. He had seen Ukiah as wholly human until proved otherwise—but that left only angel. Apparently, though, common sense was warring with his beliefs; he sounded dubious even as he confirmed that Ukiah wasn't a "demon."

"You recorded their conversations." Ukiah distracted him back to the Ontongard.

"Yes." Ice delayed saying more by taking a bite of his cod and chewing it thoroughly. After carefully choosing his words, he continued. "The conversation gives us glimpses of their plans, but it's like a large jigsaw puzzle, flung out onto the ground and then partially obscured. We've been picking up the pieces, turning them this way and that, trying to fit them together and usually failing."

"Actually, part of the problem is that there are several puzzles all mixed together." Mouse seized the analogy.

"We think." Ice cautioned Mouse with a look. "For example, they suddenly moved a seed nest to Buffalo. We saw it as an opportunity to learn more, and followed. The demons there did extensive land surveys, apparently testing the stability of the area. They killed several key employees of the local electric company. They infiltrated a truck dealership. They secured warehouses in the middle of nowhere and shipped in extensive supplies of cable and wire. There were only thirty-six demons, and we raided the nest when we knew it was practically empty. We were hoping for written plans, records, anything that would give us an idea what they were planning. Nothing."

Because the Ontongard's ability to pass on perfect memories negated the need for written plans.

"They referred to Buffalo with a word we haven't been able to translate," Mouse said, and then he cleared his throat and attempted the word, a rough guttural bark.

"No," Ether said. "It's more . . ." She got the pronunciation right and Ukiah recognized the word: Landing site/invasion point.

"You know what it means." Ice leaned forward, his gaze intense. "Tell us."

The Ontongard must have planned to land the seed ship at Buffalo and tap into the extensive power grid of Niagara Falls. Luckily, the Pack had triggered the ship's self-destruct, and all their plans were now moot. But explaining the ship to the cult, who believed the Ontongard were demons, perhaps wouldn't be wise.

The cult stirred, put into disquiet by his silence.

"Ah, it . . . it's got a lot of meanings . . . if that's really the word they were using." Ukiah wished for his brother's smooth lies. He decided on the less specific of the meanings. "I think they were using the word that means 'invasion point.' They planned to launch a massive assault from Buffalo."

"Planned," Ice echoed. "But something happened in Pittsburgh. Things went very wrong for them. And you were there."

What to tell them? He was a horrible liar. He decided to stick to a version that Max and he created to tell authorities. "They stumbled into me. They attempted to kill me and they kidnapped my son."

"And the others? Your foster father? The female FBI agent? Are they angels too?"

"No!" Ukiah bolted to his feet, spilling the kitten out of his lap. "Leave them alone!"

The cult reacted with impressive speed. Even before the kitten hit the ground, all the cultists had weapons drawn and pointed at him.

Ukiah put up his hands, warning off their attack. "Wait!" And when the cultists didn't fire, he continued, trying to keep his voice level. "They're human. You mustn't harm them. If you hurt them, they're not like me—they won't survive what you've done to me! Please don't involve them."

"We'll leave them in peace as long as you cooperate with us." Ice motioned for him to sit. "Eat, and then we'll start working."

Ukiah sat stiffly and ate only because he would need the food later, after he learned where the Ae were stored.

After a tense dinner, the cultists split into two groups. Ice, Mouse, Ether, and Link herded him like shepherds with a flock of one into the living room, which was crowded with computer equipment. The rest stayed to clear the table and relieve those who hadn't eaten yet.

They indicated where Ukiah should sit, and Mouse settled nervously beside him.

"We've got hours of recordings, broken up into shorter sound bites to make them easier to handle." Mouse handed him a headset. "What we're going to do is play a recording for you to translate. Speak into this microphone. It's hooked to that computer there with speech-recognition software. It will type in your translations as you talk."

"Okay." Ukiah slid the headset on. The word "okay" appeared on the monitor beside him.

"Here's the first." Mouse opened a folder labeled "Angel" and clicked on the first file.

A man spoke, in Hex's emotionally dead voice, a phrase in the Ontongard language: "Returning/rejoining/regrouping at gathering/den/nest."

"The speaker is returning to the nest," Ukiah said, and the words wrote themselves on the text.

Mouse glanced to Ice, who nodded. "All right, and the next one?"

They played through eleven more segments, growing longer in length, but of no great importance; all in Ontongard with no English intermixed. The speakers changed, but not the tone or delivery. Played back-to-back, it was like listening to a dozen people trying to mimic one person. Mouse

nodded as Ukiah translated them, as if he already knew what
the clips contained.

They were testing him, Ukiah realized. They were seeing
if he actually understood the language and was not just making up random comments.

After the last one, Mouse looked again to Ice. "He nailed
them all."

"Good, good." Ice swung a chair around and straddled it,
facing backward. "Play him the last call we managed to
record."

Mouse closed the "Angel" folder and picked a program
off the toolbar via an icon of a reel-to-reel tape deck. The re-
sulting program quickly scanned through the selected
recording, did a voice recognition on the speakers, produced
photographs of a young black woman and a middle-aged
white man, and rendered out a complex 3-D tree of colored
nodes. The woman was identified as Demon BU1-623-S,
alias unknown, and the man as Demon B3-215-S, alias Peter
Caldwell.

"What are the numbers for?" Ukiah tapped the numbers
for the man and was startled as a window opened giving
more information: Peter Caldwell, six-one, a hundred and
sixty pounds, brown hair, blue eyes. Nest: Caldwell and Associates Engineering, Totten Pond Road, Waltham.

"The first set is the nest they belong to." Mouse closed
the window. "This is a demon from one of the Buffalo nests,
speaking to a Boston nest."

"Since they rarely travel solo," Ice said, "a nest number
gives us a truer idea of their movements."

Mouse nodded and tapped the last part of the identifying
number. "The S indicates that these are Speakers, which
means they're the ones who usually do the phone calls for
their collective. We thought this meant the Speakers were
also the leaders, but we learned they're kind of like salmon
swimming upstream. They all react—individually or as a
mass—in identical fashion to whatever predetermined goal

they currently have locked into their collective brain. Killing the Speakers doesn't throw them into confusion."

"But it means one well-designed trap," Ether said, "presented to them individually, will trap them all."

"It's the only way we can hope to fight them," Ice said.

Phone numbers were shown. The Buffalo Get was using a phone in Butler, Pennsylvania; the Boston Get was in Waltham, Massachusetts.

"I am in Butler," the Buffalo Get reported. "Ae missing, not destroyed, thief unknown. New incursion of aware hosts discovered. Partial Get recovered."

"That's what they call us: aware hosts," Mouse said as Ether added, "We think they're talking about Eden."

"Neutralize," the Gets harmonized as they agreed on a course of action.

"Neutralized," the Buffalo Get stated.

The Ontongard then bombed Eden Court, reducing the grand mansion to smoking rubble.

"This part we don't understand," Ice murmured.

"Female host has interacted with breeder," the Buffalo Get said.

"Prime's breeder?" the Boston Get asked.

"Prime's," the Buffalo Get said.

"Capture and contain," the two spoke in duet.

"Contained female," Buffalo reported. "Incubation, nine months."

"Incubate." Again the duet.

Ice leaned in, stabbing a key to pause the conversation. "What are they talking about? Ping is the only female missing."

Ukiah had avoided all thoughts of Ping and the night he spent with her and Core. Beyond the raw emotions of his rape lay the whole ugly inevitability of conception; he was a breeder and she had been all but painted with the breeding drug, Invisible Red. All the implications—from Indigo's reaction to another woman bearing his baby to the Ontongard holding Ping—and therefore his unborn child—churned in his stomach like icy snakes.

"Well?" There was fear and hurt, but also steel resolve in Ice's eyes.

"They have Ping," Ukiah admitted. "She's pregnant. They're keeping her alive and untouched until she has the baby."

"So she hasn't been possessed?" Ice asked.

"No."

As Ice relaxed, Mouse restarted the recording.

"Breeder contamination/infection/adaptation detected in one male," the Buffalo Get reported in Ontongard. "Survival possibility excellent."

Breeder contamination? Core was dead, and he was the only male Ukiah had interacted with for any length of time. They had to be talking about the missing Parity—but how? True, high on Invisible Red, Ukiah had nearly choked the boy to death, but that was just minutes before the Ontongard captured Parity. There couldn't possibly have been enough time. Ukiah flashed back to the beating he gave Parity in the hall. Wait, the contamination was already in Parity's blood . . .

Mouse had paused the recording and the cultists looked at him expectantly.

"What did it say?" Ice demanded.

How could Parity already have been infected? Realization dawned on Ukiah. "Did Parity handle my son at any point?"

"The nephilim?" Ice looked surprised at the question. "Yeah. It bit him in the leg; he needed stitches. Why?"

"They're planning to possess Parity; he's probably one of them now. Anything he knew, they now know."

Which included everything about him and Kittanning.

"Shit," Link hissed. "At least he was just an initiate."

Ice looked troubled but signaled Mouse to continue the recording.

"Contain breeder," Boston said.

"Current whereabouts of breeder unknown," Buffalo reported. "Aware hosts more dangerous than previously thought."

"They must not be allowed to interfere with the priority project," Boston and Buffalo stated together.

"Returning to confer," Buffalo said, and hung up.

"This was Saturday morning. There haven't been any more phone calls."

"Does Parity know about this place? Sanctuary?"

The cultists looked at each other.

Mouse shook his head. "No. Until the demons hit Pittsburgh, Sanctuary was restricted to inner circle only."

"Ping knows where it is," Ether pointed out.

"She wouldn't talk," Link said.

"She's alone with the demons," Ether said. "She has to be scared shitless. Who knows how long she can hold out?"

"Go check on the fortifications," Ice said wearily. "All of you."

"All?" Mouse squeaked like his namesake.

"Yes, go on," Ice said.

Cultists scurried off to obey him, leaving Ukiah alone with Ice.

Ice sighed. "We got back to Butler to find Eden on fire. I parked across the street and walked through the gardens. Crowds of people had gathered; the entire neighborhood had come to watch the great house burn. I saw *them* standing in the crowd, like ravens among mourning doves, only no one seemed to notice them. Like they were blind to the evil beside them. There were bodies sprawled on the grass, covered with white sheets, stained with bright red flowers of blood. I couldn't tell who it was—Core, Ping, Io—but there was nothing I could do but turn and walk away."

Ice fixed his cold stare on Ukiah. "Where were you while it burned?"

"I was flying to Pittsburgh." Ukiah had managed to escape to the nearby Butler Memorial Hospital. The fireball from Eden going up had convinced the staff to fly Ukiah via the Lifeflight helicopter to Mercy Hospital in Pittsburgh. All things considered, it had been a fortunate decision.

Ice's eyes widened slightly at the news. "Oh, demons can't fly—but I guess that's part of being an angel."

Ukiah swallowed down an automatic "I meant by helicopter." It would be best not to shake the cult leader's belief.

Luckily, Ice was cuing up another recorded telephone conversation. "We'll step you backward from Saturday. We want to know what this priority project they're working on is."

"Tell me first, where are the founts?"

Ice stopped what he was doing to give Ukiah another cold look. "Why?"

"The demons created the founts for the sole purpose of wiping out humans." If the Ontongard found the highest order of native life on a planet too difficult to take over, they used the Ae to design a species-specific disease and wiped them out—settling for a less advanced species as a host. Since their own intelligence depended on their host, the Ontongard were reluctant to take such a drastic step. "They were holding them in reserve because they thought their invasion at Buffalo would work. They had been planning for centuries for that day, and until June they thought they would win."

"So why did they wait until September to check on them?"

Why indeed? With the FBI and the cult being new pressures on the Ontongard, why hadn't they acted?

"I don't know," Ukiah admitted. "But the founts are deadly. You can't use them. Don't even try."

"We've identified over a thousand demons, and managed only to kill less than a hundred. They have superhuman strength and speed, and now we learn they have telepathy. They can take massive damage and regenerate. Last Thursday we were fifty people; now we're down to twenty, and we're being hunted by demons that know all our secrets. We need to strike first, and strike hard, or we're not going to survive."

"The founts are too dangerous. You could accidentally kill everything on the planet."

"Core had a saying that truly applies: Would God give us the gift if he didn't mean for us to use it?"

Ukiah stared at him, horrified. "You can't be serious."

"God put Core at the car accident where he learned about the demons. He connected Zip with Core to give us access to the founts. A thousand little connections had to line up just perfect for us to find the founts and learn how to make them work. The chances were billions to one, and yet, we have the founts. Isn't that a miracle enough?"

What was the nature of miracles? Did the happenings have to be impossibilities, or merely extremely unlikely? Certainly it was stunning what the cult had accomplished, from decoding the Ontongard language to making advanced technology work without instructions. Ukiah could not believe, though, that God wanted the destruction of humanity.

"It's too dangerous," Ukiah said again. "You have no idea what you're doing. You're just guessing at this."

"Then help us. Surely God put you into our power so that we can use you."

He opened his mouth to say no, but then remembered that Atticus would play along, gathering information. He considered the computers around him, filled with the cult's databases. The cult didn't seem to realize that the Ontongard had genetic memory with perfect recall. While he had talked with Ice, he also overheard a conversation in the kitchen, and shouted instructions from the cultists outside.

And if he couldn't find the key to stopping the Ae, maybe he could keep the cult from misusing them.

"I am helping you," he said.

CHAPTER THIRTEEN

Temple of New Reason Commune, Sanctuary Island,
Atlantic Ocean
Thursday, September 23, 2004

Ukiah worked through the night, translating and learning about the Ontongard and the cult. The island acted as the cult's ultimate data haven, with high-speed satellite Internet service and IP telephony. The last was a frustrating temptation. The phone sat on the desk beside the monitor he used, but since he didn't know where the island lay, he wasn't sure if calling out would have any point. GPS in regards to phone service was on the crumbling edge of his knowledge of technology. Part of his ignorance came from the fact that he was still fairly new to civilization. The rest was due to his lack of interest, until three months ago when he had received Rennie's memories, in learning all of the bells and whistles life had to offer. He knew land-based phones and cell phones could be traced, but IP telephony? He didn't know. He ached to find out, but the cult never left him alone.

He was dealing with the same type of problem with the translations. While in Oregon, he had noticed that his Pack memories were disintegrating, his "borrowed" memories being crowded out as he grew toward being a full adult. The Ontongard had been guiding technology development in dozens of small high-tech firms across the country, each one building tiny parts to be shipped to Boston to be assembled into something much larger. After the pieces had shipped, the Ontongard were dismantling the companies to keep their secret. But he was at a loss as to what they were building. Either he had never had the knowledge, or it had worn away over the months of hard living and dying.

But the most terrifying hole was in the last twenty-four hours, there was a tiny gap of what he had done between Animal dying and calling Max.

He had lost a mouse.

Or the cult had stolen it.

Neither was good.

He found excuses to roam the house: going to the bathroom, getting something to drink, raiding the refrigerator, stretching his legs by pacing the large living room. On these forays he couldn't sense any of his mice, but a small collection of cells had a limited range to their telepathy. Whereas he could spot Atticus anywhere on the island and the combined Dog Warriors from miles away, he would almost need to stand on a single mouse to sense it.

In desperation, he insisted that he *knew* that Schrödinger needed to be outside to go to the bathroom, claiming inside angel knowledge, and that he could use some fresh air. The cult reluctantly agreed, but tripled his guard, kept him within fifty feet of the house, and sent Mouse along as an escort. The night was cold and clear. To the west, the moon gleamed on the ocean like a massive field of silver flowers. He was thankful the kitten did its part to uphold his ruse and buried its waste in the loose sand. Ukiah circled the house, using up his hoarded gum, picking up occasional bright pebbles to examine. The cult had drawn heavy black curtains on the expansive windows, keeping in the light so no passing boats would realize people were living on the island.

"It's really not safe out here in the dark." Mouse shivered in the freezing wind. "We've got land mines everywhere."

Ukiah slipped his most recent find—a thumb-sized disk of matte black stone—into his jeans pocket, picked up

Schrödinger, and went back in, none the wiser on the location of his mouse.

As they walked into the house, the phone rang.

Mouse froze, a look of utter terror on his face as he stared at the phone. It rang again, the noise jarring in the sudden stillness of the house.

Ice came running down the stairs and paused at the bottom of the steps. "Was that the phone?"

The phone rang in answer.

"We're all here," Mouse whispered.

Ice approached the phone with caution and snatched it up as if it were a poisonous snake, barely holding it to his ear. "Hello?"

Ukiah's keen ears caught the voice on the other end.

"Ice? Is that you? It's Parity."

"Parity?" Ice gasped as if punched.

"Parity. Only Parity—no one else. None of them. But listen—they know where you are! They're coming to get you. They're pissed as hell and they plan to make you all one of them."

"H-h-how?"

"It was so hard to think straight at first. I had to tell them something so I gave them some old addresses—places I knew you wouldn't be. I told them about the boat slip. When we found the wolf boy there, I managed to slip away long enough to clear out my head."

"How do they know about the island?" Ice growled.

"Ping—Ping told them. They've got her at Totten Pond. I haven't been able to get to her. She said something about the wiretapping. They traced the tap back to the satellite provider and you're the only connection within miles of that GPS position."

Ice glanced upward as if to see the satellite overhead, pinpointing them.

"You've got to move before they get there. They'll be

there in force—like a hundred of them. You've got to get out! I'll get hold of you later, somehow. I've got to go."

The phone clicked to silence but Ice stood there with the phone to his ear for another minute, pale and stunned. Finally he hung up, whispering hoarsely, "They know where we are. Start an evacuation."

The cultists remained still, reflecting his shock.

"Where are we going to go?" Ether finally asked.

"I'll think of something," Ice said. "Go on. Grab only the bare necessities and get them down to the boats."

"We just believe him?" Link said.

"We don't have a choice." Ice sighed heavily.

Link started to protest, "But he didn't sound like one of—"

"Move!" Ice shouted, and flung the phone at Link.

The cult scattered like a flock of frightened birds.

Ice focused on Ukiah. "Is it possible? Could he be one of them—and yet not be?"

Prime had been a mutation—a sole individual—but they didn't know why. What had caused Prime to be different? If Parity had been exposed to Kittanning, the Ontongard, and Invisible Red, maybe he had built up a resistance.

"Yes or no?" Ice hissed.

Ukiah replayed the conversation with Parity, listening to the words and the tone of voice. There had been a slight drag, but it wasn't Hex's emotionally dead intonation. There had been fear, sorrow, and true concern—things a Get seemed incapable of understanding despite its human form, its original personality drowned under Hex's alien mind. "Yes. He might be something new."

"Do you know what they're building yet?"

"No."

Ice gave a weary sigh. "We're running out of time, angel."

•   •   •

An hour later, Ice declared that ready or not, they needed to leave. "Meta, get the angel down to the boat."

The tall, burly cultist caught Ukiah's elbow and guided him toward the door. Ukiah snatched up Schrödinger, determined that the kitten wouldn't be left to the mercy of the Ontongard.

Outside, Ice pulled Mouse aside, saying, "Link, we're all out of the house. Set the defenses and come down to the boats."

"Keep to the path." Meta urged Ukiah down the hill to the boathouse. "It would be inconvenient if you got blown to pieces now." .

Ukiah wasn't sure if Meta was teasing him or not, but kept to the graveled path. Ice and Mouse trailed behind, arms over each other's shoulders, heads close together, deep in whispered conversation.

There seemed to be some kind of preplanned system, as the twenty cultists split themselves in orderly fashion between the two boats. Ukiah found himself firmly escorted to a boat called the *Ashpool.*

Ice and Mouse stood on the dock, the younger man crying openly.

"We're going ahead with the Cleansing," Ice said. "Take the angel and go south."

"South?"

"As far south as your diesel will get you."

Link came dashing down the path. "Everything's set," he said, and scrambled on board the *Nautilus.* The engine revved up and the boat started to pull away from the dock.

Ice hugged Mouse fiercely, kissing him on the forehead. "Go on. Live for us."

Ice jumped onto the *Nautilus* and the boat leapt forward away in a spray of water.

Ukiah was on the wrong boat to stop Ice.

•   •   •

They went south as fast as the *Ashpool* would take them, the cultists silent as the big engines roared. The *Nautilus* was nowhere in sight, and the island quickly vanished behind them. Ukiah huddled in the corner of the stern's sitting area, with Meta in the opposite corner, keeping close watch on him.

He'd screwed up. He should have done something, anything, although even now he wasn't sure what.

He considered his options. There was the radio, but he still didn't know where he was, where Ice was heading, nor where the Ae were, except they hadn't been loaded onto the boats. His chances of overpowering all ten cultists to steer the boat to land, which presumably lay off to the west, were laughable.

He eyed his guard. Meta was pale and unfocused, as if the heaving boat were making him seasick. Ukiah wasn't prone to motion sickness; after the first few minutes of jiggling, his body would ignore his inner ear as alarmist.

"Are you okay?" Ukiah shouted over the engine's roar. When Meta didn't respond, Ukiah leaned over to prod the cultist. "Meta?"

Meta's eyes rolled up to white and he went rigid, his arms and legs stiffening and starting to jerk rhythmically.

"Mouse! Mouse!" Ukiah eased Meta to the floor.

The little cultist appeared at the cabin doorway, swore, and hurried to Meta. "Oh, no, not again."

"What's wrong with him?" Ukiah made way for Mouse.

"It's Blissfire withdrawal!" Mouse turned and shouted for the other cultists. "Oh, God, please don't die, Meta. Please don't die."

Ukiah found himself pushed to the bow of the boat as the other cultists crowded around the fallen Meta. Qwerty had a small bag that she dipped her fingers into. She painted a glittering cross onto Meta's forehead, and then, as others pried open Meta's jaw, coated the inside of his mouth. It was doubtful Meta could be saved once the drug triggered its extermination subroutines, but apparently the cult had pulled others back from the brink, using a new dose of the drug to override the kill order. Qwerty kissed the unresponsive man, her tears falling on his face and the hands of the cultists holding him still.

Rolling thunder pulled Ukiah's attention away from the desperate scene. A 747 jet passed low overhead. Its flaps were up and its landing gear down. It vanished from sight over the shifting horizon, but he could hear the whine and roar as braking jets kicked in.

It was landing at Logan Airport. Boston was just over the horizon.

It felt heartless to take advantage of Meta's collapse, but it might be his only chance to slip away. He had to get to Boston. He had to stop Ice.

Grabbing the rail, he swung over the side and dropped into the ocean. He let himself sink for a moment, and then angled off so that when he surfaced, he was on the other side of the boat.

The cultists had stopped the boat. Mouse and other male cultists were scanning the rolling waves, presumably as the females worked to save Meta.

"Ukiah! Wolf boy!" Mouse shouted, as another male said, "I don't know how long angels can hold their breath. He might not even be down there anymore. He's an angel!"

Ukiah ducked under the water, kicked off his shoes, and swam until his lungs felt like they were about to burst, then surfaced again. He was alone in vast shifting waters with only the echoes of jets to guide him.

It was a lot farther to Boston than he imagined.

He found the first lobster trap by accident. A wave was rolling him down a plane of water as he swam and he saw a Tide detergent bottle floating in the water. Four years of Boy Scouts told him that detergent bottles made good floatation devices in a pinch. He detoured and caught hold of it, hugging it to his chest. It was a relief to float there, at rest in the chilly water. It would have been perfect, except the bottle was anchored to something far underwater. It puzzled him for a while until he realized it was a lobster trap and the Tide bottle was a buoy marker.

He bobbed in the waves, panting, weary, nothing but water in sight.

He'd been insane to leave the boat.

He knew he couldn't stay with the lobster trap buoy, but he didn't want to let go. It was starting to dawn on him that drowning was a real possibility. Strange, except for being hit by cars and shot, he'd never pushed his body to its limits before. Max had always been there, reining him in before he'd collapsed, shoving food into him, keeping him safe from his own stupidity. Any normal human wouldn't have jumped off a perfectly fine boat, blithely assuming he could swim to an unseen shore.

Atticus probably wouldn't have been so stupid.

What the hell did he think he could do once he got back to Boston? While the cult had unknowingly supplied him with information on the Ontongard, their plans remained a mystery. He had no money, no shoes, and no weapons. The Pack would have moved dens, making finding them nearly impossible. And it seemed unlikely, now, that he'd even survive to reach land.

He tugged at the knots tying the buoy to the trap, but tension and time had rendered them impossible to untie. He chewed at the rope, hoping to fray it, but several minutes of gnawing produced no noticeable effect.

Nothing to be done but abandon the tiny haven of safety and swim on.

There were a surprising number of lobster traps in Boston Harbor.

CHAPTER FOURTEEN

Atlantic Ocean
Thursday, September 23, 2004

Later Ukiah would recall the boat bearing down on him, and the blare of horns. As it was, though, the Coast Guard officer seemed to appear in the water beside him like magic. He was far too weary to do anything once they hauled him into their boat but huddle around the mug of hot cocoa they gave him.

"We're taking you to Mass General Hospital."

"N-n-no," he forced out between chattering teeth. "No hospital."

While hanging from lobster buoys, he had pieced together a plan. It was filled with things he had originally wanted to avoid, but facing death, they grew less unpleasant. Atticus was one of them.

"My brother—he's at the Boston Harbor Hotel." The Pack had plucked the hotel name from Atticus's memory during his test. "D-d-drop me there."

"We really should take you to the hospital. You're hypothermic."

"I-I-I'm fine," he told them. "P-p-please—hotel."

In the end, they dropped him on the wharf in front of the hotel. He squelched his way into the lobby and stood dripping on the marble floor as he waited for the elevator. It was easy to find out which floor Atticus and Ru were on—running his hands over the buttons inside the elevator, he found the one they'd pushed to get to their rooms. He went down the hall sniffing, smelling mostly the Atlantic Ocean soaked into his skin.

He found their rooms. Atticus wasn't there, but someone was moving around inside. Teeth chattering, he knocked on the door.

"Who is it?" Kyle called.

"U-U-Ukiah."

"Step back from the door," Kyle said.

Ukiah leaned against the far wall.

Kyle had his pistol in hand when he opened the door and scanned the hall. He relaxed once he saw they were alone. "Why are you wet?"

"I-I-I was swimming."

Kyle sniffed at the north Atlantic stench. "You need to clean your pool."

Ukiah laughed weakly.

"So, what do you want?"

"A sh-sh-shower and something to eat—f-f-find the cult—w-w-world peace."

"You mean, like, use our shower?"

Ukiah nodded, sniffing.

Kyle paced back and forth, trying to decide what to do. Down the hall the elevator dinged, signaling its arrival. The sound decided it for Kyle. He reached out, caught Ukiah by the shirt, jerked him into the room, and slammed shut the door.

"Okay. Okay. Everything's cool." Kyle motioned toward the adjoining room with a king-sized bed. "You can use Atticus's bathroom and I'll call room service."

It felt weird to be using Atticus and Ru's bathroom, the counter strewn with toothbrushes and combs and deodorant, the hotel's shampoo ignored in favor of their own. It seemed like an invasion of their privacy. Out of habit he fumbled through his pants pockets as he stripped. The cult had managed to strip him of his wallet yet again—the only things in his pocket were the gum wrappers and the pebble from Sanctuary Island. He dropped the gum wrappers into the trash, but the pebble slipped through his trembling fingers to land among Atticus's things, disappearing from sight.

Ukiah eyed the crowded counter. Where did it go? Under the toiletry bag? He lifted the corner of the bag and nearly knocked over a bottle of expensive aftershave. With a sigh, he abandoned it; he'd look for it once he stopped shivering.

Ukiah stood in the steaming hot water until he heard room service at the door. He stepped out of the bathroom, towel pinned around his hips, drying his hair, to find a stranger in the room with Kyle and the food.

The stranger glanced at Ukiah and made an exasperated noise. "Johnston's been telling me he didn't know when you were getting back."

Kyle looked over his shoulder at Ukiah in surprise. "But this isn't—"

"Zip it, Johnston," the stranger snapped. "Where the hell were you?"

Ukiah guessed that "the shower" wasn't the answer the stranger was looking for. "I was kidnapped by the Temple of New Reason."

"Where is your partner?" the stranger asked.

Partner? Ukiah froze. *What did he want with Max?*

"Takahashi is with the Coast Guard," Kyle said, making it obvious this man thought Ukiah was Atticus. "Out looking for . . . him. Hikaru will be back in a couple hours."

He felt guilty now that he had misled the Coast Guard into thinking he had only suffered a boating accident. They'd taken his name but apparently not checked if anyone was looking for him.

The stranger looked at his watch. "Fine. Call me when he gets back."

"Who the hell was that?" Ukiah asked after the door closed behind the stranger.

"Our boss. Sumpter. He came in with room service."

Kyle had ordered stuffed rabbit with peppers, pea shoots, and onions, three types of strong-smelling cheeses he didn't recognize even after several years of Max's tutelage; a plate of pistachios, macadamia nuts, and almonds; and lastly, chocolate desserts. Protein, protein, protein with a shot of pure sugar.

Kyle fidgeted in silence as Ukiah ate, and finally fell into report mode, as if he wasn't comfortable with carrying the main bulk of the conversation. "I sent your clothes down to be washed. They said they wouldn't be ready to be picked up until tomorrow morning." Realization dawned on him. "I guess I should get you something to wear until then."

Finally given a task, Kyle ticked down the needed clothes, providing T-shirt, boxers, sweatpants, socks, and a pair of tennis shoes out of Atticus's luggage. None of the suitcases were unpacked, only canted open, ready to be zipped shut and taken at a moment's notice.

"Where *is* Atticus?" Ukiah asked around a mouthful of the rabbit.

"He and Ru are out searching for you. The coast guard is flying them to various islands where the cult might be hiding."

Actually this worked well with his plans. Atticus didn't have Pack memory; he didn't know the dangers that the Ontongard represented to the world, so it was extremely unlikely he would help Ukiah raid one of their dens. Nor did Ukiah want to put his brother's "family" at risk, not when the Pack was available to help instead.

"Can I use the phone?" Ukiah didn't wait for permission, glancing at the instructions for getting an outside line and then dialing Indigo's number while Kyle was still trying to form an answer. Without a vehicle or money, his only hope of contacting the Pack was via whoever was guarding Indigo. Unfortunately, her number dropped him straight into voice mail. "It's me, Ukiah." He paused, not sure what else to say—he wasn't sure how long he'd be staying in Atticus's hotel room. "I got free of the cult and I'm safe. I'll call you back."

"I don't know—" Kyle managed to get out as Ukiah pressed the reset button and dialed Max.

"Bennett." Max answered the phone with a snarl worthy of the Pack.

"Max, it's me."

"Ukiah! Where the hell are you now?"

Ukiah explained about his kidnapping and escape, which got an "Oh, Jesus, Ukiah, you didn't!" from Max and a "You just jumped off the boat?" from Kyle, who up to this point had been pretending not to listen.

"You're lucky you didn't drown," Max snapped. "Who's there with you now?"

"Kyle," Ukiah said. "He's one of Atticus's best friends. He knows everything. Max, I know where the Ontongard are holding Ping."

"You want to rescue Ping? After what she and Core did?"

The curse of a perfect memory meant it took only one mention of his rape to shove Ukiah back to the night that Core drugged him with Invisible Red and shared him with Ping.

. . . candles lit the room to a soft glow. Ping knelt on the white satin sheets of the king-sized bed, dressed in a black robe so sheer it seemed to be only shadows. Core checked Ukiah just short of the bed, and Ping stretched with false casualness, the candles silhouetting her lithe form as she arched her back, lifting her breasts. To Ukiah's disgust, his body responded. He wanted to say no, but his mouth wouldn't shape the words. The breeding drug held his will captive, freeing his body to its artificial desires. He started to growl instead. Ping parted the gauze robe aside enough to reveal her sex, and it glittered with Invisible Red.

She stroked herself there, and lifted her damp, glittering fingers to him. "Come to me."

Ukiah's legs started to move, carrying him to her, while he could only snarl in helpless anger. A moment later, he felt Core's nude body beside him . . .

Ukiah pushed the memory away. "Yes, I want to rescue her."

He had had lots of time to think, out in the ocean. He hated her for using him, and that the child she carried could destroy his ties with the ones he loved most—Indigo and the Pack. But he didn't hate her enough to wish what the Ontongard planned for her. "She was part of the cult's inner circle. She knows all their secrets. She'll know where Ice has the Ae, and what his plans for 'the Cleansing' are."

"You're not thinking of doing this alone?" Max asked.

"I'm taking the Pack—once I find them."

"Good," Max said. "So where's this den?"

"I just have a street name, no number: Totten Pond Road."

Kyle sat down at his computer and started to type as Ukiah spelled it out to Max. "That's in Waltham."

"A fairly short segment of road," Max added.

Ukiah switched over to speakerphone and said, "According to the cult, there will be six nests in a hexagonal pattern. I've got street names for all six but none of the street numbers."

"So if we find the points that link all the street addresses into a hexagon—" Kyle started.

"—we'll be able to pinpoint the nests," Max finished.

Atticus had been building to a bitter rage for hours.

Much to his disgust, they'd spent the night with Zheng, sifting through the victims from the cremation site, building a profile. Kyle had been reduced to puppy love silliness with delight. The FBI agent, however, retreated behind her unreadable mask as they sifted through police reports and grisly photographs. Normally Atticus would have been only mildly annoyed by the two, but he found himself trying to fight off growing concern for Ukiah. He didn't want to care.

Nor was he happy with the shades of moral gray his team
was drifting into by working with the Pack. With undercover
work, the danger of sympathizing with the criminals ran high;
having met the Ontongard, though, he was no longer sure that
the Pack were the bad guys. He tried to keep in mind that their
job in this mess was to find the drugs and get them off the
street.

They pinpointed a surveying company in Watertown,
Massachusetts, outside of Boston, as a possible den for the
Ontongard. Three of the victims worked for the company, and
from there, relationships spiraled outward. The police already
suspected the company, citing "odd reactions to the news"
and "seems mentally unbalanced" in reports of surviving employees. Even with Zheng's reassurance that the Pack would
be able to tell the difference between humans and Ontongard,
it felt wrong to turn the information over to them without first
checking into it themselves.

But they'd run out of time.

They had missed the cult. Luckily, so had the Ontongard.
After several cautious flybys, the coast guard pilot landed
their Jayhawk helicopter on the cult's island refuge. The cult
had left dangerous presents behind, and the Ontongard had
tripped several. The boathouse in the small bay burned, a
charred body occasionally visible among the flames. The
walls of the living room were riddled with grapeshot, and
dried blood flecked the floor. Too little blood. Something
scurried on tiny feet among the overturned furniture and Atticus sensed small and vicious eyes watching him.

In the basement they found a windowless cell. Ukiah's
scent was on the bare foam pad. The cult had provided only a
litter box to use as a toilet. Of his brother, there was no sign
whether he left the island alive or dead, alone or with others.

Agent Zheng lived up to her reputation, cold and distant
and unreadable as a frozen lake. On the flight back to Cape
Cod Coast Guard Air Station, the hopeful Coast Guard copi-
lot proved immune to her chilly silence and grated on every-

one's nerves with his attempts to break the ice. The moment they touched down, the FBI agent fled the helicopter.

"Zheng!" Atticus ducked under the still-whirling blades.

"Later, Atticus," she shouted without so much as looking over her shoulder.

He jogged to catch up with her. "We need to talk."

"Not now." She focused on getting to her rental SUV parked next to his Jaguar, walking in long, purposeful strides.

"Wait." He caught her arm and pulled her to a stop. "Talk to me."

"I can't." She turned her head away from him, covering her face with her hand. "I can't even look at you!"

It felt like she'd slapped him. She had seemed so accepting of his alien heritage. What had happened to change her mind—or had she always felt this way, and everything had been a lie to get his team to help her?

She took deep, cleansing breaths. "I need some time alone," she cried into her palm. "I'll talk to you later."

He drove back to Boston, barely holding his anger in check. Knowing him well, Ru waited until they were no longer trapped in the small confines of the Jaguar before talking.

"You're worried about your brother, aren't you?"

"No!" Atticus snapped as they stepped off the elevator. "I don't know where the little brat is, but I'm sure he's fine."

He slid the card key into the lock of Kyle's hotel room, pushed open the door—and there was Ukiah, sitting in the corner wing chair. Thrown off balance, Atticus lost control of his anger. "What are you doing here?"

"Atticus," Ukiah said, as if surprised to see Atticus in his own room.

"How the hell did you get here?" Atticus slammed shut the door behind him.

"I swam."

"From the island?"

"No, out in the bay someplace."

"How long have you been here?"

"About an hour."

Atticus glared at Kyle, who flinched under the look.

"I tried calling you, Atty, but you must have been out of the range of any cell tower."

"Out in the middle of the ocean, yes." Atticus took in the fact that Ukiah was dressed in his clothes. The room smelled of roasted meat and expensive cheese. A room service cart set for one was shoved into the corner, well-gnawed bones the only evidence of what the meal might have been. "You've made yourself at home. Why did you come here instead of to the Dog Warriors?"

"I'm not sure where they are," Ukiah admitted. "And the Coast Guard—after they pulled me out of the water—were afraid I was hypothermic and wanted to take me to the hospital. When I told them you were here . . ."

"Useless fucks," Atticus said of the Coast Guard, to have found someone with an APB out on them and let them walk away.

"Are you okay?" Ru crossed the room to press a hand to Ukiah's forehead. "You're still a little cool."

"I'm fine." Ukiah took the mothering in good grace.

"You had us worried." Ru tousled his hair and Ukiah leaned against him, soaking in the affection. Atticus realized that the boy was emotionally raw after days of battering and isolation among his enemies; now with Ru, whom he counted as a friend, Ukiah sought solace.

Jealousy flared through Atticus. "You have a lot of nerve to come asking help from us after what you've done. The ambush at the beach house. Stealing the Pixie Dust."

Ukiah flinched as if struck. "I'm sorry about that." He stood up. "I'll pay you back for the food, and I'll swap you clothes once I get something else to wear."

"What are you going to do about Ping and the dens?" Kyle asked.

"What's this?" Atticus asked.

Ukiah stared at Atticus with his feral gaze that looked the whole way through him, and said nothing.

"We were pulling together information on the dens." Kyle held out a printout of an aerial photo, one building circled in red. "Using information your brother skimmed from the cult. We—he thinks they're holding Ping at an engineering firm in Waltham."

"You think you're going off, getting the Pack, and attacking this office building?"

"Ping will know where Ice has the Ae." Ukiah looked away but his pain was obvious. "And she's pregnant with my child."

"You're not going into an office building with those killers. If you think Ping is actually there, we'll call the FBI and the police and get an assault team set up."

"The Pack exists to fight the Ontongard. Why put humans at risk?"

"Because it's their world, their laws."

"The Gets will fight to the death—and then come back. They'll shatter down to mice to escape any prison cell. They'll infect any human who's jailed with them. You can kill them only with fire and poison, and human law doesn't allow that."

"So you conveniently leave humans in the dark so they can't ever deal with the problem themselves?"

That stumped Ukiah; he tried to brush past but Atticus caught hold of him. With the physical contact, Atticus's awareness of his brother expanded—the room service meal was the only reason Ukiah was still standing. The repeated attacks, the long, cold swim, the repeated dosing of various drugs, and perhaps even starvation in the barren cell on the island had him on the verge of collapse. If Ukiah went into the water in such bad shape, it was amazing he didn't drown.

"How are you going to find the Pack?" Atticus asked, his anger falling away to concern. "You'll probably drop over just outside the door."

"I'll make some phone calls." Ukiah tried to pull away.

Atticus tightened his hold; he couldn't let his feelings jeopardize his brother's life. "Don't be stupid. I'd rather work with you than argue with you."

The fight left Ukiah with a sigh that seemed born more from exhaustion than frustration. He leaned against Atticus. The smell of the ocean still clung to him, as if the water had seeped down to the bone. The tension between them temporarily resolved, the feeling of "this is right, this is good" resounding between them, echoes of an earlier happiness, when they were one. Atticus found himself holding his brother tightly, savoring the closeness like a starving man trying to make a morsel of food last.

It was then that Atticus realized that earlier, when Ukiah sought solace with Ru, it hadn't been Ukiah that he had been jealous of. *What idiocy.*

"You say that you think Ping is there," Ru said. "Why don't we scout the location, see what's there. The cult might have given you old information."

"It would be dangerous," Ukiah murmured into Atticus's shoulder.

"We are familiar with danger," Atticus said.

CHAPTER FIFTEEN

Ukiah eyed the Ontongard den with faint dismay. It was a huge redbrick cube of an office building. Four floors tall, and equally wide, it sat behind a moat of access roads, a parking lot, and landscaping. Its tinted windows hid its secrets from anyone curious enough to cross the moat and try to spy in.

"We should be able to sense the Ontongard from here," Ukiah told Atticus as they studied the building. Their uneasy alliance was holding, although Atticus had driven from downtown to this beltway suburb with savage speed. Ukiah envied not only his skill at handling the sports car in the pounding traffic, but also the ease with which Atticus dealt with bewildering detours, unfamiliar road signage, and a toll road that required you to fling quarters into an open bin to pass. The DEA agents laid siege to the nest with practiced efficiency. After a cautious drive-by, Atticus pulled in near the front doors. Kyle parked across the parking lot in the Explorer, disassociated from the Jaguar, but connected by radio.

"I don't feel anything." Atticus's voice was flat with hostility.

"That's what I mean," Ukiah said. "Even if there were

only one Get inside, at this distance, we should be able to tell."

"If no one's home, let's have a closer look." Still Ru waited for a slight nod from Atticus before getting out.

The foyer was a vast, two-story room with a bulky receptionist's desk. Two visitor's chairs sat close to the front doors, as if visitors were encouraged to leave.

The receptionist herself was another surprise: a pixie-small girl, thin and nearly sexless. Her hair was cut and styled into spikes, and dyed a vivid purple. A collection of gold loops dazzled in her ears, right eyebrow, and left nostril. She wore a silk tunic that matched her hair, black leggings, and cowboy boots.

Despite her outlandish appearance, when she answered the phone with "Good morning, Peter Caldwell and Associates," she sounded as smooth and polished as any receptionist Ukiah had ever heard.

"Is she one of them?" Ru whispered to Atticus.

"I don't think so," Atticus said. "My spider sense isn't tingling."

"She's human." Ukiah walked to the desk and his brother and Ru fell in beside him so that they made an impressive array as the receptionist finished taking a message and glanced up.

"May I help you?"

"I'm Agent Takahashi." Ru showed the girl his ID.

"Oh, shit," she said. "I knew this job was too good to be true."

"We have information that a kidnapped woman is being held here." Ru tucked his ID away before she could see that he was DEA, not FBI. "We need to search the premises for her."

"Don't you need a warrant for that?"

"Not in a kidnapping. Can you tell me how many people are currently in the building?"

"I'm not sure." She shrugged. "This is all of the building

I usually see outside the john. People come and go—I'm not allowed to check ID or anything on them. They have new hires all the time, but after a few days they call in sick or. . . You know, this is a really creepy place to work. I knew something was wrong when they put *me* on front desk."

"What were you going to say about new hires?" Atticus asked.

"This is going to sound weird, but it's like attack of the pod people here. Bright and happy people turn into shuffling zombies in less than a week, or they just don't come back."

"You've never called the authorities?" Atticus sounded annoyed.

"Oh, yeah, like I'm a pillar of the community that the police are going to listen to about zombies from Mars."

"We're looking for this woman." Ukiah showed her Ping's photo.

"I haven't seen her." She eyed them. "Am I in trouble?"

"No, but we would like you to give us your name and address and then go home. Nor would it be wise for you to return. Your employers are dangerous men."

"Oh, I'd believe that of upper management. Most of Engineering and Accounting are okay. They're up on the second floor."

"No pod people?"

"Yeah, zombie-free zones. Just major geeks. Third floor is iffy. No one but pod people go up to the fourth floor. Past the elevator lobby, the doors are locked with card keys."

Her name was Sonya Barnes, and she gave her address in a town called Natick, which looked like *Nat*-ick to Ukiah but she pronounced it as *Nay*-ick and had to spell it for Atticus.

"I don't know if this means anything," Sonya said. "But there was a mass exodus a little while ago of the pod people."

"What time?"

"About two hours ago."

Had the cult attacked one of the dens, triggering the On-togard to abandon the rest?

"If they're moving their . . ." Ukiah paused, as Ru and Atticus both glanced hard at Sonya to remind him that she was listening to their conversation. ". . . hideout, they might have taken Ping with them already."

"We'll see." Atticus frowned at the near slip.

The DEA agent walked Sonya to the door to prevent any other slips.

"Fourth floor?" Ukiah asked.

"Let's evacuate the civilians first." Atticus shook his head, his annoyance feeling like a coat of thorns. "Just in case we get in a shoot-out."

The elevator slid open to the scent of death and Onton-gard. Ukiah growled softly as the familiar reek triggered generations of hate. He went to step off the elevator, but Atticus checked him.

"Wait," his brother commanded, pistol in hand. Ru held the door as Atticus cautiously checked the lobby beyond. "Okay. We're clear."

"Roger that," Kyle whispered from the nearly invisible earbud that Atticus was wearing.

There was a security door with a card-key lock.

"What's bugging you?" Atticus asked Ukiah as Ru produced a small electronic lock pick.

"There's something freshly dead up here." Ukiah wondered how Atticus could miss it.

Atticus sniffed deeply and then nodded slowly.

The door clunked open. Ukiah tracked death through the maze of offices and hallways. Atticus trailed behind, a bristling presence. In a small windowless supply room, they found Ping.

On the night of his rape, after Core had been called away, Ukiah had dragged himself off the sleeping Ping and showered away the drug's control. After tying up Ping, he fled the cult's commune, unaware that the Ontongard were zeroing in on it. The Gets must have found Ping as Ukiah had left her—bound and naked. They put the closest set of clothes on her: Core's black slacks and silk dress shirt, several sizes too large for her slight frame. To keep up her pants, the Gets had made the mistake of giving her a belt. One end of the belt was now tied to an overhead pipe, the buckle cinched tight around her slender neck. The slacks pooled on the floor under her dangling feet, while the shirt at least covered her body to her knees, preserving her dignity.

Ukiah stared at her, horrified, relieved, and ashamed of his relief. "Oh, God," he moaned; and stepped forward to take her down.

"No." Atticus caught him. "Don't disturb the crime scene."

"Poor thing," Ru whispered. "What do you think this mess on the wall means?"

After slicing her fingers on something sharp in her small prison, she had used the blood to paint her last message on the wall.

I misspoke and betrayed them all. Parity has fallen. God forgive me for what I must do.

Had she suspected why the Ontongard were keeping her untainted, or had she acted only to save herself from them? There were no answers on the blood-painted walls.

Above it was a word in the cult's phonetic spelling of an Ontongard word. Ukiah didn't recognize it until he sounded it out. *Zaeta.* But surely that couldn't be right.

No longer focused on the smell of death, other scents vied for his attention. He abandoned Ping to creep cautiously down another hall, following one smell in particular.

Atticus pulled him up short. "What is it?"

"Don't you use your nose?"

"Apparently not as much as you do," Atticus snapped.

"I can smell C-four. There may be a bomb up here."

"Did you hear that?" Atticus asked his teammates.

"I'll make sure the other floors are empty." Ru headed back to the elevator.

"Calling the bomb squad and signing off." Kyle's tinny voice came from Atticus's ear.

Atticus turned off his radio and then signaled Ukiah to continue. At the end of the hallway, though, Atticus suddenly caught hold of Ukiah's braid and dragged him backward. "Whoa, whoa, whoa, it's booby-trapped."

"It is?" Ukiah froze.

"The motion detector for the security system." Atticus pointed upward, not down at the floor where Ukiah had been focused. A cord dangled down off the corner unit. "We're not in its range, but we will be in a step or two."

"So how do we get around it?"

Atticus tugged on Ukiah's braid. "We don't. We leave it to experts."

"But . . ."

"Take it from your older, more experienced brother—don't play with bombs!" Atticus pulled him backward via the braid. "Come!"

Atticus didn't let go of his hair until they were on the elevator.

"The Ontongard normally don't bomb their own dens." Ukiah rubbed the back of his head where all the roots were complaining of his brother's rough treatment. "Things blowing up attracts more attention. Also, their means of communication is so loose, a returning Get is more likely to set it off than a human."

"Why did they leave in the first place?"

"If the cult attacked one of the other dens in the hexagon, then they would abandon all the rest except one."

Atticus swore. "Not the cult, the Pack. They went after a den in Watertown this morning while we went to the island."

The elevator door opened to the foyer. Through the tinted glass walls, as they walked toward the doors, they could see the police were arriving, several squad cars' worth.

"Let Ru do the talking." Atticus put a hand to Ukiah's shoulder as they walked out the door.

Ru had found some office workers, and he herded them across the parking lot to where the Jaguar and Explorer sat, screened by some low bushes. Atticus steered Ukiah toward the crowd. The police car passed Ru and pulled up to the building. Atticus ignored it, propelling Ukiah along.

"We got a call on a bomb threat," the officer called after Atticus.

"Yes, it's up on the fourth floor and it's booby-trapped!" Atticus shouted back, not stopping.

The policeman glanced at the building and then started after Atticus and Ukiah, leaving his cruiser behind, door open, lights flashing. "Were you the ones who called this in?"

Ukiah paused, only to have Atticus shove him forward.

"Yes! We found it!" Atticus kept walking.

"Hold on, I need to get your names, take your statement." The officer's hand was now riding his pistol grip.

"DEA! Agent Steele! And the number one rule of bombs, Officer, is clear the area."

As Kyle had the Explorer in the far reaches of the parking lot, they were now over two hundred feet from the building. The policeman paused, glancing back at the building and his cruiser in front of it.

"Don't you think this is a little excessive?" the policeman called.

The building exploded, floors flashing out like Chinese firecrackers, one after another. When the ground floor flared, the blast flipped the police cruiser like a toy. Atticus started to push Ukiah down and then they were both smacked to the ground hard; Atticus shielded him as the deafening noise, smoky heat, and flying glass blasted over them. Ukiah felt a dozen prickles of pain from Atticus as if they were his own.

The sound had been indescribably loud, and the silence afterward was shocking.

Atticus scrambled to the police officer while Ukiah's body was inclined to stay put—it seemed safer that way. The policeman got up, swearing, clearly no worse for the experience.

"Obviously," Atticus said, "it wasn't excessive enough."

The golden afternoon blurred with the arrival of fire trucks and police cars and various government agencies. Atticus tried to keep a hand on Ukiah at all times while fending off offers to take them both to the hospital. True, he had slivers of glass embedded in his back, making him feel as grouchy as a porcupine, but Ukiah withdrew alarmingly into himself. With another man, Atticus would have taken this as an attempt at duplicity, but he could feel his brother's endurance was thread thin and fraying.

He made his way toward the Explorer, pulling Ukiah along with him. Kyle was still holed up in the SUV, eyeing the crowd with dismay.

"You killed your earbud." Kyle reported, motioning to his own ear rather than touching Atticus.

Atticus found the remains dangling from his shoulder, a thin coat of his dead blood on it. Gingerly he explored his ear—a piece had blown off but it had found its way back. Unfortunately the earbud couldn't similarly repair itself.

"I've been trying to tell you," Kyle continued. "They blew the other four dens too."

Atticus glanced at the office workers being grilled by police about their missing employers. If his team hadn't evacuated the building for the expected gunfight, all seventy-some employees would have been in their offices when the bomb went off. The midafternoon time might have been chosen to ensure maximum kill. "Do they have any idea of a body count yet?"

"I called in bomb threats on all the addresses we had when you found this bomb."

"Good work!" Atticus gripped Kyle's shoulder.

Kyle grinned shyly at the praise, and then confessed, "Well, your brother stressed the symmetry of the dens, so I figured if they'd blow this one, they'd do the rest too."

Kyle had trusted a virtual stranger, someone he'd seen only twice and had every reason to mistrust, because he was Atticus's brother. Atticus supposed that was the nature of family, but he found it faintly alarming. In the old adage of blood and water, why did thickness make the fluid more trustworthy? Was Ukiah someone who could be trusted? Atticus had wanted to take the den with a SWAT team, but the plain truth was that the machines of justice moved slowly. Everyone in the six buildings would have been killed while they decided *how* to deal with perps who had already fled the scene. Would Ukiah's conviction that Ping was being held in the office building have been good enough to warrant a search? In the end, Atticus suspected, the law officers involved would have weighed their decision on the fact that Ukiah was his brother.

Atticus saw Agent Zheng stopped at the police barrier by a uniformed policeman. She showed her ID to pass it; another person of questionable reliability gaining automatic trust in the brotherhood of law officers. There had been a thawing of Zheng's arctic north; dismay registered as she saw the extent of the destruction to the office building. She spotted him and something passed through her eyes at the moment of recognition, a flicker of excitement then extinguished by something she saw in his face.

What was that all about? Did he communicate something to her without knowing?

She glanced past him and summer came to the arctic.

From behind him, Atticus *felt* an answering warm outbreak.

Ukiah—of course.

The two threaded through the crowd as if they were alone in a forest, the people around them no more interesting than trees. Ukiah took Zheng's hand, looked into her eyes, and a calmness washed over him.

"That explains much," Ru murmured in his ear.

Atticus glared at his partner.

Ru only laughed at him. "I've never seen a straight woman resist you so completely—but she's got her own little honeypot."

Ukiah's love was a deep current dragging Atticus along to places he didn't want to go. Beauty, they said, was in the eye of the beholder. Tainted by Ukiah's love, Atticus suddenly could see Zheng's glacial demeanor as Indigo's beautiful calm—serenity that all the world's madness didn't invade. A refuge.

For his brother, at least, this was the true thing, a love to die for. Did Indigo feel the same? Ukiah would give Indigo access to the Pack. It was easier to imagine her using his brother than her falling in love with him. Her strong self-control eliminated the obvious attraction: Ukiah's lean, well-defined body and handsome face. He was wolf silent with all-seeing feral eyes—what would they talk about?

"Distract Ukiah away from Indigo."

Ru looked at the two, isolated in a universe of their own making. "How?"

"I want five minutes alone with her. Think of it as a challenge."

Ru scoffed at the idea. "You owe me."

Atticus watched as Ru got Ukiah's attention by touching the bare skin of his wrist. With a smile and a nod toward the Explorer, Ru suggested that Ukiah change his torn and bloody shirt and get something to eat. Ukiah wavered, the suggestion of food fighting with his desire to be with Indigo.

With a glance toward Atticus, Indigo let go of Ukiah's hand. "Go on; I want to talk to Atticus."

They watched as Ru got Ukiah to the well-stocked Explorer before Indigo turned to Atticus.

"What is it you want?"

Uh-oh, busted.

"I want to know—do you love my brother, or are you just using him?" When she didn't react, he added, "I can promise you, one law officer to another, that anything you say to me won't be repeated."

"Normally I would say, one law officer to another, that it's none of your business."

"He's my brother."

"That's between you and him," Zheng said in her calm, unreadable way. "But your brother asked me to marry him. Last week I told him I had to think about it. This week I've been praying that I would have a chance to tell him yes." She gave him her Mona Lisa smile. "That makes you my brother-in-law. I'm telling you because that's between you and me."

She was marrying his brother? "What the hell do you see in him?"

"Only people who don't know him ask that question."

"I don't know my brother."

"Obviously." She considered him with a level look not unlike Ukiah's. "I can outthink, outshoot, outfight, plain out–brass ball most men. But men have this unwritten rule: The only women who are allowed to be stronger than them are their mothers. If you don't do the mothering routine, then they call you a grade-A bitch. With most men you can see it in their eyes as they try out the labels: hot babe, possible mother, bitch."

No, we don't have issues, do we? "And Ukiah doesn't."

"When I first met Ukiah, he looked at me, and saw *me*. Not the babe, the mother, or the bitch, just me. And I was hooked. The more I got to know him, the more I wanted him. He's the gentlest, most compassionate, wisest man I have ever met."

"Ukiah?" Those were three words that Atticus wouldn't ever have thought to apply to his brother; nor were they words that described Atticus either.

"If you spent any time getting to know him, you would see that for yourself." She said it as if it were a challenge. *I double-dare you.*

"How did you end up spending time with him?"

"He saved my life," Indigo said, and explained no more, except to add, "Believe me, there is nothing sexier than having a man save your life and then never mention it."

"So it is the hot monkey sex?"

She actually laughed and then sobered. "Sometimes it's like dating the Dalai Lama in the body of a young god. There might be a lot he doesn't know about the world, but his soul is old and patient."

"If he's so great, why didn't you say yes?"

She looked away to hide the sorrow in her eyes. "For reasons that seemed so trivial when the cult killed him and took his body."

It made him uncomfortable that he understood too well the terror that held. Of all the people who were trusting Ukiah just because he was Atticus's brother, the one he worried about most was himself. Atticus's world was too fragile to entrust it to a stranger with dangerous connections—FBI fiancée or not.

"I'm glad he went to you for help," Indigo said. "If he'd been here with the Pack, he'd have been arrested."

"He didn't want my help."

"Yes, he did; otherwise he wouldn't have come to you." Indigo reached out and took his hand. At the point of contact, Atticus felt Ukiah on her, but then lost the sense of his brother under his own touch—they were too identical for Atticus to keep separate. "And he needs you."

Atticus pulled his hand free. "I think you're confusing me with someone who gives a damn."

"Oh, this isn't the same man who no more than three

minutes ago was asking if my intentions were honorable or not?"

Sometimes keeping silent was the only safe answer.

"He's about to collapse. You're hurt too. If we're to stop these monsters, I can't take time to care for him, and if I leave him alone, the Pack will take him."

"So? He's a Dog Warrior."

"And so are you."

He glared at her, unsure of the truth. Was he?

Her eyes were gray as gunmetal. "He has a clean record, but if he'd come here today with the Pack, he'd have been arrested instead of praised. Please take care of him tonight."

All things considered, she was a good match for his brother in her ability to stare a person down.

"He can come with us. We've got an extra bed back at the hotel."

She rewarded him with a smile, and put away her steel-gray weapons. "Thank you."

Atticus decided they couldn't wait for food until they returned to the hotel. Changing shirts, they stopped at the first place at hand, a seafood place called Naked Fish on Totten Pond Road. Done in a décor of mustard yellow and splashes of purple, it featured Cuban cooking. The place was crowded with a wait for tables, but Ru—with the judicious use of a ten-dollar bill—got them seated immediately. Atticus didn't bother looking at the menu, knowing Ru would order for him. Ukiah scanned the menu with tired bewilderment while Kyle directed pouting glares at him. Obviously Kyle had also seen Indigo with Ukiah and wasn't taking the loss of his dream girl gracefully.

Ru looked up as the waiter appeared with a basket of rolls to take drink orders. "We know what we want. I'll take the crispy calamari salad, and they'll both take the *empanadas criollas de carne, gambas al ajillo,* the *valenciana* paella, and side orders of the plantains."

"They have plantains?" Atticus picked up the menu to scan it.

"What are plantains?" Ukiah asked.

"You'll like them," Ru reassured him, and ordered clam chowder and steak for Kyle. He finished with, "Two root beers, a Coke, and an iced tea."

The waiter eyed Atticus, who was clearly in pain, Ukiah on the verge of collapse, and Kyle pouting and then looked back to Ru. "Ooookay. I'll go get that order right in and bring your drinks, but we're really backed up. It's going to be a while."

Ukiah surrendered the menu. "What did you order us?"

"A beef turnover; shrimp; and a rice dish with shrimp, scallops . . . chicken and sausage and probably some stuff I've forgotten. Atty loves it; you should like it too."

Ukiah sighed, leaning his head against the wall behind him, eyes closed. "We don't have time for this."

"You're not up to anything but this," Atticus snapped.

After a long delay, Ukiah grunted, acknowledging it. He considered his bloodstained fingers. "I should wash. I have Ping's blood on my hands."

"I'll go with you—I need to go," Ru lied, probably guessing that in his condition, Ukiah would have a difficult time finding his way through the restaurant to the bathroom and back.

Atticus took advantage of their absence to fix Kyle with his gaze. "Kyle, I'm sorry about Indigo—but we've talked about this before."

"Yeah, yeah, I know. Someday I'll meet the girl of my dreams. Just got to keep looking. Blah blah blah." Kyle seized one of the hot buns and angrily tore small pieces from it. "It's not fair. The hot chicks are always already taken or they never even look at me. All you have to do—all your brother has to do—is walk into a room and they watch you."

Kyle jerked his head toward Ukiah, following Ru to the bathroom. Indeed, every woman who noticed his passing continued to, follow him with her eyes. Atticus had always been somewhat aware of the attention he received, but this time, being separate from the focus, he saw how profound the effect was. Ukiah seemed completely oblivious.

"You know it's nothing we can control. You just have to deal with it."

"Doesn't mean I have to like it." Kyle sighed. "You don't know how lucky you are to have Ru."

Across the room, Ru paused at the bathroom door and glanced back to the table. When their eyes met, Ru smiled.

"No," Atticus said. "I know exactly how lucky I am."

"If Ping is dead," Ukiah said once he and Ru returned to the table, "we're back to square one in finding the Ae."

"What about this word that Ping wrote onto the wall?" Ru asked.

Ukiah shrugged. "I think it's *zaeta,* which roughly means 'transmitter,' but that wouldn't make sense. She must have gotten the word wrong."

"Why?" Atticus asked.

"The *zaeta* works on a quantum level to achieve instant communication between star systems. It was developed by a race that had achieved three colonies in nearby star systems."

"Cool." Kyle's pout slipped away in the face of far-flung alien civilizations. "Why doesn't 'transmitter' make sense? E.T. phone home." This got a blank look from Ukiah. "They're sending messages back to the home world."

Ukiah shook his head. "No. You don't understand the Ontongard."

"Pretend we know nothing," Atticus said. "That shouldn't be much of a stretch."

"The Ontongard can't stay on one planet," Ukiah said. "Eventually they wipe out the ecology by becoming the ecology, and cannibalism follows. So they gear all the planet's industries toward building seed ships. They build thousands, until the planet's resources are depleted, and then they leave, each ship traveling on a different vector. It's completely blind. One ship might travel one light year to the next star system, and the next ship could travel thousands."

"So the transmitters are used to keep the scattered colonies connected," Kyle guessed.

"No." Ukiah shook his head. "There is no home world. There is no plan. This isn't an effort to build a civilization to span the universe. The Ontongard is just one organism, reproducing mindlessly. After they find a suitable planet, they pull their ship into orbit and dismantle it, parachuting everything down to the surface in an all-or-nothing try to take over. If they succeed, they reproduce until they wipe out all life on that planet and then leave. If they fail, who cares?"

"The ones that die." Atticus felt the need to poke holes in Ukiah's theory. He found his brother's knowledge annoying in the face of his own ignorance. "It might be a long shot, but the ones here on Earth might be desperate enough to take it. Why not send out a message saying there's a perfect planet here, waiting to be plundered, if another ship was so inclined to head in this direction?"

Ukiah gave him a lost look, uncertain.

"These translations the cult had you do." Ru gave Ukiah a nudge like he would if they were questioning a witness. "They never mentioned the transmitter?"

Ukiah closed his eyes and sat still for a minute. Atticus sensed that he was flicking back over hours of spoken conversation. "A lot of the same equipment goes to building a lot of things: computer controls, monitors, switches, gauges. They could be building anything—but they *are* all things found in a transmitter. The Ontongard would have needed years to bring everything together, and I listened only to a few months of recordings."

"They're still building it, or they wouldn't be talking about parts," Kyle guessed. "Any indication how close to finished they are?"

Ukiah made a face. "It could be done now and still be useless."

"Huh?"

"Well, these things are more like cell phones than radios, if I understand human technology right. The transmitter isn't like a radio tower, where it broadcasts out and anyone out there with a radio can pick it up. It's like a cell phone, where there's two-way communication set up. There's what Max calls 'the handshake' going on—signals that go from sender to receiver and back."

"What's the protocol?" Kyle got a blank look. "How do they initiate a message?"

"They would have to . . ." Ukiah said slowly, grinding through the process, ". . . detect another transmitter first, which might take years . . . unless they know something that the Pack doesn't—like the Ontongard on the last world or two decided to set one up at a certain location, or knew of one they were going to take over."

Atticus blew out his breath in exasperation. It sounded like lots of unknowns, maybes, and dependings. He wasn't even sure why they were talking about it, since only finding the Ae mattered.

Kyle, however, was intrigued. "Let's just assume they are building this transmitter. How do we find it? What does it look like? Is it bigger than a bread box?"

"It's massive. The housing for the containment field would be, like, thirty feet tall, and waveguides are very long and straight. It's not something they'll be able to hide."

"When you say very long, what measurements are you talking here?"

Ukiah thought for a minute, translating out the measurements. "They would have to be nearly half a mile in length."

"And how thick around is the waveguide?"

Ukiah measured it off with his hands. "But there would have to be, like, twenty-five feet of earth acting as a buffer from outside interference."

"How do you know all this stuff?" Atticus asked him.

"I have Rennie's memories."

"What does that have to do with it?"

"He's Coyote's Get, who was Prime's only Get." He saw Atticus's blank look. "Ontongard store their memories in their genetics because in essence, each cell is an individual, but they function as one vast creature. The Ontongard pass mice back and forth all the time to keep all of themselves on the same page. They all remember back for thousands of years."

"But what does that have to do with you and Rennie?"

"Pack is just like the Ontongard, only completely different," Ukiah said.

"Well, that's completely clear."

"Have you ever seen the movie *Blade Runner*?"

"Can we have a straightforward conversation? One without all these weird jumps?"

"Max has this big-screen TV and surround sound and *Blade Runner* on DVD. When you watch it, you're immersed in that world, and throughout the entire movie it rains and rains. So at the end, when you go outside and the sun is shining, you think—for one split second—Wow, it's stopped raining."

"It never was raining." Atticus refrained from asking who Max was, since it would derail the conversation even further.

"Exactly."

"Just get to the point."

"The movie infringed on your reality, but only so you're disoriented for a moment, just a second or two, and then it all goes back to being just a movie you watched. When Pack trade mice, they can tell what is the movie and what is the real world. Where the other person's memories end, and theirs start."

"A good book that you can put back on the shelf?"

"Yeah. For the Ontongard, both your world and the

movie are equally real. You are yourself, and all the characters in that movie, and all the movies ever made in the history of the art. A million lives, all equally weighed."

"How can they think that way?"

Ukiah shrugged. "But that's really the only difference between Pack and Ontongard. We have a mutation that lets us remain individuals, with all the hates and desires and free will that implies—but the 'me' of an Ontongard host is lost under the flood of 'them.' You say that humans should deal with this. The Pack were all born human. They were infected by Coyote with Prime's mutation. They're genetically aliens, but in their hearts and souls, they're still human."

"As far as I'm concerned, the Pack are nothing but low-life slime deluding themselves that they're saving the world. They're no different from the cult. The Ontongard are convenient bogeymen to excuse the Pack's criminal behavior."

"I can show you."

It took Atticus a moment to realize what Ukiah meant. "I already had my mind raped."

Ukiah ducked his head; if he were a dog, he'd probably be flattening back his ears. "Not like that. You read me, like the Pack read you."

"No."

Ukiah locked his feral stare onto Atticus. "You want to stay blind to the danger until it kills you?" And he thought, but did not say aloud, *"Kills Ru?"*

Twin spikes of guilt and anger hit Atticus. He matched Ukiah's gaze, until he realized that Ukiah was offering to give Atticus free access to his memories. The offer spoke to him of sincere trust. "I don't know how."

Ukiah leaned close, locking Atticus with his intense gaze. "Just look."

Atticus never considered *how* he remembered before—how he could focus on a nearby wall, and yet in his mind, like transversing some invisible dimension, walk through the houses of his childhood. Vaguely he knew it was neurons firing, replaying stored information, only his recording was perfect. At some point, the past would crowd the present out of his sight with things recalled.

He looked into his brother's dark eyes with their vaguely Asian shape, marked with exhaustion. He could feel the fearlessness with which Ukiah opened himself up in a way that seemed both trustingly childlike and patiently wise. One of them took a breath, and Atticus wasn't sure which body moved.

Ukiah's thoughts traveled to a distant time and firmly guided Atticus there too.

All his life, Prime had been caged. Loose pellets of nutrients were dropped into the feeding bowl. Water flowed endlessly in the drinking trough. He and the others in his cage had learned sometime in their pasts to use the trench in the back to urinate and defecate. Their language was a dozen words, all that was needed to explain their limited world. To count was meaningless—nothing ever was added or subtracted. Day was light. Night was dark. Only their bodies changed, growing taller; things that had been challenging in the play area now seemed too simple, and they invented complex games to take up their endless time. At one point they'd learned that to copulate felt good, so they did it often. The timeless imprisonment ended after the bitter-smelling air that made him sleep. They woke with identical angry red marks on their arms. Soon afterward he felt the change work through him, a whispering of a million voices, trying to crowd him out . . .

Ukiah flicked them forward in time.

Prime was like them, but not. They seemed to have no identity other than the group self. It was as if he were immersed in the sea, their presence shifting all around him, trying to carry him away with their nearly antlike desires. Build here. Destroy here. Gather food. Distribute it. They had bodies like himself, and anywhere there was dirt, they also grew like plants and trees and moss. They were every-

thing until the planet was one vast organism, and the single individuals weren't even antlike anymore, but merely cells in a body.

He drifted through the world, resisting the local urges, masking his thoughts, utterly alone on a planet utterly alive. Perhaps he would have joined with them if not, ironically enough, for the memories they infected him with. They remembered the planet as it had been, the millions of species, the billions of his mother's people. And in comparison, utter worldwide genocide was unpardonable.

Ukiah took another step forward in Prime's life.

They had been pond scum, and later stolen the forms of brilliant, creative creatures, and all the ranges of life between, creeping slowly across the universe. If they ever chose to go back, they could find their home world, but its location was now lost in indifference, caring no more than a seed for its pod after it'd been cast off.

And yet, they remained true to the strictures of life formed on that planet.

Mindless as a dafi plant, they built their seed ships in orbit until L5 bristled, waiting and waiting until the last ship was built. He would have suspected that they had a reluctance to separate, tearing away from the planet that was now virtually one of them, except he knew they held no such emotion. Verily, they had nearly no emotions at all.

The time to sail, though, was now at hand.

One by one, the great solar sails unfurled, and the ships began to peel away, each on a slightly different vector as the planet circled the star, like the white heads of dafi seeds, drifting out on the wind. At the great distance, the ugly ships were merely darkness trailing behind their glistening sails.

If he didn't know that they were death spores drifting toward another planet to kill, he would have found them beautiful . . .

He had failed. They were making a landing on a new

planet to rape. A shimmering teardrop of a world, teeming with life, like so many worlds before . . .

Atticus recognized Earth, the North American continent under scant cloud cover. He recoiled. No, this couldn't be true. Ukiah was controlling what he saw. Maybe he was giving Atticus only the most damning of information. Besides, these weren't Ukiah's memories; they could be elaborate creations handed to Ukiah as real. How did they compare to the real thing? The Pack took what they wanted from him, so he must be able to do the same.

Let me see Oregon, he thought, and pushed his way into Ukiah's memory.

It was like falling into a deep well. There was a shallow layer of civilized confusion, and then a long silence of dappled forest. At the bottom, he found a toddler, naked, hungry, alone, and scared.

Where did you go? the child cried, and the voice was achingly familiar.

I don't know. He drew back, away from his failing. This wasn't what he wanted. There was nothing he could do about this. He couldn't even remember how he went from wolf protector to being a child just as lost and alone.

Nor did he want to dwell on those memories of being a feral child. He passed back through them, green leaves, white snow, and shaggy gray bodies. Thoughts so centered on the forest around him, the only horizon being the next meal, that they seemed barely human.

Finally he resurfaced.

The woman carefully pushed a piece of jerky through the cage bars. "I know, I know, you don't like the cage." She seemed to be in her early twenties, dark eyed, dark haired, and athletic in build. The child listening to her didn't understand the low-crooned words, but was beginning to trust the speaker. "But if I let you out, I'm afraid that you'll run away, so we're going to do this nice and slow and easy."

Another piece of jerky slipped between the cage bars.

"And we're not going to tell anyone about you. No, no, we're not going to let big, uncaring government with its Jerry Falwell ethics get ahold of you. I'm not going to let that happen to you, my little Mowgli. I'm going to keep you safe . . ."

And up through the days that followed as this woman, Ukiah's adopted mother, showed stunning patience, gaining the wild child's love and gentling him. A second woman merged into the memories, a beautiful sunny blonde, as strong and caring as the first.

"I did research on autistic and feral children. I think"— the blonde paused to accept a snuggling hug from the boy who was discovering the joys of physical affection—*"the reason the radio and television bother him is he's suffering from sensory overload. You didn't say how cute he was."*

"It was hard to tell under all the dirt and matted hair."

"Well, it's a good sign that he's showing affection."

"Thank you for saying yes, kitten; I know it wasn't fair to ask you to take on a teenage wolf boy."

Teenage wolf boy? Atticus jerked up out of the memories, to stare at Ukiah. "How old were you?"

"Thirteen."

Atticus suffered a sudden flash of guilt—he'd left the baby in the woods and it never found its way out. *There's nothing I could have done differently,* he told himself. But there were still disquieting echoes deep inside him, plans to search the woods, made and abandoned several times in the last twenty-five years. *I knew there was someone I lost.*

On the heels of that, he did the math. Thirteen? Ukiah's driver's license claimed he was twenty-one. That meant that Ukiah had been part of civilization for only eight years. No wonder he struck Ru as childlike.

"Food's coming," Ru warned Atticus, and they sat silently as the waiter unloaded his tray onto the table. Ru, though, watched Atticus closely. "Well?"

Atticus had to think back to the last *spoken* conversation, which seemed like a lifetime ago. Ah, yes, he was sneering at the idea of the Ontongard being bogeymen. "The Ontongard are complete monsters. The Pack is right to be doing whatever it takes to stop them."

Ukiah eyed his plantains and tasted them cautiously. "They're fried bananas?"

"More or less." Atticus swallowed down his unease along with a bit of the sweet fried fruit. Only eight years.

CHAPTER SIXTEEN

Boston Harbor Hotel, Boston, Massachusetts
Thursday, September 23, 2004

Atticus and his team had just gotten Ukiah tucked into the extra bed in Kyle's room when there was a loud knock at the door.

Atticus stilled and focused. In his memory, he found Sumpter's familiar stride coming down the hall, and could now catch his scent. "Oh, shit. It's Sumpter. Other room."

Atticus went last, closing the connecting doors behind him. Sumpter was knocking a second time when he opened the hall door. "We're over here."

The problem with his and Ru's room was the king-sized bed. While he and Ru didn't lie about their relationship, they tried to keep it fairly low-key, which usually meant keeping Sumpter out of their bedroom. The bed made it a little too obvious to miss.

"Where have you been?" Sumpter shied from the bed as if it were a sex act, heading for the connecting doors.

"We had a lead on the cult," Atticus said, blocking him. "But it was blown to smithereens."

"Let's go in the other room and you can brief me."

Atticus sighed. Trying to keep Sumpter in the dark would only make him more hostile. "We have a civilian sleeping over there. My younger brother."

"What the hell are you thinking?" At least Sumpter stopped trying to flee the room. "What does he know?"

A lot more than I do. "Everything."

"Everything? What you are and what we're doing here?"

It took Atticus a second to realize Sumpter meant he was DEA, not that Atticus was an alien. "The whole shebang."

"That's just fucking perfect," Sumpter snapped. "What were you thinking?"

"I think I'm doing my job. Don't come here half-assed, without a clue about what the fuck is going on, and start raking me over the coals."

"If you bothered to keep me briefed, then I wouldn't be reaming you a new one. You didn't mention this when I saw you earlier today."

"That wasn't Atticus," Kyle said quietly. "That was Ukiah you talked to."

"Ukiah?" Sumpter asked.

"My brother," Atticus said.

Sumpter looked at them as if he thought they were lying and walked into the next room. Ukiah lay in quiet testament that they were telling the truth. "Well, I'll be damned. But why the hell did you bring him into the middle of this?"

"The cult kidnapped him," Ru volunteered, weaving truth and fiction. "They took his wallet and threw him overboard to drown. The Coast Guard picked him up while we were at the cult's hideout this afternoon. He has no money, no place else to go, and a lot he can tell us about the cult."

Sumpter gave Atticus a look that was both calculating and suspicious. Chances were, he was wondering if the entire case was a vendetta to wreak vengeance for Ukiah's kidnapping.

"Can you trust him to keep his mouth shut?" Sumpter finally asked.

"Yes," Atticus said.

"So where do we stand?"

•　　•　　•

They did more than dance around the truth. They dressed up half-truths and waltzed them past Sumpter to divert him from the things they were covering up. It proved useful, though, as it focused on what they knew without the distraction of all the weirdness.

"We know that the cult is using the drugs to fund their terrorist activities. We've heard rumors that they plan something large-scale aimed at the companies they've been wiretapping. Today's bombings were at the offices of six of those companies."

"Why them?"

"We don't know," Atticus lied. "We think it might have to do with a construction project that is common to all six companies."

"The cult thinks they're *eeevil*," Ru said, dancing closer to the truth.

"This was the island where the cult was hiding." Atticus gave Kyle the GPS coordinates. "It wasn't on Indigo's— Agent Zheng's—list of cult properties. We should find out who owns it; it might lead us to other sites. According to what they told my brother, their drug lab is somewhere in the immediate Boston area."

Kyle nodded and focused on the search. "I think I found it," he said after several minutes. "The same account that bought the island also purchased a warehouse and pays for the electric and such. It's in South Boston, just across the channel."

Ukiah woke alone. On the doors and the bathroom mirror, post-it notes commanded: *Stay Put!!!* Triple exclamation points and no clues as to where they'd gone or how long he should wait.

The thing about his perfect memory was that it didn't turn off while he slept. There, stored with the shifting shadows across his closed eyelids, he found their conversation with Sumpter. They talked about a warehouse in South

Boston, planning to put it under surveillance, and what they
would need to get warrants and enlist backup from the police to stage a raid.

They had taken Kyle's laptop—source of a nearly con-
stant clicking of keys—and the maps they'd crinkled and
rustled, but left behind a series of satellite photos printed
onto plain paper. The grainy photos zeroed in on an untidy
sprawl of warehouses and parking lots beside a dry dock and
rimmed by water. While the address meant nothing to
Ukiah, one of the photographs jogged recognition. The cult
had a similar picture with a building circled in red and labeled VB6. When he saw it earlier, there wasn't enough in
the photo to identify the location, but linked to the other
photographs, now part of a whole, Ukiah could guess where
the site lay.

And it wasn't where Atticus was heading.

Using the hotel phone, he called Indigo.

"Tell me that you're still safe with your brother," she
commanded.

"Well, not quite." Ukiah explained the situation while he
searched through his brother's luggage, looking for anything
to use as a weapon. He found a twenty-dollar bill still tucked
into the pants pockets of the jeans Atticus wore the day before, but nothing else of use.

"Either way, this is bad," Indigo said when he finished.
"The coast guard found the *Nautilus* drifting in the harbor.
It appears that the Ontongard caught up with the cult. The
boat is riddled with bullets and there's blood everywhere."

"Ice and the others?"

"We've got one John Doe—we think it's Boolean—and
that's it."

"There were ten people on the *Nautilus*."

"There's no sign of them."

He sat on the end of Atticus's bed, stunned by the news.
"When . . . when did it happen?"

"Around noon."

Ukiah glanced out the window at the rain-dark night. Hours ago. Any of the cultists taken alive by the Ontongard would have already been infected. Ice and the others were all gone.

Noon, though, would have given the cult time to set up Loo-ae. It could be somewhere even now, slowly filling the air with poison.

"I think I know where they intended to set up Loo-ae." He described the aerial photo and the street map. "Have the Dogs meet me there."

"Be careful. The Ontongard might already be there."

"I know. Tell the Dogs to hurry. I'd wait for them, but I'm not sure there's time."

He used Atticus's twenty-dollar bill to take a taxi to the empty corner of Fish Pier and Seaport Boulevard, a few blocks from the target building.

"Here?" The cabbie swept his hand to take in the deserted pier, the empty parking lots, and a tangle of highways disappearing into a tunnel entrance. Obviously an industrial area—there were no apartments or open businesses in sight.

Ukiah hushed him and scanned the surroundings for Ontongard. If he pushed, he could sense a small group of them distantly, moving invisibly in the darkness beyond. He pulled back into himself. Being only one person, he'd be harder to detect, but it was possible that the Ontongard would sense him if he continued to blindly reach out. "Yes, here."

"There's nothing here."

"Yeah, that's good." Ukiah handed forward the twenty, which the cabbie took warily. "Do you know what that building up there is?"

The cabbie gave it a quick glance. "It's one of the ventilation buildings for the Big Dig. They blow air down into the tunnels with big fans to keep the fumes from killing drivers. There's, like, ten of them, all over the city."

Big fans? Ukiah shuddered at the thought of Loo-ae tied to such things, distributing the airborne poison. He'd hoped the cult would have the machine in an enclosed space, where there was a slim hope of containing the viral biotoxin.

Ukiah paid the fare and slid out of the safety of the cab.

In Pittsburgh, there would have been hillsides and deep weeds anyplace that wasn't paved over, but here there was just a flat wasteland of cement and plowed earth. A storm wind was blowing off the black ocean, scouring up dusty ghosts of demolished buildings and roadways. Water slapped against stone, a restless murmur.

"You sure you've got the address right, kid?" The cabbie seemed suddenly friendlier, and Ukiah realized the man had thought Ukiah planned to rob him in this empty place.

"Yeah, this is the place. I'm meeting some friends here." Ukiah waved toward a dark boat moored to the pier. "They get off at midnight. Thanks!"

The cabbie eyed the boat and shrugged. He put the cab into gear and drove away, leaving Ukiah alone.

At least with the oncoming storm, the sky was cloaked and the shadows deep.

Avoiding the pools of light thrown by the overhead streetlights, Ukiah moved wolf-silent toward Ventilation Building Six. It was larger than he had expected—on the photo it had been a small square smudge beside a rectangle of water. In truth, it was built on a giant's scale, several stories high with truck-sized doors. Despite its utilitarian function, an effort had been made to make it pretty. The air shafts rising like chimneys from the roof had been stylized into wedges and tipped with something that gleamed with reflected light.

He sensed something wrong with the building and stilled. He stood downwind, in a heavy flow of hot fumes, as if one huge engine were pouring out its exhaust, and caught the scent of blood. Stalking forward, smothering down a growl, he found a human-sized door ajar. Leads bypassed the security sensors in the door's sill, and just inside a night watchman was sprawled out dead—the source of the blood.

The cult was already in the building.

They'd left the guard's gun in its holster. Ukiah crept forward and slid it out.

At the slight noise, the prickle of Ontongard brushed over him.

"What are you doing here?" a voice asked, coming out of the darkness.

Ukiah recognized Ice's voice, though it sounded raspy and hoarse. He reached out and felt Ice, his scent mixed with sickness and Hex's reek. Parts of Ice were still human, but the rest pushed against Ukiah's senses like sandpaper. Ice was becoming a Get.

Ukiah growled low.

"What are you doing here?" Ice asked again. He staggered down the passage, hand on the wall, sweat pouring from him. "You haven't come to stop it?"

"You're infected."

"Yes." Ice licked his lips. "Evil is inside of me, crowding me out. I'm barely here. I'm barely me."

Ukiah could sense the Ontongard presence growing inside of Ice's body, a coil of hate. "I know."

"You must have power over the evil. I can feel how much he hates you. Can you save me?"

"No." There was a machine that could reverse the process, but it was on the West Coast; Ice would be a Get long before they could bring him to it. "Where is Hu-ae?"

"We sold it to John Daggit—the philistine—for access keys to this building." Ice dismissed Daggit with a wave of his hand. "He's making arrangements to move it and what's left of our inventory out of our warehouse on Summer Street. God rest his soul."

"He's dead?"

"Hmm." Ice pursed his lips together, thinking. "By now, probably. I had to use him as a distraction for the evil. We'd set up Loo-ae on a remote, so we'd have a chance to be clear of it when it started up. A running start. The demons—the Ontongard—caught us at the docks. Everyone else is dead, some with cleaner deaths than others. They knew we stole the Ae." He pressed fingertips to his forehead. "They started to rummage through my mind, trying to discover what we'd done with the Ae, so I gave them Daggit and Hu-ae to save Loo-ae." He laughed softly. "Hu-ae. Loo-ae. Listen to me. I'm using their real names."

Ice had made a small gesture to the shadows beside him. Ukiah looked and with a start recognized Loo-ae beside the huge bulk of a giant ventilation fan. A hole had been arc-welded into the metal sheeting of the ductwork, and the Loo-ae's exit chute was duct-taped into the air shaft.

"You can't use Loo-ae to stop them."

"I rekeyed it." He lifted his left hand and showed off the bloody stump of a pinkie, already trying to grow back. "I managed to slice off some of the evil and used Loo-ae to change it from your genetic key."

So they had taken one of his mice to program Loo-ae.

"Are you sure it was pure Ontongard? Even a few human cells, and you'd kill off everything on the planet."

"What do you want of me? Look!" Ice indicated a cut along his cheek. "I tried to kill myself, put a gun in my mouth and pull the trigger, but he's already too strong. He stopped me."

"I'm sorry. There's nothing I can do."

"Fine. Then I'll kill them all, even as I become one of them."

"This machine won't stop them."

"It might—that's all I care about."

"You can't do this. You'll kill millions of innocent humans."

Ice wavered. "The evil wants me to smash it. Is that enough of an answer?"

"No."

"They're finishing the transmitter today. They've had the detector done for years and found a source months ago. They'll be able to start sending messages out tomorrow. Sunday at the latest. What's a few million to the fate of the world?"

Ukiah edged sideways, hoping to get closer to the machine. "We still have time to stop them without Loo-ae."

"No!" Ice pulled out his pistol, aimed at Ukiah, and fired. At the last moment, though, his hand flicked to one side. Ice screamed surprise and anger as the bullets plowed through Loo-ae's casing to blast holes into the delicate circuitry inside. One of the bullets hit the power supply, and electricity arced in a miniature electrical storm.

They stood for a minute staring as the machine died, and with it all the hopes of the cult. Like all who had fallen to the Ontongard over the millennia, the cult had failed in the face of the sheer resilience of their enemy. Again and again, the invaders could recover from any blow, while the native-born either died or—infected—betrayed their own race.

Ice stared at his traitorous hand. "Oh, God." He dropped to his knees. "Wolf child, please, give me mercy. Kill me before they take me."

And take him they would. With Ice would go all the knowledge of Ukiah's world. Max. Indigo. His infant son. Nor was there time to consider long. While Atticus might physically survive the Ontongard's ambush at the cult's warehouse, if Ru was killed or worse—and more likely after years of close association with Atticus—made one of them, Atticus's fragile world would be crushed.

Ukiah couldn't let that happen.

Still, it was the hardest thing Ukiah had ever done, to pull out his newfound gun and point it at a person he knew. To keep it aimed between Ice's pale blue eyes. To pull the trigger. In the enclosed space, the gun thundered. The bullet smashed Ice to the ground. Gunsmoke and blood filled Ukiah's senses. All he could see was the sprawl of Ice's body. Still, the mostly Ontongard heart struggled to save the host. With a sob, Ukiah aimed at the pounding heart and fired again and again. The body jerked under the blows and went still. Life continued to exist, but could no longer steal Ice's form and memories.

Why, Atticus wondered, couldn't anything be simple anymore? There was a time—strangely just last week, but it seemed much longer now—when it was a straight and simple good guys versus bad guys. No werewolves, angels, demons, or aliens. Planning a raid seemed to offer the return to comforting routine.

The warehouse sat in a flat, treeless area; a desert of an industrial park. Dusk was running before heavy rain clouds, leaving behind a windy night full of the promise of rain. While the loading bays fronting Summer Street remained closed, one of the doors to the back alley had been wedged open. A black pickup truck blocked the narrow alley, as if the driver had tried to back it to the door, discovered it wouldn't fit, and left it at a drunken angle. Apparently someone was loading up with all haste.

"Looks like they're bolting." Ru took out the night-vision binoculars to scan the warehouse.

Atticus grunted. So much for an easily orchestrated raid. "Not surprising with the pod people breathing down their neck. Grab the cash cow and run." He checked his pistol, made sure it was fully loaded, and patted his pocket to check on the extra magazine.

"Speaking of pod people, you feel anything with your super spider senses?"

There were times when Ru took things a little too easy. Atticus grunted again in annoyance, but he closed his eyes and tried that weird "other" sense. "No."

"Hello? What's *he* doing here?" Ru murmured.

Atticus opened his eyes and peered across the street. John Daggit came out of the warehouse carrying a cardboard box. Since his right hand was a painful collection of metal braces for his broken fingers, Daggit juggled the box awkwardly with his left hand.

"Call for backup?" Ru asked.

"Let me scout the area." Atticus dialed down the interior lights so they wouldn't turn on when the door opened. "See how many people we're dealing with."

Daggit dropped his load into the pickup's bed and hurried back inside. Faint thunder rolled around in the sky as Atticus eased out of the Jaguar and into the chilly wind. Instantly the omnipresent fish-and-salt smell of the ocean filled his senses. Keeping to the shadows, he crossed the street and crept to the pickup. Battered and muddy with steel toolboxes built in, the vehicle was obviously used for construction. A tarp and bindings lay ready to cover up the load.

Liquor boxes sat in the truck bed, perhaps a dozen in all, shoved as far as Daggit could easily reach, leaving a glittering trail of Invisible Red. Atticus slid on a plastic glove and gingerly tipped the nearest box to peer inside. Plastic bags of the alien drug filled the box. Based on what Daggit had sold his team, the boxes represented several million dollars' worth of drugs. What was Daggit doing with it? Where was the cult? But most important, where were Hu-ae and Loo-ae?

Atticus skinned off the gloves, dropped them into the already contaminated pickup, and stalked quietly to the back door to listen intently. The wind and the distant murmur of waves combined to make a deafening white noise. Taking out his pistol, he slipped inside.

The warehouse was silent. Its vast interior was stacked with great beams of hand-hewn wood. There was half of an old sign leaned against the wall near the door, painted with *years after the* Mayflower *took the Pilgrims to America, it was stranded and purchased by a farmer who towed it up the Thames and dismantled it to build this barn.* The ghost scent of cows hung in the musty air.

There was something ironic in the fact that the cult had hidden an alien invader's tool in among the bones of their own ancestral invasion craft.

After several minutes of listening closely, Atticus was fairly certain that Daggit was working alone in the dim warehouse. He leaned back outside to signal to Ru. Thunder boomed, closer now. As the sound faded, there was an odd metallic noise within the building and the warehouse seemed to suddenly breathe out, the exhaled air warmer than the night around Atticus. Daggit had rolled up one of the great steel doors to the loading docks. Had he heard Atticus?

He waved to Ru to head Daggit off, and charged inside.

Daggit had run out of boxes. A small stack of plastic bags were piled in front of the tall door meant for tractor-trailers. A cube matching Indigo's sketch of the alien machines sat by the loading dock—but only one was in sight. Daggit struggled one-handed with a *Mayflower* timber, apparently planning to use it as a ramp to load the Ae once he pulled the pickup around.

The biker looked up as Atticus ran toward him, and swore. He fumbled out his pistol with his left hand. Atticus kicked it away. Compared to the Ontongard, Daggit moved ponderously slowly. Even as the big man started to react, Atticus whirled, caught Daggit's wrist, and took him down to his knees and then stomach while twisting Daggit's unbroken hand up behind his back.

Ru squealed the Jaguar around the corner and to a stop in front of the dock, flooding the area with light. He got out, hidden by the glare of headlights, and pulled his gun. "Solid?"

"We're solid." Atticus kneed Daggit in the back, keeping him pinned.

Daggit preempted the questioning with, "I don't know where the little bastards are! They called me. Sold me that damn machine, told me how it works, took the money, and ran. I don't have a clue where your brother is."

"My brother is back at my hotel." Atticus took out his handcuffs. "He swam ashore."

"So it was always about the fucking drugs?"

"Yes." Atticus cuffed the biker. "As far as we're concerned, it's always been about getting the drugs off the street and shutting the lab down. John Daggit, you're under arrest for drug trafficking, possession of controlled substances, and anything else we can tack on you."

"What? Are you kidding me? You're Pack."

"No." Atticus flipped out his ID and shoved it under Daggit's nose. "I'm DEA."

Daggit exploded into profanity as Atticus patted him down, ending with, "You're going to be so dead when the Pack finds out."

"They know." Atticus liberated a set of car keys, a switchblade, and a stash pistol. "They don't care. This hasn't been about the drugs for them."

Daggit grunted as if struck and then muttered darkly, "Those bastards, those fucking bastards," in an endless litany.

With a growing murmur, the storm front moved over them, bringing a downpour. Ru left the Jaguar's lights on, slammed the door, and scrambled up to the shelter of the loading dock. "Is that it?" Ru asked, indicating the alien device sitting next to Atticus. It was a waist-high cube of something that looked like brushed steel, with the "Hu-ae" symbol. Not totally what Atticus expected, but it matched Indigo's drawing. "Where's the other one?"

"I want a lawyer," Daggit said, assuming the question was aimed at him. "I know my rights."

"Look, you idiot." Atticus kicked Daggit harder than he intended. Daggit, he realized, had a trace amount of the drug on his hands, and it was affecting him. "The other machine is a bioweapon. It produces enough toxin to kill the entire city. If you're sitting in a holding pen when they turn it on, you're dead meat. Understand? Now where the fuck is the other one?"

Daggit considered in silence and then said quietly, "They took it away. They didn't tell me where they were taking it."

Atticus felt a tendril of fear uncoil inside him. Having seen Prime's world through his memories, Atticus now understood the scope of possible destruction that the Ontongard and their tools could create.

His fear awakened concern in Ru. "What do we do?"

"We contain this mess, get him into a holding tank, and find the cult." Atticus indicated Daggit. "There's drugs smeared everywhere. Just watch him—I'll handle things."

"I've got gloves on," Ru pointed out.

"Good."

Rain beat on the warehouse roof, a low, endless roar. Atticus just reached the truck when panic swept over him. He stood for a moment, panting from the sudden adrenaline rush. What was wrong? Why did he feel this way?

Then another person's will slammed into him. *Get out! Go! Run!*

Ukiah?

His brother was closing at a fast run, his fear racing out before him. Knowing his brother, there were only two things he'd be running from. Atticus focused on his new awareness of others like him and found the Ontongard nearly on top of him.

"Shit!" Atticus ducked back into the long warehouse. Silhouetted by the Jaguar's headlights, Ru stood over the prone Daggit. The falling rain formed a sheet of gray beyond the open doorway. "Ru! Get him out of here!"

Behind Atticus came the cough of a grenade launcher. In a burst of heat and sound, the truck exploded. He was smashed from his feet by the concussion.

Well, damn, the Ontongard were sick of losing, he thought. They'd come to the fight armed to the teeth. He scrambled to his feet, knowing that the stacks of ancient timber would go up like kindling.

In the far doorway, Ru turned toward the explosion. Daggit twisted as he stood up, snatched one of the plastic bags stacked by the door, and spun, swinging the bag of drugs at Ru.

"No!" Atticus cried, helpless, too far away to do anything but scream.

But somehow Ukiah was close enough to do more than that. He was suddenly between Ru and Daggit, shielding Ru with his own body. The bag struck Ukiah midchest and burst on impact. The transparent drug covered him instantly, setting his nerves on fire.

Atticus felt the drug blast through Ukiah's system as if his own body were washed with white fire. Ukiah had reflexively flung up his hands to protect his head. He screamed, arms flexing tight so muscles corded, and toppled—still screaming—into a fetal position, a fire victim wrapped in invisible flames. Atticus stood stunned, lost in another's pain, as the cloud of drug particles glittered in the light over his fallen brother. Ukiah's screams sucked the Blissfire into his lungs, and Atticus could feel the fire move through his brother's core.

Guns spat into the dim warehouse, bullets dancing Daggit backward, but all Atticus could hear was the deafening, endless bell-like chime of Bliss. The taste of red filled his mouth.

The Dog Warriors flowed into the warehouse even as another grenade exploded somewhere close by. Then the universe whited out and Atticus couldn't sense his body past the pain, although he knew he was moving his legs.

And then like a star going nova and dying to a dark cinder, the blaze of pain that had been Ukiah flared out.

Atticus stumbled at the sheer absence. Only Ru's support kept him from falling. Somehow they'd gotten outside, into the bitter-cold rain—a full block from the gunfight in the warehouse. The timer on the Jaguar's headlights had finally tripped, and they turned off. The fire shone through the open doorway like a baneful red eye, growing brighter.

He panted, trembling, feeling hollow, as if the experience had burned the core out of him.

"Atty?" There was fear in Ru's eyes.

"I'm fine. I'm fine."

Ru followed his gaze. "Ukiah?"

"He's dead." The words dropped into the hollow place like stones.

Rennie came out of the warehouse, Ukiah's body slung over his shoulder. At the corner of the neighboring building, a broken downspout showered rain past a spotlight, creating a glittering spray of water.

. . . a halo of dust . . . a million prickles of pain flashing into one flare of agony . . .

Shaw crouched in the shower, shifting Ukiah to the ground, letting the torrent wash the shimmering drug from the boy's body.

"You said this stuff is harmless!" Atticus shouted at Shaw. "That it only killed humans."

"Harmless to Pack." Shaw stripped the sodden clothes off of Ukiah as the water pounded unheeded on Shaw's shoulders and back. "Not to him. Not to you either. Not at that amount. His body shut down, rather than spread the poison completely through his system."

"He'll recover—won't he?"

"I don't know," Shaw snapped. "Poison is one way to kill us, as is fire."

. . . a blaze of pain like white fire and then nothing . . .

"Oh, fuck." Atticus couldn't bear looking at his brother;

he stared instead at drops of rain sparkling in the spotlight. "What are you going to do with him?"

"He's our son; we'll do whatever needs to be done." Rennie stood, lifting Ukiah like a sleeping child.

The empty feeling grew, eating Atticus from the inside. He recognized the emotion now: grief. He found himself walking away, trying to put distance between him and the pain.

. . . another's pain filling him—a complete union of a soul that once was one—and then nothing . . .

Ru walked beside him, one hand on Atticus's shoulder, a spot of warmth in the cold rain. "He'll be fine." Ru's voice betrayed what the rain hid—he was crying.

Atticus steeled himself with anger and kept walking. He just met Ukiah on Sunday. Five fucking days—just enough time to leave a wound that would never heal. Humans were the lucky ones. They forgot the pain and hurt, given enough time. In vivid slices, he could still remember parts of being a wolf—a moment here, a moment there—from what it was like to run on all four legs, to having a tail, to seeing the world in black and white. After he became human, every agony was locked into place. Despite being less than a year old at the time, he still could recall his adopted parents in exacting detail, had every moment he spent with them etched into his perfect memory.

. . . and then nothing . . .

They'd come to an enclosed bus stop. Ru pulled him inside, out of the rain. In that enclosed womb, Atticus took out his Swiss army knife and opened the blade.

"What are you doing?" Ru asked.

"If I live the rest of my life with the moment of his death locked into my memory . . . I'll go mad." He cocked his wrist, placed the blade on the blue line of his vein, and cut deep.

Ru groaned and sagged against the shelter's wall, looking away.

The blood ran hot over Atticus's rain-chilled wrist and gathered in his hand. He willed it to form a mouse while staring at the ceiling, trying to think of nothing but the slow drumming of the rain on the roof. They say if someone tells you not to think of a polar bear, it becomes impossible not to. If he thought about what he was trying to drain out of himself, it would embed itself back into his memory. So he thought about the sound of the rain, scanning through his perfect memory for music that matched the rhythm. He found one in the mournful ballad of "I Am Rock" and filled his mind with its somber words. *I won't disturb the slumber of feelings that have died . . .*

   . . . If I never loved I never would have cried.
   Atticus blinked, aware that tears were in his eyes, but having no idea why he'd been crying. He was in a bus shelter, rain drumming on the roof, an old Simon and Garfunkel song running through his head. For a panicked moment, he was worried something had happened to Ru, but his love was right there, on the wooden bench beside him. Mice whiskers tickled his fingers. He glanced down and found his knife in his right hand, a healing cut on his left wrist, and a mouse cupped in his palm, anxious about its fate.
   He hadn't drained out memories since he was a child. *Oh, God, what happened that made me do this again?*
   "Kyle?" he asked fearfully.
   "No," Ru whispered huskily. "Your brother died."
   "Again?"
   Ru gave a shaky laugh, and then hunched over and began to weep.
   Atticus spilled his mouse onto a floor strewn with cigarette butts and gathered Ru to him. "Hush, hush, I'm here."
   What had happened? he wondered with dread. His brother must have gotten himself totally fucked-up if Ru was worried. The mouse climbed his shoe to press against his sock, fearful, aware of being cast out. Atticus had

learned the hard way that he did this to himself for good reasons; taking back the mouse would be worse than being ignorant. His brother was dead—that was all he really needed to know to function. Perhaps all he could handle.

Tentatively, he probed his memories.

He could remember splitting up possible drug lab sites with Sumpter. After that, images of driving to South Boston and finding Daggit packing stuttered through his mind, ending with the Ontongard bearing down on them, and Ukiah racing toward them, and behind him, sweeping in on motorcycles, the Pack. At the time, he'd been too caught up in the roar of explosions to even notice the Dog Warriors. Distanced by time, now, he could feel them moving as one creature, with Ukiah as its heart and soul. They resounded with one will, one thought: to protect Ru. *It would kill Atticus to lose Ru.*

He had one clear memory of Ukiah shielding Ru with his own body, and then his recall ended, as if sliced out with laser precision. Practice made perfect. He could guess what followed. Even without the memory, knowledge that his brother sacrificed himself for Ru made him feel sick even as it confused him.

Why had Ukiah saved Ru? Why had he cared?

On the heels of that, he realized how close he'd been to losing Ru. Ukiah had acted with inhuman speed; Ru wouldn't have been able to save himself. The potential loss opened up a canyon of grief, which he could look into but—because of Ukiah—not fall into. If Ru had died, draining out a day's worth of memories would not have helped. To go home to an empty house and empty life, to go back to his life as it had been while he was growing up . . .

Ukiah had been right—losing Ru would have driven him mad.

It was stunning and humbling that his brother guessed what he hadn't known about himself.

Worse was the knowledge that he'd created the danger

himself. He'd known the Ontongard had been tracking the cult, and in any direct confrontation between human and alien, the aliens would win. Yet he had not taken Ukiah with him, admitted the truth to Sumpter, nor contacted Indigo. He'd been a fool.

This wasn't just about the drug anymore. It couldn't be. He couldn't accept that huge a gift from his brother and then let all the pieces of Ukiah's life fall to the ground. There was the second Ae, the rest of the cult, and the transmitter to find. But his team couldn't do it alone. They had to get help.

CHAPTER SEVENTEEN

Summer Street, South Boston, Massachusetts
Thursday, September 23, 2004

The rain tapered off, leaving behind streets that gleamed like black silk. A wild wind rushed through the darkness, chasing the storm front. The warehouse burned with bonfire ferocity; they could feel the heat even where they stood, a full city block away. The smell of burning diesel and human flesh tainted the honest wood smoke of the *Mayflower* timbers. Assaulting his senses, fire trucks wailed past them, lights cutting with razor intensity through the rain-black night.

Atticus noticed that the Jaguar sat across the street from the bus shelter, tucked back into shadows, far away from all the excitement. Had the Dog Warriors moved the car, or had he done it himself during that time of not remembering?

He could feel the Pack around him, numbers growing as more arrived, but scattered and well hidden. Shaw came out of the shadows, smelling of slaughter and smoke, the fire reflecting red in his eyes.

"Where's my brother?"

"Bear, Heathyr, and Smack took his body back to Pittsburgh."

Atticus flinched. "He's not going to recover?"

"It's too soon to tell. Even if he does, he'll be weak as a

kitten until the poison works out of his system. I wanted him safe regardless of what happens here."

It dawned on Atticus that Shaw loved Ukiah dearly. The human race had always confounded him; even the most hardened of criminals often had someone they loved. Someone they would protect. Someone they would die for. It seemed that the Pack retained that in their vestiges of humanity.

The shadows danced as the flames leapt through the warehouse's roof, brightening the night with flickering reds. The colors moved across the wet asphalt like running blood.

"Daggit said the cult took Loo-ae away," Ru said, changing the subject.

"Our Cub destroyed it." Shaw explained that Ukiah had called Indigo to let her know he had figured out Loo-ae's location and arranged for the Pack to meet him. The Dog Warriors arrived to find the device full of bullets and Ukiah far out ahead of them.

"And the cult?" Atticus asked.

"No sign of them," Shaw said.

"How did he know we were walking into trouble?"

Shaw gave him a look that made Atticus realize the Dog Warrior was lying about something but wasn't about to betray Ukiah.

"We're about to hang our asses way out over the line to work with you. The Ontongard are working on a transmitter. Ukiah showed me Prime's memories. I know we have to stop them, and I'm committing to do whatever it takes, but I need to know everything. Tell me what happened."

Shaw assessed him with a long, hard stare. "The Gets caught up with the cult this morning. We found Ice's body with Loo-ae; he was within a few hours of transforming fully into a Get."

What Shaw didn't say—would probably never say to a law officer—was that Ukiah had killed Ice.

Atticus pushed through the flash of anger at his brother.

He was jumping to conclusions in thinking it was a cold-blooded murder. Given how he had first found Ukiah, self-defense was entirely possible. "We need to pool knowledge."

Something exploded in the warehouse, drawing their eyes.

"Not here." Shaw jerked his head in the opposite direction. "Let's find someplace quiet to plan."

They gathered under a highway overpass slated to be torn down as part of the Big Dig. Indigo arrived, flanked by her Pack guard. The Dog Warriors drifted into the shadows to stand watch. Indigo had once again wrapped herself in her arctic zone. She saw Atticus watching her, and said, "It's not like I haven't been through this a dozen times before," to which Ru nodded.

He and Ru had pried Kyle from Sumpter, distracting their supervisor with Hellena Gobeyn in her tight leather pants and camisole top. The alpha female promised that she wouldn't break any bones and all Sumpter's bruises would fade within two or three weeks.

The meeting was deceptively small. To the humans, it probably seemed that Rennie Shaw was the only addition to the combination of DEA and FBI forces, but Atticus could sense the rest of the Pack spread out around them, listening in.

"The cult had learned that the Ontongard set their nests up in a hexagonal pattern." Kyle spread out a map on the Explorer's tailgate, showing that the Waltham site formed one corner. "Ukiah said that the cult also had an algorithm to figure out where they would move to if one nest was destroyed; basically this pattern would swivel on the nest opposite of the nest destroyed. Since the Pack attacked the Watertown nest, it would have made sense for them to destroy the Waltham nest, and these, but they should have left this one."

"So they've cut the thread."

"Stone cold."

"Maybe," Zheng said. "I've noticed one thing about these nests: They're all at companies that have to do with large construction projects."

That niggled something in the back of Atticus's mind. "Well, if they've built this transmitter someplace, they would need construction companies. This thing is supposed to be huge."

"Much bigger than a bread box," Rennie agreed.

How do you hide something so big—especially with it just hours from being finished?

Atticus gasped and flipped the map. "The Big Dig. It's the largest construction project in the country, perhaps the world, at the moment. If the Ontongard infiltrated the right companies, they could just add the transmitter to the design specs."

"Okay." Kyle took out a highlighter and marked up the map until the downtown area of Boston bled pink. "This is an old map we picked up from the D.C. office. These highways here are what got buried."

Rennie was already shaking his head. "We've been all over this area. Hell, your team has been sleeping almost on top of it. The Ontongard aren't down in these tunnels, and I can't see them leaving the thing unguarded. It's not Hex's way to trust humans."

Atticus studied the highlighting. There had been plenty of Ontongard at the warehouse just hours ago, and there had been Ice, halfway between the two races. "Where did Ukiah find Loo-ae?"

"Here." Rennie pointed out a point just on the water's edge. "Ventilation Building Six."

Kyle typed in a search. "VB-Six pulls exhaust out of the Ted Williams Tunnel." He paused to draw a line across the harbor. "And feeds in fresh air."

"Loo-ae was duct-taped to one of the intake fans," Rennie reported.

"Intake?" Atticus said. "The cult wanted the poisons down *in* the tunnel?"

"We haven't been out on the water," Rennie murmured. "If Hex somehow added to the tunnel there, under the bay, his Gets would be well hidden from us."

"I saw a documentary on how they built these tunnels," Indigo said. "They actually built large tubes down in Baltimore, floated them up the harbor, and sank them to make these tunnels. It seemed like an insane way of doing it to me."

"The transmitter's particle tubes need precision you're not going to get tunneling through rock." Rennie tapped the map at VB6. "But there were no Ontongard with Ice at this building."

"If it's number six," Atticus said, "there's at least five others."

"One on each end of the tunnel." Kyle spoke without looking up, searching through files on his laptop.

"So what if, knowing that he couldn't get Loo-ae into this building"—Atticus pointed to the far end of the Ted Williams Tunnel—"he put it in this one and counted on the poison being sucked through?"

Rennie went still, but Atticus could feel him expanding outward, becoming all of the Pack, tapping their memories. "That peninsula is all man-made land in the last few decades. We forget it's there. They made it to build Logan Airport. We've always had little need for planes. Wolves are meant to run on the ground. None of us have been out to that part of the city."

"So they've hidden the control center someplace out here." Atticus ran his finger along the tunnel and up to the man-made land. "We need to find it and destroy it."

"In a nutshell, yes," Shaw said. "One very big and hard nutshell—and the clock is ticking."

Kyle made a noise of frustration. "There's a ton of info on the Big Dig, but for as-built drawings and actual information on access doors and security protocols and locations of cameras . . . we're talking hours for me to get anywhere."

"Then let's go to the source." Ru grinned. "DEA with FBI backup? We can glide into anything tonight."

Operations Control Center, nicknamed OCC, was in South Boston. Flashing badges, his team and Indigo bullied their way into the building, sans any of the Pack—but only after being sure it was innocent of Ontongard. The bulk of the building was dedicated to keeping watch over the intricate roadway. In one huge room, employees sat bathed in the glow from over a hundred monitors, dominated by blue images of light gleaming off ceramic tiles lining miles of tunnels. It felt like walking into a missile command center. It was running on a skeleton shift of three employees.

"I don't understand," the nominal supervisor stuttered as Kyle made nice with the two techno geeks. "What exactly is the nature of this alleged emergency?"

Obviously this guy was in charge because he had a degree in political babble.

"We've been dealing with a dangerous religious cult, the Temple of New Reason." Ru wove his half-truths. "We believe they're linked with the bombings that took place earlier today. We've learned they might have plans to attack the tunnel system."

The man gasped and waved toward a bank of monitors, all of which seemed to be dead. "The camera system on the ventilation buildings went out this morning. We've been running diagnostics on it all day. It looks like some kind of virus."

"There's a possibility, then, that they've gotten into the maintenance access areas," Ru said, as if he knew for certain there were such things.

"We've pulled together some undercover agents who are

familiar with the MO of these perps," Atticus said, using copspeak to confuse. "I'm going to lead a team of them to sweep for signs of forced entry and sabotage. We're going to need your full cooperation."

"Yes, of course."

Kyle held out a headset to Atticus. "Here, this is ready to go. I've added a low-light camera to our two-way radio, in case I need to see what you're looking at."

Atticus clipped the headset onto his ear.

Indigo took a sharp breath, but said nothing.

What was that about? No time to ask, though.

Ru walked him to the door, murmuring, "I still say I should come with you."

"Ru, if these were humans, I'd want you with me. But these monsters—it's like trying to stop floodwaters with bullets. You'll be in over your head and dead without making a scratch on them."

Ru looked away so Atticus couldn't read any hurt or resentment on his face.

"Ru, you're a last line of defense here. I think Indigo kept silent all this time about what she knows because of my brother, but I don't want to count on her alerting the right people if the shit hits the fan. Kyle wouldn't be able to do it. You'd be able to make people listen to you."

Ru looked at him then, eyes full of pain.

"Besides," Atticus forced himself to joke, "you know how Kyle is at giving directions."

And Ru forced himself to smile. "Yeah, there is that."

They avoided the Ted Williams Tunnel so as not to give warning to their approach, instead going the long way around the bay. The Pack raced before him on motorcycles, like hounds before the hunter, while Ru murmured in his ear.

"OSHA inspections—got to love them. Apparently our friends haven't been able to infiltrate them or block them, so the inspectors had full access to the construction site. After every inspection, new areas are added onto the as-built drawings. Unlike the other ventilation buildings, the one you're heading to—VB-Seven—has a rat maze under it. No wonder this project is so overbudget and late being completed."

"You've got an entrance for this rat's nest?"

"Yeah. Here." Kyle demonstrated the need for Ru on his end.

"Take the next left," Ru clarified, giving detailed instructions for the desired door. "The electrical as-built schematics show a camera on that door, but there's no monitor for it. It's possible, though, that someone rerouted it for their use."

"Understood."

The entrance was a heavy steel door on the blind back corner of the building.

"We're going to need a battering ram," Atticus called to Rennie as he got out of the Jaguar.

"We've got a battering ram." Rennie worked the pump on his shotgun as a tanker truck with a steel I beam wielded to its prow turned the corner and roared toward the door. "Get ready; we're going in."

The Pack gathered around the doorway as the truck sped toward it, weapons ready. The ram slammed into the steel door, which folded under the blow, its hinges popping. The bent door fell inward, followed by the frame and parts of the wall around the opening, revealing a dark stairwell. The Pack flowed into the jagged hole. Muzzle flares strobed the darkness.

The stairwell was bare cement with two flights of steel stairway. The gunfire thundered and echoed in the close confines, the ricocheting bullets sparking as they whined off the walls. By the time they hit the bottom, the steps were slick with roiling blood. Atticus sensed that the fight continued on that cellular level, Pack blood fighting Ontongard.

Even as the dozen Gets on the stairs lay dead, the blood-spattered walls and steel seethed in anger.

They needed another ram for the door at the bottom. As a police-issued ram was passed down from above, Atticus noticed that the bodies, body parts, and forming rats of the Ontongard Gets were being dragged back up to ground level.

"What are they doing with them?" Atticus asked.

"We're putting them in storage," Stein, one of the Dog Warriors, told him as the Pack male reloaded. "We're sticking them in the tanker so we don't have to fight them a second time."

"Is there an opening on the tanker large enough to shove a body through?"

"Does it matter?"

"Forget I asked."

The leather of Stein's jacket was chewed away by shotgun blasts to expose body armor. Atticus glanced around him, noticing that others who led the charge wore bulletproof vests, all heavily damaged.

"Body armor?"

"Keeps you kicking butt longer." Stein grinned. "A little trick we learned off the Cub."

The ram reached the door and Atticus tensed, readying himself for the upcoming fight.

The door smashed open into a large, bare cement room, cold as a grave, littered with sleeping bags, heavy with the stench of sickness and death. Another twenty Ontongard Gets tried to stand against the flood of Pack.

"Get the doors!" Rennie shouted. "We've managed to take them by surprise, but we're about to lose that advantage!"

As the Gets disappeared under the snarling Dog Warriors, the other fighters sprang to the other exits from the room to bar the doors shut. All around them, the Ontongard gathered in an angry swarm, like bees from a kicked hive.

Atticus cupped his earpiece to lessen the noise of the fighting. "Ru, we're down the steps! Can you tell which way we should go next?"

"Big room, six exits total?" Ru asked, and then clarified with, "Counting the door you came in?"

The door directly in front of him boomed as Ontongard threw their bodies against it.

"Yes!" Atticus shouted over the din.

"They're in this room," Ru murmured to the others with him.

"Which way?"

Some of the dead had been there before they arrived. Atticus recognized the cultist Ether, stripped of her clothes, sprawled in a puddle of vomit. Mice had chewed holes out of her abdomen, the transformed flesh escaping the dead body.

"Looking, looking, looking," Ru chanted.

"This area is deeper, more extensive." Kyle's voice carried over Ru's side of the connection. They had to be hunched close together, poring over the same architectural drawings.

"No, I say this way," Indigo countered. "That area had work done by noncompromised contractors, whereas this area was totally done by the Ontongard."

"Ru?" Atticus trusted his partner.

"Okay, with your back to the stairs you just came down, to your left, on the same wall as the stairway, is a door," Ru said. "It leads to a long hallway with lots of doors off it. Ignore them all; go to the end."

"You sure?" Atticus said.

"No," came the answer from all three federal agents on the other end.

"All the other doors lead to fairly small areas," Ru explained. "At the end of the hall, though, is another stairway into an large area isolated from everything else."

"Look at these electricals." Indigo must have produced drawings to support her theory; paper rustled loudly.

"Oh!" Ru was convinced. "Atty, there's a shitload of power lines going into that area. It has to be the right place."

Atticus hurried to the door, aware of Rennie moving to join him. The Pack leader had been shot in the left arm; a gaping hole punched through the muscle and the arm hung useless at his side. The wound, though, was already healing closed. A mouse clung to Rennie's shoulder.

They'd lost ten of the Pack fighters to the thirty-two Ontongard dead, which was surprising, since they seemed so equal in strength.

"We value our hides." Rennie tucked his shotgun under his useless arm to load, doing it with an ease that suggested it wasn't the first time he had had to work one-handed. "So we're better at protecting them. But there's only a hundred of us and they've got us outnumbered two or three times over. We have to get this done before they overpower us."

Atticus nodded and indicated the door. "We think the transmitter is this way."

Rennie's mouse took advantage of the moment of stillness to scurry down into Rennie's coat pocket. "Let's do it then. Dogs, to me! The rest, seal those doors and get the dead contained."

A four-foot-square steel plate barrier was brought forward. With speed and efficiency no human team could match, the Dogs readied around the doorway and behind the shield wall. No sooner was the last person in place than they battered down the door and opened fire. Gunsmoke formed a cloud.

It was an expensive win. Of the fifteen Pack who pushed their way down the hallway, only Atticus, Rennie, and Stein were left standing at the end. Yet Atticus couldn't sense any Ontongard beyond the last door. He cautiously opened the heavy steel door and found an empty stairwell.

"Wait!" Rennie caught Atticus's shoulder before he could step forward, pulling him back away from the door.

"What is it?"

Rennie pulled out a handful of loose coins and flung them at the open doorway. With a crack and the sudden smell of hot metal, the coins rebounded to the floor at their feet, blackened and twisted. "They've got an energy field up."

"Oh, cool," Kyle said over the radio. "But that's not on the as-built."

OSHA wasn't going to like that. "How do we get through it?"

"We don't." Rennie shot one of the slightly dead Ontongard who had stirred back to life. "Nothing on Earth can penetrate it."

"Where the hell did it come from?"

"The scout ship; Hex stripped out the armory. See if there's a way around it."

With that Rennie and Stein worked back down the hall, stomping on hapless rats and shooting the fallen Ontongard in the head and chest—anything to keep them dead. Fighting broke out in the large center room, an endless thunder of guns backed with the snarls of the Pack. Atticus noticed for the first time that neither side shouted or cursed or screamed other than short yelps of pure animal pain.

"Ru, is there any way around this?"

"Actually, there is, but you're not going to like it," Ru said.

"How?"

"Go back to the first door. There's a small odd-shaped room that doglegs around the fresh-air ventilation shaft leading down into the Ted Williams Tunnel. There's an access panel into the air shaft. On the other side of the shaft is an air duct into that area."

The room was a supply closet, stacked haphazardly with construction supplies and tools. Atticus pushed through the equipment to the far back corner and unburied the access panel. The metal panel was secured to its frame with screws; he shot them out and pried off the panel.

Night air rushed out of a pitch-black shaft.

He found a flashlight in the clutter. He turned it on and discovered that its battery was nearly dead. He tried shining it into the shaft. The darkness swallowed the feeble beam. By holding on to the edge and leaning through the opening, he could make out the opposite wall. The shaft seemed to be about ten feet square. Fans roared somewhere overhead, and the sound of traffic echoed up faintly from the darkness below.

"Are you sure, Ru? I don't see anything."

"Opposite wall. It's smaller, and maybe to the . . . to the left."

He played the light across the far wall and found it. "Oh, shit."

"What is it, Atty?"

"It's like two and half feet, maybe three feet wide."

"It's the only way, Atty," Ru said.

"I know." He fixed the spot in his mind and pitched the flashlight aside. "Here goes nothing."

Atticus leapt into the darkness. He hit the wall hard, clawed at the darkness, found the edge of the air duct, and scrambled madly to haul himself up into the tiny crawl space. "I'm in!"

The only response to his news was a relieved sigh over the radio link and the thunder of guns behind him.

Ru told him that the air duct went only fifty feet, but it seemed longer, crawling on his stomach through the tight, square passageway. The other end opened onto a vast room filled with a bewildering array of equipment. Pipes from an inch to a foot in diameter bisected the room into grids. Besides pressure gauges and meters, nothing was labeled. Scattered around the room, in seemingly random order, were racks of computer equipment. Nothing seemed centralized. Nothing looked like the heart of a machine. No convenient big red switches.

He dropped lightly down onto a catwalk that ringed the upper level of the room and stared around him, suddenly feeling like a caveman asked to stop an aircraft carrier. No, worse—like a flea inside a supercomputer, whose only possible act of sabotage would be throwing himself on a random circuit and hoping that his death would fry an important chip.

Unfortunately, the room wasn't empty of Ontongard, and he'd been noticed. Three Gets started up the catwalk toward him. One was the missing Iron Horse from the DVD of the Ontongard attack on the Buffalo DEA team, the big, black, sleepy-eyed David Toback. The two others looked like construction workers, and were nearly as big and muscular. They carried short lengths of pipe; apparently they were loath to fire guns in this room. They split up, heading for the two ladders up to the catwalk, planning to catch him between them.

This was going to hurt.

"Can you see this?" he asked his team.

"Yeah, we're picking it up." Ru sounded as disheartened as he felt.

"I'm open to suggestions at this point."

"I don't know what to do," Kyle admitted while the other two remained silent.

"Not a clue?"

"Atticus," Kyle whined. "It's not like I can download a user file on this in PDF format with diagrams. It's an alien machine!"

"Shit!" Atticus charged toward the first construction worker to the right as he climbed the steep ladder to the catwalk. He did a flying kick, connecting with the Get's head as it cleared the top step. He heard the crack of bone, and the Get dropped backward.

Catching the handrail, Atticus let momentum spin him around and landed back on the catwalk. On the second-floor landing below him, the Get lay in an awkward sprawl. Atticus pulled his pistol and took careful aim. Fighting alongside the Dog Warriors had taught him how to maximize his damage. Two bullets into the skull kept a Get down the longest.

Toback had climbed the other ladder and rushed him now. The second construction worker was close behind him. Atticus aimed at Toback and fired. Even as he squeezed the trigger, the Get dodged aside, the bullets whining past harmlessly.

Damn, he read my mind!

And then Toback slammed into him like a linebacker. They tumbled, Atticus struggling to clear his mind even as he fought to break away from Toback. The construction worker swung at his head and he ducked. Still, the glancing blow rocked his consciousness, flashing darkness through him. He sensed a second hit coming and threw up his right arm to ward off the blow. He felt the blow shock-wave through his body and his hand flew open, releasing his pistol. It went skittering across the catwalk, just out of reach. From the numbness of his arm he knew the bone was broken. The Get swung his pipe upward.

I am void. I am nothing.

He twisted on his left shoulder and heaved Toback's head into the pipe's path just as the pipe came down. Blood scented the air, and Toback went limp. Rolling, Atticus kicked out, shattering the Get's kneecap. Pain as brutal as someone driving a spike into his bone lanced up his broken right arm. Snatching up his pistol with his left hand, he turned and fired awkwardly.

He missed with the first two bullets. The third and fourth took the construction worker in the chest. He put two more in the Get's head, just to be sure. Then he shot Toback twice, leaving himself three bullets. The three Gets were down, but that was bound to be temporary.

He had to destroy the transmitter before the Ontongard recovered. He reached out mentally to the Pack. They were far fewer in numbers than he'd hoped. *"Rennie!"*

"I can hear you. No need to shout."

"What part of this is the most critical to it working?"

"Let me see."

Rennie pushed into his mind. Atticus resisted automatically, and then, gritting his teeth, let the Pack leader in. Rennie leaned against the cold cement wall of the central room, panting in the gunsmoke, ribs bruised from shots taken by the body armor. He ached in his heart and soul as those he loved died around him—they were losing. If they had to pull out, anyone left behind would be at the mercy of the Ontongard.

Rennie closed his eyes, shutting out distractions, focusing on Atticus.

"Turn your head, Boy."

Atticus carefully scanned the room, and Rennie gazed out over the equipment, recognizing it, knowing how it was built and how to take it apart. Knowledge transferred to Atticus. The three-story cylinder housed the dimensional containment field for the exotic matter. The faraday cage, waveguides, and EM pumps extracted exotic matter as Earth moved through space. The long corridor lined with waveguides was used to puncture a pinhole in the M-brane, the exotic matter bleeding into the hole to keep it open long enough for interstellar communications.

Rennie focused on the tall cylinder. *"Hex must have salvaged most of the exotic matter from the sled's drive. Crack the housing open and not only will you destroy this setup, but there won't be any rebuilding."*

"Okay."

"First take the barrier down." Rennie picked out the field generator, and knowledge of how to turn it off filled

Atticus. *"You'll have, like, a minute, maybe, to get out of this rat maze, and then the fireworks will start."*

"A minute?" Atticus shut down the barrier.

"If you're lucky."

The tide of the battle turned for the worse. Rennie dropped the mental link to fight. Atticus felt strangely alone and hated it.

An acetylene torch sat in one corner of the room; he wheeled it to the containment housing.

Backing up to the door, he took careful aim with his left hand. He had only three shots to get it right, and then he'd have to get closer to set the stupid thing off. He wasn't sure what the dark matter would do once the containment field went down.

"Atty?" Ru whispered. "Are you okay?"

"I'm fine." And then, because it was dawning on Atticus how desperate their situation was, he added, "I love you, Ru. You've kept me sane."

"Oh. Oh, Atty, no."

The first bullet ricocheted off the cement floor.

The second shot hit and the acetylene exploded in a hot white flash. He was flung backward on a wave of flame into the stairwell, and an instant later everything went pitch-black and the grave-cold air of the maze rushed back over him. He scrambled to his feet and stumbled up the stairs.

There was a great howl of white noise, and it felt as though he were moving through heavy surf, invisible water trying to drag him backward. A deep, ominous rumble grew louder as the staircase quaked underfoot. The rumble changed to a roar of rushing water, and the smell of the ocean raced before the floodwaters. The first wave slammed him off his feet, and he tumbled into the black water. It swept him into a corner, smashing his broken arm against a cement wall, jolting agony through him. He flailed, disoriented.

Suddenly someone had a hold on him, dragging him against the current.

"This way, Boy." Rennie guided him through the raging seawater.

Wild, dark minutes later, they heaved up onto the steel stairway to the street. Hands pulled them upward as Atticus coughed up all the silt-filled water he'd swallowed.

The Pack waited on the street outside, guns aimed at the door, ready to shoot anything that crawled out of the water that wasn't one of their own. Most of them were battered, bleeding, and bruised, but only the dead weren't armed.

Atticus lay on the cold asphalt, panting.

"You okay, Boy?"

"Yeah. You came back for me?"

"You're our Boy. We wouldn't leave you behind."

CHAPTER EIGHTEEN

Boston Harbor Hotel, Boston, Massachusetts
Friday, September 24, 2004

In all the confusion, Atticus managed to forget his brother until they'd dragged themselves back to the hotel and slept for a few hours.

A knock at the door woke him. "Housekeeping."

"Need towels," Ru grunted.

So he got up, padded to the door, and after verifying that it was indeed the maid, opened the door. "We just need fresh towels."

The maid handed him a stack and he bolted the door. It felt very wrong to return to normalcy after so much madness. He put the towels on the shelf, feeling numb, and used the toilet. Ru came into the bathroom for a glass of water.

"What's with the rock?" Ru indicated a small pebble that had been sitting under his toiletry bag.

Atticus grunted his ignorance and picked it up. For a moment he thought it innocent of all human traces, and then realized Ukiah had dropped it there. Why? There was nothing special about the stone except that he found it pleasing. A child's treasure.

"Atty?"

Atticus blinked to clear his eyes. "I need to go find my brother."

•   •   •

The address listed in the Pennsylvania Department of Motor Vehicles for Ukiah led them to a huge house in an affluent city neighborhood.

"This can't be the right place." Atticus eyed the stone house, all gables and ivy.

"Bennett Detective Agency," Ru read from the bronze plaque by the hand-carved front door. "Business must be good."

Pressing the doorbell sounded eight muffled tones inside, an impressive door chime to go with the impressive house. After three tries with the doorbell, Atticus walked around the house, peering into the windows. The décor matched the outward appearance of the house—cherry-wood desks, silk drapes, chestnut burl paneling, granite countertops in the kitchen with stainless steel appliances, and a security system keeping all of the above safe.

"You've got to be kidding me," Atticus growled when he rejoined the other two. "This is a fucking mansion."

"I'm just getting an answering machine." Ru paused to wait for a tone and said, "Yes, this is Hikaru Takahashi; can you give me a call?"

Kyle sat on the porch step, Web surfing on his PDA. "Max Bennett's driver's license lists this address too. It says he's thirty-eight to Ukiah's twenty-one. Maybe he's Ukiah's father?"

Father or not, they'd last seen Ukiah with the Pack. There was no reason to think he wasn't still with them.

As Ru left his number on the answering machine, Atticus reached into that empty place he'd been avoiding. No whisper of his brother pressed against his senses.

He closed his eyes and focused. He should be able to feel the Dog Warriors protecting Ukiah.

"Atty?"

Atticus lifted his hand and pointed in the direction of a faint *something*. "Let's head that direction."

•   •   •

Going in a straight line proved to be impossible. There were rivers, gorges, hills, valleys, and one-way streets to contend with. They climbed an impossibly steep hill with a street pretending to be two lanes, but it was actually just one lane with haphazard parking. Downtown Pittsburgh lay across the river and far below, providing a view that was stunning but, judging by the dogged appearance of the houses around them, too common to raise property values. The Jaguar drew stares; it was out of place in this blue-collar neighborhood.

The Pack presence led him to a house on the overlook, seemingly abandoned and boarded up. He followed local custom and parked by mostly blocking the right side of the street. The boards on the front door had been pried up and then pulled back into place, to give the appearance that the house was still unoccupied. The house had been built with its back to the street to take advantage of the view, so the front door actually opened to the kitchen. Someone had been renovating recently, and plaster dust scented the air and covered the floor. The vinyl flooring matched that of his adopted parents' playroom, a pattern of random terra-cotta-colored squares. The street-side windows were boarded shut, the kitchen and the hall were night dark, the living room off the hallway was a distant rectangle of light. No one came to greet him, so he stood in the darkness, reexperiencing the night of his adopted parents' death.

He'd never gotten completely over that loss. He braced himself and walked into the darkness.

The living room been remodeled and painted before the house had been closed up. The wall overlooking the city was mostly glass, drenching the room with sunlight. The floor had been swept clean, and a gypsy camp of futons, quilts, and bright-colored pillows had been set up. By the floor-to-ceiling window, wrapped in blankets and propped in a battered leather chaise longue, Ukiah slept.

Relief punched through Atticus, making him breathe out

a surprised laugh, which he instantly regretted. He didn't want to wake Ukiah. Quietly, he crouched beside the chaise to watch his brother sleep, hoarding this last perfect moment.

What juxtaposition: the mansion and this abandoned house. Atticus wasn't sure what he would have thought if he'd seen only this ruin without the manicured luxury of the mansion, but witnessing both, he realized that from the moment Kyle pulled up the FBI database on the Dog Warriors, he'd assumed the worst for his brother. He'd let suspicion poison every word between them. He recalled all that he'd said—what he now wished he could take back. Ukiah opened his eyes to peer at him in mild confusion. "Atticus?"

What should he say? Could he even breach the gap he'd created between them?

"Don't be stupid." Ukiah reached out to pull him into a hug. The sense of "this is right, this is good" resounded through his soul. *"Between us, we don't need words."*

Wen Spencer

The Legend of Ukiah Oregon

ALIEN TASTE

Living with wolves as a child gave tracker Ukiah
Oregon a heightened sense of smell and taste.
Or so he thought—until he crossed paths with a
criminal gang known as the Pack. Now, Ukiah is
about to discover just how much he has in
common with the Pack: a bond of blood,
brotherhood...and destiny.
0-451-45837-0

BITTER WATERS

Tracker Ukian Oregon must put his skills to
the ultimate test—because kidnappers
have taken his son.
0-451-45922-9

THE GLASSWRIGHTS' SERIES
by
Mindy L. Klasky

THE GLASSWRIGHTS' APPRENTICE
If you want to be safe...mind your caste.
In a kingdom where all is measured by birthright, moving up in society is almost impossible. Which is why young Rani Trader's merchant family sacrifices nearly everything to buy their daughter an apprenticeship in the Glasswrights' Guild—where honor and glory will be within her reach.
0-451-45789-7

THE GLASSWRIGHTS' JOURNEYMAN
Rani Glasswright is home in her native Morenia, and her quest to restore the Glasswrights' Guild is moving forward again. But there are those who benefit from having the Guild shattered—and Rani is a threat to their plans.
0-451-45884-2

THE GLASSWRIGHTS' TEST
Glass artisan Rani's loyalty to the Glasswright Fellowship is tested when she is asked to kill the Morenian Queen.
0-451-45931-8

Available wherever books are sold or at
www.penguin.com

R418